THE ART LOVER

About the Love of Art and the Art of Love

by

CARL PICKHARDT

ISBN: 978-1-963565-96-6 (Paperback)
ISBN: 978-1-963565-95-9 (Ebook)

Library of Congress Control Number: 2025903574

Printed in the United States of America

Published by:
info@thequippyquill.com
(302)-295-2278

CONTENTS

Chapter One
THE SEPARATION

Dear Kate –

I suppose if there is one mercy in your going away it is that the fighting between us is over, at least for a while. How could a mother and daughter who love each other so much hurt each other so deeply? As I think back over our life together there has been so much closeness. Perhaps this was the problem.

No matter what others from larger families may think, it is not easy to parent an only child. You were my first child and last child all in one, the only chance for mothering I had and I wanted to do it right. It has been lonely work. Even with your father there to talk to, decisions about your welfare have been mostly mine. Not that he does not love you nor did not want you. We simply agreed upon this division of responsibility. He would provide the livelihood, I the major parenting. He misses you of course, but I feel the loss more. As though in leaving you tore some part of me away which only time can repair, and only then if it brings more understanding and forgiveness than I have now. Wounded is how I feel. And I know beneath your anger and disdain you feel wounded too. If you did not care you would not act so cold and injured. Yet I believe it is easier to be the person leaving than it is to be the person left behind. You have this extraordinary opportunity before you while I have only hurt to dwell on if I choose. What else is there to choose?

Perhaps this is getting closer to the truth. I wanted you to have this chance. I fought you for it. Yet I resent your accepting what I encouraged and worked for you to have. I am angry life should play this trick upon me. Giving you to me only to take you away before I am ready. Would I ever have been ready? At the last perhaps I am so angry because my mothering, which seems to have recently begun, is so soon over. Here you are barely seventeen.

Where have they gone, all the close years when you and I were best companions? In the years before the change came. I don't mean when you started school, although I missed my constant companion even then. And you did change, withdrawing from taunting classmates, bringing that withdrawal home. If they would not play on your terms, you would rather play alone. Although not agreeing, I respect your decision.

No, we changed, you and I, when your father at last acknowledged your talent and took you up, enlisting Phillip, your beloved Kip, in your education. Began the three harrowing years with Savocek when I hardly saw you. When you would hardly speak to me except in anger, whipping me with rage you felt toward him. Then, most painful of all, there was the powerful attraction of the Countess in your life. How the cultivation of your gift has grown you away from me! I, who wanted that gift cultivated.

As you looked more at others you looked less to me. When I demanded continued recognition as your mother you dismissed me for not understanding the passion your life was coming to be about. True, your talent and commitment to it did outstrip my modest comprehension of such things. I have never been at home in the world of art. Only resided in that foreign place because my husband made his living there. But to be dismissed from intimacy because I lacked knowledge of what you loved was to treat my love as a mere convenience, of interest to you no longer. How callous! You wonder at my anger. Is this the return that I deserve?

To get back in is why I fought so hard with you over things that did not matter. I would not be pushed away nor cast aside. Silence was your way when I came after you. And sullen obedience. Were it not for memories of good times we had and hope for better times to come I would not have survived these past three years.

With too much family responsibility to have friends as a child I have, as I now realize, never really made friends as an adult. Your father, your Uncle Phillip, and you: such has my social circle been. When you broke away, as part of me understands all children must, those two other friends, although loving and listening to me still, could not comprehend how wrecked my world became. Collapsing without you, I fell in upon myself.

Recognition of your talent snatched you from me, and literally carried you off at the airport yesterday. I watched your plane rise and bank and turn out across the great ocean to begin the adventure in which I shall play no part. Stared until my eyes ached from the strain of following a speck after it disappeared. Even then I wouldn't look away, wouldn't let go. Would still be fixed to the spot were it not for the Countess. Yes, it was she. Of all people to come up behind me at such a time! The effect of her speaking was to break my final connection with you. Not what she had to say, but the sound of how she said it.

I hesitate to share this with you for it may only strengthen your attachment to that terrible woman. However, I must live with myself, and doing right by you, painful though it may be, is less painful than doing wrong. In anger, you used to accuse me of having to be a 'perfect' mother. You were mistaken. I simply wanted to do the best by you I could. Career mothering an only child, a gifted one at that, has been unforgiving work when doubt has questioned or guilt punished a decision I have made. It is conscience, Kate, not perfection that has driven me to be so unyielding with myself, and as a consequence with you.

It is conscience now that dictates my declaring this. I would have you cognizant of <u>all</u> the caring left behind to help sustain the lonely apprenticeship you now undertake. The Countess, I believe she was crying. Or as close to it as such an unfeeling woman is ever likely to get. At least the usual commanding assurance was choked out of her voice, grief at your going making it difficult for her to speak.

Until this moment I would have sworn the woman with whom I have done silent battle over so many years was incapable of caring for any human being but herself. Now I believe she has come to care for one other. You. Although how you allured her I cannot possibly imagine. Why do I tell you this? Why, after resenting her the more these past three years? Because I do not want you leaving with misunderstanding which may burden you with needless anger.

It is true she used you to get the master drawing, holding your future ransom for its release when no amount of money would have tempted your father to otherwise have let it go. Even so, this deliberate extortion does not diminish her caring for you, Kate. Of this, I am emotionally certain. Her acquisition exacted a price, your departure from her life, which I suspect she did not anticipate.

Do you know what she asked me? "Mrs. Germaine, isn't it time we became friends?" I was stunned. Through the blur of my tears, she seemed to soften, but only for a moment. Then history welled up inside of me and I knew I could make no peace with this woman who has always been my rival. First, for my husband's loyalty through her patronage of his work. Second, for my daughter's affections when separation was causing you and I to grow apart.

There are limits to giving and forgiving, at least to mine. "Countess," I replied, "I have had you as an enemy too long to want to know you any other way."

It was a studied look she gave me. As though she was intently appraising some art object, considering it for purchase, and wanted to make no mistake. There was none of the usual haughtiness or contempt that had marked her treatment of me in the past. At length, she nodded. "You are right. Now is not the time for invitations. In the spring I shall call you for lunch. The courtyard is quite lovely then. Daffodils. Yes. I shall call you when the daffodils come into bloom."

Aggravating. She had not heard my refusal at all. No matter. She never listened to me before so why would she listen to me now? One thing surprised me though. I had assumed she had come to the airport alone, but I was wrong. As she turned away and I watched her go, sweeping the world before her like royalty on parade, out from the gate hobbled LaValle, the broken little man who has always been such a puzzle to me. She stopped. They exchanged some quiet conversation. She took his arm and off they went together, she adjusted her long stride to accommodate his peculiar shuffle. Do you know, after almost thirty years of acquaintance with the man it is 'Mrs. Germaine' he still calls me. And beyond the social courtesies when he comes to do business for your father, we have never meaningfully conversed.

This too is part of my pain. I have remained an outsider to your father's world. Although never troubling our marriage, when you entered that world into which I never sought nor gained entry myself, I don't know which, I felt like I was becoming an outsider to you. As I am with LaValle.

And now you are about to gain admission into one of the art world's sacred shrines, into the household, into the very studio of the Master himself. By what means did the Countess secure you such an opportunity? No one has been allowed in there for years, not since rumors circulated about his failing health, about how all remaining time was dedicated to producing the last great work. Even I know the public mythology that surrounds the great man. All the stories that have been told about Riablo. I guess you shall find out how true they are.

Kate, I wish you well these next two years. Looking back I hope you know even at my worst I was doing my best, and that I am trying to know the same of you. From time to time I shall write. Please only write me when you want to. Not when you feel you should.

I love you,

Joanne.

Chapter Two
THE BEGINNING

In stubborn silence, too private to let her unhappiness be known by others, she stood before the mirror rocking from side to side, first one hand clenched and then the other, squeezing strong fingers deep into each palm until the wincing pain caused her eyes to squint shut, momentarily interrupting the flow of tears down her angry red cheeks.

Vehemently she addressed her image in the glass.

"You're a plain one you are, Plain Kate Germaine! You're lucky they don't sing a song you to death with the name. And they would too, except you're too proud to show you care, so they leave you alone. No wonder. Just look at how you look!"

And look she did, coldly appraising her appearance with the cruel honesty of a twelve-year-old girl who knew well enough the standards of physical attractiveness to which others aspired to know she met them not at all.

Overlarge and squarely built, thick-limbed and sturdy, she was more powerfully made than most boys her age, while her face was thickly featured as well, dark heavy eyebrows and her father's strong nose which both looked handsome enough on him but homely on herself, like the broad mouth, firm jaw and other physical characteristics which from birth had unmistakably marked her as the Artist's child.

Just as no adults, not even her parents, had ever called her 'cute' when she was younger, neither had they ever called her pretty as she grew older. This omission became less easy to accept as she entered the age when prettiness was firmly wed to popularity and compliments awarded to other girls, but never to herself, hurt like old insults still occasionally revived by bored classmates in search of idle fun. 'Boxcar' they called her and 'Freight Train Germaine', nicknames that years ago she had done fruitless battle on the playground to dispel until she realized the harder she fought the harder they would stick. It was then she began not responding to provocation and concealing pain, skills developed to such a high degree by junior high that her tall frame and blocky shape, tempting targets though they continued to remain, were largely socially ignored along with the rest of her. She was no longer satisfied with teasing since she refused to act upset.

Turning away from the mirror at last she cast her eyes instead upon the bedroom walls postered by her mother with drawings by herself, drawings that cheered her up as the contemplation of her own creativity invariably did. Thank goodness for drawing, for loving to draw. She could not remember when she did not love making lines on paper when her eyes did not take delight in watching her hands at play as line led to design and design to the finished composition. There was something magical about beginning with a blank sheet of paper and ending with a completed picture. There was something so satisfying about stepping back and enjoying the moment of separation when the process was over, the drawing stood apart, from her but no longer of her, an affirming reflection of who she was.

Gradually her body relaxed and the fists which were ready to fight released fingers now restless to draw. She wiped the stains of grief from her cheeks as best she could, although the telling inflammation was evident to her mother when the girl entered the kitchen and sat down at her drawing table by the window. Her father, preoccupied as always, affectionately stroked his hand across her broad back as he passed by, at once caring and unnoticing, oblivious to the distress that his wife could plainly see but about which she said nothing.

It was the hardest part of mothering this sensitive child, seeing her hurt but avoiding comment unless Kate chose to share whatever misery there was. Joanne simply caught her daughter's eyes long enough to communicate awareness of the girl's distress and willingness to listen if that would help, then went back to what she was doing. Admittance to her daughter's world of inner experience had become less frequent over the years as teasing at school had caused her to become more emotionally guarded at home.

Being an only child in a home with two adults, Kate did not consider herself a child for very long. Early independence was rewarded with approval as seeking to be like them she imitated their independent ways. Playmates when she was very young, they soon became peers when she began to acquire speech which she precociously did before the age of two, by age three conversing confidently with each parent addressing them by the first names they addressed each other, Galen and Joanne. If she was conscious of any marriage between them at all it was one in which she was full partner, one among a triad of equals in which being so much younger in no way diminished her standing. To call either by the title of 'father' or 'mother' would have only called attention to her title as 'child', and where was the advantage of that?

Not until the first day of kindergarten did significant unhappiness enter her world. At recess, she had stalked up to a group of children on the playground and demanded inclusion in their game. Sand thrown in her face was their reply, and then laughter because she had sand all over her face. Worse, when she burst out crying they laughed harder which threw her into a fit of rage attracting other children who gathered around to join the fun. Insulting names were called, and the one which stung the worst would stick all year, 'Crazy Kate', a tribute to the fury of her temper. Now humiliated as well as hurt, she demanded justice from the teacher who was not about to let a high-handed five-year-old tell her what to do and directed the child to wash away the dirt before resuming her seat in class. By the end of the day, Kate had enough.

No more of this. She wasn't going back, she told her parents in no uncertain terms. But they reacted unexpectedly. They were sorry it was hard but she had to go to school. She had no choice. No choice? Didn't they love her? Didn't they care? For the first time, they asserted their authority. In tears, she fled their presence to her room. Meanwhile, downstairs her parents were grieving as well. At their mistake. In keeping her so much to themselves they had kept her from learning how to get along with people her own age.

It was a long grueling year which, by stubbornly opposing the hardness of it, Kate made harder still by making no friends but becoming the most popular and satisfying person in the class to tease. It infuriated her to be mistreated, fury which inspired the mistreatment to continue. Yet she refused to change, torment only reinforcing her resolve. At stake was conducting herself on her own terms. This had been her birthright at home and she was not about to give it up at school. At the age of five, she was willfully unwilling to live any other way.

The social place Kate made for herself in kindergarten was one she was to occupy for many years thereafter, and its name was isolation. When Joanne pleaded with her to be more social, the suggestion was rejected.

"But Kate, if you won't change you won't make any friends."

"Then I won't. They treat me meanly so why should I want to play with them."

The same conversation repeated many times at last reconciled Joanne that there was little she could do to change her daughter's life at school. There was little she could do but watch her daughter become more inward and guarded, the girl bringing home complaints less and less frequently. By fifth grade, Kate drew strength from not complaining, from presenting an uncaring exterior through which provocations could not penetrate. She put this image on each morning before going to school and did not entirely take off when she was done in the afternoon. With daily practice, the role she played became a role that stayed until junior high, although the taunting had subsided, this aloof exterior remained.

To outward appearances, the bad social experience seemed to outweigh the good as her attitude toward school became permanently, negatively set. She grudgingly went, she sullenly did her work, and she gratefully came home. She remained unforgiving of some classmates and unreceptive to the rest, conforming to rules and complying with instructions of teachers whose authority she fundamentally did not respect. Only through a deliberate act of introversion was she able to turn the bad back into the good. As her antipathy toward formal education grew, so did her capacity to endure it until she could stand what she hated without exhibiting any signs of disaffection. Teachers began to note on their report cards that her attitude had improved from the preceding year. What they did not note was the reason for this improvement. This was her secret. She had discovered the prisoner's freedom. By learning to pay partial attention to teachers, she gave her mind permission to escape elsewhere. Unbeknownst to them she began excavating a world of imagination into which she could retreat during the very act of doing classroom work itself. As succeeding grades became duller, more regimented, and routine, her refuge became more elaborate and fanciful, leaving school each day with an agenda of playful possibilities for the next.

"How was class today?" was a question Kate could not adequately answer because time had been spent in such contrasting ways. "It was awful as usual and wonderful as always", would have been the most accurate reply. But what sense would that have meant even to Joanne, the person who understood her best? The experience of school oppressed and enriched her beyond measure. As for coming home, that meant coming back to the world she loved an external world in which she was free to be loved for how she was and free to do what she loved doing. Most of all, free to draw.

More than Galen it was her mother who had recognized and nurtured Kate's inclination to draw. Joanne, it was who could remember how the love of drawing first began. By accident. On a mother's whim. In infancy, Joanne had sat Kate down in the middle of a large sheet of paper and placed colored crayons in her tiny hands. This was done to enjoy the baby girl's surprise at seeing marks magically appear as waving arms accidentally struck small fists upon the floor. Magical it was because the infant did not connect the sudden strokes upon the paper with her own spasmodic movements. To the little girl, it was one more miracle in a world of sudden appearances and disappearances that defied understanding. To her mother, this was a wonderful joke, the child ignorant of authoring her own delight which, had she known, would have destroyed the very mystery she found so entrancing.

More deeply satisfying still for the girl was simply holding the crayons themselves, which she did with the assurance of one whose hands were made to grasp such instruments of expression. One was never enough. Indeed, she would loudly complain until a second had been inserted between the empty fingers of the other hand. For a while, Joanne feared lest her daughter would suck or teeth upon or even eat the colored wax, but none of these mishaps occurred. Holding them was enough. Until one day, crawling through the kitchen the child accidentally noticed dark lines flowing from her hands as she pulled herself across the floor, dragging the crayons as she crept forward.

It was one of those wondrous moments of awakening that altered the course of someone's growth and her mother was there to see it. The girl immediately stopped, sat up, and looking down expected her hands to do it some more, which they did not. At length losing patience she commenced to crawl again and once again the lines appeared. She stopped and sat up as before, now resolved to wait however long it took for her hands to grow more lines. At last, as they became restless and wandered about the floor at her sides, this time they finally did, very lightly but plain enough for her to observe the marks originating not from her hands but from the favored objects which she held, from pressure which her hands applied.

At that instant, so it seemed to Joanne looking back, Kate claimed the power of self-expression for her own, and drawing as her medium of choice. For the next two hours, the child was totally absorbed, celebrating this discovery by hitting her fists upon the linoleum, scribbling where she sat, and moving on when an unmarked space to rub was wanted. By evening the entire kitchen floor was covered with scrawl, replacement crayons having been required to complete the task. Joanne had been astounded that one so young could concentrate so long. The investment of energy finally told as the child became too tired and cranky to continue, was fed, and then put down to rest, only consenting to relinquish play and give in to fatigue when she had been allowed to carry two fresh crayons with her into bed.

Thus it began, this passion for making lines, or at least such was how the mother saw it begin, knowing the true origins were gifted to the child long before. Over a period of months, the woman carefully nurtured this enthusiasm by washing the kitchen floor each night so the next day Kate could have a clean surface upon which to work, finally training her to butcher paper that Joanne pulled off a roller from one side of the room and stretched across to the other. The little girl loved dragging lines behind her creating a record of her travels, halting occasionally to look back over where she'd been before moving on, the final outcome a kind of map documenting her journey for the day.

The artist himself, her father, had been impressed by the mural-sized drawings, by someone so small working on so large a scale unafraid, although he could discern in them no coherent sense of design or form. 'Ramblings' he called them. What fascinated him most was the boldness with which she put her whole body into what she drew, using both hands to draw as naturally as she would soon be using both feet to walk. The parents joked about 'having another artist in the family,' a possibility which the mother took seriously while the father did not, dismissing this display of early interest with the explanation that all children love to draw if given half a chance.

Kate, however, was not given half a chance. She was given a whole chance. Joanne saw to that. Having never been encouraged expressively herself she was committed to her daughter having unobstructed easy access to drawing whenever the urge came upon her. The kitchen, the place where expression first began, was made into Kate's studio. From the outset of elementary school, returning home in the afternoon, the girl found by fresh paper on the table by the kitchen window a display of instruments waiting to be used. In addition to her beloved crayons, there were pastels, pens, colored inks, markers, pencils soft and hard, brushes and paints, all of which Kate took special care to preserve as opposed to the drawings she produced. Her interest in these lasted only as long as they were in process. Once finished they were tossed carelessly aside. "Because I like the next one better than the last," she explained to her mother, once more coldly stating "because I like live drawings better than dead ones," by which apparently were meant those killed by completion.

The girl did not object, however, to her mother sifting through the day's production and selecting out some drawings to post on Kate's bedroom walls, creating an ever-changing gallery of current work from which Joanne would further select an occasional few for a portfolio about which Kate knew nothing.

Two or three times a year would stage a display for Galen to see. The artist enjoyed these private exhibitions primarily, he supposed, because it was his daughter's work. Never having viewed much children's art he had an insufficient frame of reference for appreciating the precocity Kate's drawings began to express. That her interest could be serious or her talent significant did not occur to him. After all she was only a child, and a girl besides. True, each year some teacher would comment on Kate's artistic capacity and several times she had even received local awards; however, according to Galen, this was to be expected since she devoted so much time to this hobby. 'Hobby' was what he considered it, while Joanne grew less and less sure.

Kate herself, as she had declared to her mother, valued the process of drawing more than the drawings themselves. The act was its own reward. Compliments and recognition had no power to strengthen the connection that the love of doing had firmly established. It was herself she sought to satisfy and no one else. A blank sheet of paper was a temptation her curiosity could not resist. What new possibility for self-expression did it offer? What would the lines decide to do this time? And who would make this decision?

The older she grew the more she wondered what mistress her hands served. Easy to answer 'the brain', yet the process as she well knew was no simple transfer to paper of a picture first visualized in her mind. At least as far as she was aware, she drew without preconception, never knowing what was going to come out and not wanting to. Although she never told him, Kate considered portraying the image of people accurately on canvas, the kind of art her father did for a living, to lack the spontaneity that she loved.

Better to do it her way, the mind having no preparation for what the hands might do. Only after they had begun playing out lines did her thoughts begin to influence developing design, suggesting she try this possibility or that, causing her to compose a picture to meet a very vague and certain intuitive standard. Either the finished drawing 'worked' or it did not.

In this judgment, she came to have absolute trust. It was an evaluation based not on logic but on feel, based not on rational understanding but on visual sense. She simply 'knew' whether a line, a shape, or a relationship between forms felt 'right' or not. When it felt 'wrong' she moved to adjust it. Sometimes this intuitive guidance allowed her to make a poor drawing better. Other times it caused her to make a good drawing worse.

On such occasions, Joanne had to look away lest she rush in and rescue a drawing from destruction by its creator. She wondered at Kate's capacity to care so much for the process of drawing itself that she cared not at all when an individual sketch fell casualty to a failed attempt to improve it.

Only at one point did Joanne dare instruct her daughter, encouraging her to continue using both hands interchangeably and interactively when she drew, for however long this duality felt comfortable. It did not seem wise to the mother to abandon what had from the outset been so natural, even though others were advising the girl to do so. School kept trying to make Kate declare a preference and write with one hand only, limiting her drawing the same way. Hence the intervention Joanne made every primary grade and at which she succeeded. Each of those early years she did battle with the institutional convention which dictated a child was better off relying on one hand than utilizing two, marshaling the same unassailable evidence to support Kate's freedom to continue using both hands as she chose. Whether authored by left or right the girl's writing, although differently expressed by each hand, was equally fluid and clear.

Kate herself could not imagine drawing without the freedom dual-handedness gave. Indeed, she felt disabled using only one. Not just a common facility shared by both, there was a uniqueness peculiar to each which the other could not duplicate. She could tell a 'left' influence or idea from a 'right', could sense the expressive strengths each individually possessed and which, when combined in a single drawing, would later create a collaboration of extraordinary power.

It did puzzle her sometimes, this inclination of each to work differently. The left for example tended to sweeping and expansive lines determining the larger form, while the right applied fussy detail by using broken strokes to shade or model with great intensity. Most often it was the right which would begin a drawing and the left which would finish up. By force of discipline Kate could reverse the natural bent of each hand, yet undeniable resistance made her aware at a young age how both hands possessed some autonomy of their own which her mind did not control. They were independent of her yet connected to each other at the same time.

Bewildered was how she felt watching the left hand pick up a line begun by the right and continue it unbroken, the hands now switching back and forth with no loss of momentum or disruption of design, connected by some obvious kinship which excluded her, outsider to their conspiracy of play. Even to her own eyes, the tension between their differences could be unsettling, a definite antagonism that completion of the drawing would momentarily resolve into a unified composition in which a quality of tension typically remained. Art teachers would often remark on this telling dynamic in her work with a certain ambivalence. The girl's competence could not be denied and yet...and yet...what was it? There was something unconventional about her drawings, a singularity hard to define that set her work apart. Then they would relent. Oh well, let her draw as she likes. At least she wasn't being disruptive.

While Galen was too absorbed in his own commissions to consider his daughter's self-absorption anything out of the ordinary, Joanne found it cause for continuing concern. She felt loneliness on Kate's behalf. Through elementary school and junior high, the phone never rang. Friends did not come by or invite her over. She attended no parties.

At an age when other girls were surrounded by friends who could turn into enemies at a moment's notice, when rivalry and jealousy, intrigue, and rumor were all beginning to wreak social havoc in their lives, Kate lived peacefully and undisturbed. No one gossiped about her, tried to cut her out, or contested for her attention. In some ways, junior high was a good time not to have friends. Kate didn't have to deal with the social complexities that preoccupied her peers. If anyone did speak to her she spoke back. If they did not she did not appear to mind. She let others be the way they were and they accorded her a similar respect. Self-possessed and quiet she was for the most part content, except for her occasional painful encounters in the mirror when she privately compared herself to other girls.

Joanne, for whom the demands of home allowed no time for friends when she was a child, longed for Kate to have more companionship in school than she herself had known.

"Wouldn't you like to have some classmates over next weekend? Or go out somewhere with them? I'll be happy to take you." She would make this offer several times a year, re-testing Kate's desire to socialize.

"No, Joanne. I don't have friends that way." A blunt admission that the girl made not to elicit sympathy but simply to report the unchanging character of her relationships at school. Hearing this Joanne would turn away, which Kate recognized as her mother's effort to conceal disappointment.

"What way do you have friends?" Joanne finally asked her daughter.

The girl only smiled shyly and repeated what she'd said before, "Just not that way." Then Kate looked down at her hands resting together in her lap. No way for her mother to understand these were her friends, these two hands who still drew with all the passion they had exampled years ago in infancy upon the kitchen floor.

Chapter Three
THE COUNTESS IS NOT PLEASED

My Dear Miss Germaine:

Our farewell was not as I would have it. Permit me to correct the attitude you then expressed. It is enough I am to be distanced from you physically without having to endure estrangement as well.

I do not indulge in displays of strong emotion myself (why give others the advantage of knowing how one feels?) and I expect you to exercise the same maturity of judgment with me. In anger, you accused me of 'using' you and so betraying the friendship which has grown up between us. I tell you I betrayed nothing and our friendship need not be altered. Used you? Of course, I did. To get what I could gain no other way.

Do you not use me? Have you not? I permitted Savocek to take you on. His threat to leave my employ if I interfered with his choice of students while irritating, had no power to change my mind against my will. There were other art teachers, although none perhaps so remarkable as he. Who paid for that? And who now opens the door for you to the Master's studio?

You understand, Miss Germaine, to none of this do I object, only to your objection to the exchange. As I have tried on numerous occasions to suggest, this is the way of the world. Go after what you want, give where you must, and drive the hardest bargain you can.

The sooner you learn this lesson the better. I thought you already had, but apparently not. So learn it now. Life is a series of accommodations and arrangements that we must make. All of us.

Consider: for you to study with the Master, the Master has a price. The return of those incautious letters that he wrote to me when for the one and only time he allowed himself to be seduced away from work. An indiscretion for which I have never been forgiven. Nor forgotten. Now, nearing the end of his life, he is concerned about how history shall view him and does not want posterity to portray him in those intimately unflattering terms by which he once portrayed himself, in that foolish, vain, and vulgar prose in which he wrote to me, his amore. He wishes to be remembered for his creative energies, not his sexual ones, although only I know how inseparable are the two.

So: Riablo gets his letters back thereby protecting his future reputation from disclosure of past embarrassment. I get the master drawing. Your parents get to provide what, without me, they could with no amount of money or influence make possible for you. And you get to go. As my father would have said, all parties get just enough to make what each gives up worthwhile. The perfect deal. Imperfect all the way around. I learned this lesson the hard way when I was younger by trying to force my way and failing. In the process I made enemies, some I have to this day, among whom I regret to say is your mother.

It happened many years ago, in your home. I did not get what I was after, the marvelous drawing now in my possession. My approach, upon your father's refusal to sell, was crude. I implied a threat to his livelihood. Instantly your mother called me on it. Of course, I denied having really meant to threaten anyone. Too late. From her, I could not conceal my intention with a lie. She recognized what I had said for what it was, pushed your father aside, and drove me from her den. "Threats are unwelcome in my home. In the future, when you have business with my husband you shall conduct it elsewhere." I was shown the door. This was when your father's early portraits were first attracting public notice before you were born. The condition she set that day I have observed ever since. Too bad so many of life's lessons close doors behind us which are locked against us later on.

Because of my high-handed ways I know I am not liked by many people. So be it. I would rather command obedience than court approval. Let others abase themselves to me. I suppose I have this from my father, this determination to maintain the upper hand. As I have told you, he was a brutish man to live with; while to the world he showed a dashing and seductive charm. How he trapped my mother. She was swept off her feet by the public man only to realize she had become captive of the private one too late.

Public or private I am as I am. At least in that regard, I can disinherit his influence upon me. All this to help you understand I have treated you no differently than any other person in my life. Except for this: I have allowed you access by sharing with you how I am. Why? Because we are equal and similar and different. For all those reasons. Although two generations younger in age, you are my equal in willfulness. Just as I fear no one, you have no fear of me. Most people do, you know. And this difference besides. We each possess something the other covets but has by birth been denied. I do not have your talent, but you do not have my beauty. We are both attracted to what we wish we could have had.

So, forsake your anger and let us communicate upon those conditions that the Master has set. To preserve his precious privacy he will permit no visits to disrupt your confinement there. Only letters shall be allowed, and I was hard put to get this concession. Probably because letters, his own, have proved an inconvenience in the past. Since his lifetime is running out nothing must get in the way of what is left for him to produce. Nothing, that is, but you who are intruding into a household that revolves entirely around his needs. However, while you may not be wanted you shall be more welcome than he expects. See if I am not correct. As for his word, you are under my protection. He dare not break a pledge to me. Room and board. A workplace in his studio. Supplies as needed. In return, see you keep my word to him. Work diligently. On no account disrupt the orderly routines which enable him to concentrate on painting. In other words: fit in. Learn to live on someone else's terms.

This is part of the sacrifice you must make. As well as leaving your family, your Uncle Phillip and your father whom you will miss, and your mother whom you believe you will not. There I believe you are mistaken, treating her as an enemy to your interests. Well, it is not for me to persuade you otherwise. However, I shall interfere to this extent. I know something of your mother. She and I go back many years together. Not that there has ever been any affection between us. Hardly. Life placed us in opposition from our first meeting, each vying for part of your father. I don't dislike her, having never taken our rivalry personally, although I have reason to believe she has. What she protected limited my gain but of the two, she has had more to lose.

I will tell you this. I do respect her. If I ever had been willing to victim myself to childbearing and tie myself captive to parenting, I should in one regard have been like her. She has a ferocity with which I am much in sympathy, despite having been driven back by it on the occasion I described. She does not shrink from duty as she sees it, opposes who she feels she must as she has me, and more importantly has you. Willing to get in your way when she thought your way was wrong. Willing to stay in your way when you fought to back her off. Loyal to what she believes is best for you. Surely to take such a determined stand against your disapproval signifies caring at least and not a little courage. Think about it. I do.

Why? Because I had a mother whose courage to take such a stand was oppressed out of her before I was conceived, my very conception I am sure being more an act of submission than desire, while for her labor pains, she was punished because I was a girl and not the son my father had required. He never respected my mother before and he never forgave her after. So she never forgave herself. To make matters complete, because she could never look at me without guilt she never forgave me either, the unwanted object who had dimmed her luster in her husband's eyes. Something so simple, to produce a man-child. And she had failed because of me. However, give the woman her due. She dared one act of bravery on my behalf.

The son was to have been 'Alan' after my father so he feminized the name for me, 'Alana', for the son he never had. You know you are not wanted when the name you're given is for the child your parents were denied. I was born out of an act of failure and given a name to memorialize the disappointment. Not a very auspicious beginning you will agree. Quite different from your own. Still, she did one very subtle, very stubborn thing for me, the only act of rebellion against him of which I am aware. By persistent usage she refused to call me Alana, but Elena instead. Corrected by my father she would apologize only to err again and again until she wore his objections down and he accepted that they would each address me differently. The naming of her daughter. Sufficiently symbolically important for this meek woman to risk her ruler's wrath. Was she so stupid she could not remember her daughter's proper name? Yes. Persistently she was. Of such small heroisms is liberation made.

In the same way, I would suggest you give your mother her due. If nothing else understand this. Without her consent, no matter how strongly your father and uncle urged, you would on no account have been allowed to go. The invitation I contrived and you accepted was consummated by her permission. Why did she relent? I have asked myself the very question. Not because she was beaten down. Not because she gave up. Because I have come to believe, she was determined to act your mother to the last, apparently deciding that the greater loving was to let the loved one go. Despite all other feelings to the contrary.

Of course, this is between you and her, except in one regard. I did not arrange this tutelage for you to waste precious time with the Master by pridefully dwelling on childish grievances against your mother or myself. Simply put, Miss Germaine, grow up. You are older than your years in other ways so act older than your years in this. Concentrate on the opportunity before you.

Remember, I send you abroad for a purpose. Your uncle Phillip, Savocek, even LaValle (yes, I have consulted him, that man you do not like), they all agree you have the talent and the industry to achieve great things. And I concur. You only lack one critical ingredient without which all your talent and industry will never raise you above mediocrity. It is to acquire arrogance that I send you to Riablo, for surely no artist possesses greater power of arrogance than he.

Say what you will about spoiling a child, I do not believe you can indulge his dreams too much. The Master's parents were people of a simple faith. Nourish ambition and talent shall flourish. I met them once. Sincere, direct, loving people. Absolutely trusting in his judgment to determine the precocious path he would follow. Their job was to provide backing and then stay out of his way. Best for him was whatever he decided was best. The older children, none being so impetuous, were raised more strictly, and they resented Riablo and their parents for permissiveness not permitting them. Resentment was made worse when recognition of his exceptionality appeared to justify the special treatment he received. Resentment made unbearable by Riablo's obvious unconcern about their envy and animosity. His parents were the only people to whom he evidenced any attachment, for whom he ever showed any consideration, giving back to them in full measure for what he had received.

No goals he set were questioned. No projects were discouraged because someone else felt they were 'unrealistic'. Remember the studies for the massive murals at Prago were executed when he was fifteen and sixteen. When someone so young had no business conceiving compositions on such a grand scale. The only limits he was taught to respect were those he set for himself. Opinions others expressed about his work, critical or praiseworthy, were beside the point. He and only he would be responsible for judging and directing the course of his own work. From his parents, he had learned to serve as his own ultimate authority. And over the years which I have known him, he has never once surrendered this supremacy except to me, and then only for a while.

He has soared so high not simply because of capacity and dedication. He has soared so high because his confidence literally knows no bounds. This is the arrogance of the man. He believes he can achieve whatever possibilities he can imagine and has proceeded according to that belief. It is this quality of arrogance that I find you wanting. You must expand ambition to its outer limits. If you learn nothing else these next two years but this you shall have learned enough. Until you can conceive on a grand scale you shall not be able to create on a grand scale.

I go now. You shall write to me because having come to care about our friendship, I do not tolerate our parting very well. Should Riablo ask about me, tell him as little as you can.

Countess Elena D'Allessandro Ricci

Chapter Four
A WORLD OF MAKE BELIEVE

It began innocently enough. A child making up characters for companionship and entertainment when her parents were unavailable, two self-absorbed adults who expected their only child to be the same. She did her best. Dolls and toy animals, however, of which she had been given a few, had no life of their own. And the one pet she had tried, a puppy named Peter to whom she felt her father paid more attention than to herself, and whose unhousebroken habits it was her responsibility to clean up, created competition and caused demands both of which she found not to her liking.

So what remained? At first, invisible friends. These offered the convenience of coming and going at her command, but proved ultimately unsatisfying because when she honestly evaluated their worth she had to admit that believe in them as she might they still could not be seen, a deficiency which so visual a person could not easily overlook.

What was wanted, she realized, were living friends obedient to her wishes and submissive to her needs. Unfortunately, other children at school did not meet these requirements. They wanted their way when she wanted hers, which was not acceptable. Kate was not about to sacrifice self-interest for the sharing and compromise that peers required.

The solution that unexpectedly offered itself to the lonely girl proved imperfect because the friends she found, or who found her, she was never sure which, while possessing sufficient substance and vitality, and loving more than anything else what she loved, unhappily maintained a degree of independence that resisted her control. They enjoyed a primary relationship with each other in which she was never allowed equal standing or full participation. No matter how responsive to her they were, she still felt treated like an outsider. Their first meeting Kate never forgot.

It was in her ninth year on a rainy Saturday afternoon. There she was in the kitchen perched cross-legged on a stool at her table bent over a sheet of paper on which blue and brown pastels had interwoven an intense fabric of intricate design contained within a strict curvilinear form. On impulse, feeling pleased with the composition, and since no one was about to hear her, she thought to compliment her hands on the playful work they had so artfully accomplished.

"Oh well done! I like it. I like it very much."

To her utter surprise there came an immediate, albeit irritated reply.

"Well, she's finally noticed. I never thought she would!"

Looking away from the drawing to her clenched right hand with which she somehow identified the offended voice, the girl stared.

'That's right. I said it to her and I'm not sorry. All this time and only now does she pay us appreciation. What has she been thinking? Not that I care!"

"Now, now," came a more conciliatory voice which she associated with her left hand laying open to the other side. "She was only using us as she would any other part of her body."

"Then let her draw with her feet and leave us out of it," came the snappish reply.

The girl was too astonished to be offended by the criticism she had just received. In the silence which followed doubt began to form in her mind questioning whether she had actually heard anyone talking or not. Reluctant to move, she held still, not wanting to break the fragile communication so mysteriously begun. The silence continued. It was her own turn to speak, she supposed, having been spoken to or, more precisely, spoken about. But it felt a little awkward talking to her hands. Free though she felt with imagination, this required a further stretch of fantasy than she had ever taken. Dare she? Looking around to confirm the room was truly empty, she lowered her voice and quietly asked: "Did someone speak?"

"Hear her! Did someone speak? Did we? Did we draw? Do we not do her a thousand little services every day? And she asks did someone speak. Not I!" And the right fist turned angrily away.

Now the left put down the brown pastel it had been cradling.

"Come. She met your condition. We did not speak in front of her until first spoken to. Now she has taken notice. What more do you want?"

"I don't know. Something. Yes I do. I want names, names for us both if she is to keep talking with us."

Kate now found words easier having found them once before.

"Why don't you name yourselves. I'll call you each by any ones you like," she offered.

"See! See! Hear her? Hear her? What did I tell you? Making fun of us because we cannot name ourselves!"

"It sounded like an offer, not an insult," came the calm reply. "Be patient."

"I'm not impatient! Why if acting depended on you, nothing would get started!"

"True. I don't deny it," agreed the other. " Reacting is what I do best. How I'm most comfortable. And finishing. Completion is my job. Beginning yours."

"I've noticed that," interrupted Kate. "How the right hand always starts while the left is always last to leave the paper."

"There, you see. She hasn't ignored us entirely." It was the hand that spoke with the voice of reason.

"Names! Names! Names! Names! Nothing she has done about names. Ignoring I call it!"

"What kinds of names would please you?" asked Kate trying to be considerate.

"Shouldn't like whatever she chose, I'm sure of that!"

"But we would accept them nonetheless."

There was a grudging silence.

"Hers to choose, hers to use. Wouldn't use them myself. Nor would you. But at least we'd be acknowledged!"

"Very well," agreed Kate beginning to comprehend whatever she did was not going to receive unqualified approval. "I shall do as you ask."

"Hear her? Not asking. Not me. Don't want her help. Wouldn't take it. Mentioning is all I did. If she heard, if she acts, well it's no business of mine!"

Tricky, the girl was finding it, talking to those who would not talk directly to her, responding only to each other when she spoke. So she stopped speaking to search for names fanciful enough to fit such fanciful acquaintances. Closing her eyes as she often did to protect her thinking from distraction, she looked around the clutter of impressions and ideas that stocked her experience at the moment. Nothing. No appropriate titles laying about. Reluctantly she opened up the door to memory, a very shallow repository since she bridled at remembering upon demand and so did not naturally demand it of herself.

Too young to appreciate the value of her own history, or simply disinclined, her sense of past was a small agglomeration of recent events which had stuck in her head of their own accord. Yesterday seemed a long time ago so she looked there first, scanning the morning, afternoon into the evening when her mother was reading her to sleep. Something clicked. What was she being read? A story? No. A poem. Some poems from the Red Book. A single line drifted back. "Of all the friends the best by far were Anastan and Cuscubar."

Anastan. Cuscubar. She repeated the names over and over to herself. Fanciful enough, they were, and with repetition felt fitting. But which for which hand? Another fragment came mysteriously to mind. "Anastan kept stirring up what Cuscubar calmed down." There. Perhaps memory was more useful than she supposed. It was settled.   The temperamental right would be Anastan, the unemotional left, Cuscubar. With some trepidation she introduced each hand to their respective names, correctly anticipating an immediate objection from the right.

"So, it's done is it? I hope you're satisfied! I told you she wouldn't give us sensible names, not her. Shan't ever say mine, I promise you. Whoever heard of such a name? As for yours, well I suppose since you must wear it you shall grow to like it. That's the way you are, I know."

"I am. Best to learn to like what you can't change."

"Better to reject it, you mean!"

"Now, now, you're just saying that because you're feeling hurt."

"And you don't care because you're not! And now see what you've done! Picked a fight by making me fight back and she has seen it and shall think worse of me because of you. Really! Sometimes you are so provoking I could almost stop drawing with you!"

"No you couldn't. You can't resist drawing with me any more than I can with you. We work together because we can't work apart."

Caught between the heat of the right and the coolness of the left, and beginning to understand how each could antagonize the other, the girl felt a need to mediate between the two extremes. In this spirit she offered what she came to realize was the only reconciliation both would accept.

"How about a fresh sheet of paper?" she suggested.

Immediately she felt her right hand relax and her left tighten up. Like partners they seemed preparing for a dance, poised for the music to begin. Previously she had wondered about the gathering of tension before a new drawing was begun and now, she felt she understood.

Out jumped Anastan striking the paper hard with a soft pastel, making unequivocal contact, moving in short, swift, energetic strokes building up color and claiming more space until Cuscubar, the time having come, stepped into the picture and took command of the larger design, circumscribing Anastan's intense detail with clear, unbroken sweeping lines, each hand moving now in conjunction with the other. Absorbed in the unfolding creation the girl joined in, expressing encouragement and suggestions some of which were taken and some not, Kate feeling very much a part of what she was not partner to, free to talk while they worked on in concentrated silence. At last Anastan paused and then withdrew to the paper's edge, watchful Kate felt as Cuscubar gave final structure to the drawing, reinforcing lines upon which unity depended. Then Cuscubar withdrew as well. All three were quiet now, contemplative, reflecting upon what had been created.

It was the only time, and it did not last long, when Kate felt peace between them. A matter of minutes before the critique which followed caused discord once again to build. In a cold, analytic manner Cuscubar would dispassionately probe the design for weakness to which Anastan would defensively react as though personally attacked, championing the drawing's merits. The resulting debate did not alter the conviction in each that the other was wrong, fueling the conflict upon which their quarrelsome collaboration depended. Again Kate came aware of how much inner contention contributed to her experience of drawing. This was why the process was never restful, always demanding, a matter of keeping herself together when adversary forces were pulling her apart. This was why drawing was such a strain. Joyful, but a strain. Enlisting opposing forces for a common purpose, always in the same order of creation: feeling first and form after.

Something else about her own inclinations was revealed. Having reached their assessment of a drawing neither Anastan nor Cuscubar were disposed to go back and make repairs, even when both agreed about the flaw. Nor did they want to save a drawing that turned out particularly well. Indeed, when she once questioned this disinterest in correcting or keeping finished drawings, she immediately found both hands arrayed against her.

"What an idea! Who gave her such an idea, did you? As though a drawing could be bettered by reworking it. What nonsense! Improvement comes from being free to do the next one differently. Not by doing over one whose time is past. Doesn't she know about letting go?"

"She may not," answered Cuscubar. "Remember, the work we do she can only watch. Keeping is her way of holding on. She believes it's for the best."

"Best indeed! Best is how a drawing comes out. While for the best is getting rid of the last to make room for the next."

Before making their acquaintance Kate had claimed right of authorship to all she drew. Of her, from her and for her. To reflect herself and be noticed by others, perhaps admired for what she had created. Reasons enough to keep what she had made. All arguments which she posed to Anastan who became doubly insulted.

"Hear that? To think the work belongs to her! And then to care what others think! The doing is what counts. Better we'd never let her in at all!"

For Kate, however, particularly during the early difficult years at school, to be admired for something, especially by her chief tormentors, eased the daily hardship. Why shouldn't she accept some good when so much else was bad? Stubbornly asserting her right to credit and her need for affirmation she found the two friends would have none of it. After an initial challenge had failed to win Kate over, Anastan simply refused to discuss the matter any further.

"Let her worship her reflection if she must. I don't care!"

Cuscubar, however, would not give up so easily.

"We cannot go freely forward when she is always looking back. All drawings die at birth. We must teach her to let dead drawings go, that the next matters more than the last."

Repeat and repeat and repeat Cuscubar did, gradually wearing down Kate's desire to keep before her what she came to accept must be put behind. That Joanne did not understand this and would insist upon saving and displaying finished work for Kate to see was a source of discontent the two partners, on their side, reluctantly accepted as part of the larger world over which they had no control. However, they succeeded this far: Kate's attention did become wed to the drawing in process, the process itself becoming everything. Finished pictures became 'dead' in her eyes, empty of the vital energy that once caused their creation.

From this time on her parents noticed a change in their daughter that was confusing, a disregard for her work coupled with increased devotion to it. There was a new absorption with herself, a new distance from them. This was puzzling because they saw no reason for it, only the coincident occurrence of a new habit, talking aloud to no one in particular when she was drawing, but never loudly nor clearly enough for them to understand what she was saying. At most they caught an indecipherable mumble which grew softer the closer they approached convincing them whatever was going on was meant to be secret. Even from Kip, her beloved Uncle Phillip, to whom she confided everything and who once asked to whom she was talking when she drew.

"To myself. I like to talk to myself when I draw." And she went back to work, her lips continuing to move. Silently. A signal that whatever was going on was not for him or her parents to know, and they all respected that.

Meanwhile Joanne watched with undiminished amazement at how her daughter constructed a picture using both hands alternately and simultaneously, turning her head from one to the other in seeming dialogue with each. Kate coordinated her two extremities with the practiced ease of a performer making music on a piano, one hand accompanying the other, the emerging whole greater than the sum of its parts. This image Galen also used to explain his daughter's new behavior.

"She's just like a musician singing while she plays. If it pleases her to do so, what's the harm? Like whistling while you work."

No harm, Joanne agreed. Yet she felt her husband's glib interpretation did not sufficiently enlighten the darkening interior of Kate. His explanation did not satisfy. Of course, she could try to force her way into the girl's privacy, except from past experience she knew that force was futile. There was a wall of silence behind which, by age nine, Kate could withdraw and withstand a siege of questions without disclosing what she wanted to conceal. Even with her mother she was stubborn about not relinquishing secrets she held dear, stubborn as well with her new friends about one practice which they disapproved but she would not give up.

The house had forever been littered with art books laying open and stuffed in bookcases in every room, even in the bathroom. Browsing through photographs and reproductions of great art from around the world had been a way of pleasuring herself since early childhood. Art books were her picture books, while the pictures themselves deeply instilled her love of art. Trips to his museum with her uncle, Kip, further enhanced her joy from looking at what others had created, stimulating her own desire to create in the process.

"A waste," her two friends called it, urging her to abandon interest in what others had accomplished, warning her away from this subversive influence that could encourage imitation. This was as senseless as paying attention to her own dead drawings, which she had given up thanks to them. Kate tried to argue them out of their prejudice by explaining how beholding great art inspired her own desire to work. It was to this argument that both hands took immediate offense. If she loved dead others so much perhaps she'd rather draw with them!

Then Kate understood. The two were jealous of her attachment to these rivals for her attention, a jealousy made worse by arguing. Therefor she stopped arguing at once so they could not argue back, and so she could continue what she loved to do, refusing to be converted to their belief. Great objects from the past spoke to her with voices she could not ignore, siren voices alluring her to join them if she could.

Like the one master drawing that hung in the hallway of her home.

Chapter Five
ʃEAVING ONE ʃHOME FOR ANOTHER

My dearest Kip--

I have written to no one until now because I have not felt able. The confusion of feelings from my departure and the confusion of arriving here have been so great, and this household is so different from what I have known. I struggle to understand what is expected of me and what my leaving home has meant.

Late at night in this little room high up in a house so much larger than I am used to, I sit before an open window staring out into the darkness listening to waves I cannot see break against the rocky shore below and think and think and think. The pieces of me feel all out of place. There are the old pieces that are now disarranged and the new ones that must somehow be fit in. I do not believe the whole of me, if I grow back together again, will ever be quite the same as you and I remember.

What a puzzle my life has suddenly become! I have never wanted to sort it out before, never felt the need. Now I begin to understand Joanne appropriating time each day to focus on herself, time undistracted by the world around her. When I was young I would complain. Why must she take time from me to be alone? Her response never varied. "Because I lost myself once to what was going on around me and I promised it would not happen again. Not even for you."

I would get so angry when she told me that, jealous really she should value being with herself above being with me, her only child. How dare she? How I resented the separation knowing she enjoyed it while I did not. Even worse, the more upset I grew the more infuriatingly serene was her decision. You know how composed she gets once her mind is made up.

To this day I can remember looking up at her (it must have been when I was very small) pleading to be allowed in, vowing no ripple of noise from me would disturb the stillness of her meditation. To no avail. I was assured in an hour she would be out. The door closed, cutting me off, leaving me alone because she wanted to be left alone. Oh how I would tantrum to get in, beat against the study door to press my grievance, demanding attention unlawfully denied me. It was an outrage and I wanted her to know. But she would not be moved. Not even when I threatened never to love her again. How long my protest lasted I don't recall. It felt like forever. However, I do remember it coming to an end, accepting and adjusting to her privacy and finally learning to enjoy my own, although not in a meditative way.

Now I am grateful for the lesson I bitterly resented then. Solitude was not what I wanted. It was frightening. I felt abandoned. Only as I came to discover ways to keep myself good company did I appreciate what a gift it was. No artist can do without it, that I know. Strange to realize I have Joanne to thank for giving it to me. No thanks then. We were so close I thought my wholeness depended upon our constantly being together. Now separation feels better than being close. I do not miss her. Instead it is she, I think, who misses me. And it is I who have shut the study door. Only it shall be more two years before I come out.

We did not part well. I was angry, am angry still. I had to fight her for my freedom and now, to get it all, must send myself away. Why couldn't she have let me have my independence at home? But no, she was forever pushing and picking, constantly doing small things to me to prove she was still the parent and I the child. Even when I was not there I felt her eyes watching over me, dreading the inevitable questions on my return. What happened? What had I been doing? Questions I knew she would ask. It drove me crazy how she would leave me alone but not let me alone. I fought off her interference with angry silence and angry words, feeling guilty when I saw her hurt by my withdrawal or attack. I didn't want to hurt her. I just wanted her to stay out of my life. More than anything I resented feeling guilty for claiming what was rightfully mine.

Toward the end it became really bad between us. She seemed more enemy to me than mother. Every little incident was a cause for battle between us. No chance for truce. No hope for peace. All out war. It was then I realized to win my freedom I must give up the fight and leave. When Galen, wearied by our hostilities, must have persuaded her to let me go.

It was a cold embrace Joanne and I had at the airport. Holding each other so closely reminded me how great was the distance grown up between us. Our eyes avoided contact. It was stiff and awkward and formal and awful. Neither of us had anything to say. No words at a time like that!

As for the Countess, that was another angry good-bye, although I did have a few well-rehearsed words for her. Did you know Galen gave up the drawing to her for this apprenticeship of mine or whatever it is meant to be? You probably did know. It seems only I did not. I trusted the Countess to do from caring what was simply one more scheme to make a profit.

Both have written to me. I scarcely read what they wrote. And I have not written back. I feel bruised by them each and gather they feel bruised by me as well. May this separation do us all good. Heal our hurts. Thank goodness I do not feel hurt by you. Except for missing our walks and talks together in your museum.

Oh Kip, how you would marvel at the museum here! Which is what the Master's studio and house have become. Rooms overflowing with paintings and sculptures and assemblages and ceramics of all kinds, works by Riablo the public has never seen and even he himself has forgotten. I know he has forgotten because on several occasions now I have seen him wander through a room, jerk to a halt, his eye caught by the corner of some canvas jutting out from a stack of other canvases against the wall. I have seen him stop abruptly, pull it out first smiling with delight at the creation he has rediscovered, then more seriously contemplating the design to extract from this reunion with his past some contribution to his current thinking.

He is such a mix of work and play it is hard to tell one from the other because he brings the same devotion to each. Whatever arrests his attention captures it entirely. There is no differentiation between the more and less important. No facet of his life is trivial. All of it nourishes the man. Meaning, instruction, inspiration are everywhere to be found which is why, I believe, he leads such an isolated, spare and ordered life. He cannot afford to do otherwise. Additional complexity would be overwhelming. More richness than he could bear. Without the protection of stark simplicity, social remoteness and fixed routine his work could not go forward. Without Marcella and Jesus, the two other inhabitants of this house, to provide this protection, too many choices and too much outside interference would distract the Master from his painting. Marcella and Jesus. Servants at first they seemed. Then guardians. Now something more. Much more than they appear.

I have discovered the secret of how the Countess negotiated my sharing studio space with Riablo. Upon entering that room he entirely encloses in himself, the absorption so complete he doesn't know I'm even there. I am shut out of his awareness. The Countess wrote she hoped I would learn ruthlessness from Riablo since I lacked sufficient quantity myself. If by ruthlessness she meant the concentration with which the Master centers on himself, to the exclusion of anyone else, I can already appreciate how much of this intensity I lack. And his determination to live as it pleases him.

For example, because of him I am not called the name I came with. There is no Kate Germaine in this house. Instead, he gave me a name of his own making. I believe Jesus and Marcella knew he would do this and so waited to formally address me until I had been rechristened by the Master. So awkward at first. But not for long.

Deplaning at the airport I stood outside of customs with a suitcase at each side waiting to be recognized, having been told I would be met but not by whom. "Jesus" was all the man said as he swept away my bags and speedily began to weave through the thronging corridor. For a moment I was at a loss. Immediately recovering from my surprise I followed after running because I did not want to lose the one guide I had. Now I know how Alice felt falling down the rabbit hole. Only frightened until the unpredictable came to be expected. By the time I reached the outer terminal my equilibrium was restored, through the doors and there were my belongings strapped on top of a small sedan parked by the curb. Getting in, however, I will admit to being a little put off by the sunburned stranger at the wheel whom I assumed was the same man I had met too briefly inside to recognize again.

"Jesus?" I asked. He nodded slightly and off we drove in silence winding our way out of city traffic through suburban neighborhoods into the rolling countryside, passing lush farmland and quaint towns in one of which we stopped to eat mid-afternoon. Then we drove on, towards evening turning down an unmarked road along the coast which led at last up to a great walled house upon a bluff. Barely squeezing through the narrow gate way we were enclosed in an enormous courtyard where we stopped. I have arrived.

"Marcella!"

I looked through his window to see whom Jesus was calling but he was looking back through mine, so I did too. There, wiping red wet hands on a bright apron was a woman smiling, beckoning me out. I smiled back and stepping out stood up whereupon she enfolded me in her thick arms, crushed me close, then gripping my shoulders held me at arms length and drank me in with her eyes. It makes no sense, I know, yet I felt like some departed child (which I was) returning home (which I was not). And this is how I have been treated. Not welcomed, but welcomed <u>back</u> to a place I've never been where I feel like I belong.

Her stout arm around my waist, Marcella steered me into the house through a kitchen which smelled of freshly baked bread and spices, into a hallway then up three flights of stairs (I was breathless, she was not even breathing hard) opening onto a small landing that opened in turn on a small room with a single window looking out across the sea. Laid across the bed was a freshly laundered muslin smock in which I understood I was to dress. She held it up against my body to convince me of the fit. Then, as she was about to leave, she cupped her hand and drank which I took to mean I was to change and come directly down to supper.

I assumed little was spoken to me because I was ignorant of the language. No. I have since discovered little is spoken here because speech itself is valued very little, a communication of last resort when looks or actions or gestures will not suffice. This is a house for making and creating. Not for talking and discussing. It has taken some getting used to; however, I have come to like it. The purity of the quiet like the purity of the air off the water is invigorating and empowering. I feel fresh energy and focus with new clarity.

Rarely speaking relieves me from having to think about what to say. When I am with some member of the household I don't feel impelled by courtesy to make idle conversation. Quite freeing when there's no social obligation to talk. As though we had all taken vows of silence with each other, and of obedience to the routines which allow us to go our separate ways together. One effect has been a heightened awareness. My capacity to attend what is going on around me and within me has become acute. I feel, I see, I hear, I relate with a sensitivity I have not known before.

Noticing more, I find myself staring at objects or patterns, attuning my eyes and ears to what I previously have been blind and deaf. Have you ever listened to waves? I mean <u>really</u> listened so what used to be an indistinguishable roar becomes discriminated into an intricate arrangement of continually varying sounds. Have you ever looked at a shadow? I mean <u>really</u> looked as you taught me to do at pictures. You know, by opening the outer eye and then the inner so the images can enter and play upon the mind. Like that. You of all people will understand, you who have patiently opened my eyes and enlarged my vision, you and your museum. Now I realize you were not simply teaching me to see pictures, you were actually teaching me to <u>see</u>. Well that, and more than that, is what is happening to me here.

I wonder if the deaf see more acutely than those who can both hear and see? I know silence has helped me see. Not all silent. There is, after all, the music. I have not told you about the music, have I? Or the dance. Or my new name. So much to tell!

Back to supper that first night. When I reentered the kitchen the heavy square table which had been bare when I came in was now set, and seated on either side of the Master, who was standing, were Marcella and Jesus, all apparently awaiting my addition to their number.

Something in the Master's gaze commanded me stop and stand still just inside the doorway. Out of respect for the attention he fixed on me I did not move while he satisfied his curiosity about this new member of his household. I was curious too, so found myself staring back at him with no less curiosity myself.

Photographs had not prepared me for the man I beheld. Much smaller than the giant such towering genius would suggest, of slight build, almost frail in repose. Transformed by movement, he acts with animal quickness, his arms and neck swelling with sudden muscularity I found surprising in one so old. Although I am coming to understand whatever else he may be he is surely the master of surprise. One simply doesn't know what he is about to do or create because he doesn't know himself, doesn't want to know, granting himself full freedom of spontaneity, moment to moment deciding what inclination he shall follow next.

I do believe he was surprised by me. Whatever the Countess had communicated to prepare my way it had, either inadvertently or on purpose, and I suspect the latter, misled his expectation of the visitor who had come to stay. I was not how he anticipated and he was delighted. With a broad smile, those black eyes alive with pleasure, he raised in one hand his glass to me and with the other gestured toward the empty chair which I took. As I sat down the other two stood up, all three toasting me, three glasses raised, the Master intoning "Iliana! Iliana!", to which first Marcella and then Jesus echoed in turn "Iliana! Iliana!" as though the name they gave me was more than a name. It was a gift.

A blush every bit as deep as the red of their wine swept over me with such a rush I felt grateful for the chair beneath me. Embarrassment did not cause me to color thus, but the excitement of my sudden change in name. In one bold stroke the old name by which I had been known and known myself, was stripped away and to clothe my nakedness a new one immediately bestowed. Which had the greater impact, the loss or gain, I am not sure. Only that I felt emboldened by a sense of enormous possibility. I was struck how a name signifies much more than a label by which a person is addressed. It comes to represent a host of meanings gathered over time until the very mention invokes those qualities descriptive of who the person has become. What a lot of baggage is a name!

Kate. Now what kind of person is a Kate, I ask you Kip? A one syllable person. No nonsense and no frills. Not musical. Not pleasing to the ear, probably not to the eye. Plain sounding and plain looking. Plain Kate Germaine. What I have been all my life. Plain sounding, plain looking, plain spoken. A name such as one might give an object of simple and reliable use. Like a digging or cutting tool sturdily made of strong stuff, able to stand up well under daily toil, to hard work, a hard working name. A stalwart name with which to brave oneself through the perils of childhood. A name with hard edges at the beginning and the end. Not a soft cuddly name. Not a name to pick up and pet. A name to give a certain distance and respect.

Kip, that name, that person is not who I am here. Iliana, whoever she is, is a very different name and a very different person, or the same person coming to live very differently within myself. In this prison of isolation a new freedom is held out to me. I feel safe and vulnerable and frightened and excited all the time. While the name itself has become emblem of my purpose here. I believe I am sent to this place to become Iliana.

Did the Countess know, do you think, what a turn she would be giving my life when she cleared the path to this door? I wonder. She has been so open and covert with me perhaps she has been crafty in this. How implicated is she in what happens to me here? Perhaps I had best follow the advice you gave me long ago when she first took me up. Be careful, you warned. Don't try to fathom her motivations and designs. Accept that I shall always be out of my depths with her. Deal directly and trust she will not injure me unless I threaten her well being or stand in her way. Recalling your counsel now, perhaps I should write her once as she requested. Such a powerful friend she has been to me, such a powerful enemy she could become if I caused our friendship to end. And even in my anger I do not want that.

But I have not told you about the food. After my name was duly entered into the household register they sat down and Marcella removed the lid of the great earthenware pot simmering on the center of the table and ladled into bowls before us heaping scoops of steaming casserole. There were great chunks of fish and fresh vegetables in a dark savory broth which smelled so delicious I would immediately have fallen to except the others did not eat, deferring whatever appetite they had to inhale the fragrance before they enjoyed the food, treating the enticing aroma as the first course to be savored before the actual tasting which came next. Time was taken to separate the two and relish them each as I am learning time is taken to luxuriate in the most ordinary parts of life, simple enjoyment being raised to extraordinary pleasure. Either I have never tasted food so good or I have never truly <u>tasted</u> food before. Over a month now since that meal and I can still recall and linger with pleasure over it as freshly as I did on my first evening here.

When the great pot was removed and the places cleared away Riablo stood up, taking from behind one of his ears what on first impression from the doorway I had mistaken to be one of his horns and held out to me a black wax crayon which I accepted, unclear about what I was meant to do. Then from behind the other ear he extracted a second crayon and with the practiced confidence of someone who could compose anything at will, in one sweeping motion of his arm drew upon the table cloth a perfect oval so smoothly joined I could not detect where the line had originally begun or finally ended.

It was then he nodded to me. My turn to draw. Seeing he was not going to offer me more than one crayon I broke mine in two, equipping each hand equally for the task we had been given. It was within this oval I knew he wished us to draw. Me to draw. A space which, because it was neither square nor rectangular, did not oblige me to design with reference to horizontal or vertical, up or down.

You would have thought, I would have thought, I would have felt intimidated drawing before the Master, but I was not. The reason? Because I felt from him not the slightest hint of judgment, only open interest in whatever I would do. Glancing once into those eyes in which the pupils are so dilated the irises appear black, I proceeded to work on the surface before me.

You have often told me how watching me draw is like witnessing an altered state.   Yes.   Something conscious slipping away, something unconscious taking over. 'The dance of hands' as you call it began as I disengaged from those around me and let impulse out to play. Never any music to this dance, although I felt the dancing pleasure of my hands leading and following, following and leading, switching active and reactive roles, building to a point where there were no more steps to be taken, no more strokes to be made. The picture was finished. The dance was done.

I looked up. The Master was not even looking at my drawing. He was staring at me. Puzzled. As though in need of some explanation for what he had witnessed. With his right hand gesturing back and forth between my hands he questioned my preference.

I clasped my hands together to show they shared equal responsibility.

He frowned in perplexity first at my hands then at his own, dropping the right and closely examining the left, relaxing his wrist until the hand hung loose, limp and incapacitated, as though of no use. Shaking his head in disgust as though this hand was nothing but an incompetent paw, he shuffled outside muttering something under his breath which I barely caught, muttering a name to blame for his confusion, "Elena! Elena!"

You can imagine how I felt startling, perhaps offending the Master. Why? Why did the Countess not inform him I drew with both hands? Because she wanted him to make his own discovery to this effect. Even at this distance I was a tool in her hands. A tool to demonstrate how she could move Riablo if she chose. Such resentment I felt! How I hate being party to her intrigues. How could I repair whatever injury I had in ignorance done? I was about to give myself over to this question when I noticed Marcella, arms hugged tight across her breasts, trembling with silent laughter barely contained, her body racked with convulsions of delight. At what? I looked at her for explanation of the joke in which I had stupidly been implicated and saw no humor. She simply shook her head and smiled, giving me to understand I was not to blame nor to understand.

Wiping tears from her eyes and cheeks with her apron she rose unsteadily to her feet and followed Riablo out the kitchen door. Only then did I notice Jesus had already left. Glancing first at the drawing from where I stood , I walked round the table finding to my satisfaction the design held together from whatever perspective I viewed it. My first drawing in the Master's house! Done with crayons and in the kitchen too, just like old times, just like I began. I felt at home, starting over, and the feeling was good.

I live through my eyes so much it surprises me when another sense takes over as it did next. Suddenly my ears were pierced by the sharp pulsating notes of a bird song undulating in through the open door. Irresistibly drawn to the sound I turned from the table, the sweet trilling growing more insistent, more impatient it seemed, calling me out. More than calling. It felt like a summons I could not refuse and so obeyed.

From the stone landing I saw at first no further than the kitchen light cast from behind me could reach. The bird continued singing now in a lilting, playful manner. Or was it another bird, the song changing, becoming varied and musical in an un-birdlike way.

Curious to locate what was enthralling my attention I moved away from the light to better penetrate the dark. Peering more intently now I could just discern the looming outer walls when nearer to me another shape became distinct, a human shape swaying back and forth in the center of the courtyard. Jesus it was, the song sounds rising from him, hunched over cradling some pipe or set of pipes he must be playing. Now he had tamed the wild bird songs into an artless melody such as a child would compose loving the repetition of a simple tune.

As the piece became more rhythmical, another figure, also clothed in silhouette, sprang from out of nowhere and began to dance around Jesus in a large circle, crouching and leaping, prancing and bounding, like some imp of fancy which the night had just let out to frolic in the dark.

That I did not immediately recognize Riablo was because such strenuous activity seemed inconceivable to me given his age. However, whether it was by some enchantment of the moon or of the music, or some transformation conspired by them both, he could has well have been a spirited child sporting to the changing melodies sporting with him, until I could not tell whether the dancer danced to the music or the player played to the dance.

Then a third figure, unmistakably Marcella, for I knew her by a shape so like my own, joined the circle slowly stepping effortlessly turning, reaching high her arms, bending first this way then that, a ballerina freed to perform only to please herself. I could not believe a body like mine could move so elegantly when all these years I have begrudged myself dance because I was large and clumsy, lacking slenderness and grace.

Content to simply watch and marvel, before I knew what was happening each dancer caught me by the hand, would not let me go, and round and round we spun, the ground spinning beneath us scrambling the stars over head until I felt so dizzy I didn't know what I was doing, following their lead because I lacked the strength to do anything else. Releasing their hand hold of me because now they held my entire body in thrall, my sense of direction depending on them, Marcella behind me, Riablo led us in a strutting march along the circle's edge, legs lifted high, chest out and head thrown back, arms pumping, all three of us on proud parade. I followed his example, she followed mine, then we were back into another dizzying spin this time breaking with Marcella leading, slowing us into a stately processional, gliding forward on the balls of our feet, long strides skating over the ground and not upon it, back into a spin only to be broken with myself at the front. My turn to lead the other two!

Kip, I froze. The last time I danced was in second grade when I swore never to dance again, preferring punishment for refusing, to being teased about how awkwardly I moved and bulky I looked. 'Freight Train Germaine' is what it amused them to call me seeing my face color with humiliation, not seeing the shame which bled inside. Did you know? Freight Train Germaine is how I came to view myself. Until this night.

Perhaps darkness gives permission which the light denies. Or perhaps it was the music of Jesus, soft and wavering, breathlessly gentle. Or perhaps it was the two behind me waiting with no impatience, simply pausing as if hesitation were part of my dance and so part of theirs. Even the music hesitated, a long measure of silence belonging in the composition, before I ventured a tiny step to a single tentative note, then another, several notes accompanying it, momentum building as I began moving through the motions I had learned, prancing like Riablo, swirling like Marcella, then miraculously creating motions of my own, known to my body all these years but not before now claimed by me. Dancing! Kip, I was actually dancing! I did not even feel like Kate Germaine. Iliana, indeed!

How late the music and the dance continued after this I cannot say. The moon was well up, I know, because we cast shadows from her light before we were done, our shadows tireless partners in our dance. At the last it was we three holding hands in a tight ring about Jesus who played us into a final frenzy up an impossibly high scale of notes I'd never heard, tumbling slowly sweetly down one by one for us to linger over every sound that had accompanied our celebration this first night. Silence at last.

A deep silence that still resonated to music beyond hearing but not beyond recall. I strained my ears not wanting to let go. Too late. Our hands relaxed and then released. Riablo bowed to Jesus as one Master to another. Marcella did the same. Then myself, as if accustomed to ending each evening this way. Jesus, panpipes embraced to his chest like a beloved child or perhaps a lover, bowed back. It was over. Whatever had bound us so closely was broken now. We each wended our separate paths to sleep.

I did not realize how tired I was, unused to exercise as you know I am, and having traveled so far in a single day, from one world it seemed into another. Ascending the stairs my legs rebelled at climbing, cramping in protest, but I overrode their objections with my craving for rest. I must not have even undressed because when I awakened late next morning, it was almost noon, my body flung across the bed, the smock gathered about me like a gown.

Oh Kip, there is much to tell and I shall write again. To keep you in touch with me. To keep me close to you.

With love,

Kate, now Iliana

Chapter Six
PORTRAIT OF THE ARTIST

On a darkened wall of an interior hallway, removed from direct sunlight that could fade the ink and further deteriorate the paper, hung the small drawing, a few extraordinarily suggestive pen scratches on brown rag paper made centuries before by an artist whose name had been lost, but whose work had miraculously survived through this fragmentary relic of a great, anonymous talent.

With the exception of LaValle the dealer who was at any moment prepared to broker its sale, Kate's uncle Phillip, the museum director, for whom it would be a star in the crown of that collection, and the Countess who simply coveted it for herself, visitors to the home paid the little masterpiece scant attention. They preferred to notice works in progress on other walls and portraits of the family whose members themselves gave the dark little drawing only passing heed, except for Kate. For her, it had provided unfailing inspiration during the secret early years when her own talent was developing but not yet recognized by those who thought they knew her best.

When she asked how such a treasure came into the family's possession, information that Kate received was very incomplete. A paternal grandfather had discovered it among the effects of his uncle's estate into which the drawing had apparently fallen, after much relocation, from the dissolution of an art collection assembled generations earlier in another country by some landed ancestor with a taste for beautiful objects and the wealth or power to procure them. Certainly the drawing was beautiful, exquisite in its portrayal, economical in its means, subtle in its expression, stylish in a manner unaffected by changing tastes over time.

What amazed her as much as the genius of the drawing was simply that it was, after so many years, still undestructed. Surely there had been infinite opportunity for it to be torn, soiled, rotted, thrown away or lost. Yet none of these eventualities occurred. As unknown, and as remarkable, as the artist who created it were these shadow figure who time after time rescued it, secured it, passed it on to another whose appreciation would provide one more small human life span of protection for great art, ever an endangered species.

And the collector, the ancestor, what of him? Kate could only imagine, and did, picturing a great baronial figure striding through stone halls hung with heavy woven tapestries to a library in which, among religious artifacts and ancient books, this drawing held an honored place. What other treasures did this man accumulate, and how came he by them? Through purchase, theft, trickery, or plunder? The history of collecting as she had been told by her Uncle Phillip, 'Kip', seemed more like piracy than anything else. Unsuspecting countries boarded at night, who did not awaken to the value of their cultural heritage until after it had been stolen away. And yet, without collectors to preserve the past and patronize the present so much creative achievement would disappear.

Once Kate asked her father: "Galen, what is the drawing truly worth? How much?"

"Money you mean? I don't know. LaValle has told me in the current market, which is not so favorable as fifteen or twenty years ago, the drawing would still fetch a great price. He if anyone would know the exact answer, although he would never be so unguarded as to specify a sum. I have only been told he represents a number of collectors eager to buy it should I ever be willing to sell. So, what <u>is</u> the answer to your question? Like any piece of art it's worth whatever anyone is willing to pay. The art market has always been a free market, half over the table, the other half under, LaValle trading in both. The prices fluctuate with fickle shifts in public taste, rising and falling with demand that this creates. First and foremost demand. Then quality, history, rarity and condition."

"But you would never sell it," asked Kate concerned.

"No. Not unless there was a dire need or some great purpose to justify the sale. It's a trust to which I'm obligated, the care and keeping of this master drawing. One day the responsibility shall pass to you."

It was during a sitting for her annual portrait they were speaking thus. On these occasions he talked more to keep her moving less. Once a year the girl came into intimate contact with her father, a man not by nature conversational. Normally when he was painting it was understood his studio was off limits to his daughter. She was not to breach the wall of silence that surrounded him each day. Therefore, yearly admittance into his private world created an opportunity that she greatly valued, as did he. At these sittings she would receive his prolonged attention, feeling the full concentration of his observation upon her as he scrutinized her every physical and psychological detail. Kate felt treated like a client first and daughter second, accorded the same respect he would and did accord any other subject.

More than intimacy from his notice, however, she prized the intimacy from conversation as he chatted about himself and his work to divert attention from her natural impatience at remaining motionless and quiet. Posing she found to be an exhausting process. Freedom she decided was being able to move when one chose.

"It always surprises me," she said during a welcome break, " how difficult sitting for my portrait really is. It looks so easy and then quickly becomes so hard. How professional models like Joanne ever learned to do absolutely nothing for so long is more than I can understand." And Kate wearily resumed her pose.

"You're right," Galen agreed. " It's learned, not given. Practice over many years did it for your mother. Habit forming. Discipline building. What requires effort for you takes very little for her. She grew used to it, her body tolerating positions it had been exercised to accept. Like you, it goes against my grain. While with Joanne stillness became second nature, maybe even first." Then he laughed.

"That's how I first met your mother, you know. She was the model for an art class in which your Uncle Phillip and I were second year students. We each had a different reaction to her at the time. Or maybe the same, differently expressed. Entranced by her composure he did about the best sketch I ever saw him do. But me, I was fascinated, challenged by her self-possession. Still as a statue, physically naked, emotionally hidden from this circle of student artists gathered to observe her. Some mischief in me couldn't resist trying to break down her concentration. I simply had to get her attention. So for an hour and a half (we were prohibited from approaching her during the breaks) I did my damnedest. Staring, sudden noises, making faces, but nothing would distract her. No success whatsoever. Ask your mother sometime. She remembers. Ashamed to say I resorted to spit wads at the end. Kind of childish when I look back at myself acting that way, but how was I to know I was falling in love? I couldn't help it. She was more provocation than I could resist. Ended the period without even the outline of her figure on my pad.

"Immediately at dismissal, she stood up as supple as you please and without even bothering to slip on her robe stalks over to me, gets in my face, tells me never to do that again, grabs the charcoal from my hand and in bold strokes on my pad writes the word 'JERK'. Then down in the corner the address where she lived. Adding: 'Pick me up at 7:30. For an <u>expensive</u> dinner. You owe me one.' And that's how our romance began. Of course I've sketched her many times since then, but no more making faces or throwing spit wads."

Kate was delighted by this and other anecdotes her father freely shared, appreciating how it was not reticence which kept him so much to himself as preoccupation with work. A predisposition to act more than talk, to listen more than speak.

"Well," she sighed, "I shall never have Joanne's endurance for sitting no matter how often I do it."

Her father laughed again.

"No you won't. You were born active, a doer like me. I've tried your mother's way and she's tried mine. We fit together because we compliment each other. Opposites are what we are. Being is her way of doing and doing is my way of being. I love to keep busy, she loves to keep still. I don't meditate and she doesn't paint portraits. As much as we love each other we love the difference between us. More than that, I have a need which your mother doesn't. I'm a maker. I need to see some concrete outcome for my efforts and receive some notice from the world. Not so your mother. With her the process is enough. No traces left when meditation or reflection is done. The moment is what matters. She's free standing in a way that I am not. Here's what we are, Kate: she's Dickinson, I'm Dickens. This family, we're all she cares about. And of course your uncle."

"But Kip isn't really my uncle, is he?"

"By blood, no. And yet, what really matters? Devotion does. And loyalty. It began with he and I and almost ended with your mother. Phillip and I became best friends in college, darn near breaking up over her. Rivals the instant we saw her. He was terribly hurt. To this day I'm not sure why she chose me. He had more social skills back then and cut a more engaging, promising figure than the dull plodding student I was. Everyone liked Phillip and expected great things of him. When he switched into art history they knew it was only a matter of time before he would curate himself up into a major directorship somewhere, although no one would have predicted such a prestigious museum as this at such a young age.

"Really he's done wonderfully. The job is impossible, you know. The ever-present financial problems, fund raising always a necessity in addition to all the other responsibilities. Organizing shows and educational programs to bring the public in, attracting volunteers. Managing the politics of a board and the vanity of donors. Graciously negotiating the social mine fields of charity events, the sensitivities of the socially prominent, all the while firmly orchestrating a large organization of employees each driven by their own agenda of ambitions and discontents. Yet he never wearies of it, loves it all."

Noticing Kate nudge a shoe off one foot with the other and splay her toes to relieve a cramp, Galen smiled.

"Why don't we take a break. I could use a stretch. How about you?"

Gratefully Kate unfolded her body, kink by kink, reclaiming control she had given up.

"Is this why Kip never married? Because Joanne chose you and he never loved anyone else?" Looking over her father's shoulder at the canvas she saw the outlines of herself beginning to take on shape and character.

"That was the reason why he did not marry then. Since, I believe, there has been another."

"His work?" Kate asked.

"Perhaps. He'd have to tell you. In any case, your mother has ever been 'the woman' in his life and I his oldest friend. The summer following our engagement he fled to Europe on a traveling fellowship to visit great collections there, and when he returned the pain he'd left with had somehow been absolved. There was no awkwardness between us. Ever since he's been the dear caring man who is closer to you than I. Not a father. Not a parent to you, is he?"

"No. More of a confidante and friend. I've always felt I could tell him anything, and have."

"Yes," agreed Galen, "that captures it. He's the most trustworthy person I know. What you just said about Phillip is what your mother and I would say too. He probably knows more about all of us than we do about each other. So there's your answer: blood may be thicker than water, but intimacy is thicker than blood."

The sitting gave Kate freedom to ask what she pleased, inquiring as deeply into her father as she chose, just as he, through portraiture, inquired deeply into her.

"Why did Joanne choose you, Galen?"

"Back to your prison while I think about your question," he replied. "You all set? It's your face and neck and shoulders so hold them as quiet as you can. Perfect. Well, she loved me, I know that. But she loved Phillip too. Besides, your mother is not a woman to be swayed into marriage simply by love. Judgment ruled her then as it does now. I think I fit what she was looking for, a partner who would make very few demands on her because of my devotion to my work. You must remember, she was running a family when she was your age, acting housemother to younger children when she was mere child herself. Doing without her own childhood so they could have theirs, but warning them she would be leaving to take up her own life after high school, a warning they chose to ignore. At age eighteen she kept the promise to herself that had sustained her through so much responsibility. Scholarship and part time job in hand she moved out, embittering those behind who called her selfish and irresponsible. They never forgave her and she has never forgiven them. In one parting stroke the connections of a life-time were severed and your mother was alone in the world. The experience was a terrible rejection and a tremendous relief. The first year at college she kept to herself, the second she let your uncle and I into friendship, and at last me into marriage. Why me? I think Phillip's social life was more demanding than she was willing to share. He was too public a man for a woman who passionately desired privacy. She wanted a cloistered life, and with me she found it." Now he stood up, a signal Kate could do the same.

" But if she was so tired of being a mother, why did she want children of her own?"

"She didn't," answered Galen truthfully. "She wanted only one child. A daughter. You. To mother differently than she was mothered. To mother differently than she had mothered her brothers and sisters. She got her wish. You came true."

Kate resumed her pose.

"Just like I come true in your portraits ?" she asked.

Galen laughed.

"Yes, all my portraits of you are predictions. A chance to see where you are growing. It's always a surprise."

"For me too. How you see into my future." She rubbed an itch on her chin with her right shoulder, then settled back into position. Four years old when the portraits began, spring sittings soon became a special occasion to which she looked forward each year. What she wore, the accessories she wanted to include, even the pose itself were up to her, how she wanted to present herself. But this was the surprise. No matter how certain she was about the image to be portrayed, her father's rendering was discrepant in a disturbing sense. Oh it was her likeness, always that. But added was something more. He caught her older than she appeared to herself, than she appeared at the time to him. By the next sitting, however, her growth over the intervening year proved the last portrait's prediction correct. By what intuitive power he could foretell her development she didn't know. Nor did he.

"Just because I have this sensitivity doesn't mean I understand it. This talent to render psychological insight in visual terms. I don't know how that's done, getting the surface likeness and then the play of personality beneath. Strange business I'm in. Portraiture gives one the license to stare into people. How many lines of work allow you to pry? Usually my subjects are surprised. They'll ask me to put words to my interpretation. However, I make it a rule never to explain my portraits."

"Because it spoils the mystery?" Kate wanted to know.

"No. No mystery intended. My paintings have to stand on their own terms. Any picture in need of verbal support isn't much of a picture. And any subject as talkative as you is very hard to paint.

Now Kate, one great stretch and then you must statue yourself for the last few minutes."

Kate did as she was bid, extending her arms and twisting her trunk, bending way over, crouching down to drive the stiffness from her legs, standing slowly back up into position.

"You'll never be a spectator, Kate. The audience life is not for you. Your body won't sit still for it. And yet, if what I sense about you is correct, you have some capacity for stillness waiting to be discovered. All of us are a mix of opposites, walking contradictions. Even you. In the best of my paintings I capture that inconsistency, working on two surfaces, not one. The first is likeness, what is readily apparent. The second is more subtle, often hidden and disguised. The subsurface where opposing traits collide. The secret sadness of a happy man. The vicious anger of a gentle woman. The inward extrovert. The serious joke teller. This last the power of the clown. What are we to make of such discrepancies? Out of them I make my living. By casting my subjects in contrasting lights I draw their contradictions out. That's the mix I'm after, creating ambiguity so people come away feeling ambivalent about the person I've portrayed. Feeling conflicted, they can't quite make up their mind. In my finest portraits, the paintings become memorable because the contradictions hold."

All the while he talked Kate pondered the artist, her father. So self-disclosing with her now. Then the studio door would shut for another year and he would become inaccessible as usual. Until next spring when, like a spell, another sitting would once again allow her to briefly know the inner man. How curious was his work...It kept her out but it also let her in.

Chapter Seven
THE INCEST SURVIVOR

My dear Miss Germaine:

If I allowed obstinacy from others to deter me from pursuing my desires, I should not have gained all that I have. Therefore, in the absence of receiving any encouragement to my previous letter, having in hand no word from you to which I can reply, I shall use this opportunity to correspond about myself, continuing to use you as the confidante you have become.

As you may have already been informed, I approached your mother at the airport with an offer of friendship that she declined with admirable spirit. As you may not know, I pressed the invitation again more recently when she surprised both of us and accepted what she had first refused. That I like her goes without saying or else I would not have put myself in her way.

Why do I like her? Because the very characteristics that have rendered her objectionable in your eyes have raised her in my own. For years I excluded her from the circle to which I kept because she had no name except her husband's and no reputation outside of family. Possessing no power to socially advance me I saw no material reason to waste attentions that could be more profitable invested elsewhere. I was wrong. The fault was mine. The loss as well.

Preoccupation with personal gain caused me to overlook value for which I was not prospecting but am now, thanks to the generosity of your mother, being given a second chance to enjoy. As with you, I value the frank interchange between personal equals in which honesty rudely ignores courtesy by confiding only the truth. Not always easy or pleasant, yet rewarding. Occasionally altering. With the harshness of her insight, your mother has already caused me to reevaluate what I had long ago dismissed as worthless, the mothering I received. Perhaps it takes one mother to fully appreciate the contributions of another.

Certainly, I have never appreciated mine. She was so impotent. When father was about, her attention was devoted to his bidding, providing pleasures he wanted, accepting whatever temper he was in while I was kept out of the way lest my presence offend the great man. Even so small an irritation as myself could cause him to erupt.

The world accuses me of being haughty, I know. Certain enemies, I am told by their enemies even have a pejorative for me, La Grande Damn. That they only use this name behind my back is proof of the fearful respect in which I am held. Like my father, I have had few enemies to my face, your mother and Savocek being the notable exceptions. From my father, I learned how to hold my place in the world by assuming authority. You yourself took offense at my haughtiness when we first met. Remember? But that was my father's first lesson: put yourself above others unless you want others to put themselves above you. So I learned, first practicing with my dolls, then with my image in the mirror, then with the enemy himself --my father.

Initially, it amused him to look down on a little mite like myself acting with such adult command. 'Putting on airs', he called it until he realized I was serious. You cannot imagine how furious he became. This great bully of men is unable to intimidate his six-year-old daughter! I was not very tall, not compared to him. However, I drew myself up to full height, such as it was, and responded to his rage with the one provocation I knew he could not endure -- unwavering, impassive silence. Even then I knew my advantage lay in saying nothing and appearing unfazed by the storm of anger he unleashed upon me.

The louder and more threatening he became the quieter and more unthreatened I appeared. In the extremity of his frustration he finally drew back his hand to strike the impertinence from my face when, at the very last moment, he restrained his impulse. What a blow! What a loss! I had him. Victory was mine. Had I not betrayed its coming with a smile of triumph, he would have proceeded unmindful of his danger. As it was he caught himself just in time, perceiving how he was about to win the battle and lose the war.

Then he regarded me with undisguised interest. I was more comfortable with his anger. This was when our understanding of each other truly began. Check almost mate. I nearly had him. But he detected his immanent defeat from my premature smile and elected for a draw. If he had only lost control to gain control I would have ended up in control. Alas, I was only six and lacked the wisdom and restraint to keep my anticipation from showing. I know better now.

All this while my mother stood frozen with dread, fingers of both hands clutching her mouth open in horror, wide-eyed, her helplessness exposed. Immediately she became a target of his attack. 'You caused this!' And then he flogged her with wrath meant for me. Under his lash of cruel words, she cowered and whimpered and apologized until he felt restored and ordered her to his bed. Turning to me as he left to take his pleasure he threatened: 'You'll pay for this later!' We both knew that was a lie. I never did.

Some scenes from childhood never fade. You'll find this for yourself if you have not already. The specific event takes on symbolic meaning representing something far beyond what actually occurred. For me the day I stood up to my father forever redefined our relationship and irrevocably committed me to the course of independence I have honed to ever since.

Describing this encounter to your mother, we seem to do a lot of reminiscing, she made an observation, used a single word to describe my mother that has radically revised that failure of a woman in my eyes. For the life of me I cannot see her in the old way any more. 'Countess,' your mother said, 'you never told me that your mother was so <u>sly</u>.' 'Sly?' I asked, not understanding her meaning. 'Yes', she replied, 'the way she tricked your father into neglecting you so you could have the freedom she did not. How she diverted his anger and protected you in the process. How she governed him with helplessness, arousing then quenching his desires.'

What? That scorned image of the victim woman against which I defined myself was shattered. In her place stood revealed the mistress of her fate and benefactress of mine. Sly she was. Subtle and devious, using her powers of passivity and compliance to control an aggressor undetected, to shield me from his overbearing influence, to give me freedom of an active kind that she gave up. All this within an instant I perceived. And something more. It was not simply him she fooled. It was also myself. Her complaints to me only misdirected my attention from the calculated way she exploited his dependency upon her. My vision shifted from contempt to admiration to indebtedness I did not know I had, as I confessed to your mother. 'Yes,' she agreed, 'you were doubly blessed. From your father, you learned to force your way. From your mother, you were taught how to play the loser and win. You come by your deviousness honestly, at any rate.' I took this as a compliment.

Understand, however, this re-evaluation of my mother has not been unalloyed with pain. While I am grateful to acknowledge half a heritage previously denied, I find myself regretting I cannot thank the woman whom I previously misread. Regret. What an unpleasant emotion that is, the more so because it is often unnecessary. The sin of omission. An opportunity offered and not taken, in my case recognized too late to rectify the loss.

I know you are young, Miss Germaine, and life stretches out before you in such future abundance time seems to have no end. But it does. And the name we give it is Death. You and I, we have never discussed the strained relations between your mother and yourself. I do not presume to open up with you what you were not inclined to share with me. Yet I feel impelled to suggest this much. My mother is beyond recall. Yours is not. It was judgment of my mother that ended my relationship with her before she died. It was her death that renders my reappraisal so tormenting now. I hope, not for your mother's sake but for your own, you do not in anger sever a relationship for which reconsideration comes, as it has for me, after the door to reconciliation has been closed. Enough said.

My father. He well knew his influence upon me because it was deliberately applied. Having described him to you in unflattering terms let me amend this impression to this extent. In turning me against my mother by cruelly complimenting how she and I were much alike, galling me with similarity calculated to offend, he turned me toward himself, down his path away from hers. You often told me about Savocek and the duress of his instruction. I did not tell you about my father and his education of me.

After our first encounter he apparently decided my sex was no longer to be held against me. Not for my sake, but for his. Recognizing in me his dominating spirit, I was treated as an extension of himself. Thus he would not allow the world to thwart me because that would be tantamount to thwarting him. Being a professional investor, a gambler with his own and other people's money, he decided I had growth possibilities. I was a challenge and an opportunity. How close to the image of himself could this girl child, with his training, become? Quite a narcissistic venture. So much for paternal love. However, we both knew this from the start. It was a bargain plain and simple, though we never wrote it out. How much could I learn from him was what both of us were determined to see. Vanity was his objective. Power was mine.

Within a week of the occasion when I took his measure and he took mine I was ushered into his study one evening, my mother summarily dismissed, and was directed to sit down on the opposite side of his great desk with the peculiar inlay of checkered squares in the center. He awaited my response. I gave him none. Only silence. 'Good,' he said, leaning back in his chair surveying my small presence. 'Life is a game, Alana. Last week you challenged me. Tonight I take your challenge up.' Then he leaned forward and pulling open a drawer to his left began extracting gold and silver ornaments, some of the figures adorned with jewels, placing the gold upon the squares before him and the silver immediately in front of me. Still I showed no surprise. Said nothing. My last experience with indiscretion made me determined not to repeat the error of my ways. He would have to tell me what he wanted me to know. I would not ask. This was one rule by which I was going to play whatever his game turned out to be.

Chess. He was not simply a passionate chess player, he was a devout believer in the religion of chess, in lessons the ancient game had to teach. It called to his spirit and taught him, as he declared, how to play the game of life, specifically the skills and strategies and temperament required for manipulation which is how he viewed the unfolding process of each match, the pieces always in sight, the intent always concealed. A mix of move and countermove culminating in entrapment of oneself, one's adversary, or of both in a stalemate where neither gains the upper hand. How many pieces were sacrificed in the campaign was the critical calculation: how much was one willing to risk losing to win? This is why after each game he would have me assess the loss in pieces for victor and vanquished. 'No victory is worth winning at all costs,' he told me. I still believe that. 'There is no benefit in fighting to win once losing has become a certainty.' He taught me to cut my losses as well.

At the time I thought he put too much of life into the game to play it well. Not so. Years later I discovered he enjoyed high unofficial standing in the international chess playing community. Not a grandmaster himself, he had on more than one occasion taken games from these venerated men, even devised an opening that still bears his name. After he died I received letters from several of them paying tribute to the gifted amateur they had come to respect. One compliment I remember: 'Your father played the game as though it mattered.' Indeed he did.

A man who led many private lives of which chess was only one. Who knows how many other passions he secretly indulged? I've not trusted a man who travels for a living ever since. Freedom from surveillance at home is too easily abused on the road. Except LaValle, whose entire life is one invisible itinerary around the globe, and I only a single port of call. Yet I trust him. And in one respect trusted my father. As a teacher. I was an apt pupil. The game came naturally to me because it naturally made sense. The combination of feint and parry, bluff and calculation, diversion and attack, jockeying for slight advantage, thinking ahead, exploiting weakness to win. All this I instinctively understood. Patience and concentration came easily to me, as well as masking feeling and intent.

We played the games with no respect for time. It was mate, concede or draw, however long it took, and it lasted till after midnight on many occasions. Even then the lesson was not done until I had reckoned the costs of victory and defeat. Never once in those years did he indulge my inexperience. Never once did I yield effort to discouragement. Never did he let me win. Time and again I lost but never lost my determination to prevail. One sign of gain was a satisfaction to me. As I grew older I bloodied him more. His victories took longer to accomplish and he had fewer pieces left to fashion my defeat. Finally I fought him to a draw. That night he did the reckoning instead of I. 'Luck does not strike twice,' he said. A year later, almost to the day, we drew again. There was no reckoning that night. Instead, he simply put the pieces away, by which I was given to understand we had played our last game. Of chess.

Next evening I was summoned to appear before my father as usual, only I knew it was not going to be as usual. By age thirteen, however, I was no more likely to betray curiosity or surprise than he. Once again the desk was bare. Stubbornly I stood until he was forced to invite me to sit down. 'You will never be a chess player, Alana.' This was how he began. I signified neither assent nor disagreement. 'However,' he went on, 'you demonstrate potentialities of another kind. Now we shall see to what degree you can fulfill their promise.' So saying he withdrew a legal folder from the filing cabinet to his right and handed it across to me.

'This is another kind of game. It is played by negotiation, sealed by contract, and the score is kept in money. Profiles of the players, financial data, legal assurances, offers and counter offers, proposed agreements, modifications, the final document, evidence of subsequent performance, it's all there. Each folder is a casebook in the craft I ply. I am an opportunist, Alana. By helping others I help myself. A dangerous way to live. Reward depends upon risk that is only moderated by restraint. A certain temperament is required to do it well, an aptitude for advancing one's own interests at the expense of others. You have demonstrated the necessary inclination. Now let us see if you have the intelligence as well.'

It was with extreme self-control that I concealed the excitement that his words aroused in me. My mask of unemotionally did not slip from my face. He nodded to show he saw beneath my mask, and then proceeded. 'After thoroughly reviewing this material you are to tell me why I entered such a business arrangement and how I could have made it better. Understood?'

I nodded back and rose to leave. He stayed me with his hand. 'One rule must change between us. One of your rules. While questions are confessions of ignorance and ignorance is unwise to display, they also inform the other person of what you need to know. Not everything is in the folder. It is stupidity not to ask me for additional information you may require. Therefore I make this contract with you now. Questions pertaining to each investment shall be freely answered without penalty of criticism from me.' I nodded again. He was as good as his word.

So began the practical training that has enabled me to transform a substantial inheritance and widow's settlement into a considerable fortune. I was more than a week studying what my father had given me, sequencing the order of events, identifying the players, puzzling out legal and business terms in those same dictionaries he consulted, comparing numbers, assembling the puzzle around missing pieces of the picture, assigning questions to what needed filling in.

It may have been comparable to what you experienced with drawing, discovering with certainty what you were made to do. The art of manipulation and negotiation for material gain. Of sizing up and seizing opportunity. Although I never worked so hard it was no labor. Chess had been absorbing, but actually creating a deal had practical possibilities no mere game could simulate. The rewards were so tangible. The risks so real. So much to figure out. And through it all I could discern the strategy my father followed as he planned and improvised and gambled to get as close to what he sought at a price he was willing to pay.

It was, I decided, a fair exchange between us. If he were willing to expose his inner workings for the sake of my instruction, I would risk the vulnerability of learning what he had to teach by declaring ignorance with questions, feeling inept when I made mistakes, willing to look foolish in his eyes, even submitting to his evaluation when I was done. However, there was no good sense in putting myself to his test before I was ready. Therefore I took my time, scheduling a first meeting for my questions, delaying the next until my thoughts were in order. 'Reviews' he called them. I shall never forget my first review. He placed me at every disadvantage. The notes I brought with me he demanded, crumpled up and dropped into the trash. Then he directed me to stand just inside the door so I had to speak up loudly for him to hear from across the room.

Today I am known for, among other things, the firmness of my demeanor. Little do my detractors appreciate how long ago this discipline of self assurance was acquired nor by what trials learned. My father already knew I could stand up to him, but could I withstand the severity of his examination as well? Or could he disrupt my composure and disarrange my thoughts? Since they were mine I knew he could do neither without my permission, and I was not about to give him that. Having prepared for the worst, notes were no more than superfluous props since I had memorized my speech and practiced the words out loud often enough so saying them louder imposed no additional hardship.

As for this first case, I do not recall the details. No matter. It was not details I was supposed to master. It was strategy. Like so many of his deals I subsequently examined, this first was a rescue operation. A good business fallen on hard times, besieged by creditors, abandoned by lenders, desperate for money to pay off its obligations, ease pressure of indebtedness and procure emergency capital that would enable recovery to begin. God forbid I should ever be in such dire need I would accept, even welcome, the exploitive assistance he gave. With minimal investment he would acquire a controlling interest so when the reinvigorated company was turned around he could sell his share of the stock back to the principals at an inflated price or to new ones if the original owners refused his extortionate offer. He came on the scene in the guise of a savior and left like the scavenger he was. No one could ever accuse my father of charity. And never did.

I did not dilute my opinion with tact, declaring he was profiteering off the misfortunes of others. He agreed. I told him if he had allowed the misfortune to worsen, if he had waited longer before committing, he could have gotten in with less money and out with more. He disagreed. And for the next hour discoursed to me about the timing of his decision, about those 'human factors' to be considered that I was ignoring. Human factors? That he was sensitive to such niceties seemed a contradiction of those terms on which I daily knew him. Yet as I listened it became apparent he was acutely sensitive on two points of professional conduct with people. First, he never pushed them too far. And second, he always left them slightly better off than before he came, although they paid an exorbitant price for the saving of their business lives.

Two years of reviews followed the first, each case more subtly complex than the one preceding, leading me on, leading me up to something. What? I felt my father was stalking me, waiting before springing the next stage of preparation upon me. On the evening of my fifteenth birthday it arrived.

To commemorate the occasion I had allowed my mother to dress me up as she wished. Once a year I would consent to act her doll because I knew it pleased her to play with my appearance. No vanity causes me to say I was a very beautiful young girl. It was the striking, undeniable truth. Nor was it altruism that caused me to bear the offending touch of my mother's arrangements as she costumed my body, coifed my hair and deftly applied cosmetic touches to further dramatize my dark good looks.

Disdain her as I did, I respected her in this. She was truly mistress of the preservation arts. In figure and face she had not aged ten years in twenty- five. Her fragile beauty lasted like a delicate flower that miraculously never went out of bloom. Why she did it I understood even then. By holding time still for herself as my father grew visibly older she further enhanced the power of attraction that he could not resist. How she did it, what secret regimen she followed to make a lie of passing years, I never discovered. Only the hint of her secrets would I glimpse at these annual makeovers when my possibilities would become actualized by her imagination and craft.

This particular year she was at the height of her powers. My long black hair pulled back, swirled down around the nape of my neck then braided up and coiled like a crown, my eyebrows slightly arched, my cheekbones dramatically accented to emphasize the angles of my face, the portrait of myself in the mirror barely recognizable to my childish eyes. Gazing back at me in what I distinctly felt was a condescending manner was an aristocratic young woman, commandingly attractive in a severely forbidding way. She appeared sophisticated beyond any sophistication with which I felt familiar. In the corner of the glass, out of the corner of my eye, I thought I spied a fleeting smile of triumph as it sped across my mother's face. A look of pride on my mother? Impossible.

Just then my father burst in to give some parting order to his wife when beholding me he stopped in mid-sentence struck speechless by what he saw. Immediately recovering he took charge of the situation by demanding I parade the perimeter of the room so he could view me at his leisure, which he did. At first, I was not discomposed by his evaluation. After all, I had grown used to it and had nothing to fear. Yet after he appraised my bearing and my dress he was not done. His gaze still lingered. He was not satisfied. His eyes began to search and pry for more. He was no longer admiring my mother's handiwork, he was admiring *me*. Thanks to the ministrations of my mother I had caught his fancy. I felt empowered and endangered both at once. How to use his interest to advance my own without falling victim to his designs? Vigilance became the watchword with my father from that moment on.

'Alana,' he suddenly announced to my mother, 'shall accompany me out this evening. We leave in fifteen minutes.' I looked to her expecting some sign of disappointment since the celebration she had planned for me would be postponed. There was none. 'As you wish,' she obediently replied. Now I understand it was how she wished.

Thus began my initiation into the glittering world of social events and fancy dinners that my father regularly attended for pleasure and mined for business.

As was to be the case whenever I went with him to functions of this kind he escorted another woman, never my mother. I did not find this remarkable or inappropriate since I knew my mother was too self-effacing to shine socially. The kind of woman he selected for these occasions, and there were many different women whom he chose, were all as worldly as she was not, all au courant with gossip and intrigues among the prominent and well-to-do of which she was entirely ignorant. By his command and her consent, she fulfilled only two of his needs for female companionship, beauty, and duty. Outside of this narrow definition, she served no useful purpose in his life and had no place.

Curiously, I did not consider him unfaithful to my mother at the time, although in my adulthood I realized he certainly was. But as a child it only seemed natural she be excluded from the great commercial enterprise of which she was prisoner and beneficiary, but in which she played no active part. My inclusion was another matter. This was a continuation of my preparation as each time we went out I was placed under the tutelage of his partner for the evening who modeled social graces, insinuating charms and conversational wit I was encouraged to emulate, encouraged by these women themselves who were instructed to smooth off any rough edges left from my childhood and bring me out. Over the next few years I came along wonderfully, and who would not given the teachers I had? Professionals all. Poise and mien I learned, and the capacity to read deeply into other people, particularly men, because these women were expert at the penetration of men.

As for my father, I saw a side of him invisible at home, winning ways he never wasted on us. An entrancing speaker, a sensitive and seductive listener, the center of attention, he attracted those who were charmed to pay for the privilege of his friendship by admitting him into their privacy. Unawares, they betrayed more than they knew, divulging information money could not buy that ,shrewdly managed, he could turn to a considerable profit, and often did.

During this period there was little communication between my father and myself. We spoke seldom, yet I felt the object of his observation as never before. The more worldly I grew, the more of his world I became. Aware of this and taking heed I made a resolution: not to delay too long gaining independence from his care lest I become trapped in more intimacy with him than I desired. A calculating man, he miscalculated me. That fateful trip to Europe and beyond on which I was to acquire my final luster of sophistication in his eyes was, I felt certain, my last chance to put a safe distance between us. So as he prospected for business opportunities I prospected the marriage market fortunately securing the escape I needed in my departed husband, Antonio D'Allesandro Ricci.

Such a shock! My father had spent so much on me only to lose what he had put at risk to our elopement. How do you suppose he displayed his disappointment? Not at all. As he well knew the game was not over until the play was done, and if he could not have me in one way he could still enjoy me in another. One of the maxims which he lived by I have followed since. 'Loss is a great creator of opportunities, Alana. Don't waste time grieving. Look for the gifts.' True to himself he did just that. He picked up the new hand I had dealt him to see what good fortune new cards might bring. His single response to my bridehood was a scornful one. 'So, Alana, you lower yourself to acting like a woman after all.' Not one word further.

Later, when I was widowed by Antonio and pensioned off by his family into financial independence, it was as if I had never been married, with this difference. Whatever allure I once held for my father had died. I believe my virginity mattered a great deal to him. Having lost it with my husband I could not offer it to my father. He had wanted me untainted, planned to be the first despoiler himself, had sexually protected me with this return in mind. The only reason why I don't hate him more is because I understand him so well. After all, I am my father's daughter.

Without further reference to my loss or gain he took me up from where we had left off, only this time it was as partner in his ventures. As his associate was how he treated me and introduced me in subsequent business transactions. Never as his daughter. He solicited my opinion on everything and tirelessly argued with me over any points of disagreement, arguments I never won but in which I had full say. When it turned out I was right and he was wrong I would receive a larger share of the winnings from which I understood first that he acknowledged my superior judgment in this case, and second that, correct or incorrect, the final decision was his alone to make. So we traveled on sharing the same business conveyance but at his expense until, shortly after my mother gave up and died, the ground rules of our relationship shifted one final time.

In his words it was 'the opportunity of a lifetime', by which he meant the enormous potentiality for gain justified placing all his assets, but none of mine, at risk. The final throw of the dice. Myself, I saw the opening for which he was playing, yet the timing needed to be so precise, the approach so meticulously well calculated, the opposing players were so dangerous, the tolerance for error so minute, I should not have dared the speculation he was prepared to make. As was now usual, I accompanied him every treacherous step of the way. Many steps there were because the investment was enormously complex and the negotiations tedious and long. The smallest items at issue were endlessly debated because even the slightest advantage was worth fighting for, the sums being extraordinarily large.

Almost two years in construction it was to be his masterpiece. He was at his boldest and I was present to see every masterstroke which came down, as his deals inevitably did, to one crucial meeting where final sticking points must be removed before a deadline after which any possibility for consummation would be lost. Across the expanse of mahogany table in that dark paneled conference room I can still picture the faces of those five predatory men, each my senior in age and experience, all of us awaiting my father for the last act in this drama to unfold.

I was precisely on time. Never early, never late, as I had been taught. Ten minutes. Twenty minutes. The five grew restless and began to show the signs of irritation and uncertainty that such man, accustomed to control, display when they are helpless to change conditions they do not like but cannot afford to reject. With so much at stake and so little time remaining the stress upon them mounted minute by suspenseful minute. The more palpable their anxiety became, the more relaxed I began to feel as the emotional advantage swung in my direction.

Softy the door pushed open behind me. The stare from the five almost drove the young messenger from the room before he could discharge his commission. I did not look around. The paper he handed me was moist with perspiration from his fingers. Instantly I knew what my father had done. As always, his instructions were concise. 'You know enough. Now see if you can bring it off as well as I.' In my entire life, time never moved as mercifully slowly as it did then when I desperately needed to order my thoughts.

They fixed their stares upon me. What was happening they yearned to know? They watched my fingers then my face for some telltale sign of what the note portended. I gave them none. Instead, carefully refolding the paper to feign calmness I did not feel, I deliberately picked up a book of matches from a large crystal ashtray and striking one, picked up the paper with my other hand, lit the corner afire and let the message burn completely out scorching my forefinger and thumb, crumbling the ashes as if I felt no pain. Now I had their rapt attention. 'Gentlemen," I smiled, 'these are our final terms. Contest even the smallest detail and you may consider our interest in this matter at an end.'

After shaking hands with each of them I returned home and delivered the signed agreement to my father whom I interrupted deep in chess with an old adversary half way round the world from whom he had just received threatening move by mail. 'Keep the contract with your papers,' was all he had to say on the subject. 'I shall dine alone this evening. He thinks he has outmatched me; however, where's there's a will there's a way. Where there's a will, Alana, there is always a way.' Four months later he was dead. I did not miss him. We both knew he had taught me all he could.

So there you have it, Miss Germaine, the story of a nontraditional education, but an education none-the-less. You had your Savocek. I had my father. No love lost in either relationship, and yet a great deal gained.

One last word on a subject incongenial to you, the great drawing. Unlike the Pharaohs I have no use for treasure after death. Consequently I have made provisions that it shall revert to you, moneys from my estate defraying any taxes such a transfer may entail. It was never my wish to interfere with your inheritance, only to enjoy the pleasure of the object's ownership while I was alive.

Know then that what I forced from your father shall be returned to his heir. The rest of my collection, both public and private, I have endowed the Villa to house as a museum, your uncle consenting to act as first managing trustee. According to LaValle, who should know, no one understands museum directing better than Phillip Gambrell.

As for your lack of correspondence, also know this. It discourages me not at all.

I remain as I am,

The Countess Elena D'Allessandro Ricci

Chapter Eight
THE MUSEUM DIRECTOR

For Phillip Gambrell, social companionship was the breath of life. Almost suffocated from want of it as a child, he toiled endlessly to satisfy it as an adult. His job as chief administrator of such a large museum meant there was a continuing assault of people clamoring to meet and speak with him. Each day was sumptuous, overflowing with calls to return, consultations to provide, and meetings to attend, all placing him at the center of a vast social web that never stopped vibrating for his attention. Each day overflowed with demands spilling work into the next, never enough time to get it all done. Spirits high, exhilarated by the exhausting pace, he would run from one locus of decision-making to another through long hours that would have depleted anyone else, but rejuvenated him. Truly a man who had found his natural element, Phillip loved the constant conviviality required by his position.

It was not always so. The family circle into which he had been born was a broken one pretending to be whole. His mother presented a brave face to the world, a smile that swore they were a happy family when his dreamer of a father would intermittently escape the burdens of responsibility by fleeing from home. Occasionally on payday, he would take the money and run, returning from his binge unshaven and rumpled a few days later, remorseful, bearing gifts. Gifts to whom? Not really to his wife. To himself. Painted glass and porcelain souvenirs from where he'd woken up, sentimental figurines from an idealized world in which love and happiness and peace and comfort were naturally ordained. And Prettiness prevailed.

His father adored prettiness, although he did not call it that. He called it 'beauty' instead, while for his son this display of fragile ornaments upon the mantle piece was the first gallery of art to which he was exposed. He came to love these trinkets too. Their contemplation would transport him into the untroubled world they inhabited, also moving him to envy the creativity behind their making. So it was he decided one day to become an artist himself, a dream he kept with all the other family secrets to himself. He would please the eye and raise the spirits of others as craftsmen of these delicate objects did for him. This was his father's unintended gift: a love for art.

Yet in the end, fatherhood was denied. One memorable day his mother, reaching the end of her forgiveness finally ran out of patience and gave vent to the accumulated frustration of years by turning not upon her husband but upon his prized possessions. All her words of complaint and pleas for change had been exhausted because none of them had any lasting effect. So to show him what she meant, and that she meant it, she appealed to action as a last resort, smashing every precious figurine upon the mantle not just once but repeatedly until they were reduced to a rubble of shards and dust.

Unused to exertion she grew faint from want of breath, her great chest heaving from the violent exercise as she steadied herself by leaning heavily upon a chair swearing to him: "There!....that's what....that's what I....think of....think of your gifts!...Bring any more ....into this house and....and I'll do the same to them!"

Did she know that by this act of destruction she had destroyed the only reason left for his father coming home? Did she know she was obliterating the inspiration for her son's redeeming dream? Did she? Phillip never found it in himself to ask. Without a word the man who was not much of a father, but the only one Phillip had known, took one long stricken look at the demolished objects that he loved, not at his son or wife, then turned and quietly departed, a vision of wreckage drowning in his eyes. Phillip never saw or heard from the man again.

This was when he was in high school, leaving just the two of them, mother and son, to carry on, she now seeking her own escape into service. To avoid personal sorrow, his mother immersed herself in the sorrows of others, becoming beloved for her extraordinary selflessness, day or night available to minister to the victims of Life's onslaught, to the fallen, to the wounded, to the survivors of the slain. Before his eyes he saw his mother canonized by a growing community of dependents for whom she provided inexhaustible succor when they were weary of failing or hurt or of simply feeling lonely for want of someone to talk to who would understand. And listen. Saint Listener she became, beautified to this degree by those whose lives were made more bearable by the supportive presence she provided for everyone. Except for Phillip. Never for Phillip. Why should she? Where was the need? Never complaining, he had been listener to her. Ever the strong one he had been rewarded for his strength by being left alone, sparing her the looking after. He was a gift, a truly self-sufficient child. Unlike her husband with whom every day of married life had been a trial, Phillip had always been a perfectly easy child. No need to spend concern on him.

So when the time came for Phillip to leave home, neither mother nor son had much sense of loss. Her parting words helped him to part without obligation or reluctance. "Take care of yourself, Phillip. I know you will. You always have." Then she broke off their farewell to answer the phone. This was his last view of her, absorbed in listening to the disembodied distress of someone, probably a stranger since so many strangers called, ignoring him her son for someone she did not even know. "Yes," she murmured, "yes, how awful! I know just how you feel. Yes, that's all right, just keep talking, take all the time you need. This is what I'm here for." Phillip had stared in fresh wonder as she took on the suffering of yet another. "Christ!' he thought, then left without saying anything after all.

College graced Phillip's life with endless opportunity for association. Gone were the constraints of loyalty to family that had kept him unnaturally reticent in outside relationships for fear of betraying the unhappy reality at home. No more necessity to protect reputation and perpetuate myth by keeping to himself. Now he could freely circulate, using the large university to indulge his insatiable social appetite. By mid-semester, if a freshman poll had been taken, Phillip would have been voted most widely known. He introduced himself to all his classmates and because he was so outgoing and attentive others were genuinely happy to make his acquaintance. Before long a social circle formed around him in which he felt he belonged, this belonging beginning to fill the void that childhood loneliness had wrought. As he shone warmth on others, they sought Phillip out to enjoy his acquaintance.

Then Phillip fell in love. Not until spring semester had core requirements thinned out enough for him to take his first art course, 'An Introduction to Western Painting from the Middle Ages through the Renaissance'. His professor was wise enough to know her students were mostly like Phillip, unexposed to much beyond what high school and occasional visits to local museums might have seen fit to provide. She also knew that since pictures were not painted with words it was well to keep words to a minimum and let the greatness of the paintings carry their own message.

Her job was to select the slides and orchestrate the presentation of masterpieces in an all out visual assault upon the students' eyes, hopefully impacting everyone, imprinting some and inspiring a few. She played with their perceptions, building up to the total composition of each piece of art by first presenting pieces of it in detail before projecting the whole. She clearly constrasted one artist's style with another only to confuse them with similarities, varying exposure from a few seconds to several minutes, keeping students wondering how much time would be allowed, watching closely lest they miss what she was teaching them to see. Her manipulation of the slides was deliberate, meant to open up their eyes to the visual experience that artists had designed, and for a fortunate few it did. Phillip was one of the chosen.

It was a costly conversion. Giving himself over to this rapture for fine art meant giving up the images of pretty beauty that had originally captured his aesthetic sensibilities as a child. The magnitude of this discrepancy between what he had supposed and what he was now discovering art to be about was beyond belief, as he kept muttering in class when wonder after wonder was displayed for him to see.

"I don't believe it, I don't believe it," he chanted over and over until the young man assigned the adjoining seat, a quiet, occasionally humorous, mostly serious art student named Galen Germaine tapped him on the arm and asked:

"What don't you believe?'

Phillip had gotten acquainted with him slightly in the fall, as he had with so many other students, and smiled his smile of welcome, also smiling in embarrassment because he had been unaware of talking to himself.

"I just thought you might like some company in your conversation," Galen smiled back. "What don't you believe?"

"How many great artists there have been. How much there is to see. How little I know."

Galen understood this feeling of awe because his own exposure was no less limited than Phillip's

"That's why we're here, right? That's why I'm here. That's why college is here. Only the ignorant need apply."

Phillip laughed.

"Well I certainly am in the right place."

"I'll tell you what," Galen offered. "We'll do it together if you like. Pool our ignorance and share the excitement of what we find. We'll dive in and not come up until we've seen it all."

"And if we drown?" Phillip asked.

"Why then," answered Galen, "we'll drown together. Now, what do you say?"

Without knowing why Phillip felt the need to signify agreement in more than words, so he extended his hand, and as Galen clasped it to seal their compact, doing something he had never done before. By now he had many social acquaintenances, but Galen Germaine became his first personal friend. Not a commitment to be taken lightly, and Phillip never did.

The friendship began based upon the shared love of art between them, just as they would later share another love for Joannne, although that was over a year away. By then they had spent hours together looking through art books, collecting their own small library, creating a gallery of reproductions in the third floor apartment they let that summer, visiting every museum and attending every passing exhibition within reach. In the process they became close as young men do less by confiding than companioning each other, building up a history of shared experience together, relaxing into an easy familiarity with one another.

Temperamentally well suited, compatible in their orderly habits, the adjustment to becoming room-mates was smooth and unconflicted. More outgoing, Phillip continued to expand his social network and enjoy the increasing press of invitations upon him, while Galen, often invited too since people knew they were best friends, usually declined, preferring time alone to draw. Figure drawings were what he enjoyed doing first, but then caricatures of people in the news, occasionally contributing a drawing of some visiting dignitary to one of the campus publications that he began to do more regularly, gaining a certain notoriety in the process. Students first, but then professors in the art department, some artists themselves, began to recognize Galen Germaine's gift for catching likeness and something more, revealing an underlying character that gave his satirical portraits a compelling depth.

Phillip, meanwhile, began suspecting his old dream of becoming an artist was just a dream. Through his studies he saw mastery he could not achieve, yet realized he would never be satisfied with anything less. He watched Galen dedicate free time to drawing that he himself reserved for socializing because solitude was not congenial and being an artist was solitary work. Then came junior year and the life drawing class. For the one and only time he reached the limit of his drawing talent, creating an undisguised expression of idealized love for the young woman who could dress in nakedness and still preserve her modesty, unmindul of the attention focussed upon her, mindful only of herself. Phillip was captivated and projected onto her his image of perfect womanhood because he did not know her. Later, when he did come to know her, and know her well, he still clung to this idealization for the pleasure it gave him, despite the pain it caused.

Senior year was both high and low point of his college life. First he and Galen were driven to see the Riablo show by Joanne's impatience with their refusal to view the leading exponent of abstract art they so freely criticized. She accused them of being prejudiced by ignorance and not open to artistic experience as they claimed. The joy of his awakening to an appreciation of Riablo's work was surpassed by his discovery of appreciation itself as a viable career in art, one that did not condemn him to the isolation of becoming an artist. He could create awareness in others just as he had experienced this day, organize shows, perhaps even direct a museum itself. At last he found the perfect occupation for which he did not know he had been looking. What a gift!

Excitement over this revelation, however, was short lived. Within weeks came the announcement from Galen and Joanne of their intention to marry. Distraught over Joanne's choice of his best friend over himself, although he had never dared propose, Phillip reeled from the force of this rejection amplified by old rejections growing up. The force staggered him to the brink of despair where, in the surrounding darkness before dawn, he vascillated precariously, gazing longingly down on the mercy of destruction offered by the turbulance of rushing water far below. He debated life and death and death and life, if in living he could bear the dying deep inside. Salvation came when, eyes squeezed shut, his body wavering for balance, illuminations of great masterpieces began to flash continually upon the drawn screens of his inner lids. Those images first viewed in freshman year rescued him now, some part of his mind or spirit retrieving them to rapturous effect. Excitement overwhelmed despondancy and this greater loving saved his life, although it did not alleviate his suffering.

The loss of Joanne was the more terrible because it threatened potential loss of Galen unless Phillip could let go his unrequited love for her and unforgiving envy of him. Most agonizing was his knowledge that Joanne deeply love him, but as a friend, not as a husband. He had to get away. Living together crowded in the same apartment was out of the question, although they wanted him to stay. He chose to relocate. They understood. Not far enough. He chose to flee the country. They did not understand. How could they? Phillip kept them innocent of the warring emotions that he needed an ocean of separation to pacify, hoping to diminish one passion by indulging another.

The travelling fellowship had many applicants, many students with richer backgrounds and better grades than he. None, however, in the opinion of the committee, had comparable devotion to the field or were more likely to be enriched by touring those museums that held originals of objects to which no reproductions could ever do justice. Without seeing them first hand his professional preparation would be incomplete. Ten months to worship at such shrines as the British museum, the Louvre, the Prado, the Uffizi, even the Hermitage, a pilgrimage of a kind, just the kind he needed to distract himself from loss and recommit to his first devotion.

Desperate and courageous, it was a journey of redemption, a crusade to reclaim friendship from the ruin caused by loving it too much. And it was an expedition that succeeded. Burdened he left, a free man he returned. The happy outcome was due as much to the prayers of those two friends left behind as to his own determination, Galen and Joanne who mourned his going and worried over his coming back. Right away, after embracing at the airport, taking one good look at him and he at them, they felt relieved. What could not work before could work now. All three were elated. Only one thing Phillip would not do. He would not move back in with them as they invited. Even redemption had its limits, and he had gained sufficient insight in to himself to know where these were. For all their sakes, he would not he would not put his fragile recovery at risk of more intimacy than his heart informed him was wise. They deferred, allowing him to define the terms of reengagement, welcoming the daily visits and fellowship while he remained, never urging him to stay when he felt inclined to go.

The years that followed were reaffirming and restorative ones. Graduate preparation launching both men into their careers, while Joanne and Galen discreetly got married without inflicting on Phillip the pain of knowing precisely when that civil ceremony was. They let the new reality settle gently around him until what he had once dreaded became comfortable and his place within the marriage felt secure. But marriage was not enough for Joanne. She wanted more, while Galen was willing so long as she agreed to undertake most of the child's care. On this they agreed.

News of the impending birth drew Phillip closer to his friends as anticipation of the birth filled them all with excitement. Miracle this child was for Phillip, gifting him with restoration of what had previously been lost, membership in a loving family. A chance for him to belong, the subject of his belonging, unbeknownst to him, being the topic of long conversations between Joanne and Galen as they calculated what ceremony they could devise to 'bring Phillip in.'

Although Phillip had expected to be notified when labor began, had expected to await the birth at the hospital, he was caught off guard when, arriving there, Galen instructed him to wash up and put on the protective green clothing and mask required of those present in the delivery room.

"Order are orders, Phillip, now do as you're told." Galen was firm, then led his friend to Joanne's beside, her smile of greeting contracted with pain, laughing to see Phillip's alarm, grasping his hand and squeezing hard until the contraction subsided.

"Now you are here," she said, " there is no need to delay any longer." Both men walked behind the nurse who wheeled the bed into the sterile room where the doctor, who had presided at more deliveries than he could remember, could not remember presiding at a delivery like this. However, times, he told himself, were always changing, and besides what business was it of his which man fathered the child so long as the child had a father willing to claim it? His job was to see the baby safely freed from its mother, the mother safely delivered from the act of bearing, the infant examined for minimal signs of health and then given to the mother. Although not in this case, since he had been instructed on her authority to do otherwise.

So he held the swaddled baby out to Phillip who was uncharacteristically at a loss for speech.

"Come Phillip," urged Galen, "you must be the first to hold her."

Awkwardly Phillip did as he was commanded, the tiny weight almost more than he could support. The doctor stepped back but not far, having seen grown men faint in delivery rooms before and not about to risk this possibility now without being able to rescue the child if the man should fall.

"Now comes the hardest part of your job, Phillip," Joanne continued as though she were orchestrating the entire scene, which in fact she was. "Name her. She is yours to name. She will carry the name you give her now for the rest of her life."

"I'm not prepared," Phillip stammered overwhelmed by the responsibility, overjoyed by the responsibility. "Give me a moment." His mind raced through family names, none suitable because none had the power of namesake that he sought. This little princess must have a royal name, a name which could command a future as illustrious as its past. Unbidden, his mind opened the catalogue of great artists whom he knew and loved and were as real to him through their work as if he had personally known each one. All men. Back to royalty. Royalty. Back to his favorite museum in his favorite city in the world, Leningrad. The Hermitage. Birthed from the palace of Catherine the Great, patroness of the arts. Now there was a name! If one girl could rise to such supremacy, why not another? "Catherine," he murmured, looking down at the quiet child appearing to look expectantly up at him.

"What?" Galen asked. "I didn't hear."

Instinctively Phillip made a decision. The significance of the name, its origin, would remain secret from the child and her parents lest in declaring it the power somehow misguide. "Kate!" he proudly announced. "Kate Germaine!"

'Kate' was a suitable disguise under which an infant might begin a journey to distinction.

Chapter Nine
AN ENEMY BECOMES A FRIEND

Dear Kate --

Your uncle tells me you have found a niche for yourself in this new household. I am happy for you. It has been a while since my last letter, and although I have not journeyed to another continent like you, I too am in a much different place.

The grief and anger when first I wrote have both been eased by time and by a friend of yours who is fast becoming, of all things, a friend of mine. How to explain

The Countess, Improbable, is it not? What a bold woman! Not three months ago she barged into my peace and quiet with an invitation to the Villa. I refused her at the door. She persisted. The conversation grew between us. The more we talked the more we had to say. Finally, this public sharing became so personal I invited her inside, into the privacy of my home. There! Now what do you think of that? At your old drawing table, we sat. Not an elegant setting to entertain such an elegant guest yet it felt fitting to us both. As though you were there in spirit and, who knows, perhaps you were.

Poor Galen! Happening in on us, the shock of disbelief on his face was enough to make me wish I was a portrait artist myself, at least for the moment. He is so rarely thrown off balance, such a steady man, it was truly funny to see him wavering in confusion as I told him later that evening. He only muttered something about my having a strange sense of humor. Then added he was glad to see my humor returning even if it was at his expense.

Caught my attention, his observation did. Had I become so seriously despondent I had lost my sense of humor? I'm afraid so. Apparently, we escape our own notice more easily than we escape the notice of others. Well, it feels good to be getting my own glad company back again. It also feels gladdening to have the Countess to talk with.

Not humorous by intent, nonetheless she does cause me to laugh. At myself. In her approach to life, there is a surgical mercy. Why medicate the symptom when you can operatively remove the cause? Quick and deep she cuts to the heart of matters with a sharp bluntness to which I am unaccustomed. No regard for suffering, her own or anyone else's. Not when it comes to making difficult choices or confronting painful reality.

Here I was swathed in mourning over my loss of mothering and she told me I was indulging in self-pity. Not what I wanted to hear, but unerringly correct. The protest was my immediate response. I challenged the justice of such an accusation, yet something like a smile lit up inside me when she said it. I felt enormously relieved. My bloat of seriousness had been lanced by her stab of truth and I realized I had a choice, to keep feeling sorry for myself or to stop. The Countess was not being critical, only honest. Probably the most honest person I have ever met. The only time she is not honest is when she lies when lying serves her purpose better than truth, as I told her.

You know her better than I and so will not be surprised to hear she readily agreed. More than that, do you know what she said? 'Lying is not a wrong, Mrs. Germaine. It is a skill.' Good heavens! I replied human society would be a conniving and untrusting place if that belief should ever take common hold. She only laughed and shook her head like a world-weary adult at a naive child, adding: 'As for trust, that can be as much a failing as a virtue.' Really Kate, did she ever speak to you like this? What a cynical outlook on life! I told her this too. Then she chided me with the remark that has opened a way for us to coexist in friendship. 'Mrs. Germaine, rather than feel obliged to defend our own view by judging or trying to change the other's, let us instead enjoy the differences between us such as they are.' And for the most part, this is what we have done. We share without fear of contradiction.

In case you wonder, we talk very little about you even though you are much in our minds and hearts. By unspoken consent, we have not, since our first conversation, discussed you save on one matter that the Countess may take up with you upon your return. Or she may not. As you well know, only the Countess dictates what the Countess shall do.

Much to her dismay, I am finding her to be a wise counselor, although she does not appreciate that term. In fact, the other day she summarily dismissed the notion. 'I am too self-centered to help anyone but myself. If you derive more than social benefit from our association, Mrs. Germaine' (she has yet to call me Joanne, preferring formal to informal address) 'please consider it accidental.'

Still, she casts a new perspective on my life and says I do the same for her. Perhaps. However, this is not my intent. We seem to mirror for each other, often receiving back an unexpected image of ourselves. Not necessarily pleasant to see, but usually illuminating, some facet of ourselves we did not know or did not want to know before. I can't speak for her, but I am always a little anxious when we meet. Eager, yet anxious for the next unwelcome learning to occur.

The Villa. Galen had told me much about it over the years. Phillip too. Yet for my first visit, I was totally unprepared. I am used to our modest level of comfort, not to luxury, certainly not to the opulence of such an old-world kind. She received me in the inner courtyard. As promised, the daffodils were indeed in bloom, their brilliance giving the open space a golden hue. We sat at a round white table on chairs of matching color, three stories above the skylight filtering down warmth from the sun blazing high overhead.

We both felt awkward. And in what I now realize, knowing her better, was an act of generosity, she did not use her practiced charms to gloss over the discomfort we both shared. I am no match for her in self-control, not being able to mask emotion so completely; but on this occasion, she allowed her unease to show. The embarrassment caused me to contemplate the table setting where I observed her long fingers playing nervously around the rim of her teacup tentatively circling, searching for something to say. So I glanced around me, not at her, silenced by the space and grandeur of richly furnished rooms that I could glimpse through stone archways on every side.

Graciously she initiated conversation. 'Do not be misled by the trappings of my life, Mrs. Germaine. I am a woman no different from yourself, despite what this ornamentation may suggest. She who sat in your kitchen is the same who sits before you now. Only the scenery has changed. As for the vanity of this display,' and here she casually waved our surroundings away, 'it is only that: display. One must do something with money after all. While with a great deal of money, one must do a great deal more.'

It was difficult not to feel overwhelmed by such a grand residence, I admitted.

She agreed. 'Overwhelming visitors and guests is part of the design.   Appearances are a great source of power in this world, particularly those that can impress. I hope I have not succeeded so well with you that we shall fail to continue the communication so promisingly begun.'

Have you ever noticed the stilted manner in which she speaks? I don't mean what she says, but how she says it.   So arch in her expression, her style of speech like her style of living sets her apart. Not an easy person to get close to.   How you managed it over the separation of so many years I don't pretend to understand.   It must have been a shared love of art or else some positive chemistry that differences struck between you.   I am certain of this.   She would never have sought out friendship with me had it not been for her friendship with you. So it seems I am in your debt. Thank you, Kate.

Still, we groped for a path of conversation to follow. I told her I also had been looking forward to continuing our acquaintance, but just at the moment did not know how to carry it forward. 'Since words are failing us,' she suggested, 'suppose I take you on a tour. I have one or two items which may please you, being a woman who obviously has a taste for the aesthetic, wife to one artist, mother to another.'

How little she understood the truth about me I did not say. Only that I should be delighted to receive an introduction to her home. After all, it would hardly have been polite to declare sincere disinterest in what she had spent so much of her life accumulating.

It was a quizzical look she gave me, comical, like a great raven cocking its head at some curiosity suddenly observed. Instantly I knew what she had spied, the lack of true enthusiasm in my obliging tone. So much for the dishonesty of tact. 'Why, you are not an art lover, are you Mrs. Germaine?' No, I declared, making restitution with truth, then confessing how natural creations always called to me more than human ones. As for being married to an artist, it was not for love of art, but for love of him; while I had supported your passion for drawing out of responsibility for nurturing your gifts. Surprisingly she seemed to understand. Further, she then proceeded to make an extraordinary disclosure. 'Nor am I, Mrs. Germaine. Nor am I.'

I objected but was immediately overruled. 'As my father's daughter, Mrs. Germaine, my tastes are necessarily subordinated to one master need, to achieve dominance at whatever I do. Certainly, the treasures that I have assembled in this place are worthy of the universal admiration they receive. I venerate them as deeply as anyone. Just not for their own sake. First, I am a woman of business who has used collecting to establish a position of influence to which even leaders in this world or art pay tribute. Their deference is testimony to the excellence of objects I have won.'

I found her definition of collecting abhorrent, as though winning the competition for a piece of art were more important than the art itself. From your father and uncle I knew better. A passion for appreciation was what drove true collectors, not some egotistic desire to better their rivals. Otherwise collecting became no more than a means of keeping score.

She only laughed. 'Show me a serious collector who does not keep score as you put it, and I'll show you a minor collector who is destined for the mediocrity he deserves. No, Mrs. Germaine, I am afraid you have failed to grasp the lust for possession that a work of art of the first magnitude inspires in the hearts and minds and loins of collectors once that work becomes momentarily available in the market place. This is why a man like LaValle is so valuable. Through his contacts he is given advance notice that enables those few of us for whom he consents to serve as agent to act before the competition is aware. Collecting? Dr. Johnson said it best concerning the great pyramids in Egypt. "A monument to the insufficiency of human enjoyment." So, too, collecting.'

I suppose, Kate, she has spoken this way to you. As for me, my grudging admiration for her patronage of art was lessened by the lack of love she was confessing. So mercenary! Your father and Phillip derive such inspiration from great works of art. I felt, by comparison, she was cheapening what I have come to vicariously believe myself. Surely art's chief value is a spiritual, not a material one as she insisted.

She was looking at me now very intently, weighing I thought the impact of her words upon my attitude. 'Have I disillusioned you about me, Mrs. Germaine? I see I have. Then let me do it thoroughly. When I do a thing, I do it completely, else why do it at all? Half measures only satisfy the uncommitted. I will now give you such a tour as I have never given anyone, a tour of the collector, not the collection. When we are done you shall know me at my worst if you cannot refrain from judgment. Or, if you can, you shall know me on those more tolerant terms that we previously discussed.'

She was correct. By comparing I was judging her, and by judging disallowing differences to freely exist between us. I promised to be more forbearing. She demurred. 'Do not be premature. After I am revealed, you may yet decide I am not a woman to befriend. Besides, promises are no substitute for performance. Either you shall accept me, or you shall not. My father could never resist a single throw of the dice. Nor can I. It's all of me or none, Mrs. Germaine. I know no other way to play. Not being an art lover primarily for the love of art, that is my first unveiling. Now for the second: how I traffic in art for the sake of prominence that great collecting brings. When I told you this was vanity you did not fully credit what I said. I encourage you to do so now. I am known for my collection. Without it I would simply be very rich, and what distinction is that? Cloak new money in old art, however, and wealth gains a respectability no other kind of purchase can confer. With all his material worth, my father never gained an enth my reputation. So keep in mind what I shared earlier. Everything you are about to see is calculated to impress.'

Standing up she invited me to follow as the tour began. Impressed I was, by the sheer volume of possessions if nothing else. I wondered to myself how anyone could want to own so much. She must have heard me. 'Art collecting, Mrs. Germaine, is a kind of mania. Like hoarding beauty. Why else would someone be driven to own so much in excess of what they could ever fully enjoy? Any one of these objects has enough subtlety to enthrall a lifetime's examination and still not yield all the harmonies of its creation. No, there is no reason to justify this accumulation. Only a very ancient sin, one of the Seven I believe, alive and well: Greed. If anything, private collections such as mine, and there are not many, illustrate how insatiable a collector's appetite becomes. The more one feeds it the more the craving demands to be fed. Like an addiction. Where does it end, do you suppose?'

I had no idea. My feelings at the moment were those I have described to you when visiting Phillip's museum. Soon overwhelmed by the glut of richness, I lose sensitivity to individual pieces. All come to feel alike, none standing out with the uniqueness each one possesses. For this reason I have never cared for museums. They are too much of a good thing. The more I see the less I see. One object at a time works best for me.

The Countess, since I gave no answer to her question, answered it herself. 'It ends, Mrs. Germaine, when the collector becomes satiated or dies. I myself have gorged to the point of satiation several times only to be offered some new delicacy that aroused my appetite afresh. What sensualists we collectors are! Did you ever read Balzac, Mrs. Germaine? No? A pity. I believe he understood human rapacity as well as anyone. At least he would have understood mine. Even surrounded by this bounty which you see, I remain dissatisfied. Even with all this I cannot bring myself to utter that simple command of self-restraint: "Enough!" '

Then began the vile catalogue of her acquisitions. True to her word she was selective, picking the very worst examples, the most diabolical deals and unconscionable intrigues through which this unprincipled woman secured some of her greatest objects. No means was too corrupt to secure a desired end. All legal, I suppose, but ruthless beyond what I had imagined. If her purpose was, as she declared, to unveil to me the darker side of her ambition, she certainly succeeded. What a consummate manipulator! It made me wonder: through some calculation was she now manipulating me?

At one point we stood before an enormous tapestry hung along a hallway on the second floor. I'm sure you know it. A medieval scene with mounted and dismounted hunters pursuing prancing stags in flight across a woodland meadow decorated with woven renderings of the most delicate flowers. She had paused, I assumed, because this genuinely pleasured me. The idealization of nature was uplifting and I hoped she would not break the spell with yet another crass tale of procurement. Having already heard more war stories than I wished, I felt in need of no further illumination. Her pattern of doing business was becoming clear, her formula generally the same. Seek out the desired object and then find ways to squeeze the owner into allowing its sale at a bargain price. It might be a fellow collector fallen on hard times or one about whom she had secured some secret of extortionate value. Either way, she got what she wanted; while they were grateful she had not squeezed them harder still.

Finally, when I had looked my fill at the tapestry I became aware she was awaiting some response from me. What? My obvious puzzlement seemed to genuinely puzzle her. 'You are not familiar with this masterpiece?' she asked. I was not. 'Nor the story behind it?' Again I replied in the negative. Keenly she searched my eyes for an assurance of honesty, I thought. Why would I lie? Turning away at last she murmured to herself something about laboring under an obligation she did not know she had, about someone really being the soul of discretion. There was more. I didn't catch it all. What she meant I do not know, except my ignorance had meaning for her.

'I've saved the most telling for last,' she announced as we entered a small gallery on the third floor in which her statuary is displayed. I must say, for a woman so cold and calculating she has surprisingly sensuous tastes. Of all her possessions I believe I liked her sculptures best. How is it possible to craft the soft illusion of human flesh from substances as hard as bronze and marble I asked the Countess. She gave an ironic reply. 'The same way it is possible for something as weak and frail as a little girl to be shaped into a hard and unforgiving woman. By craft. Come, Mrs. Germaine, now tell me what you think of this.'

Here she directed my attention to an empty alcove specially architected into the wall, lit from above, furnished with an empty pedestal apparently awaiting some precious object to support. I asked when this niche in her collection would be filled with whatever it had been designed to receive.

'Probably never', was her stern reply. 'Unless extraordinary opportunity knocks twice, which is unlikely.' Then why did she not fill it with something else? 'Because vacancy keeps memory of loss alive.' This sounded unnecessarily harsh. Surely it would be kinder to let go losses which cannot be reclaimed? She met my proposal with a refusal that struck me as brutal, yet for her was realistic. 'Kinder perhaps, but foolish to forsake the protection great losses can provide. Some wounds bear keeping open to prevent reinjury. So long as I remember this once in a lifetime acquisition that I foolishly sacrificed for price, I am not likely to make the same mistake again. And I have not. Every strength is double-edged, Mrs. Germaine. Because I bargain so well I bargained once to often. In the delay created by my counter-offer, a rival bid the prize away.'

From this last gallery she led me through her private chambers, magnificently appointed, out to a balcony which overlooked the beds of daffodils blazing far below. I was struck by how distance amplified their color by creating a collective intensity no single blossom possessed. She agreed. 'Yes, the Impressionists understood the tricks perception plays.' This was the opening she wanted. 'Now tell me, Mrs. Germaine, having seen the tigress in her lair and glimpsed her fierceness, as I once glimpsed yours, what is your impression of me? Do you find me sordid? It can be an ugly business, can it not, this business of collecting beauty. So, pronounce your verdict. The prosecution rests. As one non-art lover to another, shall we continue to be friends?'

Don't ask me why, I do not know myself. Perhaps it was the absurdity of self- incrimination being her best defense. Whatever, I burst out laughing. In triumph she did the same. What a truly horrible woman! It made no sense. No. It made nonsense, why it was so funny. We laughed and laughed until at last I caught my breath enough to gasp an answer. 'Why not?' And then we laughed some more.

When I arrive home Galen, worried at my swollen eyes particularly in light of where I'd been, asked if the Countess had made me cry. Yes, she had. Was I all right? Yes, I was. Righter than I'd been in a long time. He gave me one of those analytic looks reserved for clients, steady and invasive. Yes, he agreed. Yes, I was. Even closing this letter to you now I am smiling. Can you tell?

I love you, Kate.

Joanne

Chapter Ten
BREAKING THE ONLY HOUSEHOLD RULE

Had it not been for Phillip taking her to the Riablo exhibition, Kate would never have committed the violation that subsequently occurred. With virtually no prohibitions constraining her freedom at home, to deliberately break the only one was unthinkable to her parents, hence her father's shock and her mother's outrage.

"Kate, is this _your_ work?" Galen had asked in disbelief.

"How _dare_ you have done this?" was Joanne's question which ironically contained the answer she was seeking.

Daring in fact had caused their daughter's inexplicable behavior. Not, however, daring to disobey them, although it was to this that Joanne took offense. She treated the infraction as defiance instead of the act of risk taking that it truly was. Kate was daring the perhaps-possible, while doubting whether she had power to carry it through. That her mother of all people could not comprehend this, troubled Kate. Was she growing beyond reach of Joanne's understanding? Kate shuddered at the thought. Fortunately, after recovering from his surprise, Galen grasped the significance of what Kate had done, giving her more freedom in response to freedom she should not have taken. As for Joanne, she began to feel her daughter pull away.

None of this had Phillip intended when he took Kate to see the Riablo show. He had simply wanted her to experience the Master's paintings because they had been of so much significance in his own development, marking a turning point in his career. Certainly, he was aware of how agitated she became because of what she saw. Her abrupt desire to leave told him that. However, he had no way of knowing to what end this agitation would lead.

The beginning had been ordinary enough. He had come by to pick Kate up after a day's sitting with Galen who was painting the thirteen year old's portrait, quietly conversing with his restless subject to keep her still when Phillip entered the studio.

The artist looked up.

"She's been a fidget today, Phillip. You'll have to run her up and down the stacks of steps outside your museum a few times to wind her down."

"Oh Kip! Thank goodness you're here." Kate fled the riser upon which she had been marooned and gratefully hugged her rescuer. Then they both inspected her emerging likeness that her father was creating.

"This doesn't look like me at all," she complained. "You always paint me older than I am!"

Galen smiled.

"So you can have room to grow into whom you shall become."

"And if I refuse to obey your predictions for me? Kate asked.

"Why then you shall become as obstinate as the young woman in this picture here," he answered.

"Do you paint everyone's future or only mine?" she wanted to know.

"I don't even paint your future, just possibilities."

"Sounds simple to me," Phillip volunteered. "All you have to do is --- Galen, what *do* you have to do?"

"Trust your instincts mostly," Galen answered, removing one canvas from the easel and replacing it with another. "You're asking the wrong person about how an artist creates when you ask the artist. I've done this too long to understand how I do it. Besides, if following one's intuition could be explained we wouldn't call it intuition would we? How does Riablo do what he does? 'I do not seek, I find.' That's his answer. Profound, but not very enlightening. More to the point, you're taking Kate to see the Master himself. I'd go with you but I'm having a devil of a time getting this pose of the Benefactor right. What do I have? Five weeks until the dedication of his new wing for your museum? I'll have his portrait ready for your opening, Phillip. One mercy in this business, you don't stay stuck forever. Not like I've been this past week. But it's been an education making studies of the great man, I will say that. From poverty to privilege to social largesse. Such a savage man to have so sensitive a side. With one great donation, the greater taker becomes a great giver, and a social reputation is reversed. Now he'll be remembered not for how he made his money but for how he gave it away. And I have one pose to capture it all. I do not find, I seek. Have fun you two. Phillip, be sure to tell Kate about our first exposure to Riablo. If he has anywhere near the same impact on her we'll all have to watch out."

On route to the museum, Kate asked her uncle what Galen had meant.

"Only that Riablo has been a pivotal artist in both our lives. He caused us to fundamentally shift the focus of our work. A long time ago, now. The Institute Show, a watershed event in the history of art, although we didn't know it at the time. Since then, Riablo's name has become a popular and unpopular byword for modern art. Before, with the exception of a few admirers, he was largely discounted as a rebel, not accepted as the true revolutionary we think of today.

"Myself, a young art student in love with the classical past, I loathed Riablo. He was doing violence to the visual orthodoxy in which I believed, to the very heritage in which he himself was steeped and trained. Why the early Riablo was hailed as legitimate heir to this tradition, gifted with sufficient genius to carry it on. When he changed direction on them, the art community that had taken him up felt betrayed. They threw him down, cast him out, made him a pariah. Important galleries and museums would have nothing to do with him and demand for his work almost dried up.

"Fortunately there were knowledgeable few connoisseurs who could see in the new work what devotees of the old could not. Their purchases kept him alive. He has never forgotten this patronage. When Riablo's work came grudgingly back into favor as the force of his vision literally wore popular resistance down, those early collectors found themselves sitting on a treasure of rapidly rising value, while their reputation for taste and shrewdness was enhanced. Foremost among them was LaValle. He established his wealth and standing as an agent by acquiring for others, as well as himself, the very finest of Riablo's transitional paintings. This is why LaValle has favored status with the Master today, brokering most of what is let out for sale. I'm curious what effect first hand exposure to Riablo's ideas will have upon your eye. Very different from knowing him through reproductions you'll find. The real thing."

Kate was reasonably well acquainted with Riablo having poured over art books at home that reproduced his paintings and drawings.

Already she respected the strong linearity with which figures were defined, solid like sculptures, elegantly designed with a strict simplicity. The later work, however, lacked appeal by affronting her sensibility with twisted, distorted and misshapen forms. Barely recognizable for what they represented, hard to like, harder to forget. Yet it was this later phase of work that was on display. Mostly she was curious to discover the secret of Riablo's impact upon her father and uncle. Hence she asked to be told more about what Phillip remembered.

"Well, as I said, Riablo's disregard for the aesthetic I valued caused me to loathe what I considered the deliberate ugliness of his work. My limited taste was offended. As was your father's. Like two gossips tearing down someone they loved to hate, we considered our slander enlightened conversation. Late at night, after class over coffee, we'd reinforce our mutual dislike until we couldn't put off studying any longer. Then came The Institute Show. At first we refused to attend. Why should we? Our minds were already made up. What could Riablo and a few of his contemporaries have to teach us? Indeed. But your mother made us go. She grew tired of our steadfast refusal to waste time seeing what we wasted so much time railing against. She accused us, us of all people, of having closed minds! Well, we weren't about to plead guilty to that charge so off we went, intending to confirm the bias we carried with us."

"But you didn't," interjected Kate, knowing how the story ended.

"No, Kate. No we did not. How to describe the experience? How to explain it? The key was your mother, with her stinging criticism of our prejudice. To pacify her and to redeem ourselves we agreed to take a token look, and that reluctant willingness cracked the door. A glimmer of light from the brilliance that hung before us was let in. Then it was all over. We were both physically affected. In sudden wonder our eyes became un-skinned. For the first time we could begin to comprehend what the man was about. We saw him in his terms, not ours. Therein lay our conversion. His terms became our own. By the end of the day, and every day thereafter for the duration of the show, we were groggy with astonishment, shaken with excitement, exhausted with stimulation. The revelation we received caused us both to see differently and to correct the courses we had been following. I changed from wanting to be an artist to wanting to curate shows that could do for others what this show had done for me. As for your father, his painting changed over night."

Feeling a little nervous about her own reaction Kate began to take more seriously the experience she was about to undergo.

"Am I to be changed as well?" she asked.

Phillip honored the seriousness of her concern with a serious reply.

"I don't know, Kate. This is for sure. By now your eye is sufficiently well educated to take in some of Riablo's genius. What impression is made, what outcome produced, is up to you."

"Yet you say it changed Galen's work," she wondered. "I can't see any resemblance between the two."

"Oh yes you can," he answered. "You just don't credit the similarity. The constraints of conventional portraiture which Galen had religiously followed were torn away. You're right, he doesn't abstract visual reality like Riablo. No, Galen does it psychologically by combining dissonant characteristics into a single portrait, making the subject every bit as jarring to the eye. You know how Riablo will combine front and back views into the rendering of a single figure that articulates despite the contradiction is contains? Well your father does the same, integrating opposing human traits into a consistency the viewer can accept. In both cases, logic tells you it can't be done, but your eye is persuaded to accept what reason disbelieves."

"Is that why people like Galen's work?"

"Like it or dislike it, they don't usually forget it. And they wonder why. I'll tell you. Gaze at one of his portraits long enough and your impression of the subject will begin to shift as you come to see many portraits of the same person fused into one. Like applying glazes, he overlays aspects of personality upon each other enriching depth of character with each succeeding layer. I've told him, when the history of portraiture in this century is written, he will be counted among the innovators. And I'm not alone. It's no accident LaValle took up your father's work, nor that the Countess followed. They esteem Galen's paintings more highly than he does himself."

"You make <u>him</u> sound revolutionary when he is only quietly going about his work." Phillip was not describing the father whom she knew.

"Yes. Well the quiet revolutionaries are the ones you have to watch out for. They go unnoticed until one day you turn around and they explode sudden awareness in your face. Not like Riablo. He burst on the scene when he was not much older than you and has been bursting ever since. Just when critics and art historians get him fixed and typed he breaks definition and challenges them to understand him anew. He's the exception to the rule, the prodigy who keeps his early promise. An engine of creativity that won't slow down. According to LaValle, one of the few people who gets in to see the recluse any more, Riablo's still going strong. Well, here we are. You ready?"

Kate thought so, and at first she was, joining the promenade of onlookers winding their way through three large rooms of increasingly abstract compositions, each gallery devoted to a different period into which scholars, not the artist, had divided up the artist's work. Cutting up the body of Riablo, Kate felt, dismembering it, making it difficult to comprehend the whole.

"I wish you'd mixed them up, Kip. I wish they had been hung together."

"Why?" he asked.

"Because I feel like I am missing something when they are kept apart."

Ever obedient to Kate's desires Phillip immediately consented to what not even she would have presumed to ask.

"Easily remedied. Pick three. From each room one painting that you like the best."

"But Kip," she protested. Too late. Her wish had now become his command.

"Do as I ask." He was firm, so she was forced to abide by her request. However, even with her quick eye the task was difficult. Kate found herself forced to focus deeply on her responses because each picture was surprisingly unique, each playfully exploring a new idea. It took an hour or sorting and weighing before she could decide on her final selections: a reclining nude, a coastal village, a spare still life. While subject matter of each was ordinary the variety of pictorial invention astounded her.

"Wait here," Phillip ordered as he whispered something to a guard who, because it was closing time, had begun herding everyone else out of the exhibition, reentering several times to retrieve the lingering few who required encouragement to leave.

"All right. Close your eyes." Taking her hand Phillip led Kate back into the furthest room where, rehung on one wall, were the three paintings she had chosen.

"Now you can open."

And open she did, as completely as she could. Although tempted to view them individually she resolved to take them in together, forcing her focus to embrace them all at once. He eyes ached from the strain of what she was commanding them to do. They resisted, but her will prevailed.

To Phillip, watching her, this concentration of effort was impressive and alarming. Stalk-still she stood, arms stiff, hands clenched at her sides, forcing herself to -- to what? What was she trying to do? What had he done? What should he do? She was insensible to his concern. Curious, he leaned forward to get a more complete perspective of her face. It was drained of expression. The eyes were unobstructed, utterly receptive to whatever impression she was taking in. To whatever impression was being made. Which was? He had no way of knowing, and this ignorance was causing him anxiety. About to awaken her to awareness of his worry, she woke herself.

"Well?" Phillip asked, relieved she had regained consciousness and could talk.

"He takes everything apart and puts it back together in a new way, doesn't he?"

"Yes," Phillip answered. "Totally unafraid to experiment. If one approach doesn't work, he'll simply try another. What begins as a horse can end up as a landscape. Unrehearsed. Spontaneous. Where he starts has no sure bearing on where he ends up. As much a reinventor as an inventor. He takes familiar concepts and techniques from everywhere and recreates them in his own idiom. Critics charge him with stealing ideas from the entire history of art. Riablo makes no apology. "All art belongs to me."

"He gives himself so much freedom. I would be scared." And Kate meant it.

"He only gives himself as much freedom as he has skill to control. Don't let the freedom fool you. It's really discipline in disguise. Genius counts for a lot, but not as much as effort. Practice is the invisible foundation. Riablo makes it look easy. Hard to remember that the great drawing which takes minutes to execute is actually the outcome of a lifetime's training."

"I see that," Kate's confession of recognition was spoken soberly, almost sadly. In comfort Phillip put his arm around her broad shoulders, hugging her to his side.

"What you are feeling now is something very special, Kate. Difficult, but enormously beneficial if you can hold onto it. Humility. The same effect Riablo had on your father and I. Acknowledging his genius, we both realized neither of us had his gifts. We had to accept our modest capacities and do with them what we could. There's no substitute for knowing your limitations, Kate. Then you can live gratefully in the land of giants who dominate the history of art without feeling obligated to be a giant yourself. It's kind of freeing in a way, at least it freed me to know my best was going to good enough."

Kate nodded. Her uncle had followed her feeling to where it lay, awestruck and humbled.

"But not daunted," she added aloud, filling with excitement at her own possibilities.

Phillip could feel her change of energy.

"Not daunted," he repeated, excited by her possibilities too.

"Kip: what do you value most in Riablo's work?"

"How he sees. Beneath the surface of ordinary things he discovers the elemental forms. Then he designs configurations that are more real than the reality they represent. Plus the message he sends to those who can't see beyond figurative work: all art is fundamentally abstract. Still he offends more people than he pleases. You and I, Kate, we're among the lucky ones. To have our vision pleased and not offended."

"Kip, take me back. Now!"

The sudden urgency of this request caught Phillip off guard.

"Is something wrong or have you had enough?"

"Neither. Take me home!" She was frantic to get back to work.

Pulling up at the house she kissed Phillip good-bye, threw open the car door, thanking him over her shoulder as she rushed down the walk into the house, into the kitchen, setting down on her familiar stool by the table, gratefully picking up two crayons and commencing to draw. And draw and draw, shaking her head in silent refusal when Joanne announced supper, absorbed by an overpowering need to draw her energy down which she finally did after her parents had retired to bed

What happened to her? Why had she forced herself to look full face into the Master's brilliance and not shy away? What streak of pride or stubbornness caused her to challenge Riablo through his work? She had lost. Humility told her that. Or had she? Closing her eyes she reflected on herself. Something felt different. Either she was unable to purge all the excitement from her body or something had stuck that she couldn't get rid of. Something was still causing her excitement. A measure of freedom she hadn't felt before. The magnitude of Riablo's originality had inspired her own. Kate heaved a sigh of relief. So that was it: she felt capable of more.

Now she gave in to feeling tired. Gathering up the large pile of drawings that had accumulated on the floor she stacked them on the table. For the first time in a long time, she had drawn without conversing with her friends. "Thank you,' she said to each, but neither would give her a civil "good night." No doubt she would hear from Anastan tomorrow.

Down the hall past Galen's studio where a light had been forgetfully left on. Her father had apparently paid his portrait of the Benefactor a late night visit in hopes of visually solving the riddle of that contradictory man with a single telling pose. No luck. Galen had left without success. Kate was looking in from the door always left open and always forbidden to her except at sitting time. From the confusion of charcoal lines upon the white, freshly prepared canvas she understood the difficulty her father was having trying to get the standing figure to articulate. How to lean him back against the mantle in an expansive gesture of generosity, while hunching him forward just enough to suggest the wary animosity of a man who, despite all his wealth and comfort, still lived life with his back against the wall? She understood her father's problem. And the solution. What? Yes. It was true. What eluded Galen was obvious to her. The illusion could be managed by thrusting the left leg and shoulder forward just enough to establish this potentiality for instantaneous attack without violating the reclining stance. To accomplish this, one half of the figure would have to be slightly foreshortened without dividing in two what must be rendered whole.

Action followed instinct without thinking. She did not hesitate. Boldly marching up to the easel she armed each hand with a piece of charcoal, forcing them into service. Immediately they began redesigning the subject according to her plan, overlaying firm dark lines upon the tentative strokes made by her father in his futile search for a representation that worked. It was done in a matter of minutes. Stepping back she spoke aloud to herself.

"There. This captures what he's after!" But other voices protested.

"Now she's done it! What made her do it?"

"There's something the matter with her. She doesn't feel the same."

Kate heard them, agreed with them, yet felt no regret over the crime she had knowingly committed. In denial of consequences she knew must follow, she felt elated, empowered by forbidden freedom she had taken. Turning out the studio light, she went directly to bed falling peacefully asleep until early next morning when she was awakened by a tone of voice that had never been used to her within the family before.

"Kate! Kate Germaine! You come down here this instant!" It was Joanne, her usually soft voice now overcome by anger. "Right now! Get up and come down here right now!"

As she was ordered, Kate did, silently barefooting into Galen's studio where her father stood studying his portrait with some perplexity.

"Kate, is this <u>your</u> work?"

"Yes." She could scarcely hear her own voice. Then her mother attacked with a force of feeling Kate did not realize Joanne was capable, that she was not later to forget.

"How <u>dare</u> you have done this?" It was both a question and accusation and commanded a reply.

"I saw what needed to be done and I did it." Kate spoke as calmly as she could to calm her mother, despite not feeling calm inside herself. She felt frightened by Joanne's anger battering against her, yet felt protected by knowledge that while she had done wrong she had also done right.

But her mother's outrage was unrelenting.

" Do you know how important this commission is? Never mind entering your father's studio without invitation and defacing his work. We'll get to that. In five weeks your uncle opens the new wing of his museum when the Benefactor's portrait is to be unveiled. Now, by vandalizing your father's painting, you've set him back I don't know how much time. You've made a very difficult commission more difficult still. How could you do this to your father? To your uncle? And to me? It's your father's studio, but the one rule was as much mine as his. Well, what have you to say for yourself? And don't say you're sorry! Apologies for inexcusable behavior are not accepted. You knew it was wrong before you did it!"

"I won't." Now Kate was angry. She was unused to criticism no matter how well deserved, and she didn't like being berated. One wrong did not justify another. She refused to be passive any longer.

"I won't apologize!"

Unfortunately, by denying Kate permission to express repentance, Joanne deprived herself of the remorse she wanted to hear. Thus blocked by her own prohibition she appealed to Galen.

"Well, you say something to her!" then in a softer voice she addressed herself. "She's not even sorry for what's she's done. I don't understand it." Joanne didn't know what to do. To have Kate behave in such a rebellious fashion caused her initially to feel angry, but left her ultimately bewildered. Where had her mothering been remiss? Where had she been inattentive? This was not the Kate she knew, yet who knew Kate better than her mother? And if she did not truly know her daughter, then what did this mutiny portend? For the first time, vague fears began to gather, clouding the relationship with her daughter. Could it be they were not as close as she supposed?

Meanwhile Galen had finished examining the altered canvas and was examining the offender herself. Thirteen years old. Soon to be fourteen. Her love of drawing, he had always known about that. But this? He felt bewildered too.

"Kate, have I missed something? I know we don't often talk. You saw what I was trying to do and couldn't, so you did it yourself?"

"That's right." While her mother was punitive her father was receptive.

"Where did you come by the understanding? And the execution. Who taught you to draw?"

"I guess I taught myself," not mentioning her hands.

"Yes. Of course. That's how it's done. Growing with practice all these years. Your mother showed me your drawings from time to time, and I glanced them over. I should have given them a better look. So: you've caught my eye. Now what?"

"I don't know," Kate replied. And she didn't.

Joanne had heard enough.

"What are you two talking about? Galen, don't you see what she did? Respond to that!"

"I do see, Jo, and I am responding. We need Phillip in on this."

"She ruined your study, Galen!"

"No, Jo. No, she didn't. She made the study work."

"What do you mean?" Joanne only saw a child's scribble on her husband's work.

"I had created a problem for which I had no solution. Kate found a way through. Jo, we need to take her drawing more seriously."

Too much. Now Joanne exploded at Galen.

"Take Kate's drawing more seriously? Who has always taken her drawing seriously if not I? Not you. You just dismissed her drawings as child's play. Don't you dare tell me to take Kate seriously!"

"I know,' Galen confessed. "I admit it. I've been wrong. I should have given her more notice and encouragement. But you're missing the point now, Jo, you really are. I'm going to call Phillip. We need his advice."

There was a stubborn streak in her husband that only became apparent when disagreement drove a deep enough difference between them and this vein of obstinacy was struck. Joanne could tell they had reached it now. From past experience, she knew no argument with him would prevail. It was a matter of him deciding what would happen. Nothing to do but wait for Phillip, hear his counsel, then influence the outcome if she could.

Phillip took the side of neither parent, instead taking them to task.

To Galen: "I hope this is a lesson. Don't ever underestimate Kate again."

To Joanne: "You have no business getting angry at Kate for showing what she can do."

Always her advocate, Phillip was not about to fail Kate now.

"So, where do we go from here? Is that what you are asking?"

Chastened, both parents nodded. While they loved their daughter, in some way they knew Phillip loved her more.

"Very well. Since Kate has chosen to enter your studio, Galen, and behave like an artist, then treat her like one. Move her out of the kitchen. Make a place for her to draw in here. Let her observe you at work. Answer any questions she is curious to know."

Galen turned to Kate.

"Would you like that?"

"I would," she replied.

Joanne shook head.

"It doesn't seem right. For a punishment she gets a reward. Are you sure, Phillip?"

"I'm sure," and Phillip was.

"So be it," Joanne sighed as much in defeat as consent, feeling the sadness that underlay the sigh: she would miss her kitchen companion. Funny how she had gotten used to the drawing table by the window. Not so funny. The vision of it empty and deserted heaved up a swell of emotion that she swallowed down. Then came another vision, not voluntarily conceived. A vision of a ship, of Kate as a ship sailing away from her. Not far, but away none-the-less, to anchor in a nearby harbor. Galen's harbor. Departing one influence and entering another. Sadness? Joanne was sensitive to her own emotion. No. It was grief.

So began Joanne's letting go her only child.

Chapter Eleven
A List of Personal Dislikes

Countess:

Yes, no doubt you are dissatisfied with my manner of parting as well as not writing you back until now. However, I do not take injury lightly, particularly from someone I have come to trust. Since you and Joanne have become friends (and I do not begrudge either of you this) ask her. She can testify. I do not let mistreatment go unanswered. You betrayed me, Countess. I told you this before. And I shall not allow our friendship to hurt me again. This shall be my only letter. You may write more if you wish. I do read what you write, underlining parts I do not like. They keep me mindful of how you are. As for now, I bring news of Riablo. Knowing him, you may appreciate what I have to share.

'Escampobar' is engraven on the gate of this great house. I do not know the meaning of the name. Set high on a rise overlooking the sea it is surrounded by wild and uninhabited land. In every direction is stunted growth, beaten down by the ocean wind. Most of the trees are weathered silver-gray. Twisted and dead, they look like crooked crosses in an unkempt graveyard. The location is so remote and forbidding it keeps strangers away. Our one connection to the outside world is a narrow road that winds across the grassy hills for twenty miles before reaching the nearest town. From there, Jesus retrieves those few necessities he cannot make and Marcella cannot grow.

Nothing is fancy here, yet nothing is wanting. There is enough without abundance. There is comfort without luxury. And there is order and simplicity except for clutter from the Master's work that crowds the corners and the walls of every room but one. Marcella claims the kitchen, and Riablo leaves her space alone. Together Marcella and Jesus run the house. Younger than he, yet they are his guardians, protecting him from care, and preserving him for work.

One aspect of Riablo I can understand. He values work more than the work produced. Quickly he sets completed work aside to make way for the next. You should see his face light up at the prospect of some new idea. And yet just before the light, a darkness falls. Only for a moment. Right after completion. A softening of his eyes, a saddening of his face. For this brief time, he appears to me as he does at no other. Old. Aware the picture he has painted is one closer to his last. Then he draws himself up into an attitude of defiance. To what? To the End, I think. I can almost hear him challenging the Enemy. 'Take me when you will, but you must take me at my best!' Then he hurls himself forward into the next picture, carrying his brush before him like a lance. I believe he is determined to die at the height of his powers.

I may be wrong, yet I've inherited some of my father's eyes. Enough to see beneath the surface. And in Riablo's studio, I am free to stare since he is blind to me. I stare not just at him, but at his paintings too, scenes from another world in which the structures are so monumental they defy ordinary scale. They communicate a brooding, emblematic power. I do not know the meaning of his final vision nor, I believe, does he. Only playing his creative instincts out.

Such vitality! How much less vigor I possess. I thought the young were more energetic than the old. Not so with him. I think it is because he uses himself wisely, never losing sight of his priorities.

By comparison, I have a lot to learn. One thing you said was true, about living as though my future had no end. I know better now. Like Riablo, every drawing I make is one closer to my last. So there is no life to waste.

I can promise you this. I won't spend time fighting with Joanne any more. Not because I have forgotten or forgiven because I haven't. All that pointless conflict. Nothing was resolved except to keep on fighting, anger drawing us together and driving us apart. Well, she started it by forcing me to Savocek. I only wanted to be left alone to draw from inclination and for pleasure. But no, she drove me into his instruction. Now that man's lessons are set so deep within me I cannot move them out. I've left my teacher, but his teaching carries on.

Dislikes. Since I'm on the subject I'll add one more. LaValle, that man you and Galen and my uncle all esteem so highly, though I can't see why. I've never liked his secrecy and prying ways. Nor the way he looks. I know, I know, it's through no fault of his. Galen has told me the story a hundred times, about artistic promise broken by a tragic accident. But why must LaValle wear his disfigurement so openly? I never know whether to look at him or look away. Sometimes I think he uses this discomfort to his advantage. All stooped over peering up into your face, his shaking fingers clinging to one of those awful cigarettes. Reeking from the smoke. Talking in a whisper so you have to listen closely when he speaks. But Galen will hear none of my objections. He calls LaValle the resurrected man. Vanishing for seven years after the accident only to reappear as the most well-connected agent for foreign acquisitions in this country. More important, with a growing reputation as a connoisseur. No one's opinion of his work does my father rate so highly as LaValle's.

To rid me of my prejudice, Galen asked that I consult with you. He said you and Lavalle were once romantically attached. Before the accident. Did that end more than his artistic career? None of my business. However, he did suggest I ask to see LaValle's early water colors, the ones you acquired before they gained their current value. Perhaps when I return. Galen hopes liking the work will cause me to appreciate the man.

As for what you wrote about your father, yes he sounds like a dangerous man. But you knew this at the outset. While he never altered for the better, he never changed for the worse. He was bad from the beginning. Not so, Joanne. If any mother can be said to be ideal it was she, everything I could have wanted. More. Giving me space to nurse my wounds from school. Providing space for me to draw. Always ready to listen when I wanted to talk. Countess, this was the sensitive and supportive mother I had.

Then I was given another. At first she just suggested I try studying with Savocek. I said I'd rather not. Ordinarily this is where she would have left it, respecting my wishes and letting the matter drop. Not this time. After I declined, she insisted. I began to argue, she to demand. Since my arguments, although well founded, would not change her mind, I simply refused. That was when she transformed.

Her eyes hardened, her mouth became grim, her voice dropped, and her words became cold and measured. I can still hear her command: 'Kate, in this you shall do as I say.' 'You can't make me,' I answered defensively, stepping back. 'Oh yes I can," her face now in my face. 'Don't try me, Kate,' she menaced. 'I ruled my brothers and sisters, and in this I will rule you.'

Feeling ferocity I never had before, I began to feel afraid. Afraid of my mother! Afraid of what? That she was prepared to do whatever she had to do to get her way with me because at that moment all that mattered was my obedience, not my love. There was no trace of caring in her face, only purpose, and she drove me with it until out of fear I finally gave in. To do what I hated, hating myself for yielding and hating her for changing from the mother I had known. The worst part of Savocek, although God knows he was bad enough, was what it took to make me his student.

So, which am I to trust? The good mother or the bad? Two faced she has become, like the Little Goddess in my uncle's museum whose appearance changes depending on the view. One face is all I have, although there have been times when I wished for another more pleasing. Even you have only one face, never pretending to be anything except acquisitive with me. My error was refusing to accept you as advertised. Well, I know better now. I trust you no more than that man Lavalle. Who knows how many faces he wears? As for me, I do learn from my mistakes. Therefore, when we resume our friendship, be warned: I shall remain upon my guard.

Until then,

Kate Germaine.

Chapter Twelve
DISCOVERING A TEACHER

Kate first heard mention of Savocek when Phillip began taking her to the State exhibitions of high school art. These were held annually at his museum to recognize winners of district contests and the instructional programs in which those students were trained. Since Galen was usually asked to be a juror, Kate would accompany them both to preview the entries. This was an event she looked forward to because both men would solicit her opinion in finalizing their own evaluations.

On one occasion Galen paid tribute to his daughter's taste.

"The vision of a child, Phillip. You can't beat it. She goes right to the heart of the matter. No education to confound her instincts. Not like you and I, all mired down by what we've learned -- too informed for our own good. The image simply strikes her eyes and reflexively, like a camera, snap goes her judgment and immediately she knows whether the work has any particular merit or not. She's always done my pictures this way. No hesitation. I'll have eight or ten studies I'm evaluating, and it's only a moment's effort for her to pick out the truest rendering and most apt design."

And this was true. For it seemed to Kate that her father and uncle took forever selecting the few outstanding pictures from the many that were simply very good. What were they considering? What took them so long? It made her impatient, particularly when, as usually happened, in the end their choices coincided with her own.

"Galen, I disagree." Phillip had a habit with both parents of taking up for Kate at unexpected times. "A child's eye is one thing, but she has more than that. It's not just innocence from lack of sophistication. The young lady has a lot more artistic understanding than you give her credit for. She's gifted that way. Don't you dismiss her talent as some ordinary aptitude of youth."

As far back as she could remember, Kate was not simply a child to her uncle. She was distinctly female, accorded special courtesies he felt her sex deserved. 'Young Lady' was how he regarded, respected, and behaved toward her. Courtly, deferent, considerate, this was how he had been taught by his mother to treat women, all the ways her husband had never treated her.

Recipient of her uncle's delicacy and consideration from earliest childhood, Kate came to expect it as her due until the world of school betrayed her into believing otherwise. In consequence, she treasured Phillip's treatment of her the more, especially on these annual occasions when she was treated as another juror, on equal standing with the artist and her uncle, standing that enhanced her opinion of herself. As she deferred less and less to them from one exhibition to the next she gathered faith in her power of judgment, becoming stubborn in her own artistic taste. Although she did not insist they adopt her view, neither would she be governed by theirs. Just like her mother, Galen confided to Phillip. Flexible up to a point, but immovable thereafter.

As for the judging of the high school exhibition, this was blind, there being no information identifying from where in the State each entry came. And yet year after year the same small high school kept producing winning work until Phillip grew curious to know who was responsible for the instruction. A long-distance phone call to the superintendent's office turned up the teacher's name, one J. Savocek. Follow-up calls to the high school, however, were never returned, although the secretary promised all messages had been delivered. This lack of response only made this mysterious figure that much more intriguing to Phillip.

"Savocek again, Galen. Now what do you think of that? Six years running his students have carried off top honors."

"Well, at least we know it can't be coincidence or luck," the artist replied. "The man must be quite a teacher to coax this quality of work from a bunch of small-town kids. Why don't you invite him up for a special award?"

So Phillip did, receiving the response he anticipated -- no response at all.

"That's it! I've offered every inducement to communicate with me, but one. If he's going to play hard to get then I'll play hard to avoid. I'll go to him if he won't come to me. Either he's very busy or has no interest in personal recognition. Before I go, however, I want you and Kate to glance at the display I've put together. The winners of the last six years, all of them students of Savocek. Come look at this." He had them lined up against his office wall. "Well, what do you notice?"

After scanning the makeshift gallery, Kate was first to speak.

"They're serious. Not by students at all. By artists."

"She's got it," agreed Galen. "The talent has been disciplined and deepened by some commitment. Not easy to extract from young people with a lot more on their minds than art. You'd think they'd rebel or become discouraged, but apparently not. He must be a skillful taskmaster to push so hard and still keep them on his side. Quite a touch."

Kate's was the final word.

"A heavy hand, not a touch at all. I bet he drives his students and they don't like him for doing it. I wouldn't. When drawing becomes so serious it stops being fun then what's the point? I bet he takes the fun away. Who'd want to study with a man like that?"

Phillip eyed her as she said this, but said nothing in response so she had no way of knowing her antipathy had confirmed the decision he had already made. The next morning early he was on the road driving west four hours to a town he'd passed through upon occasion, never before considering it a worthwhile place to stop. A citified man, the country offered only natural beauty that could not compare with the great creations housed in his museum.

The high school was not hard to find. He knew what it would look like without any previous introduction. There it was, an old three-story brick block of a building with not even the slightest architectural ornamentation to soften the hard institutional lines. Clearly, it was an example of form following function to its logical conclusion, all function and no form, at least not of an aesthetically pleasing kind.

The principal was a bluff, florid-faced man, red and blocky and unadorned as the castle he ruled. An all-state center in his youth, for many a year a successful coach, now the well-liked administrator of a high school in which he gave no one any trouble so long as they did not trouble him. He was a man used to running his team smoothly, a team that never questioned his benevolent control. And he loved to hear himself talk.

Phillip, who did not know him, recognized him at once and felt recognized in return. Both seasoned administrators, they were expert in sizing people up. Introducing himself, Phillip declared the purpose of his visit.

"I would like to meet Mr. Savocek, your Art teacher. His students have repeatedly won the State competition held at my museum, yet he has never accompanied them."

"Doesn't surprise me," smiled the Principal. "Awards wouldn't amount to much for him."

"Why so?" Phillip asked.

"Best I can tell you is the man's a winner who plays the game for its own sake. All he cares about is working with students. Or maybe just the students' work. Not a socializer, he mostly keeps to himself. Only here in the afternoons. We're such a small district, Art has always been a frill we couldn't afford until one of the board member's children took a class with Savocek down at the community center. The kid's mom is a real firebrand. I guess every board has to have at least one. She got the other parents so excited, that about seven years ago we bought us an art program. Amazing how there's no money until someone finds something they want money for. But that's another story. The point is, I hired him and he's scored for us every year since. I kidded him one time, early on when I didn't know he didn't have a sense of humor. I said: 'If I could find a football coach with your record of wins we'd have a stadium by now.' Any other member of my staff would at least have faked a laugh, but not him. That told me a lot about the man right there."

"So records don't interest him either?" Phillip could feel his curiosity more aroused.

"Not as near as I can figure," the Principal shook his head. " No more ambition than humor to Savocek. He couldn't care less."

Phillip knew how to keep a talker talking.

"Then what does he care about?"

The Principal leaned back in his chair.

"Not about other people's opinion. Maybe after you meet him you can tell me. Teaching is the only thing I've found. He's pure teacher. Takes students with no particular interest or talent and shows them what they can do with what they didn't know they had. It's no free ride, I can promise you. Those kids pay for what they get. What gets them first is a surprise. You'd think by now Savocek's reputation would have gotten around. But no, they think the E in 'elective' stands for easy, another blow-off course offering an easy grade. So along about mid-semester, not only do they find themselves working harder than expected, even worse they find themselves barely hanging on with a 'C', in spite of ten hours of homework a week. Homework in art, can you believe it? That's when they start coming to see me, wanting to transfer into some less demanding, more rewarding class."

"What do you tell them?" asked Phillip.

"I don't tell them anything," the Principal answered. "I just listen and watch. It happens with four or five students a year. The kid will come in ready to quit and then Savocek shows up with a portfolio of her work under his arm. While she's expressing her discouragement, Savocek is just sitting right there, right where you are, leafing through the student's folder. Then, when she's had her say, he looks up, never once at her but at me and asks would I be interested in viewing some of her work. By now I've come to understand that's my signal. I say sure I'm interested, and he proceeds to show me what she's produced. I should explain to you, no offense intended, art has never made any difference to me. I don't know the good from the bad. All the stuff on the walls at home my wife picked out, hand painted pictures of places we've been. Souvenirs, you know. Nice reminders, and they beat looking at an empty wall. But even I can see as Savocek talks that this kids has covered a lot of ground in a short time. More important, as he talks the student can see it too. The learning didn't come easy, she worked hard, and she accomplished more than she ever dreamed. Those pictures are hers, and she starts feeling proud to have made them. It's a pretty impressive display. Mind you, there's no word of encouragement or praise in what he says. No promises of better things to come. Just straight talk to me about the pictures and what he calls the problems the artist was trying to solve. You see Savocek doesn't have students. He won't use the word. If you're in his class then by definition you're an artist and you better treat yourself that way. Seriously. Finally, when he's gone through the last picture he leaves the portfolio open on my desk, on top of the pile, on top of the last picture, a blank sheet of paper signifying, I guess, what could come next. Then with never a glance at the kid he ups and leaves the office, leaving the three of us behind -- myself, the student and her portfolio. Now I don't say a word 'cause I know I don't have to. Waiting is my job. Pretty soon the kid will get up, eyes fixed on that blank sheet of paper. She'll carefully gather together the pieces of her portfolio as though they mattered to her and mumble something about how she'll come back to talk later on. But she doesn't. They never do. Seven years and of the students ready to quit this man's class not one of them ever has. Now you tell me what he cares about."

Deeply moved by what he had just heard Phillip resonated with the spirit of the man he had yet to meet.

"He sounds dedicated, whatever else he may be. Parents must appreciate this even if his students don't."

This time the Principal laughed.

"You're wrong there. The honors? Sure, parents love that. Particularly the Board. But his grading system? That's another story. You take a high achieving kid ambitious for college, his parents willing to sacrifice to make this dream come true, then give him a 'C' in Art. Why before the ink's dry on that report card, those parents are storming in here infuriated their son's or daughter's grade point average has been lowered by some class as no account as Art. How dare I allow this teacher to ruin their kid's future?"

"What do you say to them?" asked Phillip, wondering what he himself would say if placed in the same position.

"Say? I say I'll call in Mr. Savocek and let him explain. I didn't give the grade. After a while in he comes in his own good time. Nothing shy about the man. Sure of himself in a manner that can offend people who expect to intimidate their public servants. As his principal, I know the feeling. He works for me, but he teaches for himself. On his terms or not at all. His attitude was maddening at first, but once I adjusted to my loss of authority I've found our relationship kind of refreshing. I can trust him to be honest and direct with me. No flattery or manipulation. He says what he believes, not what I want to hear, which sets him apart from most other staff. They resent his independence. The jealous ones can get pretty vicious, some of the rumors they circulate to attack his reputation. Getting all these awards hasn't made him any friends on the faculty, I can promise you that. Not that he cares. Hell, he probably doesn't even know. Who's to tell him? Not me. But they'll get him. Sooner or later the nonconformist gets beat. Last election the Art program lost one supporter. Next election it will lose another. It's only a matter of time."

"What happens with the parents?" Phillip wanted to know.

"Oh, the parents." The Principal enjoyed having such an eager listener. "First off they ask about their son's performance in class. Did he do what was required? And Savocek answers 'yes', yes he did, asking if they want to see their son's work. No. No, they're not interested in his work. They came to talk about his grade. The 'C'. Savocek nods, yes a 'C'. This is correct. As though he doesn't see their cause for concern. They press on. If their son did all the work and it was up to standard, why didn't he get an 'A' or at least a 'B'? Now is when I get ready for the explosion I know will follow describing how he grades. A 'C' Savocek explains is for working hard and doing everything that is demanded. It's not easy to get a 'C'. 'C' is a good grade. But the parents disagree. Good? What does he mean 'good'? It's only average. Yes, Savocek , that's right. 'C' is average. That's about the best most students can do if they make an honest effort. Now the parents get angry. Does he ever give a 'B'? Savocek thinks for a moment. No. Not at this school. Not so far. A 'B' would require exceptional effort and a level of competence far beyond what most students could achieve. Well then what about 'A's? Now the parents are really fired up. Does he ever give an 'A'? Oh no, Savocek shakes his head, he would never give an 'A'. Such a grade would mislead students into believing they are doing better than they actually are. These are only beginning artists.. This is why accomplishing average work is no small achievement. The parents should feel good about how well their son has done. Are they sure they wouldn't like to see a few of his pictures? But other teachers, argue the parents, other teachers give their son 'A's. Lots of them. Savocek sighs in sympathy. Yes, he agrees, they encourage the boy to believe he is superior when he is not. Well, that's it. The parents have had it. They can't believe what heresy this man is speaking. In their exasperation they appeal to me."

"What do you tell them?" Phillip wanted to hear the outcome.

The Principal shrugged.

"I tell them Mr. Savocek gave his rationale for grading to interested parents on back-to-school night. Yes. The parents were there. Yes, they heard it. But they thought the Art teacher was just joking. If average is the best you can do, why bother? If there are no good grades to work for, why work at all? Do I, now the parents are after me, do I support instruction with the incentives taken out? In this case, I do. Then they'll take it to the Board. And they do. However, as long as the Board supports Savocek's program, I'll support him."

"And when they don't?" Phillip knew the answer that was coming.

"Then he's gone. As I've told him, Art isn't worth losing my job over, although he can sacrifice his if he likes."

From his own experience with boards, Phillip knew how capricious they could be, support given or withdrawn based on political considerations. And he felt concern for this passionate, principled man, this J. Savocek. Then a funny thought struck him and he smiled.

"You mean to tell me the State winners from his class are 'C' students? I assumed they were the best he had."

The principal laughed back.

"They are. Every one of them only average."

Then Phillip asked for the permission he had come to receive: "I'd like to see his classroom and meet the man, if I may."

"No problem." The Principal was happy to oblige. He had enjoyed their conversation. "I can show you the classroom right now, but he won't be in for another hour. Only works half time as I told you. Guess he makes just enough to pay his keep at the rooming house around the corner from the community center where he still runs evening classes. As for meeting him, most I can do is make the introduction. The rest is up to you. He's not what you'd call a sociable man, not a joiner. Not one friend on the faculty. Come on, I'll show you his space."

On the third floor at the very back of the building was Savocek's classroom, as far away from other teachers as he could get. At least this was how it struck Phillip who was curious how the Art teacher would decorate this remote corner of the school to suit his purposes. Would he texture it with prints or objects of beauty to counter the otherwise sterile surroundings? How would he go about creating a setting conducive for creation?

The answer, upon opening the door, was apparent at once. The room had been stripped bare. There was no decoration of any kind, not one single piece of art upon the naked walls. There was nothing to divert the eye or stimulate the imagination. Rows of school desks had been elevated on blocks to serve as drawing tables at which students must stand to work, there being no stools or chairs to sit upon. This was a room designed for one activity only, primitive in this respect. A room without adornments or comforts.

The one grace in the room, which Phillip could appreciate, but which the Principal did not, was the bank of windows letting in the cold, clear northern light, the most benevolent natural illumination by which to draw.

"You can stay here and wait if you like or I can bring you back in a little while." Once in motion the Principal liked to keep moving around.

"I'll wait. You've been a lesson in how to make a stranger feel at home. Thanks to you, I know much more about the man than when I came, although to be honest I don't feel I know a lot."

The Principal patted Phillip on the back commiserating one old coach to another.

"He's locked up tight as a secret. At least I haven't found the key. Good luck!" And the burly good-natured man strode down the hall sticking his head into classrooms as he went, on patrol, making his presence known with a friendly wave or word causing everyone to remember, lest they forget, who was in charge.

Alone in the empty room Phillip walked over to the window and surveyed the vast expanse of playing fields that stretched out behind the building, material evidence of the priorities adhered to by this and most other communities. So many resources dedicated to athletics, so few to art. Well, ancient Athens was no different. People admired art, but they loved sports. He left his museum and its attendant haunts seldom enough to welcome this reminder of the small world of art in which he lived, a world of great refinement and great irrelevance.

"You came to see me?"

The sharpness of the question cut off his stream of thinking. Without turning around, and without knowing why he did not, he responded.

"Yes, Mr. Savocek. I am Phillip Grambrell, Director of the museum responsible for the awards your students keep winning year after year. I wanted to meet you." He felt the presence of the strange man now standing beside him. Still Phillip did not alter his gaze, allowing Savocek's intense, unsparing and suspicious stare to thoroughly evaluate him.

"So? You have found me," spoken by the Art teacher as a statement of fact.

With controlled leisure Phillip turned to face the man he had been seeking, receiving his hostility by smiling warmly in return until Savocek finally looked away.

"To teach young people so powerfully," Phillip began, "I have wondered if you were an artist yourself?"

"I teach others to do what I cannot. Why have you come to see me?"

It was a question for which Phillip had been waiting.

"I have come to make you an offer."

"Which is what?" the question phrased like a demand.

"To teach for the Museum School. To conduct classes for young people with unusual artistic promise. Would you be interested?" Phillip expected a refusal and so was not surprised when it came.

"Why should I? I have students here. The studio you see. They leave me alone. What more could I want?"

"What more could you want?" Phillip repeated.

Now it was Savocek's play in the negotiation that was building between them, drawing them closer as they sought common ground upon which to come to agreement.

"What do you know about me?"

Phillip reflected for a moment.

"I know you are an extraordinary teacher of young people with ordinary abilities. Your principal tells me that although you are in his employ, you work only for yourself and keep to yourself. Having just met you my impression is you would like to put me off either because you don't trust me for a stranger or don't like what little of me you have met so far.'

"So? What do I know about you?"

Phillip was willing to do most of the talking.

"You know that I have sought you out and am not easily discouraged. You may not have returned my phone calls and letter, but I'm sure you received them. My presence here proves my persistence. I am a man well-versed in dealing with difficult people. My position demands it. Like you I live alone, although I have a family of friends in which I belong. I am passionate about art and make my living there. What else can I tell you?"

Savocek took a step nearer. Standing toe to toe now, their faces a few inches apart, each scrutinized the other. They were close enough for Phillip to perceive vulnerability crouching behind the stern wall that normally defended the teacher. Savocek, no less perceptive, descried beneath the director's easy going manner a strength of will that was not desperate like his own, but was of all things he had never known, gentle and kind. And he was swayed. His cold eyes momentarily thawed, shimmering with feeling, quickly averting to recover. Awkwardly aware that he had breached the privacy of a very private man, Phillip might have apologized were he not sure acknowledgment would have added humiliation to existing pain.

"To continue my offer," he said as if nothing had transpired between them, "you would be salaried above what you are paid now and given studio space to work with students --"

"Of my choice," interrupted Savocek, "of <u>my</u> choice."

"Of your choice. In a great city of our size the pool of talent would provide you pupils of the highest caliber not often available here. How you teach--"

"Is up to me," interrupted Savocek again. "I will <u>not</u> be interfered with."

"Of course," Phillip promised. "The manner of instruction is entirely up to you. It may be the person who funds your salary, we do not budget this position, would want some return from her investment. In fact knowing her I'm sure she would. Probably her pick of what students produce would satisfy."

"This is of no matter to me. Who is this 'she'?"

"An important patroness of the arts. I haven't approached her yet. However, your record of successful teaching shall be sufficient to gain her support. You would have to meet her once. She would not buy you sight unseen."

"No one <u>buys</u> me!"

Phillip immediately apologized. This was going to be tricky.

"I meant your position, not yourself. Not your freedom to teach."

But the teacher sensed an adversary waiting.

"I do not like this 'she' whom you describe. You come to terms with her without me. Better you stay between us."

"And so I shall," Phillip made yet another promise. "After the first meeting, I shall broker all further contact. But an initial meeting cannot be avoided."

"Very well," relented the teacher. "But I shall not feel obliged. Tell her I have no gratitude to give."

For the first time in the interview Phillip smiled.

" No, I don't expect you have. Now, when shall you arrive?"

"The semester ends with May. A week to move and to find a room. The second week in June I shall be at your office ready to begin."

For no reason he think of except it felt important, Phillip asked: "Do you ever laugh?"

"No. Life has been no laughing matter for me. Why do you ask?"

"Since we shall be working together," Phillip replied, "I was curious to know if you are always as serious as you seem."

"I am."

A bell clanged, an alarm signaling permission for every teacher to release their captives at the same time. A rumbling like an earthquake shook the entire building as classes changed, pent up energy pouring into the halls and crowding the stairwells. Phillip could hear the raucous sound of liberated voices approaching. Savocek seemed not to notice. Softly his door was pushed open and the first students filed silently in, leaving their riot outside, becoming orderly at once. Purposefully each walked to the desk assigned, withdrew materials and commenced to work. Not one of them greeted the teacher. He greeted not one of them.

"I won't keep you any longer," whispered Phillip. "I look forward to seeing you in June." But Savocek was paying him no attention. His work had arrived.

With satisfaction at a difficult mission fulfilled, Phillip returned to his museum. He was bearing a gift for his beloved Kate, a gift she would hate. A gift he would need influence from others to persuade her to accept.

Deliberately gave the good news to Galen in front of Joanne.

"I have him! He's agreed to teach for the museum. One of a kind. Now we'll see what alchemy he can accomplish with exceptional talent. I'll get the word out next week. There should be no shortage of applicants. Too bad Kate is set against education. Great ability so seldom has the chance to work with great instruction."

"What are you saying?" asked Joanne. "Why not Kate?"

"Come on, Jo." It was Galen's turn to speak. "You know how Kate feels about schooling. She only endures it because she has to. She has more teachers than she already wants. They're bad enough in subjects she doesn't care about. Intolerable in the one she loves. She won't do it. You know that as well as I."

Joanne didn't argue the point. Instead, she wanted to be sure. "This teacher could advance what Kate can do?"

"Like no other," Phillip answered. "As I said, he's one of a kind."

Now Joanne looked from one man to the other and shook her head. They were both good men, but to convince Kate neither one was capable of doing what needed to be done.

"She won't do it willingly," agreed Joanne. "But she will do it. If I <u>make</u> her."

"And how are you going to do that? Not without bloodshed." Galen thought he was being funny.

"Not without bloodshed is how," said Joanne, giving each man a grim look neither had ever seen on her face before. Then she repeated silently the terrible words to herself: "Not without bloodshed."

Chapter Thirteen
THE HARDEST GOOD-BYE

Dearest Kip,

I have discovered this. I do not like saying good-bye. Too much sorrow comes of it.

Of all the partings, cool and restrained with Joanne, angry with the Countess, sad with Galen, sadder with you, none were as painful as my farewell to Savocek. The more I dreaded telling him, the longer I put it off, the more anxious I became. So there I was, the day before leaving not yet having broken him the news. With no time left I had left myself no choice.

What I feared was not anything he would do, but how I would feel for quitting his instruction. He is so unsparing of himself as a teacher I have wanted to give equal measure of my self in return. But I never could. No matter how I tried, I felt his standards for himself always exceeded my own for me. Although he never compared or criticized since that was not his way. Our arrangement was a simple division of labor. His job was to teach, mine was to learn. We both worked hard, but he worked hardest.

Three years now: a long time to withstand such a force in my life. Time enough to change, and like myself less well because of it. Whatever happened to the little girl who drew because she loved to draw? Was she real or did my wishful thinking make her up? I can't imagine drawing with such innocent delight. Not any more. Installed inside of me is this teacher whom I obey for love of what he enables me to do, while hating him for refusing to be satisfied with my efforts. For him there is no enough. No matter how I stretch myself, I am told there is more that can be given, more that can be gained.

At a sitting years ago Galen told me how possibilities expand as competencies grow. 'What was Da Vinci's dying vision do you suppose?' he asked me. 'What blinding possibilities did he conceive that never reached the canvas?' He regrets how this Master of masters left so few finished pieces behind.

Regret is what I feel too. And doubt. And guilt. What I carry away from my final meeting with Savocek. An ocean of separation is insufficient to distance me from what has passed between us. Unhappy baggage has accompanied me to this new place. Start with guilt. There is the sense I have done wrong. To him? To myself? To whom?

It is this. To everyone but him I shall be coming back. Even to the Countess, although on what terms is unclear. For he and I, it was the end. Not being the kind of teacher to befriend, there was no friendship to carry on after the teaching was done. All he had given me, and yet I could not find, still cannot find, feelings of gratitude for what I have received. I could not thank him for instruction that was so oppressive. I could not thank him for what I had endured. At least I gave him enough in staying to owe him nothing when I left. Surely I had earned my right to go.

I can say this. And I can mean it. Still guilt remains. I am glad to finish what I never wanted to begin, and yet am sorry too. When I declared to him I would be stopping he made an unexpected response. 'First Gilner, then Tate. Now you. My best students desert me. Of the three, I thought you would remain.' He sighed and I glimpsed disappointment when I was sure he wouldn't care.

But I was wrong. I mattered to him! In leaving I was taking something he would miss. What, I asked him? 'I never get to finish,' he sighed again. 'With you, I thought I might get to finish. To give one artist everything I understood. Just once. But no. Like the rest you leave before my work is done. What could I accomplish with an artist who remained!'

There is my guilt. I was depriving him of this possibility. And myself. You make staying so hard, I told him in my defense. Why do you make staying so hard? 'Because every time you work harder for me, you learn to work harder for yourself,' he replied. Then you have succeeded, I said. He disagreed. 'Not enough. Now you must teach yourself. Do you think you can do that?'

There was a challenge in his question that creates the doubt which plagues me now. Can I progress under my own supervision as well as under his? Am I making the wise choice? Am I running toward Riablo or away from Savocek? Is this opportunity I'm seeking, or only an escape? So many questions to be answered.

Regret has proved to be the worst. I know Savocek is correct. My leaving is premature. I have not learned all from him I could. My worst regret, however, is what I managed to make known. Courage to speak plainly was given to me at the last. I told him, Mr. Savocek I wished I could have liked you, but I have not. You have shown no interest in me except as an artist. You have made not one concession to the demands for study from my school. You have never approved one drawing I have done in your studio. You have never expressed any liking of me. I am a person, Mr. Savocek, have you ever considered that?

'I have tried not to,' he answered. 'I care about your work. If I ignored you as a person, as you say, it is because I wanted you to do the same.'

By now, having nothing left to lose, I was willing to speak openly. I can't live as an artist first and a person second any more, I said. 'Then do not waste your time or mine pursuing art except as avocation,' he replied. But I clung to my conviction. There is more to life than art, Mr. Savocek, just as there is more to me than work! 'Not for me there isn't,' were his final words on the subject.

His response gave me some relief. My dislike had a firmer basis than before. But I knew the worst was yet to come. He was bound to ask my plans and learn about my destination. Silent for a moment after I had told him, then he became outraged. 'Riablo? Riablo the thief? Riablo the pretender? Riablo the betrayer? He who robs all history for his ideas, you go to him? Who plunders East and West and steals their inventions to create his own? You go to him? Riablo who has led the modern decline of art into senseless abstraction. The great subversive! You go to him? For what? To learn to imitate the great imitator? The great corrupter of human form. And who arranged for this to happen?' The Countess, I told him. 'Ah, it would be she!' he cursed with such contempt I saw his bitterness laid bare. Whom I dislike, he truly despises. Why do you suppose? What did she ever do to him? I dared not ask.

Riablo is not to teach me, I explained. I am only to be given space in his studio to work. 'He will teach you. He will teach you! Whatever else, he has too much influence to be ignored. Well, you have three years of Savocek within you. You have your originality. And you have the master drawings and their claim upon your eye. See if the Great Destroyer can destroy all that!'

Then he did what he had done so long ago. From the drawing table he picked up a blank sheet of paper and wetting each corner with his tongue posted it upon the bare wall. 'What do you see?' he asked. I felt like crying. I see, I replied, I shall never draw for you again. 'Yes,' he agreed, 'I see that too.' And turning away he stalked out through the open door, dismissing me from his service.

When the paper finally became unglued and fell dead to the ground I followed my old teacher out. Taking one last look down the bleak undecorated corridor I saw him at the very end where I had seen him first, only now leaning wearily against the wall, older, even thinner, perhaps unwell. Where once he had been waiting for me to arrive, now he was waiting for me to go. I had to pull myself away.

Strange is it not? The least beloved person proved the hardest to let go. And his early prophesy that I discounted now comes true: I do carry him within me after all. How you manage to enjoy the company of such a forbidding man I do not understand. I should have thought Savocek would have tried even your generous limits of acceptance. But what do I know about friendship, only having had family for friends? Unless you count the Countess, which grudgingly I do.

Certainly I made no friends at school. Too many years of teasing and torment, although the Countess says some good even came from that. She values what she calls the 'gifts of adversity', acquiring strengths through enduring hardships. According to her, my early experience with rejection at school let me stop caring what others thought of me. It freed me from the 'eyes of the world' which is her name for approval seeking. Maybe so. Except I think I shall always miss never having pleased Mr. Savocek just once.

Of course my appearance is another matter. The one part of myself I never liked and still do not. I know there is nothing I can do about it except complain to Nature which I have done so often Nature is probably tired of hearing my complaints. However, I do have an attractive mother after whom I could as easily have been modeled rather than my father. Instead I'm made like a manly girl. I know, I know, you love the way I look. But you are Kip, and here the eyes of the world still prevail.

About this the Countess is no help. She is too beautiful to understand. My growth is not over, she tells me. Plainness can mature in unexpected ways. I tell her I prefer to deal with how I am, not how I might become. Why wait for improvements that shall not occur and be continually disappointed. Better to give up watching and wishing and turn the mirror to the wall. As I told the Countess, hope is a great deceiver. Of course she disagreed. 'At least hope does not settle for misery.' But I had a ready answer. At least misery keeps its promises.

We refuse to stand corrected by each other. So when she declared my appearance to be another gift, I scoffed. However, she insisted. 'Better to have the pillars of your esteem depend on a more solid base than the superficiality of looks.' Easy to say, I countered, when she had been given what I had been denied. Easy for the rich to say money doesn't matter. Let them try living poor. Let her try living plain. Of course she has an answer for everything. 'I have played the hand that life has dealt me, Miss Germaine, and have played it well. You must learn to play your hand the same.' But mine was not complete, I protested. An important card was missing. 'Even the best of hands are incomplete,' was all she said.

She doesn't know what a prison self consciousness is. What a cruel jailer shame can be. Why my first night here at Riablo's was so magical. One spell was cast and another broken. The dancing freed me to move my body whether I liked it or not. Perhaps there shall be more magic to come.

Whatever happens, I shall let you know. Having you to write to, having you write me, makes me glad. Now let me give you a commission. Kip, do this for me. When you see your friend Mr.

Savocek, tell him Kate Germaine sends her sincere respects and that she wishes for him what he wishes for himself: to one day teach an artist with sufficient staying power to receive as much instruction as he has to give. That's all. No. One thing more. Tell him that I regret not being able to be that artist.

There, I am worded out for now. Good night, sweet Kip.

I love you,

Kate

Chapter Fourteen
IN HER UNCLE'S HOUSE

Because Kate was the child Phillip would never have, she was a greater wonder to him than to her parents. No matter how noticing of Kate they were, Phillip noticed more. No matter how marvelous they considered her ordinary achievements, to Phillip they seemed miraculous. When either parent acted abruptly with Kate in his presence or, heaven forbid, presumed to be slightly disapproving, Phillip would rush to her defense. He was her champion long before Kate ever realized she needed one.

Her earliest recollection of Phillip was of a devotional presence emotionally distinguishable from her parents. With him she felt a degree of specialness she did not with them. Cherished and prized she was given patience without end. He would play with her whatever games she wanted until she, not he, became exhausted. And he would play them not just at her home but at his.

How she loved his home! Before she could actually count she had memorized the number of terraces leading up to it. There were three. And the number of steps in each stone flight. There were twenty-two. Before going in, they would play climbing games out front until her legs became so tired he would have to carry her inside.

For many years Kate believed he lived on a top of a mountain, she being so small and the ascent so long and steep. Invariably taken there during the early morning hours when the museum was closed to the public, she had innocently assumed this vast place must be his private residence.

"Is Uncle Phillip a King," she had once asked Joanne.

"Yes, you may think of him that way if you like," she had replied. So Kate had done as she was given permission, and the affectionate name 'Kip', for King Phillip, had been born of the child's instinct to simplify a complicated title by contracting it.

To live in a palace of treasures seemed a delightful thing except for the one rule, the only rule that he ever imposed upon her. Nothing was to be touched. All play must be with her eyes and he would teach how this was done. Although she was given one freedom accorded no one else, freedom to skip and gallop down the unending halls. They were irresistible. Long marble race courses waiting to be run. With his voice he would sound the starting gun. "Bang!" and she was off, immediately accompanied by a host of invisible Kates competing at her heels, echoes of their footfalls crowding up behind her as she flung herself toward the finish. He grew as out of breath from excitement as she from the actual exertion. They would joke about who won and how many contestants there were, he having tried to keep count as echoes echoed echoes until he lost it and she laughed and laughed in triumph at running so swiftly she could outrun his counting rushing to keep up.

The one rule was not new since she was told the same at home, particularly not to touch her father's paintings. As for making drawings of her own, well she liked doing that; although once a picture was made it was no fun anymore, as she told her uncle. But he gently disagreed. Every object in his palace could be fun, he explained, if she would let the object invite her eyes in to play. She laughed and called him funny for his funny ideas and he laughed too.

Yet she also listened and began to do as he suggested, gazing at an object until her eyes relaxed and allowed themselves to be led into the object's arrangement, into its shapes and lines, contours and spaces, textures and colors. Until she was let into the picture or piece of other piece of art and began to appreciate the nature of its construction.

Not just her eyes were moved. There was a deeper pleasure that she enjoyed, a new kind of excitement.   Like exploring a hidden place and discovering secrets about how the place was made, as she confided to Phillip to whom she told everything.

"Yes," he agreed, "this is the first step a person takes when they venture beyond simply looking at art and begin to *see* it."

"See what?" she asked.

"The games of design each artist plays," he answered, for he knew she loved the fun of games. Then he added an inducement to her seeing more.

"You win," he continued, "by discovering as many of these games as you can. The more you find the greater your enjoyment shall be."

And so began the game of games they played that invariably started with the invitation: "Tell me what you see." And was followed, never preceded, by his sharing what he saw, which increased her appreciation for subtleties the game could offer. Not accidentally selected, the objects for this play were chosen carefully, starting with those whose excellence was easily accessible as he gradually trained her eye to pierce the obscurity of more difficult pieces, which in time she learned to do. He had only one wish for the game: it should not be played when she was tired. This would spoil the fun, and spoiled fun might spoil the game. So she must tell him when she grew weary.

When she did, a less demanding play replaced the game of seeing. The game of stories. This was Kate's to initiate.

"Kip, tell me about it," she would begin, referring to whatever object they had been delighting with.

She loved his knowledge. A fluent and fascinating conversationalist by trade, and an art historian by training, Phillip could make scholarship so entertaining the object would become unforgettable, which was his intent. When she was very young these stories were told with a simple charm that grew more complex as she grew older when he began adding a wealth of historical detail. And just when she thought she had finally seen everything in the museum (for she had now come to understand he was not a king and this was not his palace) he would surprise her with some new discovery, none more dramatically introduced than what was to become her favorite treasure of them all.

By now their visits and revisits to the museum had changed from when she was a little girl. The game of seeing had given way to simply sharing insights into what they saw, while tales Phillip recounted grew more compelling for Kate as her curiosity about the world of art became more aroused. The more he told, the more she wanted to know.

In the early mornings, wandering down brightly lit corridors, floors buffed shiny from the night before, Phillip would talk continuously about the work he loved, she loving to listen, interjecting questions when she wanted more. Sometimes they'd stop to peer in darkened galleries, lowering their voices, self conscious about making noise in the huge still emptiness around them. Except for a passing deferential guard they were alone. Silently Phillip would acknowledge the friendly greeting back and then, the two of them alone once more, he would lead their way through the labyrinth of rooms and halls and floors in search of what he wanted her to see, her trusted guide.

"The Museum has many riches, Kate. We have been fortunate in our patrons, gifts and endowment. Of course the great proportion of our collection is never on display. We haven't space to show it all. Most of it is stacked away and packed away in vaults where even I have never fully inventoried everything we own."

She was dismayed.

"What a waste! To keep so much hidden from the public. Why don't you sell it or loan it or just give it away?"

Phillip understood her objection.

"You're right. Keeping art from public view should not be what a museum is about. However, your solutions oversimplify the problem. Many of the bequests we get are on condition the art is never sold. Then there are the collections we agree to accept. Most contain only a few really distinguished pieces, but to obtain these few we must take the lot. Collectors usually don't want their life work broken up. Giving to us assures a place of permanence for what they have assembled. A collection is a creation in its own right, Kate, particularly the great founding collections that originated the reputation of this museum. Given to us by great collectors, gifted visionaries who brought together in one place supreme examples or a genre or period previously ignored. In doing so they opened the public eye and educated its taste, preserving beauty that would likely have been lost."

"You sound as if you admire the collectors as much as what they collected," Kate observed.

"I love it all. The art, the history, the creators, the collectors, all woven into the fabric of this place. You know, there's something very American about how this museum was built, on three collections of non-American art. These wealthy men decided since we had no history of art comparable to East or West, by God they'd go out and buy it, and they did. Also in a typically American way. The world became their marketplace before the world knew it, and being skilled in commerce they had no difficulty plying their trade in countries that they raided. Token sums they gave for artifacts which no amount of money could buy today. These early merchant and manufacturing princes were as far-sighted as the countries they plundered were blind. Or at least asleep to what guile on one side and greed on the other were conspiring to slip across their borders. Too late, these nations awoke, but in time to stop total cultural loss."

"Why did they awaken at all?" asked Kate. " And if the art belongs where it originated, why is it not given back?"

They sat resting on a bench in the central rotunda talking thus.

"Good questions," Phillip replied. " The first is easier to answer than the second. In one case the collector, after having stowed on board his last railroad car of temple statuary and shipped it off, actually called on the Prime Minister to describe how the Country was being looted of its ancient heritage by outsiders like himself trading trinkets and paying paltry sums for treasure. How about that for audacity! But when you've made your fortune exploiting labor, ruining rivals, and buying political influence, I guess offending a foreign dignitary isn't anything to shy away from. Like the robber telling the victims to lock the door behind him so they don't get robbed again. Immediately laws were made that have remained in effect ever since forbidding unauthorized traffic of such items on penalty of death. This was how seriously they took it."

Kate felt a little better.

"Well then the collector did a good thing. You make him sound like he was only after personal gain."

Phillip nodded and shook his head.

"Yes and no. It was good for the country, but not exactly an altruistic act. You must remember this collector was a businessman, highly successful, well versed in how to protect his investment and make a profit. He knew, for instance, that as the supply of a desirable commodity goes down the demand and its associated price goes up. By closing off further trade in what he bought he was ensuring scarcity of what he had gotten away with. There is literally no collection anywhere in the world, outside of the country itself, to rival what the East wing of this museum contains today."

"But the country," argued Kate. "Wouldn't they like their art returned?"

Phillip did not disagree.

"I'm sure they would. However, art is just one form of human treasure, Kate. No different from any other kind in one regard. It only belongs to its owner so long as he or she can defend against its loss. Collectors are treasure hunters. Like the Countess. Like LaValle and the secret list of buyers who retain him. The means they use to gain their ends can be legitimate, but often times are not. An unregulated enterprise at best. What cannot be bought on the open market can be procured illicitly. For a price. These early collectors were more piratical than those we have today, but they were not the worst.   Go further back in history and art was one of the spoils of conquest. Sometimes the victors took what they wanted and saved it in the process, other times they systematically demolished every piece of art they could find to annihilate the culture and subjugate the people. That's the great tragedy! All the great masterworks that have been destroyed which we shall never know. This is why, despite all their shortcomings, collectors and museums are important, preserving what little has survived. This is what you must understand. Infinitely more has been lost than has been rescued and preserved."

Kate had never thought of collectors and museums as rescuers before.

"I suppose even Mr. LaValle serves some useful purpose then," she grudgingly admitted.

"Indeed he does," said Phillip. "A mysterious man in a mysterious occupation. He was a broker for the object I want to show you this morning. As fine and rare as anything we possess. I believe you are ready to see it now. The only piece for which we constructed a special exhibition space. Look here."

He pointed to a small archway darkly gaping at the end of a long hall. They had passed it before, but never gone in. She had barely noticed. This time it caught her attention and her curiosity.

Entering now through an opening built so low she had to duck her head and her uncle to stoop, she stood up again her eyes adjusting to the dimness. Upon the walls she could just make out stone reliefs softly illuminated which caused her to shudder. It felt like she was trespassing into some tomb or sacred place of worship where outsiders were forbidden and spirits stood on guard. Then her eyes were directed to the center of the small gallery where two spotlights, recessed into the ceiling, shone down on a solitary object. Glass encased it was mounted on a pedestal of black marble.

Kate used her eyes as she had been trained to do, responding to the form before recognizing the object, a standing terra cotta figure of a woman about three feet tall with two heads joined onto a single neck. The body was at once draped and naked, thick legs planted so firmly she seemed to grow from where she stood. Her swelling waist swept up into arms outstretched, one in a gesture of giving, the other in receiving, small breasts pulled up and back by broad shoulders that were the center of tension for the entire design. Neither head was clearly featured, yet each was differently expressive, one face perhaps smiling, the other perhaps not.

"What is it?" Kate whispered.

Phillip whispered in reply.

"We don't know for sure. She looks magical. From what little scholars have been able to determine she may have been focus of religious observance. Perhaps she is a goddess, recipient of some mystical devotion from a very ancient time in history. The culture out of which she came is largely unrecorded. No similar statue survives. There are a lot of theories to explain the two heads and differently gesturing arms, but as you would expect from scholars the fine points keep them from reaching total agreement. Of course back then it was Goddesses not Gods who ruled religion and society, there being no separation between the two. Priestesses and queens held the power. Men were only fit for serving. This is how far back she dates. Unique. Enigmatic. Most of all crafted with a subtlety and grace which is unmatched. Notice the economy of scale. Three feet high and she could as well be eight or eighty feet tall. Size her up or down and the proportionality holds. Look at her long enough and actual dimensions fall away. She could be a colossus. So tiny to be so commanding."

"And LaValle found her for you?" The more she learned about the man, the more she realized she didn't know.

"Yes," Phillip recalled. "He called me years ago late one evening when a private collector apparently balked at the price and the seller grew impatient to find another buyer. I came to his office at midnight. It was darkened, with only a table lamp shining on the Goddess here. Took my breath away. He put up his hand to stay any questions I might have. 'Do you want it?' was all he asked. Then he gave the figure. Non-negotiable. Within five hours I'd awakened board members who had secured the necessary funds. Over early morning coffee he and I closed the acquisition of a lifetime."

"How did Mr. LaValle come by it in the first place?" Kate was hungry for the object's recent history.

Phillip shook his head.

"I never knew. Nor whom he represented. In his business secrecy is part of the service he provides. For their own reasons sellers and buyers may prefer not to be publicly identified. The buyer may not want to announce his prize, while the seller may not want to disclose her profits. This was one of my earliest transactions with LaValle. I've had others since. There is no phone call I return more promptly. No dickering over price. Quality and authenticity never questioned. He plays a close hand, does LaValle, but he is absolutely reliable. And he has marvelous taste."

"That's why I don't like him," confessed Kate. "It's hard to trust someone who never talks about himself. Though Galen doesn't mind. He says Mr. LaValle knows his work better than he knows it himself."

"Probably so. And like your father I trust him implicitly. Even the Countess relies on him for guidance, and you have heard how stiff-necked she can be. Now there is a collector for you! Although she doesn't have the range of objects we do, her collection is of uniformly higher quality. She has been extremely selective. Have you ever seen her Villa?"

"Once," Kate replied, still studying the Goddess. " Several years ago, Galen took me along when he and Mr. LaValle were meeting with her to discuss some commission or other. When I was noticed she made it clear I was not welcome and ordered me to remain in the entry with my hands tucked in the pockets of my skirt. I don't think she likes children. I know Joanne doesn't like her. This is why Galen meets with her away from the house. He told me she and Joanne had a falling out years ago and neither wishes to mend the relationship."

Phillip smiled.

"No, I fancy your mother and the Countess would not be a congenial match for one another. While knowing Galen, I'm sure he wouldn't relish getting caught in between, the Countess demanding subservience and your mother refusing to bow to any one's authority. Better to keep one's wife and one's patroness apart and honor the claims of each separately as he has learned to do. Do you remember what you saw at the Villa that day?"

Kate remembered well.

"Yes, how old everything looked. And how rich. Mostly it felt peculiar to live alone among so many beautiful things with only art for company. I knew everything was wonderful, but I came away feeling lonely."

Phillip paused to consider, weighing what Kate had said.

"I'm sure there's a measure of truth in what you felt. I wouldn't put it past the woman. She's capable of anything, so why not loneliness, although I've never thought of her that way. Here. Since you've given me something to ponder, I'll share something about the Countess in return, but you must keep it in complete confidence. Something she once did to me. I tell you on the off chance you should ever have any dealings with her later in your life. Be mindful of how ruthless she can be."

Now Kate turned to listen to her uncle.

"It was a medieval tapestry, a tightly woven panorama of a hunt, executed in exquisite detail, which unexpectedly came on the market when knowledgeable authorities believed everything of that quality had already been permanently placed. Quite a furor of interest was created. Bidding for the Museum, I was in a position to secure it when I received an invitation to the Villa for dinner. This was not uncommon since the Countess frequently summoned members of the art world to appear for her social pleasure. What was different this time, however, was my being seated at her right hand for the first and only time. Well, the evening proceeded as it always does with sparkling wit and deeply satisfying intellectual exchange until we were about to adjourn the table for liqueur in the courtyard when she stayed my rising by gently but firmly pressing upon my arm. Of course, I immediately sat down as the others left. When we were by ourselves she spoke. 'Dr. Gambrell, I want you to withdraw your bid for the tapestry so I may purchase it myself.' I was about to politely decline when the stare from her eyes stopped me cold. Then, as her long porcelain fingers picked up a butter knife I felt an actual chill as if she were about to place the point of a stiletto against my heart. I can still hear her words to this day. 'If this were the Fifteenth Century and I was a Medeci, do you suppose, Museum Director, I should have to ask for what I wanted more than once?' I wish I could describe to you the danger of her velvet voice. The absolute intent was to have what she wished at whatever cost to me. With certainty, I knew that my life, whether personal or professional, it did not matter, was at stake. Survival made my mind up in an instant. I smiled as graciously as I could and lifting up my napkin gently laid it over the threatening blade. 'Countess,' I responded, 'consider the tapestry yours.'"

"You let her get away with that?" Kate was astonished.

"Yes, and have never regretted my decision. Although I had hell to pay with my board of directors to whom I had to defend the withdrawal of our offer after I had sold them on the extravagant purchase in the first place. However, they finally understood my change of mind, even congratulated me in fact. I told them we could get the tapestry at the museum next door, available at close proximity at no expense. As for the Countess, why I am still invited there regularly for dinner. Her courtesy to me is unfailing. And although I have never again been asked to sit at her right hand, I now have sympathy with whomever is selected for that dubious honor. I tell you this as a caution. Should you ever have contact with the Countess, Kate, take it seriously. She is not to be trifled with. Certainly not to be crossed. Hopefully you shall never stand in the way of what she wants. Working with the rich and powerful, I have developed a delicate touch, none more so than with her. And whatever you do," he laughed, "never sit at her right hand."

"I don't see how you can make light of what happened," Kate scowled, angry on her uncle's behalf. "She sounds like a terrible person. Joanne is right not to like her."

Now Phillip grew serious.

"She is a terrible person, Kate. So terrible she's not afraid to show how terrible she is. And yet I bear her no ill will because there was nothing personal in what she did. I was simply an obstruction. Once removed to another square our relationship became as cordial as ever."

He glanced for a moment at the Goddess as though deliberating.

"Here," he said at last. "I'll tell you one thing more I know about her, for whatever it's worth. Being in this room reminds me. She never comes to the Museum without paying a visit to this gallery according to the guards, who are my eyes and ears around this place. If others are present she waits until the space has cleared and she can have the little Goddess to herself. For a communion of kindred spirits? Who knows? If so, this relic of ancient femininity may be less benevolent that it appears."

Chapter Fifteen
IN FRIENDSHIP'S NAME

Dearest Kate--

was it your parents or yourself who decided to conceal from me that you were being teased at school? This is the first that I have known. Had I been told, I would have spoken to the powers that be and put a stop to such cruelty at once.

I see you smile. The notion of my authority stopping anyone strikes you as improbable since you only know me as 'Kip the Agreeable.' Mostly I am. However, I am also a boss. There are times when as Director I must be as forcefully outspoken as at other times I must proceed with utmost tact. You would be surprised by the diversity of roles that I perform. The ways I act. Kip the actor. Now what do you think of that? How little you know me! You have never seen me reconcile a fractious board of directors into agreement over a divisive issue. Or court a donor. Or inspire weary volunteers to want to give more when they feel given out. Or override an angry curator's refusal to purchase what disagrees with her taste. Or chastise a careless staffer with such severity he does not repeat the same lapse of responsibility again. Come Kate, do you recognize me in any of these scenarios? I doubt you do.

Dr. Gambrell is a more complex person than your dear old Uncle Kip. I'll tell you what we'll do. On your return you spend some time with me at the Museum not observing artwork, but observing the Director himself. This would be on condition, of course, that you hold none of what you see against your affection for me. I wonder, shall you be able to detect the actor from the parts he plays so well? We shall see. In any case this will be a different Kip than you have known.

And a different Kate for me as well. I have thought much about this. How you come home will not be as the girl who left. Not as a child at all. As a young woman. Goodness, what sadness floods me at the thought! How I regret not bidding the child Kate good-bye, taking time to honor the passing of your childhood and the golden times we had. Just you and I. King Phillip! Remember when you were still innocent enough to believe the Museum was my castle and I was fanciful enough to indulge your innocence?

To play a King to a beloved child. Talk of roles! Of any I assumed before or since none have been so deeply satisfying as Ruler of the magical world

which you adored. To open up the gates of my kingdom and behold the brightness in your eyes sparkling with wonder at the treasures I possessed! Whose joy was greater, yours or mine? Then later, when my crown was removed and my castle had been reduced to a mere museum, still the joy went on. Only the game had changed. I became Lore Master regaling you, my apprentice, with history of any object that excited your curiosity. On to the further education of your eyes, playing the game of seeing. Now I was Guide and you my follower. Together we searched for illumination, first in the likely then in the unlikely places where insight was required to expose the beauty hidden there. Every step in the search for judgment you kept pace, never lagging behind, never losing interest, following my lead until the Riablo show when you became my peer. Fellow travelers ever since. What a pleasure to journey through life with you! I wish we could begin all over again, but cherishing these memories is the best I can do. Kate, I loved your childhood and my part in it.

So, is it agreed? We shall continue our friendship on more 'grown up' terms when you come back. As for my friendship with Janovar Savocek, everything you wrote about him I believe is true. He himself would certainly disclaim none of what you said. While not a man to communicate about his past, in the present he is forthright to a fault. About the future he is unconcerned. Tomorrow is more time than he is willing to consider. He is either very focused or very fatalistic, I don't know which, treating every day as though it were his last. 'Now' is all there is, while even that is very circumscribed. Outside of certain subjects, he will not communicate and when I try he immediately cuts me off. Not with words but by withdrawing behind a wall of silence so profound I may as well have disappeared. To reconnect and become visible again I must reintroduce a subject within his tolerance range. If ever a man lived on an island it is Jan Savocek. More than an island, it is the extent of the world he is willing to acknowledge. Yet within the confines of his narrow borders an enormous richness exists.

One passion rules his life. What he lives for: his passion for fine art. Works of art elicit from him a response I have not ever witnessed before. No wonder he is such a resourceful teacher. Again and again as he and I marvel at one great object or another he actually takes me into the stages of its manufacture, how from inception to completion, from vision and revision, the work was accomplished. How does he know this? Does he know this? I believe he does. What an extraordinary gift! This is an approach to seeing I have not practiced, inferring from a finished composition the stages of its construction until the final artistic problem came to be resolved. The effect of Jan's instruction has been to enrich my understanding. Now I am learning to integrate an object with the process of its creation. Learning day by day because this is how we start each day, sharing early morning coffee in contemplation of some object of study, exchanging impressions and contaging enthusiasms, invigorating our spirits before our respective chores begin. His passion arouses my own. This is the friendship we have formed and I feel more complete because of it. Social though I am at work, I am no less a loner than he.

Now Kate, I want to share one of these mornings with you. It will be of interest, since Jan's response was to an old favorite of yours, the little Goddess. Apparently he had seen her several times already because he began describing his response before we arrived in her presence. I can't remember everything he said because he was unusually stimulated by the challenges she posed to his particular gift for understanding. 'She is made differently than any other piece in this museum,' he declared. 'This is what confused me at first. I kept looking for the stylistic imprint of a single hand, but in search of one I found many. She is constructed like a monument, not like a piece of sculpture at all. When I understood this, the manner of her making became clear.'

As we stooped in and stood up in the tiny gallery the obligatory bending down to gain entry felt like an act of prostration, although demanding homage from museum goers was not our architectural intent, at least not consciously. When I said as much to Jan he answered that I had been obeying a higher authority than I knew. Spend solitary time in the womb of a great cathedral, he confided, as he did in his youth, and I would never underestimate the commanding power of religious art. Cathedral? Youth? The first breach of personal history I have known the man to make. What cathedral? Too late. The opening was closed and he began to explicate on what we had come to see.

The problem, as he described it, was how to create a figure at once clearly divided in two yet totally unified as one. Taken separately each head arose out of a body uniquely its own yet belonging to them both. Surround her by a circle of infinite views and from each perspective this fundamental dichotomy must hold. The two must be one and the one must be two. From every angle of observation both must be apparent.

How is it to be done? The secret, as Jan disclosed it, is in the diaphanous gown that provides the body just enough concealment where we can't quite determine what is raiment and what is actually skin. This continual doubt creates sufficient visual uncertainty for the play of physical tensions beneath the elusive covering to be ambiguously expressed. We don't know precisely where opposing physical strains originate or where they are resolved. Yet they are resolved, because from every vantage point the composition holds. This is one magic. There is another he described.

When we walked around the little Goddess he showed me how she seemed to dance. Static yet she became dynamic as we moved. How could this be so, I asked. He showed me the trick. In addition to a slight twisting in her trunk, there is a discrepancy in the length of her arms which encourages the gesture of one to create disproportion for the other to correct. It is this compensation that created the illusion of motion as we made our circle. Her posture seemed to keep shifting, causing her to become alive, the arms softly undulating for balance, while the expressions on her two faces alternated to musical effect. Yes, I could swear that she was dancing. To have studied the little Goddess all these years and only now begin to see how truly wonderful she is!

However, it was his final observation that I think will interest you most. His verdict: she works in too many ways to be the work of a single artist. He suspects she was crafted by a community of people sharing responsibility for her creation. Perhaps in quest of a transcending vision to unite them they found what they were seeking in the image of the little Goddess, working together to give substance to what they had discovered. The preceding is speculation, he said. The following is not. She is made by the laying on of many hands. The variation in texture is not uniform. Consistency in touch which one artist would impose is lacking. The individual caress of many fingers have modified impressions made by many others until by mutual consent the modeling was declared complete. Jan believes she was ceremony-made, the process of her making bonding the makers, her perfection the outcome of their collaboration. This is what he meant when he said she is constructed like a monument. She represents the confluence of many talents.

There you have it, Kate. What do you think? Call up her image in your mind. Invoke her spirit. See if these words from your old teacher do not inspire fresh insight into that ancient idol as they did for me. And glimpse, if you can, why my friendship with the man has become so powerfully rewarding. As I taught you, so he teaches me to see, while he welcomes the appreciation that I have to give.

Of course, some differences abide, none more bitterly held than the one you mentioned, his hatred of abstraction and of Riablo for breaking with the naturalistic tradition, causing others to follow his lead. To believe as I do in the fundamental abstractness of all art places me in the enemy's camp. And I do mean 'enemy'. When he and I face off over this issue, the fate of civilization feels at stake. For him pure abstraction is barbaric, destroying recognizable reality, the human frame of reference that art is meant to be about. As for me, I am an unwitting sympathizer who aids the enemy from within. He warns me: I shall see! By dehumanizing art, abstraction shall destroy man in the end. I shall see! Sometimes I shiver at his warning. Has he witnessed barbarism similar to what he feels is threatening us now?   There is no bridging the chasm that this subject opens up so we avoid it as best we can.

In closing let me raise what I hope is not an argument with you. Rather a request. Your description of life at Riablo's sounds full of many changes, one of which I beg you not to make. Your name. Let Iliana be your travel name, a new name to wear in a new place. Leaving that place, however, leave Iliana behind and bring your old name home. I'm sure you count me foolish to weigh heavily something as insubstantial as a name, the name I gave you. However, indulge me, Kate. The name has served you well up to now and, who knows, it may yet serve you well in the years to come.

Do consider what I ask as I ask it in the name of love.

Kip.

Chapter Sixteen
A TORMENTED MAN

Much to her ongoing frustration, the Countess found Savocek unresponsive to those persuasive arts of flattery and intimidation with which she was accustomed to maneuver various pawns about her board of life. His defiance was a continuing affront to her will, and she sincerely detested him on this account. Only his capacity to elicit precocious excellence from those young artists whom he taught saved him from the banishment that she felt his indifference to her wishes richly deserved. This, and the small matter of potential profit to be made from each student if later prominence should confer upon early work any material value. With a discerning eye, she systematically selected their best studio drawings by right of patronage, enduring the teacher's insolence as part of her cost of doing business as she explained on one occasion to her faithful agent Lavalle.

"It is an investment worth the inconvenience of an insufferable relationship," she had confided.

For Phillip this incompatibility between patroness and teacher proved to be an ongoing challenge to manage. It felt like trying to prevent flint from striking steel, the resulting spark from igniting the antagonistic charge primed to explode between them. Separation worked best and, since neither sought each other out, worked most of the time. However, when an unavoidable encounter did occur, every staff member understood the Director was to be summoned at once so he could intervene if opportunity permitted, repairing damages afterwards if it did not. In either case, he was aware that any injury given or offense taken would neither be forgotten nor forgiven, but remembered for its grudging power to nourish grievance each devoutly cherished toward the other. Why they loved mutual hate was beyond Phillip's comprehension, but he knew they did. No meeting with either passed without the other's name being taken in vain.

For his part, Savocek kept himself in a constant state of mutiny against "this Bligh of a woman", as he was fond of calling her, who would dictate oppressive terms of his employment if he let her, which he did not. Instead he took his stands for freedom early and hard, plainly communicating to her that while he loved teaching art he loved liberty more. To make his condition of noninterference perfectly clear he even insisted, against the mighty woman's wishes, on teaching the Germaine girl, or else he would teach none of the other students. He went so far as to take a student he didn't want just to prove his point. This deliberate extortion infuriated the Countess who hated wasting exceptional instruction on such an ordinary talent. However, having nothing to give, withhold or take away that mattered to the teacher, she felt obliged to capitulate. After all it was better to lose face than the opportunity to turn a profit.

After this defining confrontation, the only one Phillip deliberately chose not to mediate, lesser hostilities still continued to disturb the peace. However, having gambled the two antagonists would resolve their major difference in his favor and won, the Museum Director now redoubled his efforts to patrol their relationship as vigilantly as possible. He wanted to protect the opportunity that he had covertly created, having secretly recruited Savocek for Kate's education.

As for the teacher, why had he consented to accept Phillip's offer? Not from any material inducements the Museum had to offer, since money had no allure. Nor from any desire for prominence, since prestige was of such little value. What then, Phillip wondered? Perhaps work was the answer. When work sufficed for all, as it did for Savocek, then assuredly something important must be missing. Some vital lack. Maybe the teacher had accepted Phillip's invitation to fulfill that deficiency, whatever it was.

No way for Phillip to fathom Savocek's simple motivation: it was time to move on. The omens had appeared. His tenure at the high school was coming to an end. He could recognize the signs having seen them often enough before. Once again, the forces of intolerance were spreading sedition against him with The Powers That Be. Once again, doubts were being raised about his character, about his suitability for teaching children. Questions were being posed about his unknown history that jealous rumor chose to answer. Since his success was unarguable, it needed to be used against him. At what price was this excellence achieved? Disdaining personal recognition, giving so much of himself to students of either sex, what was he desiring in return? The answers were left to the imaginations of those addressed who after a while began to suspect such gossip might not be totally unfounded, since it repeatedly came to their attention. Nothing specific was charged against the man, yet in a community concerned with the welfare of children such innuendo could not entirely be ignored. So as watchfulness increased, Savocek began to feel himself watched. This was the first omen and the sign.

In the beginning, as in other jobs, friendship was extended to the new employee, warmly extended until it was rejected, then coldly withdrawn. Clearly this man wanted to be left alone to do his work. By itself this antisocial entry would have simply discouraged further association, and at first this is what it accomplished. However, by adding state-wide recognition to the repudiation of his peers he earned one thing more, their envy and resentment. After all, many senior teachers had devoted their working lives to the school and yet received none of the acclaim this interloper was awarded over the short duration of his stay. It wasn't fair, and so their grievance was pursued. Little known about him lent itself to easy slander against a reputation that only grew worse as it grew better, attacks increasing with success. To none of which would Savocek respond.

Contempt was what he felt and it showed. Not with words. He would no more deign to defend himself against his detractors than attend those ceremonies honoring his students. Enemies and admirers were all alike to him. He trusted no one. And it was this immunity to disapproval or approval that maddened those put down by his conceit. It provoked determination to rid him from their midst, inspiring that inevitable conspiracy to get him gone. Inevitable, because it had happened so often before. Superior performance was his passport into employment, and sooner or later became his passport out. He expected no less. It was the price of living on his own inflexible terms.

In a compromising world, he would not compromise; in a political world he would not play politics; in a workplace that demanded conformity he would not conform. Submitting to any dictatorship was tantamount to death. He knew this as well as knowing these other teachers, who could not abide his independence, did not. They accepted their captivity without protest. Compliance was their way of life. While for him every choice at his command was a sacred trust, an obligation to live freely at all costs, what he owed to those whose sacrifice had ensured his survival. But none of this history did the rumor makers suspect because they were never told.

As for being driven out, that was by now a familiar experience. No matter how far he traveled to escape their evil influence, the forces of intolerance were always there waiting when he arrived at the next stop. Thus in his new position at the Museum, he instantly recognized his ancient enemy in the person of the Countess, she embodying the ruthless spirit of that oppressive regime that had crushed his mother and father and would have crushed him too. The lesson from their example was to last him a lifetime.

Because of their patriotic independence his parents had been suspected since the occupation. Placed under paid surveillance of a trusted friend turned informant to detect even the slightest whisper of sedition, they expressed not one incriminating word. When this espionage failed, however, they were summarily arrested, incarcerated for a short time, released without explanation only to be incarcerated again, this time with their son, then all three transported under sealed orders to one of these infernal destinations to which less prominent others were simply herded by railroad car. The special instructions were plain enough for even a child to understand: 'Return unwanted.' Like all orders in this socially obedient chain of command, they were efficiently executed, except by some underground contrivance the boy was spared, although the records, they were very good at keeping records, documented he had perished with his parents.

Condemned to survive without them, he had wandered throughout the charnel house unchecked because he had no officially verifiable existence. Saved by subversion, he was kept alive by the cunning and sacrifice of others as a sign that while his parents had been killed, the passionate love of freedom for which they died was undestructed. By protecting him, these nameless preserved their one great hope that no matter how systematic the extermination, it would not be absolute.

Come liberation, the boy was repatriated back to the city in which his parents were still well remembered and revered. Much celebration greeted his homecoming. A hero's welcome they gave him, celebrating their own survival through celebrating his, crediting the child's bravery for somehow managing to stay alive, confusing him with too much change too soon, causing him to feel he had only escaped one crazed captivity into another.

He spoke little, but this did not matter since so many others were happy to speak for him and about him. Always it was in reference to his parents they spoke, dead symbols of the living faith that no matter how the forces of darkness would oppress, some small flame of resistance would remain lit, impossible to snuff out. Miracle he was for many: 'The Savocek Boy Lives!' Incarnated was how he felt, becoming what others kept telling him he stood for until he came to believe he inhabited no other identity but this.

Passed around from family to family vying for the honor of his temporary care, he would solemnly receive the veneration paid through him to his parents. He would listen blankly to stories retold about them by those who had known his mother and father in the early days of protest at the University, stories celebrated by fellow students now grown older except in memory of those awful, glorious times. From horror to glory. It was all too much. More than he could emotionally encompass, and which was he? And why? There was no sense to the questions he was asking and so no answers to hold his sanity together. From speaking seldom he retreated into silence, watching specters begin to play where his thought used to be. His stream of experience became dreamlike and strange as life itself had been, transmuting consciousness into a reverie more bearable than life. He stopped eating and appeared not to sleep. Or if he did, it was a staring sleep, eyes wide open and unfocussed, gazing everywhere and nowhere at the same time.

Having by now seen many similarly traumatized children the Doctor recognized the look of vacancy. 'Survival Death' was how he had come to call it, this withdrawal from reality into some mental sanctuary where life could not disturb nor death, for the moment, reach. Later, many years later, when asked what prompted him to begin the exploration of semiconscious states for which work he had become famous, he would acknowledge his indebtedness to these victim children who had taught him so much and set him on his path, among whom was this boy.

How the Doctor wished he could get behind those staring eyes to stare out or in and see whatever visions they beheld. With a bright light, he had peered through the dilations into where the optic nerves connected to the brain. The eyes did not squint. The lids did not blink. Searching for some neurological clue the Doctor found nothing explanatory. It was always to be thus: physical causes of mental functioning were maddeningly elusive. The connections <u>had</u> to be there, but they were so difficult to establish. He was left to depend upon whatever data the children could verbally and non-verbally communicate if they retained or recovered some power of speech or motion.

Many did not. Many simply lingered into death. Immobile for days, unresponsive to commands, in limp paralysis, fever free, pulse normal, some reflexive movement but otherwise trance still, their bodies amenable to any position he chose to place them in, volition suspended, waiting, waiting, waiting for what? For the spirit to speak, the Doctor had concluded. By which he meant, life or death was determined by some choice-making mechanism deep within each troubled child beyond the influence of any choice of his own. He could not save them. Their continuation in this world was not up to him. When the staring eyes closed, when the breathing ceased, when the small body gently expired, he felt no guilt or regret. Living was not what they wanted when they died, and dying was not what they wanted when they lived. At least this is what he told himself to make the tragedy of his work supportable.

He was only there to accompany and comfort, to play the expert people needed when he knew there was no expert. Most of all he was there to serve the interests of enlightenment as an investigator of the inexplicable. Perhaps he could advance understanding one small step and so drive back ever so slightly the terrible ignorance in which human kind was condemned to live. It was a family calling. For generations on both his mother's and his father's side philosophers and scientists had striven to enrich the ferment of ideas upon which intellectual advancement of the species depended. Not trusting religion, but needing to place his faith somewhere, it was this hope for intellectual progress that he religiously worshipped. This was as close to theism as the Doctor came, suspecting there must be a Great Knower responsible for concealing from people what they spent so much of their short life spans trying unsuccessfully to discover. Thus every patient became a possible informant whose case might instruct him so he could enlighten others. Like this boy, bearer of such a great name.

It was on a morning early in the second week of the boy's confinement when the Doctor, making his rounds of various houses of the sick, visited the one in which the boy had been lodged since his collapse. Everything appeared as usual. Only one day more frail, otherwise no change. Getting up from the bedside to leave the Doctor caught his sleeve on something, turned to free it to discover the boy's left hand clutching his cuff. The vacant eyes were focused on his own, the boy's mouth working to speak repeating an inaudible phrase the Doctor had to lean over and pluck from the dry lips to hear.

"They lie!" Barely a whisper.

Sitting back down from where he had arisen, the Doctor waited for more to be said. But nothing further was uttered. The boy was mute yet his earnest gaze clearly sought confirmation that the Doctor gave by repeating what he had been told, not as a question, but as an established fact.

"Yes, they lie,' he agreed. And in response to that affirmation of understanding the Doctor sensed a choice to live was made.

Feebly animated by this encouragement the boy chanted:

"They lie! They lie! They lie! They lie!"

"Yes," echoed the Doctor. "They lie! They lie! They lie! They lie!" carefully enunciating the charge the same number of times it had been insistently spoken, careful to intone the words with full conviction even though he was ignorant of to what 'they' and to what 'lie' each referred.

By now the boy had relaxed his grip allowing the tired arm to collapse upon the heaving counterpane, up and down, the heavy breathing caused by the unaccustomed exertion. The Doctor waited until all commotion had subsided before once again invoking the magic words the boy had given to magically unlock communication between them:

They lie."

Wearily the boy nodded.

"They call me brave." He shook his head.

"They do," the Doctor agreed.

"They make a hero of me."

"That too." Agreement encouraged the boy to speak.

"They say I am a patriot just like my parents."

"I have heard them say that." And indeed the Doctor had, many times.

"I am none of those things!"

"You are none of those things." The Doctor flatly accepted the contradiction.

"I tell you I am none of these things!" flared the boy in a fierce expression of defiance that was later to become so characteristic of the man.

"You are not who they say and it angers you when others will not treat you as you really are." The Doctor clung to the boy's meaning but substituted other words.

"They will not let me be who I am and I cannot be who they want!"

"Who they want." Now the man simply repeated some of what the boy had to say.

"I am not my parents, just their son. They were brave. Resisting to the end they were afraid, but shouted none the less."

"They were afraid." The Doctor moved cautiously now.

"They shook with fear. Their voices shook. Their bodies shook. I felt them shaking when they gave me over. But I was not."

"You were not," the Doctor saying as little as he could to keep the boy conversing.

"I was not afraid. I felt no fear. No feeling. Nothing. I was there and I felt nothing at a time like that! You see how they lie? Calling me brave! Making me into something I was not. Calling me a hero. Tell me" (now entreating the Doctor for something more than understanding, pleading for explanation) "how could I feel nothing at time like that? How could I be a hero when others saved my life? Why do they do this to me?"

The Doctor did not want to say more than the boy could absorb.

"You felt nothing to keep from feeling too much. You are called a hero because others, for their own needs, wish to make you one. Your feelings shall return as you return to life. As you do now."

Already the boy was shaking as waves of strong emotion trembled through his feeble body. The Doctor simply placed his hand upon the boy's arm with enough weight to promise he was not alone and waited for the initial surge of feeling to subside.

"Once upon a terrible time," the man continued to explain, "events became so overpowering you took refuge in a place of safety deep within your mind. Now those events have passed and you are ready to come out. As you do, some of the horror shall be remembered and the pain experienced. I shall keep you company each day until you feel the worst is over, but I cannot feel the feelings for you. So you must go slowly and you must be brave."

In the weeks and months that followed, the Doctor told the boy this and, as recovery grew gradually stronger, told him more. The Doctor prophesied the degree of freedom from his past that the boy could realistically expect as he grew older. It was the truth as he had come to understand it.

"From time to time old images of violence you witnessed shall burst into your awareness uninvited, by surprise. Flashing across your mind's eye, the pictures shall carry you back. They shall <u>seem</u> to carry you back. Actually, they cannot. You must remember this as well as repeating to yourself 'these images shall pass, these images shall pass.' Do not allow emotion to convince you otherwise. Courage at these moments shall be required to prevent a natural panic which, if it occurs, shall also pass. What shall not pass, and what these images will keep alive, is the vision of life that life has given you, of man's inhumanity to man. This shall never go away, nor should it. With such a vision there can be no peace because in your sanity, you cannot make peace with evil. To survive you must find a moral purpose worth living for. I cannot tell you what this shall be, but I believe it must be worldly. Some act of service by which you feel your life is justified."

Having learned to trust the Doctor the boy attended closely to what he was told, and so the man was encouraged to tell him more.

"Of course you cannot remain here. Your story and what you represent belongs too much to this community. They will not let it go. You are their hero, their hope and pride and inspiration to cope with loss and carry on. For your survival, I must send your living symbol from their midst. They will not love me for doing this, but they shall accept my medical decision. I have this much standing among them. When you are gone, we shall memorialize your departure to keep what you have stood for alive."

"Where?" the boy asked. "Where shall you send me?"

"To a place far enough removed where your name shall not the evoke memory of your parents in those who hear it. To the care of an old acquaintance, a man as skilled at creating comfort out of extreme adversity as anyone I know. Although war ravaged the countryside around where he lives, it inconvenienced him very little. I send you to him in hopes by example he can reveal to you, among his many worldly comforts, one which may call to you. He is very rich in this regard. His heart is glad and yours is in need of gladdening. However, you will not like him for being unprincipled in ways your parents were not, and for being part of the establishment which failed your parents by not protecting them, not speaking out. I mean the Church.'

At this the boy, now physically restored, strongly objected, only yielding when the Doctor assured him Father Bruch would make no effort to indoctrinate him in the Faith because the man was not that sort of cleric.

"What sort is he?" the boy had suspiciously asked.

"The kind whose primary allegiance is to his own well being," answered the Doctor, "as he himself would tell you. It proves convenient for him to assume your charge because it satisfies the Church's need to make atonement and show compassion that was politically unwise before. Again, I am only quoting what he has said. You shall have a hard time liking him. But even harder shall be not liking him as well."

The Doctor was correct. So amiable a man as Father Bruch was indeed hard to dislike. The boy was as put off as he was attracted by the man's insinuating charm that never gave nor took offense, that slipped around unpleasantness as smoothly as it eluded controversy. The Clergyman ingratiated everyone who came under his entertaining sway, who usually invited him to share those enjoyments of good living to which the Doctor had referred.

Father Bruch was an untroubled man who had managed to remain so during troubled times by engendering the affections of parties bitterly opposed to one another, sympathizing with each but carefully avoiding being sympathizer to either. He offered hospitality to all, but sanctuary to none, creating a small island of benevolent neutrality on which he protected himself and his small jewel of a cathedral, both of which emerged from the war unscathed. This achievement impressed the hierarchy of the Church. His superiors agreed: survival of their institution through temporal upheaval was best perpetuated by loyal servants like Father Bruch.

It was the cathedral that proved to be the boy's salvation, converting him not to the love of God, which would forever be denied him, but to a love of something else. Before the boy could identify his growing devotion, the Clergyman had noticed it himself. Time and again between services the boy would enter the deserted church and stand gazing up at the nave lost in contemplation of the sacred space, swept away by the inspiring grandeur and blessed sense of peace. That mortal hands and hearts and minds had crafted such a place! Father had told him how two centuries of selfless labor had built this monument. To what? The boy had found his own secular answer. To creating beauty through the love of art.

No matter where he looked, from decorative detail to architectural design, the entire structure was human made. Enraptured, he contemplated what was surely, purely an expression of human good. This vision of creation was reflected in every carven piece of wood and stone and statuary, in every embellishment, arch and vault, and in the vast interior space gloriously illuminated by changing daylight sifting through windows of multicolored glass, at night aglow with candles mysterious and dark. A world apart had been created. A world so different from the one that human hatred built.

For Father Bruch, a man who luxuriated in the refinement of his tastes, life was for cultivating this refinement whenever he could, which was a very often because the jovial fellow was such good company. It was so gratifying to entertain someone whose appreciation enhanced one's own appreciation of the finer things. Who could forget those after dinner discourses on the aesthetic merits of this artist or that musician, the cogent disputation of philosophical ideas, not to mention the blessing of fine food and wine given by a man who had earned his reputation as an epicure. If ever a man deserved the title Bon Vivant, it was Father Bruch.

And when, the war finally over, art collections, libraries and other cultural treasures were disinterred, once again placed on private and public display, the Bon Vivant had no shortage of invitations to re-appreciate what for safety had so long been hidden. Curious to see if the boy's appreciation extended beyond the cathedral walls, Father Bruch included him along, a silent companion whose quiet was occasionally broken when outbursts of wonder overcame his usual reticence to speak. Then questions would pour out that sought to satisfy more than mere curiosity, questions that passionately desired to embrace every facet of the object and instill its beauty deep within himself. At least this was how Father Bruch, in his occasional letters to the Doctor, interpreted the intensity with which the boy ministered to this one single passion.

Once he had asked the if the boy had ever tried his hand at making art, creating what he so admired.

"No," was the sure reply.

"And why not?" Father Bruch was surprised by the rebuff.

"Because" (what a strange thing for the boy to say) "I have no imagination left."

Father Bruch puzzled over this statement many times but did not question it, doing his utmost to honor the Doctor's advice which had preceded the boy's arrival by letter: 'Don't ask about his past. Introduce him to everything you love. See if you can make him smile.' This last should have been easiest since who could resist Father Bruch's infectious good humor? The boy could and for those eight years did. He never smiled. He never talked about his past. He only spoke more obsessively about his passion as the years progressed until the normally loquacious man was reduced to nothing but listening on many occasions, resorting to lending the boy art books and arranging for the loan of others to occupy his mind and still his speech. But not for long. While fresh reproductions absorbed the boy's attention for a while, they soon stimulated his desire to converse again and soon Father Bruch would find himself back in a fervent discussion once more. Where, wondered the bewildered Cleric, would this insatiable interest tend?

The answer came courtesy of a catalogue he received through the mail documenting an exhibition of master drawings in a far off capital where royalty had amassed a collection second to none. As was by now his custom, Father Bruch showed it to the boy who, after absorbing it for several hours, matter of factly declared:

"I know how these were done."

"You could do them, eh?" joked Father Bruch.

"No," the boy seriously replied, "but I know how they were done."

"Then tell me," asked the man, and the boy took up the challenge.

For the next three hours the boy did as promised. Page after page, from one reproduction to the next, he analyzed the obvious and subtle mechanics of form and technique, the interplay of background and foreground, the integration of outline and detail, the architecture and division of space, the interaction of light and dark, the balance and counterbalance of design. On and on the boy discoursed, intuitively revealing to his more experienced elder new insights into the draftsman's art. Extraordinary! The boy didn't just have a grasp of the finished product, he could sense the process through which it came to be. Father Bruch was impressed.

"If I wanted to draw, I could learn much from you. Suppose I were to find you some students to teach?" he asked.

The boy did not object and so the man assembled a small class.

Aloof, intense and demanding, Savocek ran off all but those few students whose desire to learn was strong enough to withstand his severe instruction. Within a year the results spoke for themselves. Seeing a livelihood developing, Father Bruch encouraged the young man to consider this a possible occupation that Savocek did for the first time. But where? The Church had a school. Perhaps, suggested the Cleric, he could teach there? No. Savocek wanted to go further away. Further away? Yes, across the ocean. Did the Church have schools over there? Yes. Could a position be found? Possibly. But why go so far? Because anything less distant would not be far enough. Father Bruch requested time to consider and wrote the Doctor, by now a rising professor in a great university, for his opinion. By return letter came the Doctor's last advice: 'Let him go. Although he can never get far enough away, he must discover this himself. You have given him what he desperately needed.' Thus absolved of any further responsibility, Father Bruch let arrangements move forward.

As a parting gift he gave Savocek the catalogue of master drawings. And for the only time in his life the young man gave a gift in return. It was a pencil drawing of a dark, thin, hollow-eyed boy on gray paper, a stiff unexceptional drawing meant as a portrait of the artist who vaguely resembled the child Savocek.

"I did not tell you the truth. Once I tried to draw but this was the best I could do. I did not want to leave with a lie between us." This was his statement of good-bye.

"Thank you," Father Bruch stammered awkwardly as if he were receiving a gift from a stranger, as indeed he was.

Savocek never looked back. As was his wont, he taught not to make a living so much as to make living supportable when an undying part of him kept old pain alive because he felt he had no alternative. To do any less was to dishonor the dead, while to destroy himself would deny the sacrifice that had been made for his survival. At each job, and there were many, results of previous instruction got him hired on but only overcame growing objections to his abrasive personality for a while. Then he would move on.

Until he met Gambrell, one situation was similar to every other. Although life continued to be a torment, the Museum and its Director made existence more bearable. Like working in a holy place for a man who could be trusted not to do him harm. Except there was still the presence of the enemy, this Countess woman. Wherever people settled tyrants grew. He had no more sympathy for her than she for him as both expressed to the Museum Director on numerous occasions, although the Countess stated her side of the antagonism most succinctly to her confidante, LaValle:

"There's no excuse for such a man, there really isn't. Some people are just born objectionable, and he is one."

Chapter Seventeen
THE IMMERSION

*D*earest Kip--

over a year it's been since I've worn shoes. The bottoms of my feet are earthen brown and leather tough. Now I can beach comb with Jesus or go gathering with Marcella and not mind sharp rocks or prickly plants that guard this place against all but the most hardy intruders. From this you may conclude I am not always at my post of duty, drawing in the studio with Riablo. However, I am no deserter.

The Master's presence and paintings provide continual inspiration. His range of invention knows no bounds because he treats every culture as his own. As my old teacher complained, Riablo has robbed the whole store of human history. Like a man who adores all women more than any one, he has loved every period of art the world over. Yet borrowing from many styles, he has managed to follow none. He has obtained their secrets, but escaped their influence. By some magical power, he has turned what he has taken into his own. But this is by no means the only power in this place, at least not for me. So if you find Kate changed when she returns, the difference shall not be due to Riablo alone. Marcella, Jesus, and the ocean have all had their effect. Most particularly the ocean.

What would you say, Kip, if I told you that at night, under a new moon with only star reflection and phosphorescence from the curling tips of waves for illumination, I bask out in the ocean by myself, I who always feared to swim? It's true. The little girl who was loved too much to force her into facing what she feared has learned to love the water after all. How came this change? It happened thus.

On a usual evening, Jesus was late to give my call, so late I wondered for the first and only time if I was being excluded. Then, in through the door to the most strident song you can imagine, burst the Piper himself. He strutted around the table twice until I fell in step behind and out we marched together, the other two following me, the four of us drilling to music less suitable to circling than for travel. But to where? By now I understood the practice of this house forbids invading privacy with questions. What I wanted to know I must wait to find out. That is how my curiosity is answered in this curious place.

So I let patience rule as we tramped round the courtyard several times then out the gate around the walled enclosure and across the bluff to its very edge where I supposed we would stop, but no. Over the brink, without slackening his pace or interrupting his playing, disappeared our leader. When I hesitated for a moment, Marcella pushed me past uncertainty and over I plunged expecting to trip and fall, when to my surprise and then delight the cadence of the music kept my feet from stumbling. Skipping to the beat kept me from mishap all the way down that treacherous trail securing me a safe descent. I felt as sure footed as a goat, while behind Marcella I could hear the pitter-patter of Riablo dancing double time to every step we took, the flutter of his feet lightly drumming down what was for him was as familiar as a flight of household stairs.

Reaching the rocky shore, the music became irregular to accompany our changing progress that was awkward and obstructed. In our path were strewn great boulders surrounded by lesser of their kind, all resting on a bed of pebbles that kept shifting underfoot.

Pathways of pebbles are what we followed winding up the cobbled beach, Marcella dancing behind while Riablo leapt before me vaulting over rocks I skirted round. Way out of sight, but not of hearing, was Jesus who called to us from our destination for the night, from the rocky promontory where from my window in the early morning light I had often seen seals congregate and play.

Arriving where this spit of land reached out into the sea we were showered by spray from surf colliding with the breakwater of stone, soaking me to the skin, cooling me off. Gradually my pumping heart and heavy breathing slowed, the song Jesus was playing slowing too, becoming softer and more repetitious until it matched the beating of the waves and his playing ceased. The ocean would accompany the remainder of our dance.

But what remained? I glanced around for Jesus and Riablo, but they had disappeared. Only myself and Marcella, she scrutinized my appearance, although I knew not why. Then, as if to prepare me for some special presentation, she began to carefully to pull back the hair that had fallen down my face and chest, gliding behind me to weave an elaborate plait, my hair now long enough to braid.

Stopping to admire her handiwork, her fingers brailled the intricate design. Then she let go and began to unpeal my smock from where salt water had adhered it to my skin, straightening the fit, getting the grooming right. For what? I soon found out. Gripping hands, my left in her right, she gestured toward the end of the peninsula, a shifting line of foam marking where the great procession of boulders at last submerged into the sea. Was this our destination? I stiffened at the possibility. Then momentary fright was reassured by trust in her and by the sound of waves encouraging me on, marching me forward, the rockweed cold and wet, slippery beneath my feet. Before I knew it, we had reached the final outcropping of stone from where I could see swaying beds of kelp swirling the water's surface from below as secret currents stirred them back and forth. We hesitated, I waiting for Marcella until I realized she was waiting for me. To dive into this place? Fear was what I felt, but also the other side of fear: fascination. Jumping off into a watery world! Without Marcella I should not have dared what I both dreaded and desired.

If you had seen me, Kip, poised on the edge of a drowning sea you would have pulled me back for safety. But I am under new protection here. One that protects me from continuing how I have been. So it was to finish the dance music started and waves had carried on that I sprang into the ocean. The immersion was instantaneous and complete. With Marcella's hand still tight in mine, we plunged through the surface, seaweed caressing us as we sank down and down and down. Why panic did not overcome me? I trusted to the woman by my side, following her lead. Just when my chest began to tighten, she kicked her legs so I did mine, exhaling a stream of bubbles as we rose until breathing in we were breathing air and looking up at the stars. In wonder, I released Marcella's hand. I was adrift alone! Kip, one does not have to swim to live upon the sea! Lolling in the water, my buoyancy was keeping me afloat. With no effort, I rose and fell with the swells, yielding to the pull and sway. From trusting Marcella I had come to trust the ocean with my life, letting it wash me up between the algae-covered rocks and roll me over, then give me back to oncoming waves. I would recede with one on a voyage out, returning on another for a journey in.

Cradled by the rocking water, I lay suspended between ocean and sky as the others gathered around me each at home in their own way. Jesus lazily reclined, pipes resting on his chest, stolid as a piece of driftwood slowly ebbing toward the shore. Not like Riablo, who kept diving down triumphantly resurfacing to admire by starlight some prize he had wrested from the ocean floor. While ever drawn to circles, Marcella revolved one way and then the other, spinning whirlpools that sucked her down and then yielded her back up as the vortex shallowed out.

Our frolic seemed to last forever until the pipes began to call above the waves, Jesus, Lord of the Dance, ending our play as the rising tide and incoming swells encouraged us to shore. Washing in upon the stony beach, I placed my weight back on the earth. All unsteady, the land felt falsely firm beneath, hard and ungiving, my body awkward and heavy, my legs enfeebled. On the steep climb up the bluff, they supported me as best they could, back to the house and up the long stairs to the bedroom where I shed my soaking smock and slept uncovered for the remainder of the night. My dreams were no surprise, affirming what I now already felt: at heart, I am a sea creature condemned to land.

The ocean. She tells me when she is of a mind to receive me, and when she is not. Calm and inviting on some days, she is surly and forbidding on others. I honor her moods and do not trifle with her when she is upset. She has the power to be infinitely gentle and overwhelmingly violent. Her only constant is her beauty.

Beachcombing with Jesus, we find evidence of her destruction after every storm. An endless variety of debris torn from its origin, much of it fragmentary, much miraculously whole. How is this decided? As capricious as she is wanton, she decides. How the rocks withstand her abuse and do not complain is hard to comprehend. Perhaps because they are unfeeling. Not me. If I were they, I'd hurl myself against her even if it meant smashing myself to smithereens. And yet, I can't deny her glory when aroused. An awesome sight. The wind, thunder, and lightning goad her into a froth of seething fury until she heaves up enormous barricades of water to combat this provocation from the sky. Crashing down she heaves them up again further enraged, tirelessly fighting back until the attack is done. Oh Kip, Escampobar, this remote corner of the earth, was made for watching the sky and sea do battle. I feel so fragile on these occasions, so pitifully human in the face of Nature's power.

After such a gale, it has become our practice, Jesus and I, to search for treasure along the beach. We discover telltale reminders of what happens to those who stand in the storm's way. What do we find? Everything you can imagine is the best description I can give. All of it grist for Jesus who creates from scavenging most of the furnishings and implements in this house. They are of the most handsome and ingenious kind. His eyes envision an object's possibilities for what it was never intended. Inventor, carpenter, and craftsman of castaway remnants, pillaged from the sea, he resurrects the old and breaks into new and useful forms. In my room alone a mirror, chair, chest, and bed are all wrought by his hand from wreckage on the shore, the ocean's lost and found. My mirror is a torn piece of silver metal beaten slightly concave to hold the light. Brightly burnished it reflects imprecisely, my image only vaguely recognizable. Who is this woman looking back at me, and I am only a girl?

The sailor's chest, contrived from weathered planking that has been pegged together, is grooved at the corners, meticulously joined and precisely fitted like the bed frame and, from barrel staves, the chair. Suspended from the staves slings of the torn canvas support me like a hammock, while for the bed a tattered sail has been made to do. The spirit of this house is as much Jesus as Riablo, more in a way because upon what Jesus creates we daily rely. By this measure, Marcella is most sustaining because she prepares the food we eat.

Although Jesus brings her fish and mollusks from the sea, she also gathers forage from the earth. Without a recipe, each meal is a mix of provisions available that day. I do not know how many gardens she tills nor how many wild places she harvests, although I have accompanied her often. What is not immediately consumed is stored in the cool, dry cellar which preserves what we find long after it has been collected. Certainly, her gardens are not chosen for convenience, being in far-flung locations where circumstances favor successful cultivation. Always there is proximity to some seep or creek or spring for easy irrigation, while whatever mix of soil and sunlight she is seeking must be found. Her way of cultivation demands enormous labor.

Walk? I have never walked so much in my life. Miles there are between her gardens and once reached there is no rest before tending begins. Now I manage to keep up with her, but not at first. My body and my breath kept giving out. 'Marcella!' I called to call attention to my exhaustion. She only turned her head and gestured back to whence we came, giving me to understand I could return but she would keep trekking on. Well, I was not about to be physically outdone by a woman my own mother's age!

One of the advantages of pride. I am willing to do a lot to prevent its injury, never more than on those early outings with Marcella. At least my muscles no longer complain and my lungs are not overtaxed on these endless hikes. Nonetheless, I am no match for one whose body has been conditioned to this exercise for more years than I am old. She does not weary when she walks. Bending over again and again does not ache her back, nor heavy lifting and long carries tire her arms. Arriving home laden down she appears to step more lightly than when we left, while I require recuperation.

Keepers of the Master is how I think of them, while captive of his keepers is how I think of him. Which is barnacle and which is rock? As for Marcella and Jesus, they are bound together more powerfully than either is to Riablo. Are they brother and sister? Are they married? Are they lovers? Certainly, they are connected by some deep intimacy. At odd moments during the afternoon, I would discover them seated on the bench made from a broken skiff in the courtyard sharing quiet company with each other, she mixing seasonings in a bowl, he whittling pegs. Not quite touching yet they appear joined.

In dwelling on these influences, I fear you may wonder if I remain faithful to the purpose which brought me here. Is all my time spent staying up carousing every night? Have I committed to farming and salvage, sea bathing and dancing, abandoning drawing in favor of these new pursuits?

No, Kip. Most of my time is still spent in the Master's studio where I feel even more at sea than in the ocean. The currents that now direct my drawings are beyond my depths to comprehend. You will notice the result. They have changed the quality of the line. It has become more calligraphic. Remember the great screens at your museum with brush strokes dancing down the picture's edge? How I loved that energy of the line! Each character is filled with vitality, a tiny masterpiece. Some of that vitality is coming to me now, although not executed with the genius we both admired. How strange! Although my body is still rooted in the West, my drawing is now tending toward the East. Well, you shall see. A portfolio of my efforts shall accompany me home. Sans many of my better drawings, not that I care. One of the unsolved mysteries of this mysterious place.

I love you, Kip.

Kate.

Chapter Eighteen
To Prison She Shall Go

On that fateful morning before school, Kate had been sullen and silent over breakfast. Joanne, however, endeavored to act as though this day was no cheerfully different than any other, this day when her daughter was going to begin the tutelage that both realized would change her life, but which neither suspected would alter their relationship as profoundly as it did.

"I packed an extra sandwich in case you get hungry before coming home." Joanne wanted to show she cared, but Kate was unimpressed.

"Whatever."

Joanne kept trying.

"And don't forget. Because of the early release, you'll need Mr. Savocek to sign your slip each day for the office."

No response.

"Kate, did you hear what I said?"

"I heard."

Joanne had one more instruction to give.

"The bus leaves the Museum stop at 7:15. Catch it and you should be home by quarter to eight."

No response again.

"Kate?"

"I'm not deaf! I'm going, isn't that enough? Now leave me alone!"

Watching through the frosted window as her daughter trudged to the corner where she reluctantly boarded the bus each morning for school, Joanne shivered with the cold. This stand she had taken with Kate, was it right? Sometimes, most of the time, parenting felt like such a heavy responsibility. And right now so unrewarding. Acting for Kate's best interests against her wants, Joanne was being treated like her enemy.

Carefully, Joanne reviewed the chain of occurrences leading to this fateful day. n the most recent linkages, she had played no active part, by standing as arrangements drew Kate under the growing influence of others. First, there had been Kate's alteration of the Benefactor's portrait, a transgression Joanne had been prepared to punish to protect her husband's work.   Instead, the violation had caught Galen's attention, causing him to acknowledge Kate's ability and to enlist Phillip's aid in nurturing her talent. Together, the two men had removed Kate from Joanne's domain and into Galen's studio. Then came Phillip's determined pursuit of Savocek and his successful embassy to the Countess, causing her to hire an exceptional teacher she personally disliked, then causing the teacher to take Kate on to show he would not surrender to his new employer's will.   By pitting one side of the antagonism against the other, when neither approved her instruction, Phillip had slipped Kate through the opposition between them and she had been accepted where she was not wanted. What a gamble for Phillip to take, and he not a gambling man!

That he would stake his relationship with the Countess for this return told Joanne there was much worth risking for, a brighter future than she had dared envision, but one in which she no longer played a planning part. That must be left to Galen and Phillip. Deferring to their judgment, she swung in behind them with what she had to give, the power of her support that proved essential when Kate predictably refused her uncle's offer.

She had more than enough school in her life already, thank you very much. Of course, Kip had understood. And that should have put an end to her attending, except Joanne would not let the matter go. She kept pushing, and when Kate pushed back unaccustomed conflict arose between them. Then, instead of acquiescing, Joanne became adamant. Knowing she could not win for losing, she was determined to win a battle even though it might start a war. Committing all the authority at her command she caught her daughter by surprise, and Kate, not knowing how to cope with a mother who had become inexplicably and awesomely coercive, began to yield.

"Why must I do this? Tell me. Give me a reason!"

"Because I say so."

"That's not a reason," Kate objected. "That's an order."

"Yes, it is," confirmed Joanne.

"Fifteen hours a week of torture with this teacher no one except Uncle Phillip likes? Why? Don't I draw every day at home? Doesn't Galen help me with my work? What more do you want?"

Although Joanne was depending on authority, she had her arguments in order.

"The quality of teaching this man can give. Even you admit students catch fire under his instruction. Your father, Phillip, the Countess all pay tribute to his unique capacity. Your uncle has won you the chance of a lifetime. You must take it.'

"And if I refuse?" But Kate already knew the answer.

"The choice is mine, not yours. It is up to me. Don't try me, Kate. I ruled my brothers and sisters, and in this I shall rule you. You will go because I am prepared to make you go, do you understand?"

Kate hung her head, bewildered and beaten by the dreadful conviction with which her mother spoke. Against her wants, against her will, Kate surrendered.

"All right. I'll go. But drawing won't be fun any more. You'll spoil what I love. You'll make it serious, you and this teacher. Haven't I teachers enough at school? Now I shall come to hate what I love and you for making this happen. I warn you. I shall hate you. Do you want me to hate you?" Kate spoke from the bitterness of her defeat.

"No." Joanne did not. "But I am willing for you to hate me if that is required."

"I won't work for him," Kate threatened. "You can't make me do that!"

"No," Joanne agreed, "I can't. That is between you and Mr. Savocek."

"I won't do anything. You think because you can bully me here I shall be bullied there. Well I won't. I'll just sit and do nothing. He won't get a line out of me. I promise. And all your money shall be wasted!"

Joanne agonized to hear Kate struggling to accept submission.

"It's not our money. The Countess pays for you, since she is paying for your teacher."

"Then I'll talk to Kip," Kate reached for a last resort. "He'll understand. He'll side with me. He has before."

"Yes," Joanne nodded. "He has before. But not on this. Kate, think for a moment. Do you really suppose Phillip brought Mr. Savocek here for the Museum school? Is that what you honestly believe? No. You know better. Phillip found this teacher for <u>you</u> , Kate, and he found a way for you to have him. All this because he only wants what I and your father want: the best for you."

But Kate's retort had the sting of truth.

"The best <u>from</u> me, you mean! So you can look good as a parent!"

Joanne paused to consider. How to separate performance of the child from performance of the parent? Was she pushing Kate to satisfy her own secret ambitions? So hard to be clear. Parenting was such a murky undertaking.

Sensing her mother's doubt Kate tried to take advantage.

"How do you know what's best for me? How can you be sure about another person's life? How do you know you're right?'

"I don't know I am right," admitted Joanne. "I can't be sure. But about your studying with Mr. Savocek, I am resolved. In two weeks, like it or not, you shall begin."

Kate saw it was no use. Her refusal had been crushed, but in the process grievance had been born. Armed with a sense of outrage and just cause, Kate's rebellion against her mother had begun.

Joanne had no right to be her ruler. Joanne was not boss of her world. But for acting like she was, Joanne would be made to pay. If Kate could not prevail, she could get even. For this first day, however, she would do as she had been directed. She would go to school after school. Boarding the friendless bus she nodded to several acquaintances and took a seat by herself, shivering in anticipation of the afternoon that came soon enough.

Departing the bus at her beloved museum, she slowly climbed the familiar stone terrace, entered through the great doors and followed the sign to the basement stairs. What an uninviting entrance to an education! Two flights down, it felt like descending into a dungeon, her spirits becoming more depressed every step she took until there were no more steps to take and she was standing in a small dimly lit stairwell of gray concrete from which a single exit offered the only escape.

'*Advanced Drawing: J. Savocek*,' read a stark sign on the wall. Just enough information to announce Kate had arrived at her dreaded destination. Between the weight of the door and her reluctance she had difficulty pulling it to. Forcing herself to draw it open, she stared down a long hallway along which were a series of smaller doors opening off on either side. At the very end of the hall, tall and spare, stood a lone figure of a man staring towards her, hands clasped behind his back as if he had just been pacing up and down. Rapidly he approached her.

"I am Savocek. You are the artist Kate Germaine?"

"Yes," she answered quickly back since he seemed in such a hurry.

"You are prompt. This is good. Time is all we shall have together. How well we use it is everything. Now, I want you to examine me closely. Study my appearance until you have my image fixed in mind."

Feeling embarrassed, Kate averted her eyes. She had been taught not to ogle strangers.

"No. No. You must follow my instructions implicitly. Pay no attention to discomfort. Do as I say. You shall have over hours without me, so use these few minutes of observation well."

With this encouragement Kate did as she was bid, grateful he was not looking back, but gazing off into space. Initially what struck her was the lack of color in his dress. Prison garb is what came to mind. Gray shirt, black trousers, scuffed white canvas shoes. Then how pinched and drawn his features were. He seemed wasted by some experience or illness from which he had not yet recovered. Yet there was the feel of enormous energy in the man, as though he were held together by tension and excitability more than muscle and sinew. Fiercely alive and dangerously exhausted was how she summed him up. Having characterized him to her satisfaction, she glanced away.

"You are done?" Savocek gazed down at her.

"Yes."

"You have a quick eye. We shall see what you have taken in. This is your studio." He indicated a hall door on which were posted three names: 'Ira Gilner, Joel Tate, Kate Germaine.' Fellow students she supposed. Kate shuddered as she peered inside. Her worst fears of incarceration were realized. The small brightly lit room had all the deprivations of cell. No windows, no decoration and minimal furnishing. Against the far wall was a drawing table set with the basic tools of her trade. There were two soft leaded pencils, a blunt knife and a square of sandpaper for fashioning fresh points, and several large sheets of off-white paper. No stool or chair. No place to sit. None of the comforts of home.

"This is your work space. Here we shall meet, you bringing your ideas, I my instruction. Outside of this room, you may study any models or pictures you like. Outside. Inside, however, you will have only your memory and imagination. If the setting and conditions seem severe, this is because to disguise the artist's work in comfort would be a lie. It is lonely, arduous labor. Better to accept this reality at once than first experience it later on."

Kate felt herself harden to the hard surroundings. She neither liked the setting nor the teacher. Both were cold and harsh. She was used to better.

"To begin," Savocek intoned, "you will do a drawing of me. I will return toward the end of your time." He started to leave.

"Wait!" she cried. "How am I to draw your likeness if you are not here for me to see?"

He turned in answer to her call.

"You are not to draw my likeness. The task is more demanding. This is not photography or portraiture we are about. The picture I want is what you think about what I look like. For this my presence would only be a distraction. Already I am in your head. You must get me out. Do you understand?"

He must have asked the question because Kate looked at a loss.

"No? All right. A suggestion. Before committing your ideas to paper, compose them in your mind. Dr. Gambrell has shown me samples of your previous work. Your drawings have the strength and weakness of spontaneity. What you draw emerges as you draw. There are benefits. Immediacy enlivens your quality of line. You trust your instincts. All to the good. But not enough. Too much of your thinking is in process and not enough in preparation. You are quick to follow impulse, but lack discipline to study. So, what to do? First, understand my role. I am not an artist. I cannot teach you how to draw. But I can show you how great drawing is accomplished by explaining how old masters worked. At this early stage, your drawing is extremely limited because you only know the one approach that you have taken. I know very many. With the help of great exemplars, I shall enrich your understanding. As for the exercises I require, they must not be questioned. Each presents a visual problem for you to solve. Like today, creating a pictorial statement from what remains in your mind's eye. Do I make myself clear?"

Kate dumbly signified she understood and Savocek secured the door behind him when he left. Surrounded by the four bare walls, she stood alone. A great sigh heaved through her body and subsided. She didn't feel like drawing. She felt like running. Would he stop her if she tried to escape? Was he her jailer? Tiptoeing to the door, she silently pulled it open and peered out. Softly she stepped into the deserted corridor and began to sneak toward the exit through which she had originally entered when something stopped her. Something going on behind another studio door. The words were too muffled to decipher but the voice was unmistakable, Savocek conferring with another student. Only the tone was not what she was used to hear at school. Much more impassioned, he sounded like a preacher rousing a congregation. Although the words were unintelligible, his conviction caught her, moved her, hesitated her departure, swayed her from wanting to leave, at least for that first day. Something religious was happening. This was no ordinary conversation about art. She had known these with her father and uncle, yet neither spoke with the fervor of this voice. Here was a deeper quality of caring than she had heard them use to honor what they loved. And she was curious, moved to want it for herself while pondering the cost. No cozy surroundings for one. No loving encouragement for another. Motivation here would have to come from within.

Would he talk with her as he did this other student? She returned to her studio to wait and find out. Cautiously approaching the strange table she examined the minimal equipment provided. Instinctively she reached around for a stool such as she sat upon at home. There was none there. She knew this, but did not want it to be so. Drawing from a free-standing position felt unsupported and awkward. It left her with more to manage than just her arms and hands. Shifting from one foot to the other, she felt a vigor in her legs and trunk and shoulders which she had not used before, at least not for drawing. Fascinated, she set her feet and sensed a flow of energy rising up the length of her body into her back, into her shoulders, surging down her arms into her hands. Excited by this sense of new potentiality, she reached for the pencils when her hands rebelled. First the right and then the left refused.

"I'll not be told what to draw, not by him! You'd think she would have left when she'd the chance."

Kate looked down at her right hand stubbornly clenched in defiance of the decision to remain and follow instruction. Then she glanced at the left, equally opposed but deliberately slack and functionless. Feeling abandoned in her time of need and opportunity, she appealed for their cooperation.

"If you will just try to get along, we may learn from this man. I didn't want to at first. I love our freedom just as much as you. But if we give some of it over, not a lot, we may profit from what he causes us to do. Do try. Trust me!"

"Trust her! Let freedom go and soon it shall be given up! You'd think she'd stand by us but no, she prefers this teacher. What did I tell you. Eventually she would tire of our play!"

Under Anastan's attack Kate felt disloyal and defenseless. Turning to Cuscubar, she hoped the more reasonable of the two would come to her aid. And her left hand tried.

"Perhaps if we let her she won't like it and will give it up."

"Perhaps! Perhaps! Perhaps! Either she follows him or us. Not both. There is no in between. She had her feelings right the first time. If she begins for him it is the end for us!"

Listening deeply, Kate knew in her heart that Anastan had spoken truth. The old way of drawing and the new could not coexist. Either way, choosing was losing. And if she had to give one up, it would not be her dearest friends for a stranger.

"All right," she relented. "We'll stay together. I won't draw for him." And so saying she sat down, back against the wall, on strike, waiting out the time, arms clasped about her legs, knees drawn up to support her chin, a huddled figure of sullen disobedience. This is how Savocek found her at fifteen minutes before the hour she was due to leave.

The man appeared neither disturbed nor surprised, proceeding, as he intended, to look at what she had produced. Giving a long thoughtful gaze at the blank sheet of paper, appearing to study its blankness, he carefully lifted the untouched sheet, honoring it as her creation, moistened the top corners with his tongue and posted upon the wall above her table. Stepping back he considered it for several minutes.

"What do you see?" he asked at length.

"Nothing," Kate stubbornly replied, slowly standing up, preparing to stand up to him.

"I see that too. What a sad picture."

"Sad?" Not expecting sympathy, she did not understand.

"Yes. Do you not think so? Three hours of lifetime you shall never have again, and this is what you have to show for it. This much is certain. However far you get with the development of your art, it shall always be these three hours short. You see, the artist progresses by effort alone. There is no short cut. There is no alternative. There really isn't. So much for today's lesson. It can either make a bad beginning or a good one. Which, is strictly up to you. Myself, I lead life as though every moment is my last, having reason to know it could well be. Time is what we have and we do not have very much. For today, our time is up."

As the door swished behind him a rush of air detached the bank paper from the wall, causing it to slip back down upon the drawing table, confronting Kate with the empty outcome of her labors. She stared at this affirmation of her teacher's words that no power of argument could deny. Savocek was brutally correct. The consequences of her not working lay there for both of them to see, while the precious loss of opportunity was hers alone to feel. Shame, anger, regret, some painful mix of the three, stirred a revulsion at what she had chosen to do. Refusal proved her point, but what had she really proved? That he couldn't make her draw. Yet the victory was at her own expense, not his. An irrecoverable loss of time and opportunity. In service of rebellion, she had self defeated. Even as she bitterly reflected on the folly of her choice, her right hand rose up, up over her head the fist proclaiming triumph.

"We've won! We've won!" Anastan cheered. "We've driven him away!"

Before Kate could think, she reacted.

"Won? Lost, you mean! Lost me this time with your foolishness!"

The fist unclenched in astonishment.

"See what you've done? No. You can't. You think drawing is all a matter of play, don't you? Well it's not. It's work! Work, do you understand?"

The arm collapsed dragging the hand down with it, the hand stunned and still at her side.

"I never want this kind of talk again, do you hear? Never talk with me again!"

Too late. Words spoken in anger were beyond recall. Now one loss beget another, deeper than the first. In crushing realization of what she just had said, Kate collapsed against the wall, falling against it for support, her back sliding down until she sat upon the floor legs outstretched, hands twitching, quivering, laying limp and lifeless in her lap. Aghast, she lifted them up.

"I'm sorry," she sobbed. "I didn't mean. I didn't mean what I said!"

Except she knew she did, the guilty knowledge heaving up the hurt, convulsing it back down. Crying for relief, she softly moaned as relief was slowly given, rocking silently back and forth, mourning her loss. Silently opening the door, Savocek discovered the prostrate girl still there and quickly withdrew out of respect for the secret suffering he saw, in kinship felt, never referring to it, never forgetting it either. Like himself, she had paid a great price.

Late getting home that night, Kate was greeted at the door by Joanne who was anxious to discover how well or badly the first day went. Mother like, as she had done since the girl's infancy, Joanne quickly assessed her daughter's bearing and expression. Alarmed, she saw something was seriously wrong. The girl looked bereft. Something had been injured or broken. Clasping Kate by the shoulders Joanne, searched the red swollen eyes for explanation. This was all the invitation that Kate needed. Up and out swept her arms breaking Joanne's hold upon her, thrusting the woman several paces back, anguish from Kate's loss now given voice as fury.

"Murderer! I hate you!" she seethed. "I hate you for what you made me do! I'll go back but not for you. For me. To get something worth what I have paid. More than you'll ever know! For my sake. Not for yours. Now get out of my way!" And the girl pushed by the startled woman, fleeing to the fortress of her room. "I'll get you back for this!" Slamming the door.

Horrified by the vehemence of her daughter's anger Joanne reeled as though she had been struck, as indeed she had. Her daughter's vow of vengeance threatened to sever their relationship. Joanne had not anticipated this.

As for Kate, emerging later from her room and for many months thereafter, she was true to her angry word. In service of punishment, she withdrew affection, kept communication to a minimum, was cursory when spoken to, volunteering nothing, constantly conveying through hostile looks the unforgiveness that she felt. For however long her interment in Prison Camp Savocek lasted, she would be implacable. Hurt for hurt she would return, this was her promise. And for three surly years she was as good, or bad, as her vindictive word.

Joanne had underestimated her daughter's dedication to reprisal. Momentary anger, even a lingering grudge, she could accept for a while. But for so long? What perverse benefit could Kate possibly derive from remaining furious this length of time? The answer to which Joanne came, after much painful meditation, was that Kate was using this enmity to drive a separation between them. She needed distance from her mother. To grow forward, Kate had to break the bonds of love that held her back else she would remain a child. And time for childhood was passed. But how to justify the break? Unwittingly Joanne had given Kate the grievance that was needed. No one rebels without just cause. Even the terrifying statement 'I hate you!' made emotional sense. It meant 'I need to hate you now because I have loved you too much to let you go.'

All this in the clear light of detachment Joanne could comprehend, but detachment was fleeting and fragile. In a moment it could be obliterated by injury inflicted from her daughter's sharp tongue or taunting silence. Then perspective would fall away before Joanne's hurt at being harmfully treated by one to whom she had given so much. She felt abused. This treatment was unwarranted. She deserved an explanation.

"Kate, I do not appreciate your attitude toward me. I find it insulting. I'm not your whipping post. You have no right to take your anger out upon me day after day."

For a retort Kate substituted a look that spoke more venom than words would dare express. 'Get used to it!' her daughter's glare seemed to say.

"And I resent it when you look at me like that."

No response.

"Is this still about your art instruction, or is it now about something else?" Only recently had this possibility occurred to Joanne. "Five months is long enough to nurse a grievance, Kate. For heaven's sakes, say what it is. Let's talk. Let's put this unpleasantness behind us. You must be getting as tired as I. You can't be enjoying this."

"I didn't say I was."

"Then why keep it up?"

"I'm not keeping it up. You are. You're the one who made me go to Mr. Savocek. Undo that, repay what it cost me, and I'll stop acting angry. But don't blame me for what you started."

"Kate, I explained to you why this is so important. As did your father and Phillip. Yet you don't treat them any differently than you ever have. Only me. Why only me?'

"I'm not angry a Galen and Kip for wanting this for me. Or for Mr. Savocek for turning out to be the tyrant I expected. I'm angry at you for making me go. This was your doing and no one else's."

Joanne took this truth to heart and gave it back.

"True. They would not have forced you to go, so it was left to me to do what they would not. They love you, but not enough to fight you into doing what they know is best when you are against it. You father is only stubborn about his work, while Phillip uses others to get his way when the way proves unpleasant. And he has used me in this. I get the blame for doing what he wants for you, while he remains secure in your affections. Do you think I relished being the one to push you into this? But if I didn't, who would?"

"No one. And then I need not have gone. It's my life. It's my future. It's my talent."

"Not entirely." Since Joanne had taken the stand once she would take it again. "Not yet. So long as you are in my care, you are under my direction. I am still your parent."

"Fine! Then as your child I shall be obedient to your wishes and spiteful of your commands."

Hearing the argument wind into the interminable cycle of an eye for an eye, Joanne chose not to argue back and lend further cooperation to the well-worn conflict between them. She looked away. Then another thought occurred to her.

"I wonder if you're telling me the truth, Kate? I wonder if you are not using me too?"

"I don't know what you mean." But Kate did.

"Five months now you've been going faithfully. Only because of me?"

"No. I told you then. Now I keep going for myself. You I hate for making me go in the first place."

"Yes, but the other? Are you getting something you are not admitting because in doing so your going would not only be my fault?"

In her mother's eyes Kate saw an appeal for honesty and felt called upon to honor it.

"All right. I am learning to be serious. The play has gone. Has died. Drawing is work. A challenge, but no longer simply fun. Also, I am going because I have something to prove, that I am worthy of being there. Mr. Savocek did not want me. He only accepted me to show the Countess she could not dictate his selection of artists. Neither one wanted me."

"How did you find this out?"

"From the Countess. She strode into my studio the first week I was there and told me. We talked. I didn't appreciate what she had to say and said so. She seemed surprised. Since then she has come by a number of times. To see my work, she says. But I believe it is really to see me. She has some curiosity to satisfy. I am as insultingly polite as she is haughty. We get on very badly very well."

"How often has this been going on?" A vague foreboding began to take shape in Joanne's mind. Danger of something. She didn't know what.

"From the beginning, once or twice a week. At first I didn't like her. Now I don't know. We may become friends."

"Be careful Kate. She is a truly designing woman. If she wants friendship with you, be assured she is also after something else."

"What?"

"I have no idea. And neither shall you until the moment when she strikes to get it."

"Why couldn't she simply want to be my friend? No more than that? You've always encouraged me to have friends. Now when I am about to, you discourage me instead. Is it because you and she don't like each other? Is it because you don't want she and I to get along?"

"Kate, I am not discouraging your friendship with this woman if that is what you want. I have chosen my battle with you and it is not over friends. I am only giving you a warning. It's my belief the woman has no heart."

Chapter Nineteen
AN UNEXPECTED ALLIANCE

*D*earest Kip --

a change has taken place and I wanted you to be the first to know. It affects my future with an influence you shall approve.

One day last week, coming down from the studio in the late afternoon, my mind still abstracted by what I had been drawing, I was startled to see a fifth chair crowding the kitchen table and wondered for whom it could be. Engrossed in her dinner preparations Marcella gave no sign of anything out of the ordinary, even though in the year and some that I have lived here, we have received no visitors. I supposed the person must be a familiar one since no special preparations were being made for their reception. Were I still Kate I would have asked who was expected, but Iliana is more patient with her curiosity and so did not. Therefore, casting the mysterious guest from my thoughts, I strolled out the door across the courtyard and through the gate heading to the edge of the bluff where my feet easily found their way down the steep path to the rugged shore. Clambering around the larger rocks and over smaller ones, I reached a secluded cove of sandy beach where at day's end I come to bathe my body and cleanse my mind of work.

Quite a friend the ocean has become to me who never cared to go outdoors when I was young and feared the water because it was not land. Now it is land that I find uncongenial and water where I belong. A great mother, the sea.   I have become her trusting and reliant child. What a world of reversals I inhabit here!

Ascending the bluff without effort, I found myself dwelling again on this odd addition to our number. Intrusion is what I felt. Some outsider was about to disturb my household. Feeling protective of the routines to which I myself was once a stranger, I resented anyone complicating our simplicity. Passing through the kitchen on my way to change I noticed the table set, the interloper apparently had not yet arrived. Ahead of me climbing the stairs was Marcella carrying a pile of folded bedding to an interior room as I returned to mine.

Unwrapping, I slipped into a fresh smock and tied back my hair. Yes, my hair is longer now and probably you shall detect some other changes too when I return. But never fear, I am more recognizable than not. Although for the first time in my life, what with playing in the ocean, my excursions with Marcella and Jesus, and dancing at night, I am well exercised, my body happy with the use. Something Joanne encouraged in me the last few years that I refused, spiting myself just to spite her. How glad I am to be free of rebellion's rule! Free from the dislikes that I left behind. Now this emissary from my old life violates my sanctuary here.

The guest, of all people least expected! When I barefooted into the kitchen for dinner the sight of him brought me to a standstill. I was shocked. How to fit his unwelcome figure into this place I have come to love? For a moment I couldn't integrate the picture with him in it.   Then by pointedly ignoring my confusion he communicated his awareness of my troubled state. He greeted me with his traditional courtesy.

"Iliana, you look well."

How did he learn my name? How dare he use it!   Just what I have always found offensive in the man, how he spies other people out, how he was doing this with me. Discovering more than I wanted him to know. How you and Galen, even the Countess, manage to tolerate his secret ways I have never understood. How can you trust someone who is so prying and concealed? But I had let my aversion show. The Kate in me had been aroused. Not that it seemed to disturb the others, least of all LaValle. In fact, I had the distinct impression he was a visitor of long and welcome standing in this house from his ease with them and theirs with him.

Of course I assumed, in deference to his disablement, we would forgo our nightly dance so long as he was with us, regretting the loss, resenting him from causing it. How little I knew. If anything surprises me here it is how frequently I am surprised.

The pleasures of the meal were as usual. In silence we savored what Marcella had prepared to celebrate the passing of another day well spent. Then Jesus adjourned in his customary manner, one moment among us, the next disappeared. My God! Were they going to go ahead with it after all? I panicked on LaValle's behalf, this man I never cared for, fearful that his crooked body and ungraceful posture was about to be painfully exposed through dance. After Riablo left, I appealed to Marcella with my eyes but she didn't notice my appeal soon rising and departing, LaValle and I seated alone. As the first slow notes of music drifted in he pulled himself to standing and obediently shambled out the door. I didn't want to join the others but the minstrel would not be denied, and so at last reluctantly I followed.

As soon as we were all assembled the music changed as I knew it would, but not how I thought it would. The strangest song began, the melody disconnected, syncopated so we could not predict precisely when each note would fall, stumbling as we tried and failed to match the irregular beat, trying to catch the tempo that kept eluding us like we were caught in a hopeless game of tag.

Eluded all of us, but one. Instinctively LaValle mastered the music and the awkward steps required, while it was the three of us who looked ungainly because we could not synchronize our movements to the tune. Whether it was only LaValle who could carry the misleading melody or only him whom the melody fit, Riablo, Marcella and I kept tripping over the capricious rhythm until singly and then together we came to the same conclusion, we must accompany LaValle.

This was a difficult decision because we had to attend to him so closely, anticipating his next step, feeling what it must be to move like himself. A shuffling, meandering, halting dance of fits and starts, precariously risky, correcting one stagger with another, a constant fight for balance to keep from falling down. These were the steps we learned: lurch, stumble and recover. And learn them at last we three did, LaValle's dance, though none of us as well as he to whom normal stability and coordination were denied.

All the while the pipes played more and more arythmically, our responses becoming wild, wheeling and exaggerated, strenuous and exhausting. But LaValle would not stop. Short of breath and ill conditioned smoker that he was he kept gasping in and panting out great gulps of air, each desperate exhalation attended by screaming wheezes from his lungs like bellows pumped to leaking from their seams. And not just him. We three were pushed to bursting of our limits too. No matter. Jesus and LaValle kept us dancing on and on, while I revised my estimation of this decrepit man. His appearance is deceiving. Crippled he may be, but physically frail he is not.

Then in mid note the music abruptly ceased, Jesus collapsing to the ground totally spent as were the three of us, only LaValle still standing. The chorus of our heavy breathing rose up into the night sky like an encore to the performance we had just completed. Many minutes passed before any of us stirred. At last, slowly standing up from the heap into which all but LaValle had fallen, Jesus regained his feet. Inspired by his example, Riablo, Marcella and I struggled to do the same. After respects were duly paid the Music Master, we retreated to our separate beds for rest.

Except for myself. Though it was late and I was very weary, I wandered out to the edge of the bluff where I could hear waves prowling along the shore below. Something I wanted that I felt the wind could bring. Some answer about the dance. About LaValle. You know him, Kip, have known him much longer than I. Is this a man given to dance? You know he is not. Yet he outdanced us all until at last we danced his dance. Such a difficult dance. So hard to learn! I believe this is why Jesus played and played. For however long it took for the three of us to learn The Dance of the Broken Man.

But LaValle is not broken. I realize that now. Bent he is, but so are each of us in our own way, some more obviously than others. Now having seen him dance and danced his dance I begin to understand why he repelled me all these years. He makes no effort to conceal or improve upon his unfortunate appearance. Doesn't he care? I would. I do. Having been teased too much for lacking prettiness, I am uncomfortable around another less visually pleasing than myself. Plain is not that far from ugly. Because I do not want to get closer to unsightliness than I already am, I've treated him as though his unattractiveness is catching. There! The truth is told. I have blamed the man for my dislike only to discover it is of myself.

Not a peaceful sleep I had that night. Dreams of judgment and the suffering it caused kept awakening me, strange story forms repeating the same troubling theme telling and retelling what I didn't want to know. As I have judged myself, so I judged him. Next morning, battered by my dreams' insistence, it required effort just to rise. I had to lower my body gently down the stairs to avoid jarring my head and rattling the pain. At the table my usual appetite was lost. Listlessly I climbed back up the stairs to the studio, drained of my usual excitement for fresh expression the day would bring. Reaching the landing I paused to hear the murmur of indistinct conversation, actually just one person talking, LaValle. It reminded me of another voice heard long ago, through another closed door. Except this voice was cool and carefully reasoned, leveling with truth more than preaching about it. What truth? What was he explaining to Riablo? I waited several minutes for the monologue to end, and when it didn't, unwilling to disturb them, I returned to my room and slept away the day. I awoke for dinner rested but still uneasy in my mind.

That evening Riablo seemed strangely pensive, his black eyes dulled, turned inward, pondering I supposed whatever passed with LaValle during the morning. Our dance this time was short, slow moving and circular. It felt rejuvenating like a coming round, a coming together without effort. There was no leader and there were no followers. Instinctively we knew the step and all could do it. Used to feeling at one with Riablo, Marcella and Jesus, now I was moved to feel this kinship with LaValle. I wanted to say something to him about it, but was afraid to speak and so did not.

We parted, I in better spirits than before, feeling at peace from the union we had made. No dreams that night. I awoke next morning fully restored. After a full breakfast I hurried to the studio expecting to find Riablo already hard at work. But no Riablo was there. Instead, bent forward in a chair placed beside the Master's easel hunched LaValle, a large black portfolio leaning against the wall beside him. I shall describe what followed for you word for word. He spoke first.

"We have only until noon, Iliana. Then I must leave. Other business calls me on."

I had no idea to what he was alluding. However, my old repulsion and distrust were gone. I stood attentively before him, expecting he would have something further to say. He did.

"I am going to examine your work as I do with your father, Riablo and a few other artists. Periodically I lend them my eyes. This they find of service. Now you must determine if what I have to offer is of use to you." So saying he opened the portfolio and placing one of my earliest drawings on Riablo's easel began his review of my production at the Master's house.

How to describe the remainder of the morning? I thought I knew my own work better than anyone, but I was wrong. Certainly you and Galen, even Savocek, have been insightful of my work. Yet no one, including myself, has comprehended the larger sense of what I am about, the body of work I am beginning to create. No one has linked each drawing to an emerging whole, showing how the past is tied to the present and the present directed toward future growth. Through LaValle's eyes I saw myself at a distance close up. For these few hours, drawing by drawing, omitting some of the best, he guided me into an appreciation of where my talent lay and my vision tended. Although he was critical in separating false starts from true progress, I felt neither discouraged not diminished. I felt clarified in my own mind through the mind of another. I felt thoroughly understood.

What Galen had explained to me once when I objected to his choice of dealer came back to haunt me now. I had thought he was correcting me, but he was not. He was making an appeal. Something like this was what Galen had said. 'After you've been in this business for as many years as I have, you realize the great frustration is not being ignored or even rejected. It is not getting through. Think of it. You commit your whole working life to an act of communication no one else really understands. What is more lonely than that? So along comes LaValle who knows my work better than I. Whatever offense his manner may give is of little consequence compared with the service that he renders.' I can see what my father was saying now.

Like Galen, I have received a great gift. LaValle traced the threads that weave through my work and let me glimpse the future fabric whole. When he was done I felt full of myself as I believe Riablo was last night. Grateful, I wanted to thank LaValle, but first I felt a need to repent.

"Mr. LaValle," I began. "I have never liked you until now. I want to tell you why. I judged how you looked and then took offense at the judgment I had made. I am sorry."

He smiled.

"Yes, most people judge me by the first impression I create. Few are permitted to get beyond it. You are one."

"Why?" I asked. "Why me? Why now?"

"Because of business," he answered.

This made no sense.

"Mr. LaValle, what business could you possibly want with me?"

This was his reply.

"Iliana, the time approaches when you shall want a dealer. May I offer myself to you in this capacity now? Your father, your uncle, the Countess, Mr. Savocek have affirmed your industry and skill. Admission into Riablo's studio is testimony of his estimation as well. A service I was happy to render. Despite what a mutual acquaintance may have led you to believe, Riablo would never have permitted an apprentice had I not spoken well on your behalf."

I felt confused.

"The Countess, I thought she made this arrangement."

"Yes," he nodded. "She thought so too. And if it pleases her, why not? Much of my pleasure comes from pleasing her. However, if she thought more deeply, she might recall the idea was originally mine. No sense revealing everything when she believes she knows it all. Our secret, yours and mine. Now, to the matter at hand. Will you trust yourself to my representation? The only contract I offer is a verbal one. No other. Nothing written. To begin when the time is right."

"When will that be?" I wanted to know.

"Not yet," he answered. "Although there are highly reputable galleries that would show you now, in my opinion this exposure would be premature and harmful. You would be tempted to repeat yourself to please collectors wanting more of the same. No. Better to fly free of public recognition and remain obscure a while longer. Then I shall see you placed to best advantage. Do you accept?"

I glanced down at the manicured hand that he extended, clasping it in token of agreement. I held it tight until his shaking momentarily subsided noticing he did not squeeze back, wondering why?

"Thank you for your faith in me and for your eyes," I said. Declaring this felt strange because he was still a stranger. "Shall I get to know you better?"

"No," he answered. "My work requires concealment for success. Like others I represent you must take me as I am. A secret agent entrusted with keeping your interests uppermost in mind. The risks balance out. While the dissemination of your work is in my hands, my reputation is in yours.'

"How can I repay you?" I asked, for I was feeling in his debt.

"This is our final piece of business," he replied. "My fee shall be deducted from the price of everything I sell. I charge what I am worth."

Then an awkward silence fell between us. He had no more to volunteer, but I had one more question.

"When shall I see you again?"

"When you see me again," he said. "I look forward to a long and productive association. Until then." And he shuffled out of the studio where I remained until I heard Jesus driving LaValle off to wherever he was conducting business next. Leaving me to wonder: Kip, who is telling me the truth about my coming here? Who really caused this opportunity to happen? Was it the Countess or LaValle?

I love you,

Kate

Chapter Twenty
BECOMING A COLLECTOR

"So, Elena, you have taken up the daughter. Why?" With the Countess, LaValle did not waste words..

"Because it pleases me." She was not inclined to discuss the subject.

"No. No," he objected. "Between us, two old intimates, evasion will not do."

One thing she liked and disliked about LaValle, he would not be denied.

"Because Savocek forced my hand. Because you yourself have told me the girl does have an unusual talent. Because good turns can turn up good opportunities. Who knows? My father taught me if you must do a thing, however much to your distaste, appear to do it gladly. Gratitude, even obligation, may come your way. If something is to be made of the girl, I shall make it. I promise you my time shall not be wasted. Meanwhile, it pleases me. Now, tell me what you have found."

"Business first and business last. Always business, eh Countess?"

There was no reply and he expected none.

"It is an Imperial Bronze of exquisite workmanship, in perfect condition. The patina, more blue than green, creates a verdigris of extraordinary beauty. The entire collection, alas, is soon to be lavished on a major university. However, in consideration of past service to the family, a few chosen items have been withheld for my disposal. Are you interested?"

"Have you ever brought to my attention any object in which I was not?"

"Once," the Dealer smiled. "Once."

She shook her head to dismiss this unpleasant piece of history.

"You'll not let me forget it, will you? Ever."

Now he shook his head in return.

"Surely the lesson is worth remembering. A once in a lifetime acquisition, yet you hesitated for the most immaterial of reasons -- price. And that ancient object of religious veneration, the little statue of the two-headed goddess, goes on public display because a board of directors was able to make a decision faster than a private collector who knew far better than they the incalculable worth of such a prize. When shall I ever be able to bring you such an opportunity again?"

"Never," came the stiff reply. "And I must bear the loss. If it is any satisfaction to you, I do not visit the Museum without paying penance to She whom I let go. The memory is much alive, while the piece itself has only grown more wonderful in my eyes over the years. So I do not need to be taunted with reminders. Is this why you came? Or to make me a purchase? I notice you have been careful not to mention cost."

But LaValle could not be bullied.

"As you trust my judgment of artistic merit, you must also trust me as to price. It shall be below what the urn would fetch on the block. You do trust me?"

"Yes, LaValle, I trust you would never betray anything as precious to you as your taste. Your reputation rests upon it, and upon that your livelihood."

But the Dealer would not let her end the matter there.

"And upon my livelihood, the superior quality of your collection," he added.

"Yes," she sighed, weary of what was happening between them. "I don't deny it. In this arrangement the connection between us is still in tact. But in no other. So why must all our transactions end up sounding like the bickering of broken lovers?"

"Because that is what we are, Elena."

"LaValle, it is over. It was over long ago. I told you then. I showed you in every way I could. Yet you persisted despite all the discouragement I could devise. Never have I had to be so severe with a suitor. Not before or since. Rejection is usually considered sufficient dissuasion in matters of the heart. You required something more. I told you then. I tell you now. My love is not of the lasting kind."

"You do not know that. Elena. Had it not been for the accident changing me from what I was, my appearance and talent might captivate you still." Then he deliberately paused before proceeding. "I don't suppose I shall ever know how 'accidental' the accident really was?"

But on this the Countess would not been drawn out.

"I don't suppose. Nor have I ever been 'captivated', as you phrase it, by any romance. Attracted yes. Even enamored for a time. Once, and this was <u>not</u> with you, I confess I met my match. I was lured as irresistibly away from my self- interest as he was lured away from his. Two egotistic people for whom life could only be lived upon their own individual terms. Passion consumed and would have destroyed us had we not torn ourselves free of each other and forsworn further contact ever since. I tell you this, LaValle, to hurt you. I may have been the great love in your life, but you were not in mine. The accident changed many things, but not that. Believe what I say. Let my words sever whatever longing binds you to me. I have never been accused of kindness. However, I take no pleasure in your suffering. May the injury I give you now put an end to it."

The Dealer fumbled in his vest for the silver compact in which he carried his imported cigarettes. Slowly extracting one he methodically closed the case returning it to his pocket recovering his composure as he did so. Lighting up he inhaled deeply until the acrid smoke was drawn into the further reaches of his lungs where he held it for a meditative moment. Apparently reflecting, he was actually waiting for the blessed nicotine to enter his bloodstream before gradually breathing out. The combination of the two events, the breathing in and the breathing out, had a reviving and relaxing effect. Now he smiled at the Countess.

"Caring comes in many guises, Elena. Thank you. I am glad to know you care this much."

The Countess made one final effort.

"I value your taste and resources for what they can provide. Even more, I respect how, out of what surely would have destroyed the careers of lesser men, you have created a position of influence in this art world in which we live. More than that, there is no more."

"For now," he appeared satisfied. "All beginnings are small."

"LaValle, have you not understood a word I have said?"

"Yes, Elena. Yes I have. Perhaps more than you. And I can wait."

"One last time, there is <u>nothing</u> to wait for."

But LaValle would not be discouraged.

"We shall see. Like you I am an opportunist. What is the old French saying? 'And God created the future to surprise us'."

The Countess shook her head and the two fell to discussing business once again.

Of all the Dealer's clients, and there were many well placed around the world, none was a more astute trader than the Countess. When, as now, money could not be negotiated, he knew she would attach some contingency or consequence that could and would be bargained to her material advantage sometime later on. How she acquired this acumen he knew by occasional references to her father, although the precise nature of that education he was never told.

Since he already knew her so well, the Countess did not wish to yield any additional history that could only strengthen his hand in the ongoing game of strategy that never let up between them. He was too trusted an agent to trust too much, representing as he invariably did three interests at once -- the buyer, the seller, and himself. Besides, one unintended outcome of the accident had been to literally alter him beyond her powers of recognition. Before the misfortune he had been open and forthright. Afterwards he became guarded and deceptive, his motivations closed even to scrutiny as sensitive as hers. That she could absolutely rely on him she had no doubt; however, she knew better than to absolutely rely on any man. For this self-protective distrust, she had her father to thank. He was her mentor about men because he was her model for mankind. Her father.

From their first encounter she and her father had shared an antipathy of the most intense kind. Already similar they had grown more alike the longer they matched wits against each other. Since she was the less experienced she was more influenced by him, continually strengthening her will by asserting it against his, becoming by temperament and practice the child image of him in female form. Growing up in this fashion, she grew to believe like her father that it was better to take first, only giving for the sake of a better return, always bargaining with this profit in mind. By young womanhood, she had developed a compelling coldness, a shrewd eye, and a ruthless drive for an advantageous exchange in every relationship. Her father approved. They were bonded, he the teacher, she the protégé, this bond causing she and her mother to rift apart.

It was no great loss. Since birth had separated them twin jealousies forbade their ever reuniting. Her father was jealous of any attention the mother would give her child when he was about, while the mother was jealous of the growing intimacy antagonism forged between her daughter and husband, the girl unafraid to challenge her father in a manner the woman never dared. At most the Countess, not a countess then, did admire the perfectly attired, immaculately well kempt woman who posed, as she did everything else, as her mother. Like a model on permanent display she was prized by her husband for her ravishing appearance and yielding nature that he could not resist. It was an indelible lesson for the daughter, this power of her mother's physical beauty to exercise sexual dominion over a man who ruled her in every other way.

As his interest in his daughter's femininity grew more unfatherly, freedom from his financial control became more urgent. To escape, the young woman married early and married well. Very well. Although to the world her decision appeared impulsive, she had only known the Count a matter of weeks, the move on her part was as calculated as his was rash. For over a year she had been studiously assessing marital possibilities within the limited social circle to which her father had kept her confined. Unwittingly, when he took her abroad he expanded her field beyond what normal surveillance could adequately patrol.

Accompanying him on a tour of European investors, unbeknownst to him she was equally intent upon doing some prospecting of her own. At a formal dinner on a verandah overlooking the great valley of the Po, destiny and a deliberate unfamiliarity with the language ("How could I have misunderstood?") apparently caused her to ignorantly seat herself at the young Count's side, displacing an ambitious cousin who was maturing matrimonial designs of her own, but did not wish to make a scene and regretted this decision the rest of her embittered life.

Immediately attracted, soon fascinated, and by meal's end infatuated by this chance American acquaintance, so different from the women of his own country, the Count gallantly offered to show her the local sights as only a native could, and did. For the next several days, and nights, he was her guide, even conducting her through his family's estates and the centuries of cultural treasure that they possessed.   She was duly impressed, but business called her father on and she with him, causing her smitten suitor to follow them from city to city urging his attentions upon her that she encouragingly resisted and reluctantly accepted so artfully that he became obsessed with the notion her could not live without her, although until then he had managed very well.

At last, he professed his love with such ardent desperation she relented to his entreaty on condition they elope at once without the knowledge or permission of his family or her father, neither of whom in possession of the first would have given the second. Indeed the dalliance was only let go so far because all parents concerned were unconcerned, trusting too much in their authority and too little in the power of brazen youth to requite forbidden love.

Given the slip at chase's end, her father subdued his anger and suppressed his disappointment, accepting defeat not at the hands of his daughter but from his own overconfidence, not protesting the union since he knew such opposition would only demonstrate the impotence to which he had been reduced. Besides, her newfound wealth had distinct possibilities, if not at the moment, perhaps at some later time.

The Count's parents, however, were not so restrained and philosophical. Outraged their eldest child had been entrapped by this foreign adventuress when they had another connection for him in mind, they resorted to the law that unhappily proved ineffectual. By then, Antonio, their only son, had just reached his majority, acquiring the right to make decisions independent of their approval, of which getting married was the first. Over the telephone from a neighboring country the Count strenuously denied accusations being made against his bride, or at least as strenuously as he could. Never having been able to stand up for himself against their wishes, to refuse them now required the steel of his wife's support, squeezing strength from her hand as he made the first autonomous decision of his obedient life.

Even so, anxiety at this rebellion shocked his system, always sensitive and frail, and soon chronic ailments were inflamed. Becoming unwell he appealed for relief to his new protector the way he used to call upon his parents. Her prescription was a change of place. Back to America they should go, she advocating a different climate and distance from family pressures as curatives for what had been diagnosed as 'nervous exhaustion'. And he did cheer up, all the while languishing under her care, dying within the year from no physical cause the doctors could find and so were powerless to treat. All the while their patient had been as compliant as he was uncomplaining. Guilt at betraying his family, missing home, self-sacrificial adoration of his wife: these were the maladies about which he would not speak, lest he incur displeasure from she whom more than anyone he wished to please.

To do her justice the Countess, already finding social rank advantageous in a land that publicly disdained but secretly admired such titles, did do everything she could to shore up her failing husband. Only the more she did for him, the less he seemed able or inclined to do for himself. The stronger she acted on his behalf, the more dependent he became until her strength ran out or his weakness gave up.

To the extent she could she sincerely mourned his death, touched anyone could care for her so much, regretting this loss of dogged devotion. Out of respect for his family's wishes, and as part of the settlement she consented to accept, his remains were sent back across the ocean for burial at a private service that commemorated his life as they wanted it remembered -- ill starred and unmarried.

At age twenty three, the Countess Elena D'Allessandro Ricci was widowed, titled, and financially independent to a degree even her father could appreciate, treating her with a respect not previously warranted, considering her now an equal. However she had become well off, he admitted she had it done very well. Then she proceeded to do better, conservatively increasing the value of her estate, not squandering it, inheriting what he chose to believe was his alchemy with money. She transmuted substantial capital into a great deal more.

Lacking in her, however, was his hard learned experience at high risk investing that he offered to teach in partnership with her, pooling their funds on condition he would have the final say about how these joint ventures would be conducted. She must trust his more experienced judgment. To which she agreed, but with a condition of her own. In return for her non-interest bearing loan, she would share equally in the profits, but not in the losses. These would be his alone to pay.

"Which places the risks all on my side,' he observed.

"That is correct," she agreed. "And there they shall remain." She had endured risk enough in their relationship and was not about to expose herself to any more.

He was extremely pleased by this arrangement. It confirmed his high opinion of her. He was so pleased, that unbeknownst to his daughter he had his will redrawn designating her primary beneficiary, disinheriting his wife who later died in ignorance of the poverty to which she would have been consigned had she outlived her husband. He was prepared to leave her as destitute as he had found her many years before. She, however, left him unprotected from the consequences of those excesses to which she ministered when alive and that now ran their ruinous course unobstructed by her care. He died from complications several years after, leaving his disciple to carry on the family fortune, although regrettably not the family name.

Free from every obligation except management of her wealth, in full possession of a daunting beauty, the Countess could now do whatever she wanted. It only remained for her determine what this ambition would be. While her father was alive, she had interned herself to him in order to acquire the cunning he could teach. His death was timely. She was tired of school, grown bored of business for business' sake. Surely making more money was not money's only use. Restless with dissatisfaction, she began to look elsewhere. At first she surveyed the world around her but found nothing she desire to emulate or to possess. Then she reflected back upon herself, searching personal history for clues to what direction her future could meaningfully take.

At once the ambition to dominate at whatever she chose came faithfully to mind. That much was clear. Then she recalled the men she had known since Antonio had returned to his ancestral home. Over the intervening years, the Countess had amused herself with numerous male playthings who generally had not been amused to discover she was taking them so lightly when they thought they had made a significant conquest.

She found them a source of enjoyment during their relationship, but a source of contempt once it was over. Their sensitivity to rejection was surprising, particularly the range of their responses, reviling her reputation, turning pettish, becoming angry, a few threatening revenge, others pathetically pleading broken hearts. There was even one who refused to let her go, an artist named LaValle. He had a rising reputation and was in full possession of a wit to match her own, the closest man she found to be her equal. Pitting her intelligence against his was a challenge as was matching his skill at repartee. But when she grew tired of continuing his company, he refused to be dismissed.   Finally his persistence became so unrelenting she was forced to rid him from her life by the only means which remained, by actions since words had lost their power to convince. That seemed to work. She did not hear from him again.

Of course remarriage was out of the question. Nor was she interested in a serious attachment. What passed for love seemed to the Countess a case of emotional stupidity contracted by losing one's mind to feelings for another person, sacrificing self-interest and personal freedom. For what? At least she was proof against such folly. So she thought. Then rumor of her reputed invulnerability to men and the lure of her wealth and beauty challenged the interest of a visitor from abroad. He was another artist, an *enfant terrible* said to be revolutionizing ideas in his own country, who enjoyed sampling local delicacies at each stop upon a promotional tour, while the Countess was happy to oblige since she liked sampling foreign delicacies too.

At first taste, passion was aroused that neither had anticipated, each instantly convinced it could be satisfied by the other and no one else. Unlike previous affairs, of which both had known many, familiarity instead of eventually breeding boredom increased excitement that proved insatiable. They could not seem to get enough of each other and could think of nothing else. No matter how they satisfied their momentary appetite, they ended craving more. There was no enough. Used to ruling in relationships each felt ruled, enraptured then enraged by the captivity of their desire, alternately loving and hating each other, creating terrible fights for freedom followed by passionate reunions that entrapped them again. Finally their obsession became intolerable and severing it a mercy worth the loss. Each carried part of the other away, parts that could never be rejoined and restored because to do so would revive what had nearly destroyed the independence of them both.

For the Countess it was a humbling experience. For scoffing at Love, she had been taken prisoner to learn what it was like. Cured of boasting and convinced that tempting Fate in this matter was ill advised, she came to believe there were greater powers at work in the world than the power of her will. As for Riablo, for it was he, letters became his means for letting go, writing out all the passion that she had aroused, sending it to her in order to be rid of its dominion so he could recommit himself to work. Occasionally a phone call was risked, but only occasionally. By mutual consent they never saw each other again.

Two artists: LaValle and Riablo. Reviewing the vanquished admirers from her past, she was struck how it was artists with whom she had become most entangled. Something must be there. As her father had told her so she believed. It was foolish to blame coincidence on chance. But how to discover the significance?

As if by summons, the most entranced of her admirers obediently answered memory's call. There he was, Antonio, the one she married. He seemed to beckon and she saw him lead her once again through the great ancestral estates of his family. Castles they still seemed to her, huge and old, as indestructibly permanent as the rock that had been quarried for their construction. Each one was a treasure house with rooms and rooms of antique furnishings, decorative objects, miniatures crafted with exquisite attention to ornate detail, massive sculptures dominating great interior chambers, and walls and walls of paintings such as she believed only existed in museums. Certainly not in private homes. Certainly not. And yet, why not? The question was an intriguing one.

She had the money. She only wanted the ambition. To create a collection of comparable grandeur to those of the illustrious family to whom she had given back their son, but not their name. For the first time she thanked her husband, deceased though he was. First he had bequeathed her his title, then his money, and now he had given her a goal. But how to begin? The only way a woman of action like herself could get started, by throwing herself into the purpose to which she had committed. Indiscriminately she began collecting according to criteria which to her made sense. She used demand and cost in deciding what to buy, trusting the most to cost to determine artistic value. The more expensive the better the piece. She bought at auction whenever she could, relying on more knowledgeable competition to drive the bidding up according to the item's worth. Although it was a market place with which she was unfamiliar, it was a market place none-the-less.

As a new player in the game of collecting, evidently well financed, her name was circulated swiftly among those who concerned with the buying and selling of fine art. Without applying, she found herself on the select list to attend exclusive openings of important exhibitions where the Director of the Museum, Dr. Gambrell, insinuated himself into her acquaintance one glittering evening and extended her an invitation. Would she like to serve on the Museum's Acquisitions Committee? Indeed she would. Being an experienced prospector, she knew when it was being done to her. Apparently today's collector might be tomorrow's donor. So this was one way the game was played. Too bad she had no confederate upon whose seasoned judgment she could rely until she gained adequate expertise herself.

Time for another coincidence. She knew it was not. Late one afternoon, about to lift a telltale finger signifying acceptance of the auctioneer's last asking price for a pair of silver ewers inscribed with pictures of ancient gods, a trembling hand firmly closed over her own smothering the winning bid she was about to offer, allowing a less affluent rival to obtain the vessels for a bargain price.

Affronted by this interference but in cold control, she turned to challenge whomever had dared come between herself and the objects she was after. Turning she beheld, impeccably attired and unperturbed, a man considerably shorter than herself who seemed oblivious to the strong physical restraint he continued to place upon her hand until the sale had been gaveled down. Only then did he glance directly at the Countess, and when he did his gaze did not waver.

"Let them go," he gently commanded. "They are not worthy.'

"LaValle!" Even through the disguise of so much physical alteration, she recognized her former suitor. He had changed indeed. His voice softened almost to a whisper, he posture bent, his shoulders hunched. It was he whom she had been forced to discharge so long ago.

"Follow me,' he murmured struggling to his feet.

Unaccustomed to obeying anyone's orders, she felt no disinclination to follow his. Slowly he shuffled from the room, one foot slightly dragging behind the other. The Countess adjusted her pace to his, to her surprise adapting to the authority with which he carried himself despite (or was it because of?) the infirmities that were so apparent. There was something less about the man, but also something more.

Out through the foyer of the great auction house they ambled, LaValle frequently acknowledging deferential nods until they reached the sidewalk, she now by his side, strolling a few doors down, doors instantly pulled open:

"Your usual, sir?" Within moments they were seated at a secluded table in a private club or restaurant, she looking attentively at the man who had once been her slave and was now acting her master.

"So, Countess. We meet again. May I call you Elena?"

"You already have." Since he began the conversation, he could carry it on.

"The passage of years has used you kindly, Elena. Older, but otherwise undiminished."

"Unlike yourself."

"Yes," he smiled to feel the old directness once again. "I am not entirely the man I was."

"The last I heard you had gone away to recover. Then after years of silence, bits and pieces of your rise to prominence began to slip into the newspapers. Once there was something connected with the Museum and the purchase of an important new collection."

"Something. And now you yourself are making acquisitions. May I ask why?"

"I have decided to form an important art collection of my own." Somehow her declaration sounded pretentious, at least felt that way. Because she was declaring to LaValle? No matter, it was the truth, and in moderation truth felt safe with this man. Besides, she was curious what opportunity he was bringing into her life. Whatever else LaValle had become, he was evidently a man of purpose. If she waited him out, the Countess was certain his intent would be disclosed. Meanwhile, as in days gone by, she found the parry and thrust of conversation with the man invigorating. What she had liked most about him then she still found to her liking now. The body may have been injured, but not the mind.

"This collection," he asked. "Is it to be specialized or varied?"

"Varied," she answered. "Quality is the only consideration."

"And how shall quality be assured?"

The Countess didn't like being questioned and didn't like this question in particular. However, she felt him engaging with her and that was good. Soon he would be getting to the point.

"By reputable sellers," she replied. "By outbidding knowledgeable buyers. By bestowing value based on price. How else?"

"The market place for art, Elena, is an uncertain and fickle one. What commands high dollar today was unsaleable twenty years ago and may be just as hard to sell twenty years hence. Price is driven not so much by enduring value as changing fashion, fashion always reacting against itself."

"How else to select, then?" she demanded.

"Have you considered taste?"

The Countess did not like feeling out of her depths, which was where this discussion was sweeping her. Yet there was in LaValle something she trusted enough to believe he would not let her drown.

"Come, you disagree with my strategy for collecting. I only buy what pleases me and only after it has attracted the financial interest of other collectors. I call that taste."

"Yes," LaValle agreed. "So do I. But of an inferior kind. Taste must be educated, Elena. Taste is an art in and of itself, the art of seeing art." He paused to let his words sink in and to light a cigarette. "Lest you think this is some mystical notion of little practical value, let me assure you such is not the case. These eyes of mine, I place them for a fee at the disposal of artists and collectors who I am retained to represent. Through my discernment, they come to see their own work and the work of others with an acuity they otherwise could not. It is an accidental gift I cultivated when I was an artist. Now I trade on it to make a living. When I was forced to abandon my first profession I turned this second gift into another. Those years when my whereabouts were unknown here I was cultivating the acquaintance of public and private collectors around the world. Gradually, as they came to appreciate my taste, they entrusted me with their commissions because by now I also had connections they did not, a network of sellers and buyers who could find each other only if both paid me."

Although impressed, the Countess was also suspicious.

"If your taste, as you call it, is so valuable why do you not collect for yourself?"

"First, because I lacked the money. Second, once I began to make my living one rule became immediately clear. I could not be a dealer who collected without competing with collectors whom I chose to represent. So I only act as agent. Now, are you interested in hearing my proposal?"

The Countess had been waiting for nothing less.

"So long as it has to do with business and nothing more."

"All business it shall be."

The Countess gave her permission:

"You may proceed."

"I propose to act as your agent in purchasing museum quality objects and artifacts of such undisputed excellence that when we are done cognoscenti -- connoisseurs, scholars and serious students, eminent critics and collectors-- shall petition the Countess D'Allessandro Ricci to grant them the favor of viewing her treasures."

"Very flattering, LaValle.   I see you have not lost your persuasive touch. Yet the offer has a curious omission. Your fee."

"My fee, Elena, shall be included in whatever price the purchase bears. It shall vary according to the excellence of what I am able to procure."

"Come, LaValle, I am a woman of business. I never have, never would, sign a contract obligating me to pay unspecified costs."

A slight edge entered the Dealer's voice suggesting something hard and inflexible.

"The contract between us shall not be written. You may choose to reject any purchase I propose.   I may choose to end our relationship at any time. In this often delicate and occasionally risky business in which I trade, Elena, my word is my bond.   This is enough for others. It must be enough for you. As to my fee, I shall decide how much my efforts should be reimbursed. Not you. Not ever. You may safely assume any object I bring to your attention is beyond price.   Therefore, whatever I ask you to pay, consider it a bargain."

This felt like an offer worthy of her father.

"I see you have developed a blunt side since last we talked." The Countess was impressed.

"I know my own value, Elena, and I choose to set it for myself."

"LaValle, what an interesting, what a surprising man you have become. I accept your offer. And I begin our association with two points of business. First, what is to be done with those few items I have already acquired?"

"I shall dispose of them. Be prepared to take a loss."

"So, I am not to trust my own judgment?"

"Not yet," he replied. "In time, as your taste develops, you may begin to follow your own instincts. But not yet. The second point?"

"I want to build a structure of older design that is as superior as the art which it displays. One in which I can live. How is this to be done?"

"Thoughtfully. I shall need time to think. Give me a year. In twelve months I shall lay before you plans for the building you require. Meanwhile, purchase the largest piece of property you can as close to the Museum as possible. In the future, this proximity shall work to your advantage. Anything else?"

"Yes." And her tone of voice turned extremely cold. "Do not treat the trust I give you lightly, LaValle. Do not betray it. Do not exploit my ignorance. You need to know, I am a devout believer in revenge."

Apparently the Dealer understood since he immediately took her measure with his own.

"Then we have something else in common, Elena," he gravely replied, "because so am I."

Chapter Twenty-One
THE LESS SAID THE BETTER

Dear Kate:

As I grow more at peace I seem to have less to say. Probably a good sign. While the only news of you I hear is from your uncle who tells me you are doing well. I'm glad.

Are you still angry with me? You do not write, so I guess you are. I underestimated your capacity to hold a grudge. Or perhaps I presumed your forgiveness too much. In my quandary, I asked the Countess: 'What's a mother to do?' Her response was a typically unsentimental one. 'What she can. Some good and some not so good, I suppose. Why do you ask?'

Why <u>do</u> I ask? Because occasionally I still long for answers. Where did I go wrong that we should end so badly? Surely what cannot be undone can at least be understood. Was it overindulgence? Demanding so little of you as a child, was forcing you to Savocek too much? Did overruling your refusal destroy my loving kindness in your eyes? Did it discredit all the good that I had done? Do you know what's really strange? I never saw or spoke to your teacher, yet I destroyed our old relationship for the sake of this man I never even met! Fighting for your best interests and prevailing, I won what I did not want.

How absurd, as the Countess was quick to point out. I was agent of my own unhappiness. It's her opinion I have been shortsighted and imprudent. She says I gave too much to mothering, hence the loss that I am feeling now. According to her, I over-invested in you and under-financed myself. This is how she conceives of most relationships -- in business terms. Each relationship is a chance to turn a profit, create an opportunity, or at least gain some advantage. Never any mention of interest or enjoyment, of caring or love for their own sake. So I challenged her material philosophy of using people when it came to me. Of what benefit was I? At least my daughter had some talent to exploit, but me? All I had to offer was my friendship.

'Yes,' she answered. 'I have been curious to see what rewards simple friendship can provide.' And what have you discovered, I asked. 'That terms are harder to dictate than in business, and there is more to dislike. For the pleasure of your company, I must put up with questioning I do not want.' Why do you? I asked. 'Because as I please myself in other ways, I choose to please myself in this.'

Now Kate, why does she play a closed hand despite her openness with me? What is she hiding or protecting? What is she holding back? Since she has the drawing, I pose no further obstacle to what she wants. Do you know what I think? She is uncomfortable with her good feelings for me. The last time we met I unintentionally caused her to give evidence of this.

As I used to do with you in happier times, instead of shaking hands I refused to be kept at arm's length and gave her a hug. My hands on her shoulders I pulled her to me and placed my face against the side of hers that instantly inflamed, becoming burning hot. If one can be said to go limp and stiff at the same time, she did both. Immobilized by my embrace, she was powerless to respond or resist. Sensitive to her discomfort of course I let her go. Relieved to be back in charge, she led us inside, recovering her usual self-control by the time we were seated. What a contradiction! Here is a woman who by her own account has not been shy with men when so inclined, yet she recoiled from the touch of my affection.

Your Uncle Phillip once described her to me as 'a human fortress', implying I supposed that she was battle-wise and well-defended. Both are true, but not the whole truth I believe. In his dealings with her, he has been made to stand beyond the outer gate, while you and I have been allowed within the walls. We have glimpsed the woman with some of her guard letdown and have received a measure of her trust.

Only one other person that I know may have been given more. Mr. LaValle. On many of my visits to the Villa, he is leaving just when I arrive. Galen says this is only natural since LaValle is her confidential agent, but I believe he is about something more than simply executing her commissions. I think he watches over her and she lets him act as her protector. Why I say this is because of how he now treats me.

When I was only a social appendage of your father, courtesy was all that I deserved, although he never failed to give me that. Since the Countess has befriended me, however, and I stand closer to her than I did before, LaValle wants to be more sociable. I think to better please the woman whom he serves. So now when we meet, as we often chance to do, he will ask about my life, particularly what I have heard from you. When I reply 'Nothing yet,' he takes a moment to describe your general progress at Riablo's. How he gets his information I don't know, but he speaks with such authority I do not doubt his word. And I feel grateful to receive it. He says you are maturing faster than he predicted. I suppose he means your work. And that the climate suits your growth and you are flourishing. Never more specific, but I find his evaluations reassuring. A mother always worries that her absent child is doing well. So now each week I look forward to my 'Kate Report', and he seems to enjoy giving it. If I am late, I'll find him smoking, waiting for me at the entrance. When he sees me he greets me with a smile that feels sincere, and I smile sincerely in return.

When I told the Countess how much his consideration meant she immediately understood. 'Yes, LaValle is the master of small attentions. I should know. Over the years, he has provided me so many he has become indispensable. A convenience I can hardly do without.' So Kate, while you and I are trusted, he is trusted more.

Other news of a less happy kind is this. I don't see much of your uncle now. Most of his time outside of work is spent with Mr. Savocek who has apparently become unwell. Whatever he has caught it is persistent, some days advancing, others retreating, but never entirely going away causing Phillip to alternate between periods of worry and times of hope. Beyond the fact that it could be serious, he tells me little more. The sense I get is that the diagnosis is complicated, the treatment limited, and the outcome uncertain. Phillip confides in Galen more, your father interrupting work to listen to his friend, the two sharing with each other what evidently I am not supposed to know. This is how it's always been between us, Galen and I each enjoying a separate intimacy with Phillip as you do as well, none of us party to the privacy of his relationship with either of the others. Thus I'm not told about what you write your uncle because that is between you and him. He is closer to each of us than all of us.

He is closest of all to Mr. Savocek, closer now that his friend is fallen ill. Such a difficult person to get close to, and yet your uncle has found a way. What Galen marvels at in Phillip, his gift for getting on with difficult people. He evidently learned the skill when he was young, although he never told me so. In any case, he must have confidence in this capacity, recently placing the Countess on his Board. Much as I am coming to like her, I don't think I would relish having her on mine. She enjoys enough influence on my life already without my placing her in a position to have more.

Well, that's all for now. Except your father has just emerged from his burrow long enough to ask if I would add he loves you too. Back he goes. It's work that gives the man contentment. While the separation between you and I is gradually helping me recover mine.

I love you,

Joanne

Chapter Twenty-Two
WHEN TWO SIMILARS COLLIDE

If it was an angry three years for Kate, it was an even angrier period for Joanne who found herself the object of unremitting hostility from a daughter whose moods seemed limited to three -- sullen, irritable, and indifferent. Every weekday morning in anticipation of the afternoon's confinement, every weekday evening after her release, Kate would be sure to fix her mother with an accusatory glare, a reminder to Joanne that she was unforgiven. For what? For advancing the daughter's interests, punishment was the mother's reward. Needing some enemy to blame, Kate had chosen Joanne.

'I don't deserve this treatment,' Joanne would think to herself and then repeat out loud to her daughter, "I don't deserve your treating me this way. Stop it!" But it was Joanne who stopped protesting instead when she realized Kate was interpreting her denials of responsibility as admissions of guilt, using them to fuel ongoing resentment.

As for Kate, all she knew was that anger ruled, anger at a mother who had never merited anger before, anger that was causing separation, frightening Kate by distance she was creating. By pushing so hard against her mother, would she end up pushing her mother's love away? What Joanne could not see through her own sense of injury was that Kate's rebellion was an act of courage. Painfully for her mother and herself, excruciatingly lonely for them both, Kate was tearing free of their old attachment, anger over Savocek the grievance being used to drive them apart. To what end?

Beyond the excuse she was using, she didn't know. Nor really why. Alone in her room, bewildered, Kate would sadly ask herself the same question over and over again. 'Why am I acting this way?' Since she could find no good answer, her actions had to speak for themselves. 'Because I am.'

As time wore on, Joanne's patience with her abrasive daughter wore down. The provocation was constant. Kate contested every request, passively answering questions with stubborn silence, actively becoming antagonistic to rules, demanding reasons that she discounted as soon as they were given by charging: "That's no reason at all!" Before long the force of this resistance grew hard enough to harden the mother against the daughter. No love was lost, but protection was needed. Why should Joanne allow herself to be repeatedly rejected and continually hurt by Kate's snubs and attacks? She shouldn't. And she wouldn't. So to take care of herself, she began to redefine her position with Kate. Reducing expectations of positive return, Joanne reaffirmed her determination to maintain what was hers by right of motherhood, a full parenting presence in her daughter's life so long as Kate still lived under her roof.

Occasionally, when Kate's withdrawal threatened the mother with isolation, Joanne would initiate a demand calculated to offend her daughter, inviting Kate out for an argument. This ploy usually succeeded, the fight satisfying Joanne's need for an emotional connection, a hostile intimacy through which her daughter could be reached. While the conflict felt bad, the contact felt good. And some anger could be released.

Yet there was anger left over that no amount of fighting with Kate could purge, since it was not directed at Kate but at Galen and Phillip. To her father and uncle, Kate had not altered her traditional affection in the slightest. The annual sittings, the museum excursions were uninterrupted. Both men were sheltered from the storms of disapproval and rejection that attacked Joanne each day. Talk about unfairness! Did Galen think this was fair? Did Phillip? She had attacked them with this question, charging them with complicity in an arrangement where they enjoyed ongoing love with Kate from which she was barred. She tried them and declared her verdict: guilty. Well, how would Phillip like it if he lost his precious museum? Or Galen the opportunity to paint? Both men felt sentenced to self -punishment, caught in the middle between two conflicting loyalties, wanting a way out, wishing for resolution, blaming themselves, helpless to heal the antagonism they had helped create.

Despite his deftness with difficult people and his skill at manipulating possible outcomes from impossible situations, Phillip saw no way around or through this impasse. Having spoken to Kate of his concern and been told he should not take sides in what was not his battle, he had talked with Joanne, assuring her of his pain on her behalf, committing his support. Then he divided the friendship out, pursuing time with mother and daughter separately, since family occasions were now strained and awkward for everyone.

Galen. His refuge of work was scarcely removed enough to protect him from the spoken and unspoken hostilities that raged outside the rampart of his studio door. He entered earlier, came out more seldom, stayed later, yet no degree of avoidance or absorption could deny the reality of disharmony between beloved daughter and beloved wife. By temperament, Galen was ill-suited to the strife that beset him now.

Quietly he had tried speaking to Kate only to be quietly told she did not wish to discuss it. Loudly he had insisted on reconciliation with her mother only to get a loud unreconciled response: "Not until Joanne undoes the damage she has done!"

Patiently he had urged Joanne to let Kate alone to grow out of whatever she was growing through. Patiently, she had explained how by this request he was demonstrating the very insensitivity she found so offensive. Impatiently he had told her to do whatever she must to restore household peace because the current tensions were interfering with his concentration, a charge he was made to instantly regret.

"Your concentration?" And she proceeded to attack the self-centeredness of placing desire for work over concern for family.

Then what in God's name did she want him to do? She didn't know. Stand by her until she and Kate came out the other side of this estrangement, hopefully intimate again. How long would this take, he asked? Again, she didn't know. For now, the best he could do for her was understand there was nothing he or she could do. They could be powerless together. Could he do this? He could. And did. Faithfully, but at a cost.

Their playful times diminished as seriousness overcame his wife. Range of conversation grew extremely limited, fixated on a problem no amount of discussion could resolve. Distraction with mothering caused her to be harder to reach as a wife. Love making became more infrequent. Yet there was one blessing from the hardness of this time endured together, a deepening of commitment between them: an appreciation by Galen of Joanne's steadfastness as a mother, and by Joanne of Galen's steadfastness as a mate. She was not easy to live with, but he lived with her without complaint. He was not emotionally supportive like Phillip, but his constancy never wavered and it gave her the strength to make the statement that began to free her from entanglement with Kate.

"This cannot go on." She said it to herself again. "This cannot go on." Many times she repeated this phrase during the first year of their estrangement, each repetition gradually affirming the need to take care of herself in the face of Kate's unremitting grievance against her mother. "This cannot go on." At last a limit was reached from which new limits could be set. Joanne was not responsible for whatever depth of injury was being held against her. As this merciful understanding sunk in life with Kate became bearable. Not enjoyable. Not rewarding. But bearable. More bearable, as she let go all hope that their old relationship would somehow be restored. Hope became revealed for what it was: denial. The golden years of Kate's childhood were over. Now the hard half of parenting had begun. Her daughter had begun to grow away toward independence.

Hopeless, helpless, but not quite. In quiet daily meditations a new source of sustenance came to her rescue: faith. While hope vainly expected, faith firmly believed. While hope created dreams of bad times finally over and better times ahead, faith was rooted in conviction that if she did not break faith with her daughter, if she were constant in her love and patient, Kate would not break faith with the history of love between them. So with detachment, the abandonment of hope, and faith in faith itself, Joanne restored herself to 'some semblance of sanity' (which Galen was glad to hear) and she would have grown stronger in that state had not Kate's Saturdays with the Countess set her progress back.

Beyond warning Kate of the reputation for ruthlessness that the older woman richly deserved, Joanne had no energy left to discourage this interest any further. As for the woman being curious to meet Kate, this did not particularly surprise Joanne. After all, the Countess would want to inspect any beneficiary of tuition she was being made to pay. Joanne knew her this well. But why this invitation to the Villa?

Kate's answer had been a defiant one.

"My going to class was your decision. What I do from there is up to me. If the Countess wants to talk with me and I wish to allow it, that is my choice. If she invites me to visit and I choose to go, that is also my choice. What I began doing on your terms, I shall continue doing on my own!"

Joanne backed off because she did not want to encourage this new association by opposing it. Besides, both Galen and Phillip were in favor of cultivating the connection if Kate were willing. Whatever else might be said against her, the Countess was a powerful patroness; while exposure to the treasures she possessed could only enrich Kate's artistic experience and further educate her eye.

Had Joanne been present at the first clash between Kate and the Countess she would have had no anxiety about their relationship maturing beyond a cordial dislike. It began with a commotion of tense voices outside the girl's studio door breaking the silence sacred to Savocek's instruction.

"Since you have insisted on teaching this girl, I insist on meeting her myself! You have had your way. Now I shall have mine!"

As the door abruptly burst open Kate heard the sound of angry footsteps stamping down the hall. Turning around, she boldly scanned the older woman with unsparing attention to detail, meticulously taking in her particulars. As Galen by example and Savocek by instruction had both taught her to do, Kate instinctively prepared a mental portrait of the Countess, observing how posture, feature and dress combined to strike such an impression of beauty, none-the-less keeping an eye out for any inconsistency of a telling kind. Finding one, she fastened her gaze directly upon it.

To be admired was one thing, to be scrutinized was another. The Countess did not like this examination, particularly where it had finally become fixed.

"Well, what do you see?" she challenged in an effort to regain ascendancy unaccountably lost.

"Those burns on the finger tips of your left hand. What are they?"

Determined not to care that her only physical blemish should preoccupy the girl, the Countess held the offending fingers out for closer evaluation.

"When you have satisfied your curiosity, we shall proceed."

Kate was fascinated.

"They are so ugly and the rest of you is not. Why don't you have the scars removed?"

"Because I earned them."

"By playing with fire?"

"A rite of passage is hardly an act of play. Ordeal is more like it. Now: are you quite finished?"

Kate shrugged, then nodded.

"So. You are the artist's daughter. I am the Countess D'Allessandro Ricci."

"I know who you are."

"Indeed?"

"Yes. We have met before. Long ago. Not in my home. You were unwelcome there."

Defeat not being a pleasurable memory to dwell upon, the Countess chose to ignore it.

"I don't recall."

"With my father and uncle I came to your house when they had business to discuss. You didn't like my being brought along and had me stay out in the hall."

"I may have suggested that."

"You did. I didn't like you for it."

"I dare say. Because you were probably acting like a child no doubt I chose to treat you as one. My 'house' as you call it was not designed nor furnished with children in mind."

"I know. It was very cold and uninteresting. I remember being bored."

"Uninteresting? You were <u>bored</u>? Less a reflection of the setting than of yourself, I should say."

Whatever the Countess had expected it was not conversation with a girl whose tongue was as tart as her own. Caught off guard, she allowed herself to get angry.

"I am here to see on whom my money is being squandered. Mr. Savocek's teaching capacities are of a sufficiently high order I do not want them wasted on a talent, no matter how promising, that is destined to come to nothing."

Having recently freed herself for indignation at her mother, Kate felt no constraint in answering the Countess back in kind.

"His instruction shall <u>not</u> be wasted on me!"

"Indeed? You hold a high opinion of yourself for a girl. And so young. How old are you?"

"Fourteen."

"You look older."

"I am older. How old are you?"

"I am your superior in age is all you need to know. Is it out of fashion for the young to speak politely to their elders?"

"Not when the young are politely spoken to first."

At this impasse the conversation reached a momentary end. Rather than tolerate being stood off the Countess strode forward toward the table and perused the unfinished drawing on which Kate had been working for the last two days. It's bold strokes caught the older woman's attention, the confidence and innovative thinking they betrayed. By now her eye could recognize quality when she saw it, and she saw it now.

"So. It was not just to oppose me that Savocek insisted on teaching you. Well, I don't begrudge you talent or your desire to improve it. In fact, if you were not a girl, I would have no objection to the investment of his instruction and my money in your education."

This was the first time anyone had ever linked Kate's sex to her artistic potentiality.

"And since I am a girl?"

"The possibility of your ever becoming accepted as a major artist is greatly diminished."

From her uncle, from her father, from her mother, even from Savocek himself, she had never heard such nonsense and was not about to listen to it now.

"I can make of myself whatever I choose!" So she had always been told by those who loved her.

"Young woman, what you do with your talent is entirely up to you; however, what society does with whatever you produce is not. Much less any future verdict on your work. History decides what matters, even who matters. And the history of visual art, and the men who write it, make one point eminently clear. In the pantheon of great artists, women occupy only a minor and very occasional place. This is why, and only why, I did not wish to waste Savocek on you."

Kate had never been spoken to in these terms.

"Are you telling me a woman, because she is a woman, cannot become a major artist?"

"I am not telling you anything your experience will not tell you better, or worse. Look in the art history books. Look in the prestigious museums. Look in significant private collections such as mine. Where are the great women artists? Show me! You cannot. The art world is no world for a woman. Am I wrong?"

Kate soberly considered what was being asked and did not like the older woman's question any better than her own answer.

"It doesn't have to be this way," she sighed at last, her sad agreement softening the Countess, moved by the girl's loss of innocence.

"No it doesn't. I am right, but you are correct. Still, many changes would have to occur."

"What changes?"

The Countess shook her head shaking off the question.

"I was fourteen once. Not always as you see me now. What do you know about making your way in a man's world?"

"I don't. I never thought of it before."

The Countess fixed her with a searching gaze.

"Would you like to learn how it is done?"

Kate couldn't tell if this was an inquiry or an invitation. She looked intently back to see. The Countess had withdrawn several paces, her arms crossed not in a formidable manner but in a kind of self-consoling embrace that suggested to Kate discomfort, even pain. From what? Not that. She quickly dismissed the idea because someone so socially powerful would never want for that, yet there it was. Something of her father's eye for psychological detail she had assimilated. There it was. For all her self-assurance, the Countess was unmistakenly lonely. Imagine that! And on her side Kate softened in response.

"Yes. I should like to learn how it is done."

"Good." The Countess, arms now unfolded, resumed her accustomed carriage of authority. "Saturday, shall we say? At eleven?   Come to the Villa.   This time I shall try to be more hospitable than when I consigned you to the outer hall."

Kate smiled. Something slipped into place, into an empty place she did not realize she had. Not comfortable, yet welcome. It made no sense.   The woman was so many years older, but like the loneliness she had seen, well there it was within herself.   Not loneliness exactly, but an unfulfilled desire for a female friend.

Returning from class that evening, Kate did not flash anger as usual at her mother. Self-absorbed, she just announced in passing to her room:

"I am invited to the Villa this Saturday. And I am going."

Joanne did not protest.

"Very well."   However, from this moment suspicion began to grow. As best she could Joanne, suppressed her distrust of hope, telling herself one visit would be enough to satisfy whatever additional curiosity the Countess harbored about Kate. And upon returning home that first Saturday afternoon it initially appeared from Kate's evident disenchantment that things had not gone well and Joanne's worries were over. Then Kate, as she had done before, announced how she was going back the following weekend.

Joanne had never considered herself a jealous person. Even years ago when the Countess, at the urging of LaValle, had acquired patronage of Galen, Joanne did not fear losing her husband to this powerfully attractive other woman. Her only concern had been to prevent this outside influence from sweeping in and taking over her home, which she had successfully defended.   But now was a different matter.

This woman's untimely and inexplicable interest in Kate was threatening to take away what little connection to Joanne remained by providing a substitute attachment elsewhere.

Galen disagreed.

"Jo, whatever develops between them, you are always Kate's mother. No other woman can compete with what years of nurturing have built. Even if they could, the Countess would never be anyone's candidate for motherhood. Why she wouldn't even be her own. Believe me, I am enough a judge of character to be certain of what I say."

While comforting to hear at the time this reassurance lost helping power as, by the beginning of her second year with Savocek, Saturdays with the Countess became an established part of Kate's weekly routine. Whatever actually transpired during these visits, it was upon her own fearful imaginings Joanne's speculation had to depend since Kate would not be drawn out on the subject.

On the positive side Joanne found her daughter less provocative to live with, more amenable to requests and restraints, less likely to argue or object, generally tolerant of those irritating characteristics in her mother that had previously drawn Kate's fire. On the negative side, however, Joanne was not sure she wouldn't rather be directly criticized than passively endured. Kate's seeming indifference could feel so crushing at times Joanne would still occasionally resort to picking a fight just to impress her presence on her daughter and be acknowledged, which Kate obediently did by fighting back.

"Why can't you just leave me alone?"

Joanne could, but there were times she wouldn't.

To do her justice, Kate was too concentrated on herself and the world that study with Savocek and friendship with the Countess had opened up to deliberately try to get back at her mother any more. She wasn't even aware of the agony her mother often felt. Self-centered and inconsiderate Kate was, but calculating she was not. She hardly gave any thought to her mother one way or another, unless Joanne deliberately acted the obstacle or interfered.

Kate had ample cause to be nonresponsive. Continually adjusting to the rigors of Savocek's demands, she had come to treat him like an inspiring opponent who kept creating new and more difficult artistic problems for which she must create new and more difficult solutions. Unless of course she wished to give up, which part of her continually did and part of her did not, the stubborn part that would not be beaten out of what she wanted for herself. In numb determination she kept on, school work becoming by comparison so easy to accomplish it was scarcely taxing, while home was where she only wanted to be left alone. Her uncle, coming to the house less and more occupied with his friendship with Mr. Savocek, was less easy to see. Thank goodness for Saturdays at the Villa where she could freely enjoy a relationship apart from work and family. Time spent with someone who knew her independently of the child she used to be. A fresh start. And after the first visit, woman to woman. No condescending deference to either age or youth. Opinion to opinion, each questioning the other at will, each forthright in response, no quarter given and no offense taken, this direct.

"Why aren't you married?"

"I have been. Once was sacrifice enough. Why don't you date?"

"I've never been asked."

"Why not?"

"Other girls are more attractive. They know how to be with boys. I don't. Did you date at my age?"

"Hardly. My father would not permit it. I was socially protected by a sexually possessive man. Since he knew from personal experience what men were like, he didn't want his daughter to go out with one."

"Is that the way men are?"

"Most men at least."

"I do not think my father is. Or my Uncle Phillip."

"Agreed. There are always exceptions. Beware the exceptions, Miss Germaine, or you may find yourself trusting in those you should not. At least my father gave me a faithful rendering of the rule. For this I suppose I am indebted to him. He did his best to save me."

"From whom?"

"From no one. For himself."

"I don't understand."

"No, you don't. I hope you never will. One pleasure in confiding in you, Miss Germaine, is that our histories are different and many years come between us. You are so free from influences I am not. What a blessing to confide in someone who truly cannot understand!"

"Why a blessing? What's the point of talking if you won't be understood?"

"Yes. Yes, of course. Understanding is important too. And yet, have you never had some piece of your past too private to be shared, but too painful not to be expressed? This is what I mean. Like confessing infidelity to a truly celibate priest. He can listen, but how can he really understand? In any case, I find your innocence on some matters very soothing."

"About men, you mean. I am very innocent about men?"

"Yes. You have been spared much experience. No doubt your future shall make up the lack. I wish you a better opinion of men than I have if that is what you want."

"I don't see why you choose to dislike half the human race."

"Not half, Miss Germaine. Half of the half. Of the male human being I like the human part well enough. Just not the male. The best I can say for their darker side is that it does have its fascinations and attractions. And carefully managed, men can be useful to a woman who knows what she wants and is not afraid to enter their domain to get what she is after."

"How can you talk the way you do? As though life is some kind of war, men against women. What about the men in your life, the ones who have been useful. Are they enemies?"

"Potentially yes. However, even the most savage can be tamed. Alliances can be formed. Arrangements made. Deals struck that benefit both parties. One way to manage men, Miss Germaine, is by sticking to business. A common interest is something they can understand, while they respect hard bargaining. At least, so I have found."

"Your father again?"

"Yes. Remarkable, is it not? I learned so much from him and yet don't cherish him in the least. A narrow escape. I promise you, Miss

Germaine, if he and I had ever reached Alexandria together as he intended, I would not be as I am today. Lucky for me, unlucky for him. His unerring sense of timing failed enough in Italy for me to slip away. Luck is the Father of us all."

"I'm glad I have a father I can love."

"Yes. I'm glad for you. I would not wish my kind of father on any woman. And yet I cannot deny the gifts that he unintentionally gave me. I am strong because and in spite of the man he was."

"Gifts?"

"Lessons if you will. Better to be the hunter than the hunted. He taught me that. Watch for those men who fancy themselves great seducers because they are most easily seduced. Bait men with beauty and they shall flock around like fools to gain your favors. No wonder the art world is a man's world. Who are more susceptible to beauty than men?"

"I am not beautiful."

"No, you're not."

"Not even pretty."

"No. Not even that."

"Were you always beautiful?"

"Yes. Although today I must use tricks. When I was your age, no artifice was needed."

"Would tricks help me?"

"Tricks never truly help because they are lies. By covering up, they only keep one mindful of one's flaws. Causing myself to look younger means I am discontent to look my age."

"Well I am not content with how I look at my age. Fifteen years old and the same square shape I've always been, only taller. The same plain face. They don't tease me any more. Now it's worse. I'm not even noticed. Too large to miss and too plain to be of interest. I don't care!"

"But you do."

"Well wouldn't you?"

"Yes I would. But not enough to give others the satisfaction of knowing. I wouldn't show it.'

"I don't. I keep to myself. One teacher once told my mother I had no friends because I acted like a snob. Like a snob! Can you believe it?"

"Yes. I can believe your sense of entitlement offends. You have been treated so specially by those who love you, you have come to treat yourself with like regard."

"What's wrong with that?"

"Nothing. Much right in fact. Only you seem blind to the consequences. Holding yourself out to the world as everyone's equal can convey superiority to those less self-secure. No, Miss Germaine, the teacher told your mother more truth than you wanted to hear. Certainly appearance matters, as much to women as success to men. I would be the last person to deny the power of physical attraction. However, it does not matter as entirely as you have let it.   You set yourself socially apart, then blamed the separation on your looks."

"Easy for you to say. You have what I have not been given."

"Yes. In more ways than you know. Beauty is a dangerous advantage. What you attract, you must also fend off. When your outer surface counts for so much your inner worth is often disregarded. At least you can be confident that your achievements are not the outcome of a pretty face."

"I don't care what you say. I hate the way I look and always will!"

"Perhaps not. Growth can create unexpected changes, and you have growing yet to do. Both in appearance and acceptance."

"Yes. I'll probably look even worse as I get older!"

And silence followed until another line of sharing opened up. To this conversation, however, and to none of the many others, was Kate's mother privy. While they were not aware of how, shut out of her daughter's life, Joanne resented both her daughter and the Countess full measure for the jealousy she suffered at their hands.

Chapter Twenty-Three
DEATH OF A FRIEND

Dearest Kate--

he had been ill a long time before admitting it to me, holding back the news, I believe, for fear, I should abandon our friendship from my fear of contagion. He died knowing nothing in this world or the next could keep me from remaining at his side to the end.

What I confide in you now, Kate, I have told no one else, not even your parents who have been so supportive during his time of dying and in some ways of my own. You knew Savocek; they did not. For this reason, you have the right to know what they do not. You earned the right by tolerating the unsparing nature of the man, remaining longer with him than anyone else. You did. A tribute to your determination. And what he probably never told you: you worked harder than any artist he ever had. Others were more innately gifted and were more advanced in skill when they began, but in sheer power of industry, you surpassed them all.

He was so secretive, that I have felt compelled not to divulge to anyone what he shared in his relationship with me. Yet for my own survival now without him, I must share with someone or live on an island as he chose to do. Not that I am any novice at keeping secrets, having been trained in concealment as a child out of loyalty to family reputation. Then I was an island. No more. Not even for Jan. Here then, Kate, here is the way it was.

I believe Jan was happier with me than at any other time in his troubled life. Yet in consequence of this blessing, a terrible reversal occurred. The better off with me the worse he felt at the same time, as though some unforgiving guilt or obligation would not permit him to enjoy what we had found. I was both a joy and a torment to my friend. Then, when his illness started weakening his usual defenses, other diseases lay in wait as he began to fail. Opportunistic, they exploited his deteriorating state. Although his mind was willing, his body, besieged from many quarters, could not repel their subsequent attacks. At last, he gave in, but he never gave up.

As for his death, it was a mercy. Of this, I am now thoroughly convinced. Death relieved him from the torment of his life. We were wrong, you and I. Janovar Savocek was not a man without a past. Remember wondering about him together early on? Where did he come from? Why was he so closed to questions? Why so stern? These we asked each other, never him.

And what were those sudden interruptions that occasionally seized him, inducing that blank stare when his gaze turned inward and vacancy looked out? I always tried to react as though nothing unusual was happening, protecting his sensitivity with my obliviousness. Waiting, I would watch the tremor pass and the rigid lips relax, light once again enlivening the voided eyes. What inner thoughts or impulses were so commanding they could order his attention away from company one moment, abruptly returning it the next? Memories seem the most apparent explanation. Of what? Like lightening unpredictably striking his awareness, illumination lingered after the bolts had passed, the after glare at last fading away. Then he seemed back in the present, freed from the past.

My impression was correct. Although I cannot tell you any more of his specific history, I can with certainty say this. His origin was darker and more terrible than I imagined. At his end, I glimpsed his beginning. Not clearly. Dimly through the delirium of those final days when at his bedside power of forgetfulness deserted him, his mind too weakened by physical decay to resist recalling whatever horror it had once successfully denied. Moaning, whimpering, he cried like a child dreaming through a protracted nightmare from which he could neither waken nor be woken up.

There were snatches of murmured speech in a mix of languages I did not understand. One word beseechingly repeated, one word over and over I could identify. 'Doctor! Doctor!' And he would squeeze the life out of my hand, I squeezing back as I was able in return, affording him the intermittent relief of uneasy sleep until the next terrifying visitation. 'Doctor! Doctor!' the invocation would begin again calling up this person in whose stead I was serving.

What doctor? In what circumstances? Ministering to what devastating need? Kate, I grew so angry! Why was this man not granted peace in dying when living had required so much pain? Had he not suffered enough? I raged. Where was the justice in such punishment? For what offense? Tell me! Consenting to live when life was the least preferred alternative. Committing himself to furthering the one redeeming human grace to which he clung for meaning when all other meaning had failed. You may say I am suffering from his delirium. However, I believe Death itself was demanding a full and final accounting of his unacknowledged pain before permitting him to journey on. His dying was a reckoning, Kate. The price of dying very dear. Remembering, an act of extraordinary courage.

The doctors. The doctors were amazed a man already frail and wasted from a scourge for which they had no cure could last so long. Little did they comprehend the intractable character of the patient they attended. But you and I, we knew. We knew the strength of will that years of physical self-neglect had fostered in a man determined to survive upon the one devotion of his life and little else.

Not until the very last did the delirium partially subside. Then I was there. Then he knew me. To his stare of recognition, I responded by cradling his head to comfort him, to hold him up. 'It's going to be all right, Jan, it's going to be all right!' What a contemptuous look he gave me. What a reproof for lying when I should have spoken truth. His final words to me: 'The Hell it will!' His body rattled with a mirthless laugh, he shook his head, fell back and was finally released. I can still hear the fierce hoarse whisper of those dying words, 'The Hell it will!' He died as he had lived, in defiance. But not alone.

I held him resting in my arms for a long time. Until the warmth began to leave his body and he felt cold. Resting in my arms was a consent he would have given no one else. This was how he expressed his caring for me. By welcoming my caring of him. As close to another human being as he could get.

Much there is I shall miss, but most of all the early mornings together. The love we shared for the love we shared for art. His spirit was helpless before a great object, soaring with joy at what artistic imagination could create. Response to response, one enthusiasm urging on the other, we were able to discover an appreciation together that neither of us could discriminate alone.

His death affected me more profoundly than I expected, comparable to losing you or Joanne or Galen. A vital connection gone that has diminished my own enthusiasm for living. Mornings, as I have said, are most difficult. Getting up taxes my strength particularly after not sleeping well. I have no appetite for breakfast.

Once at work, once I can get myself to work, the demands become supportive pushing and pulling me through the day, although with a detachment that feels robotic. Mechanically, I go through motions at a job I know so well it hardly requires thinking any more. This is probably a sign I have been at the Museum too long and she deserves fresh leadership.

Day's end I cannot bear to go back to my apartment yet do not want to insist my sad presence on anyone, much less anyone I love. The choice, however, has been taken from me. Galen or Joanne, often both, arrive at the Museum to bring me home -- to their home, your home, my home. They will not accept any of my objections so I have stopped objecting. Frequently they keep me over night depending, I suppose, on how they judge my state to be. When I do go back to my apartment, they call in half an hour to ensure my safe arrival and make sure I want to stay alone. While promptly at 7:30 in the morning I am rung up to check on my night, to encourage me to the office, what they know is good for me.

Such attentive care has taken some getting used to. I am more accustomed to helping others than accepting help myself. It feels wrong somehow to be indulged in this manner, as though others are doing their part for me while I am doing nothing but taking from them. Frightening really. It feels so good I could develop a taste for it. Except that would violate self-sufficiency that I was taught as a child and have clung to as a man.

With Joanne, when the mood suits me, I talk about my grief. What sensitive support your mother gives. At first I worried I would burden her with pain not properly her own. Raising this concern, I was immediately put in my place, the second time she has ever accused me of conduct unbecoming a friend. 'You have no right to forbid my giving when you have given so much to me!' Any further hesitation to confide fled before the sharpness of her words, one guilt driving out another.

With Galen there is no talk. I enter his studio, lay down on his raggedy brown couch and say nothing while he puts aside whatever work was occupying him and we share in silence as deeply as your mother and I share with words. Between such old comrades as he and I no words are necessary to communicate. Quiet companionship is enough.

So we remain until Joanne brings up a tray or calls us in to supper. They are very intent upon seeing I eat during this time, concerned about my pallor and loss of weight, although I am not. Surely it is not unusual to lose one's hunger and color when beset by personal tragedy. Besides, before long you shall be home, and this anticipation fills me with the strength to carry on.

What is hardest now is feeling I am mourning for my friend alone. Is there no other human being in this world besides myself who cared for Jan? It seems not. The only expression of caring I receive is for myself on behalf of his loss. Kate, besides you and I and those other students who were attracted into and then repelled out of his instruction, who else was there who knew him?

Did you realize, I did not, that neither of your parents ever met him? I never made the introduction knowing how he was disinclined to socialize outside of work. As for your parents, they must have sensed this reluctance through me and so never pressed the matter further. The other students? They came and went, focused on their work as Jan intended, heedless of him who pushed so hard for their advancement. Ironically, the Countess had more knowledge of them than I, skimming off the cream of their production for her private use, you the only one in whom she took a personal interest.

There, you see. I do her wrong. I did receive one note of appreciation. Characteristic: short and to the point. From an unlikely quarter of the world, from that unprincipled, principled woman.

'Dr. Gambrell:

I did not care for your Mr. Savocek from the first, nor did I come to like him any better at the last. He was not a socially congenial man.

However, possessing as I do, undeniable evidence of his excellence

as a teacher, I feel it only just to express my respect for his life

and regret for his death. He was a worthy adversary.

Countess D'Allessandro Ricci'

Praised by his arch enemy. I wonder how he would have taken this solitary tribute? I know. As an affront. Suspicious of her motivation, treating any approach as an attempt to put him off his guard, savage in retaliation for any real or imagined attack. How they fought on those occasions when I could not keep them apart! A matched pair of foes if ever there were, she the more subtle but he the more desperate, equal in anger. Words were weapons between them, the issue ever the same. Control. She could not resist commanding someone directly in her employ. Orders? He would only follow his own. She demanded deference. He deferred to no authority. For an uncommunicative man he was surprisingly adequate with speech, as brutally direct in his way as she was sharply cruel in hers.

At the last his style of combat prevailed. In the heat of battle, she would allow herself to fight like him, capitulating to his force of character to this degree. Then bad blood flowed between them. You could see faces flush with hatred for the other, exchanging accusations and suffering insults as demeaning as a slap across the cheek. No matter how late, my arrival on the scene was always timely because neither would back down until the other backed down first. So I would physically intrude myself between them like a barrier that allowed an honorable withdrawal on either side.

Why did she not fire him? Why did he not resign? In my belief because they truly loved to hate each other. They enjoyed the luxury of fighting against a 'worthy adversary' as the Countess termed it. One who neither could not defeat and one by whom each would not be defeated. After I came to this conclusion, I took their complaints to me about the other less to heart. At last I understood. The conflict that I feared would destroy my arrangement was actually keeping it together.

So someone else did care for Jan and was sensitive enough to acknowledge it to me. To my surprise, I confess. The Countess has never struck me as a considerate woman except when it would pay her way. For this disinterested expression, however, I felt grateful and wrote to tell her so. She has not referred to the matter again.

As for the rest of the world, there has not been one word of communication, not even from one single artist who, as you have given me to understand, 'endured' his teaching over the years. Alone! Alone! Alone! The man lived so alone! Once I asked Jan if I was his only friend. 'Yes.' I didn't mean now, I explained, I meant ever. 'Yes,' he repeated. I was the only one. 'All the others had been strangers.' Wasn't that lonely, I asked? 'Yes. Existence is lonely. Strangers provide escape.' Escaping loneliness with strangers, I wondered, didn't that make him feel lonelier still? 'Yes. When it was over.' However, in the forgetfulness of escape, no matter how dangerous or illicit, 'there was a vast momentary relief.'

A vast momentary relief. What a hard way to live, Kate, when life becomes insupportable without escape. Or perhaps not. Perhaps we all rely on one escape or another to buffer the harsh realities that bound and hound us.

Thank goodness I have your parents who, during this time, have acted the parent with me. I am so grateful for the gift of a second family. I only wish life had been as generous to poor Jan. He had so little. You could see this in the few effects he left behind. In a simple room, barely furnished, his worldly belongings were contained in a single suitcase. A change of clothes, expanding file for his beloved reproductions, a few toiletries, and one thing more wrapped in a time worn scrap of velvet cloth. So few were his possessions, this must have held great value to a man who valued little. For no eyes, but his own. He had never shared it with me.

Trespassing into his cherished privacy, I carefully opened his secret. It was a tattered catalogue of master drawings from the Windsor collection, the slim volume well cared for like a beloved bible. I thought there might be some tell tale dedication, but no. Only the elegant script of he who must have been the original owner, 'Father Emelio Bruch.' His refined signature struck me a trifle worldly for a humble servant of the church, yet who am I to judge? But here's another question. Who was this man? What place in Jan's history did he occupy? What part did he play? A churchman in the life of one who loathed all religion except religious art? How is it possible to know someone so well and not know him at all? To share so deeply and be kept in so much ignorance. No answer. The little catalogue I have saved for myself. The precious file of reproductions are yours. As he used them for inspiration and renewal, so may you.

Funeral? There was none. No ceremony. No point. Who would have cared to attend but myself? Yet I missed doing something to commemorate his death. It was Joanne who gave me the rights I needed. 'Publish an obituary' she suggested. 'Notify the world about his loss.' So I have. Here's what I wrote. As close to the truth as I could get

'To Whom It May Concern.

A Teacher died today. Janovar Savocek, exact age, parentage, place of birth unknown, forsook his work as incurable disease accomplished what great personal adversity could not, defeating his will to do what he did best.

He is survived by many artists who, while they may not grieve his loss, shall not forget the principles for which he stood:

Only teach about what you passionately care;

Model through teaching the total commitment to work

you expect from your students;

Set standards of excellence by using great exemplars from the past;

Never evaluate how well students have done, only cause

them to appreciate what they have learned to do;

Challenge students with lessons of increasing difficulty

until they are driven to declare independence of your instruction;

Do not diminish caring for what you teach by coming to care

for those whom you teach.

From a friend who mourns the passing of a friend.'

I love you, Kate. I count the days 'til your return.

Kip

Chapter Twenty-Four
HARD INSTRUCTION

Although not usually threatened by adult authority, having like many only children grown up peering with her parents and considering herself their equal, Kate was intimidated by Savocek. Because she disliked the feeling, she did not like the man. Although the Countess clearly meant to rule her relationships and so was easy to resist, opposing Savocek was a different matter. Resisting him kept ending up by Kate resisting herself. It was extremely frustrating. She didn't want to obey his instruction, but she didn't want to deprive herself of its benefits either.

The ambivalence was maddening, as was the trick he played upon her again and again. She didn't understand how it worked, each time feeling trapped anew into doing what he wanted because she had come to want it to. Against her will, she did his bidding unable to withstand the temptation of growth he kept casting in her way. It felt like being preceded through life by someone who knew what she needed next before she did herself.

Not that he understood <u>her</u> at all, or cared to. It was her drawing and the process through which it could develop that he knew better than she, able to sense what exercise or problem would create a particular challenge that, if she mastered it, could test her capacity thereby increasing it. As an apprentice would fear her sorcerer, so she feared him. Attracted to his greater power, assimilating bits of it through lessons that he taught, yet by comparison always learning how inferior her own poor power was.

Several months passed before she mustered courage to speak honestly to him. She wanted to declare her reluctance at being there, so he would appreciate the effort she was making and soften his treatment of her accordingly. It was on a Friday evening, after he had finished reviewing her week's work, when she chose to confess her discontent.

"Mr. Savocek, I want you to know I did not ask to be your student."

"I have no students. I only work with artists."

"I did not ask to be your artist, then."

"No? So why are you here?"

"Because my father and particularly my uncle want me to learn from you. While my mother makes me come."

"Makes?"

"Yes. Forces me against my will."

If it was sympathy Kate wanted, she could see it was the very opposite she was provoking.

"You are made to attend?"

"That's right."

"No. That is wrong. You are not <u>made</u> to be here. You cannot even imagine the forces that can truly overpower human will. You are choosing to come here because if you don't something you like worse will happen between you and your mother at home."

Affronted at having her petition dismissed, only partially heard, Kate's natural stubbornness rose to her defense.

"Even so, I didn't freely choose to study with you."

"No. Nor did I freely elect to be your teacher. I only insisted on it after being forbidden your instruction."

Despite having already been told this by the Countess, Kate was shocked to hear it plainly stated by her teacher. Why would he not want to accept her on her own merits?

"I don't understand."

"I will not be dictated to. You are here as an example for someone else to see."

"What about my talent?"

"What about it?"

Kate was afraid to ask her next question but more afraid not to.

"Don't I have enough talent for you to accept me?"

"You have talent."

"But not enough?"

Savocek shook his head wearily.

"You have enough talent, but talent is not enough. It never is."

Now Kate was truly lost.

"What more do I need? What more do you want from me?"

"I? I want nothing from you. You have been too talented too long, and too often told so, to even conceive of the question you are not asking."

Despite the offense she had taken at not being wanted, Savocek's allusion to ignorance caused her to become curious about what she lacked.

"Go on," she continued.

Now Savocek eyed her with interest, as though glimpsing some possibility he had not noticed before.

"All right. Talent is everywhere. The world is littered with great talent come to nothing. In your case, you have been spoiled. Why have you drawn all these years? Because you love to."

"Is that a wrong reason?"

"It is not wrong if drawing is only to be an avocation, a pastime pursued for pure enjoyment. However, I do not teach hobbyists. I teach artists -- people who commit to work not simply for love, which is easy, but because it is a matter of ultimate concern. Anyone can do what they love so long as love lasts. Like depending work on inspiration. What happens when enthusiasm fades, when love grows weary without infatuation to make it easy? What happens when creative work is reduced to a tedious grind? What happens then? Nothing. Work stops. Other diversions, other pleasures call."

Kate felt obliged to defend herself.

"How old do you think I am?" she asked indignantly in hopes the answer would excuse her loving motivation to draw, while impressing Savocek with what she had accomplished so young.

"You want to tell me?"

"Yes," proudly, "fourteen."

"And what does this signify to you, this 'fourteen'?"

"That my talent, however I have chosen to develop it, is advanced for my age."

"So. You measure your talent by your years. Never mind it is not how early you begin or how fast you develop, but the quality of what you produce at the end that counts. Never mind. This is good. You disagree with me. But suppose I humbled you. Would you be able to speak up for yourself even then?"

"I <u>always</u> speak up for myself," this spoken honestly.

"Very well. Would you like to know what precocious talent looks like?   I warn you, having once seen it estimation of your own capacities will be altered."

"I am not afraid," she answered. But she was.

"Then come over here."

He opened a closet door. On the inside, stacked against the wall, were three large black portfolios. On the first one her name was boldly printed. On the others, the names she had noticed on the outside of the classroom door: 'Joel Tate' and 'Ira Gilner.' These were the two other students with whom she shared this space, had not met and probably would not since their schedules apparently did not adjoin her own. And because Savocek believed in the solitary, not the social, nature of creative work. Why he demanded his artists draw in isolation and not in group.

"First we shall look at a drawing by Mr. Joel Tate."

From the file of papers Savocek withdrew a single sheet and held it up to Kate for examination. She gasped, not prepared for the virtuosity that startled her eyes.

It was an abundant landscape executed entirely in pencil, although Kate had to keep reminding herself of this fact because she had never seen a single instrument produce such a profusion of unusual techniques, each natural component rendered with a texture uniquely its own. What came to mind were those centuries old graphic formulas developed in the East to portray natural variety, the great Japanese tableaus Kip had introduced her to at his museum years ago.

Except this artist, Tate, had created conventions of his own through which the composition and structure of each substance was uniquely depicted. Bark was not leaf, leaf was not grass, grass was not flower, each flower had its own distinctive interpretation. Sky was partly clear and partly cloud and partly in between. Stream was reflection, surface, current, and depth. Water was still, and smoothly flowing, and turbulent. Even the difference between wet rocks underwater and dry rocks on the bank was clearly communicated. All with a single pencil! Kate was awed by technical possibilities of which she had not conceived, much less ever tried herself. Such stylistic diversity unified into a single composition. Or was it unified? Stepping back, she was not sure that concentration on the parts did not detract from design of the whole.

"He captures surfaces and substance like I've never seen." Kate was truly impressed.

"A remarkable display, is it not? I myself have rarely seen the like. Next week he shall be instructed to render with pencil four balls identical in all respects but composition -- one brass, one steel, one silver and one gold. The drawing must unmistakably communicate the metal of which each is made. Can it be done? I don't know. But I am prepared to be surprised. An insidious talent, technique. A marvelous servant, but a dangerous master, hard to keep in its proper place. So tempting to let cleverness become an end in itself. Every gift has its dangerous side. Would you like to see any others? No? Then on to the work of Mr. Ira Gilner."

From a second portfolio Savocek extracted the next example. This time Kate did not want to look. Having already seen too much of what another student could accomplish that she could not, she lacked desire to see any more. Feeling compared and found wanting, she found herself resentful of Tate and Gilner for creating a competition in which she was the loser, hence the inferior. Easier to be the only student than one among many.

Patiently Savocek held the drawing where she could view it when she chose, recognizing her aversion to doing so, watching her fight against and finally overcome this reluctance.   Sucking in a deep breath to fortify herself, Kate turned to face her next accuser. She was amazed, flooded with admiration for what she saw. A single human figure it was, so brightly illuminated from front and back the absence of any possibility of shadow should have flattened the subject out, yet the figure was not flat. She looked more closely. No shading because there was no variation in light to play with. Yet the figure's volume was retained. At last, at a loss, she asked:

"How is the sense of mass achieved?"

"Examine the delineation of the shape, the quality of line itself."

Carefully now Kate scrutinized the single uninterrupted pencil stroke which confidently defined the standing body. The outline was not as it had first appeared, of uniform intensity and width. Rather it was modulated for calculated effect. In some passages it was bold and hard, in others gossamer and faint. Thick here and thin to disappearing there, capturing minimal but sufficient variation in light to create the illusion of roundness, while brightness of light itself was another illusion produced by varying darkness of the line. Kate was astounded. At last she looked away and back at Savocek.

"Yes," he replied, amplifying on her thoughts. "It is the visual artist's constant challenge. How to source and manage light. Of course, contrast is the answer. To have light one must have shade, while by creating shade light becomes apparent. A simple principle with endless variations requiring years of study to discover. Rembrandt was the master of light in Western art. Gilner here, precocious for his years. See how instinctively he grasps the interplay of light and mass. As for the problem of simultaneous illumination, this was mine. The solution his. How I instruct, by creating visual problems. Solve them and you will move beyond what you could do before. Do you wish to see any more?"

No. Kate did not. Admiration for what she had seen had emptied appreciation for herself.. In discouragement she sought to restore her diminished pride, bravely declaring:

"Well, perhaps when I am their age I shall excel as they do now."

Savocek shook his head.

"That cannot be."

"Why not?"

"You will never be their age. Tate is ten. Gilner eleven."

If Savocek had hit her forcefully in the midsection he could not have winded her more completely. In shock, in disbelief she stared at him as though she had just received such a blow. Not doubled over, but she was bent, her broad shoulders hunched forward to shelter pain where some part of her spirit had been badly bruised. Gradually she came to recognize where the injury was. In her confidence.   Feeling bereft of its support, Kate gazed at her tormentor in anguish. Impassively he waited. For what? What more did he want?

Gathering her strength, Kate straightened up.

"I must be going. It's over time. She will be worried. Mr. Savocek, you accepted me under protest. Now you have shown me younger students who are truly gifted with skills I lack. I didn't want to study with you before, but I was willing. Now I am not. Whatever the consequences may be at home."

"Good."

"You are glad to be rid of me then?"

"No. Good you have reached this point of determination. Now we can get down to work."

Kate looked at him in utter bewilderment.

"I thought you didn't want to teach me."

"I didn't."

"But you do now? Why?"

"Because you have been willing to confront in Tate and Gilner the kinds of draftsmen you are not capable of becoming yourself. Yet despite whatever inadequacy and doubt this aroused, you fully credited their work. You were able to esteem them for capacities you do not possess."

"To do otherwise would be a lie. I do not lie."

"Everyone lies. That is how they live with themselves. However, you do not lie by denying the merit of other artists. This is the point.

You can learn from what you see even when it hurts. Now, are you ready for one final artist? It will take all your honesty and sensitivity because of the three, this is the hardest one to see."

Wrung out of energy to do other than she was told, Kate limply agreed.

"Another of your artists?" she asked.

"Yes."

"Gifted too?" She hated to hear the answer.

"Yes. Are you ready to respond?"

"I will try." She braced herself.

"What do you think of this?" He held up yet another drawing.

She looked at it, then looked at him.

"Why do you do this to me?" She felt humiliated.

"Because it is time you became familiar with this work. I give you the artist, Kate Germaine!"

It was too much. Strength to stand unsupported fell away. She collapsed back against the wall. Shoulders slumped, she stared at the drawing Savocek had withdrawn from the third portfolio, hers. She remembered the assignment. 'Create a group of dancing figures with the most important one missing.' At the time she felt he was posing her a riddle, asking her to imply the presence she was omitting. Anticipating her question he had answered before she had asked. 'A shadow is not a permissible solution.' Angry at being given a puzzle for an assignment, she had grudgingly done as he had requested, with additional ill will because she hated dancing.

"Look at the drawing. Look well."

It was a disappointment. Evaluating her pencil technique and use of light she found the first limited and the second undistinguished compared to possibilities she had just been shown. Her presentation was blunt and to the point. Two women circling to their left, one hand clasped in each other's, the leading woman reaching forward as though holding another's hand in front while the following woman was reaching back clasping the forward hand of an invisible third partner behind, implying the full circle that they made.

"Well?" demanded the teacher.

Having no desire to itemize specific deficiencies in her performance, Kate made a general confession:

"It is inferior in quality to the other drawings you have shown me."

"Yes it is. If you choose to compete with the other two and compare yourself to them. Is that what you want? To be as good or better than Tate or Gilner at what they already do so well?"

"You have made it clear I can't do what they can."

"No you can't. But is that what you want?" The question came like a hammer, repeatedly beating down what was left of her esteem.

"Yes!" she finally admitted, just to get the hammering to stop.

But it would not stop.

"Is that what you <u>really</u> want?"

His relentless questioning offered her yet one more opportunity to restate her ambition. Was the man deaf to what she had already said? One more time then. Slowly, clearly, deliberately so there would be no mistake:

"No! I don't want to be better than them. I just want to be myself!"

What did she say? She appealed to him, confused. Savocek seemed to relax, and she realized how tightly wound he had become. The interrogation must have been wearing on him as well. Why? It was her work, not his. Or was it? Instruction was his work, and he could not do this without her. She needed him as a teacher, but he needed her as a student. They were bound in this way. For however long both wanted. For the fist time, she felt he desired to teacher her if, if what? If she was teachable was the answer that occurred. So she asked:

"What do you wish me to learn?"

"How competition creates resemblance. How comparison, even when favorable, demeans one's work by judging it according to the merits or flaws of another. To be as good or better than Tate or Gilner, you must become like them and submit to being evaluated on their terms. Is that what you want? No, you answer. Because through competition and comparison, individuality is lost, and of all my artists, this loss would hurt you the most. Because it is from your uniqueness that you have most to gain."

"You mean my drawing with both hands?" This was the only uniqueness Kate could identify at the moment.

"Immaterial. One hand, two hands, three hands, what difference? Only the drawing matters. Not how it is done. The hands are simply disciplined to do what they are told."

Sudden sadness swept over Kate as Savocek consigned her hands to simple servitude. Not even the slightest tremor of protest did she feel from either her left or right. Submission was complete. There was a pang of loneliness for lost companionship, and then she let it go.

"What is my uniqueness?" she asked.

"The most difficult kind for me to instruct. Originality. You will never attain the technical magic of Tate or the subtle mastery with which Gilner handles light. However, in conception and design, they are not gifted with your power of invention. A difficult gift, originality. Hard for others to understand because they have no reference. Hard to teach for the same reason. Unlike the other two, you have managed to escape the orthodoxy of education to which they have fallen victim. Now: look at your drawing with me. See how the space is organized. The dancing thrust of the two figures up and to the left is counterbalanced by emptiness in the lower right. How? Because you have made vacancy into a presence. Design implies the missing figure so dynamically the circle is complete, the dance goes round and round, the viewer's eye returning to the mysterious third dancer whose invisible company anchors the entire composition. This assignment would make no sense to Tate or Gilner, but to you it did. Why?"

Reflecting on the question, images of ancient Sung landscapes floated back to mind, panoramas where the hint of mountains and trees shrouded in mist were suggested just enough to suggest the larger natural presence the was not rendered.

"My uncle calls it 'the art of omission'. In the Chinese collection, he loves them best. They are my favorites too," she explained.

Savocek nodded. So that was where she learned to appreciate the art of leaving out.

"The trick was well learned. You took from others without giving up freedom in return."

"Is this the trick of learning from teachers too?" She had never questioned him so sharply before.

"See. Now you interrogate me. Good. It is beginning. You must become your own authority at last. Until then, I shall dictate your instruction. Why you do not want to study with me. But you have already learned too much not to want to learn more."

He was infuriatingly correct. She wanted and did not want to be there. This would never change.

"How long am I to draw with you?"

"Until you are ready to leave."

"How is this decided?"

"By your feelings. You will reach a point where you cannot take it any more."

Now it was Kate who pushed for an answer. There had to be an easier ending than this.

"I want another way to know."

"There is none. When you can bear my instruction no longer, you shall leave to become your own teacher. Rebellion shall drive you out. You shall not look fondly back on our time together. We shall argue. I will insist you are not ready to leave, that you have more to learn, that I have more to teach. We shall part badly. In anger, you will claim your independence. Your freedom, so you shall think. But I will not be so easy to get rid of. You shall take me away within you. In the discipline you will have learned. In the eye you have developed. In your understanding of yourself as an artist. Always you shall remain partly under my instruction. That is my satisfaction. Through you, my contribution shall carry on!"

Kate was sane enough to recognize the ravings of a crazy man when she heard them. Having pushed Savocek into prophesy, she realized she had pushed him too far, exposing this grandiose ambition. Far from frightening her, however, this vision of instability beneath a rigid purpose was a relief, giving her permission to accept her own frailty as well. If he could have flaws as a teacher, she could have flaws as an artist. What her first impression had suggested later experience now confirmed. For all the power and rigor of his instruction, he was a peculiar man.

From the outset Savocek, appeared to possess the emaciated vitality of a fanatic. So devoted to creativity of the mind, he appeared to neglect needs of his body. And this zealous regard and disregard extended into his teaching of her. Just as he ignored his own physical needs, so he was oblivious of hers. Four to seven o'clock each day after school with no excused absences, be she sick or laden down with homework, he expected total concentration. That she could be tired or dispirited or hungry from a full day of classes never entered his thinking enough to alter the standard of dedication he demanded.

As he drove her, so she learned to drive herself, gradually increasing self-discipline and endurance, unaware that in addition to providing instruction, Savocek also had her in training, conditioning her for the long haul of the artist's life to come. By sheer force of his commitment, he increased her own. And when, at the end of each week, he would review with her what she had completed those five days she would see without fail this evidence of growth and feel her effort had been justified.

It was both fascinating and frightening to be around Savocek's intensity. From his caring, Kate felt her own passion for art aroused. In his presence, she loved drawing more than she ever had, although she did not tell him that for fear he would respond with scorn as he did once before. She worked primarily alone. There, in the solitude of her studio, drawing was all there was, all there needed to be, all that mattered. Life was reduced to herself, her pencils, a blank sheet of paper, and what happened between them. Yet despite her absorption, she could not help but feel intimidated by is supervision, long for approval he never gave, work even harder in the vain hope she might attain it, and dread his reprimand should she fall below the standard of commitment he believed serious artistic purpose required. It was easy to become disheartened by such oppressive education except she knew what he wanted from her was no more than she wanted from herself. Not excellence, but effort.

"Because you have talent, excellence is easy. This is why talent is cheap and why it is easy to cheat on talent. The more talent you are given, the harder you must work. Practice and challenge: these are the masters you must serve. I speak for them now, so you will learn to follow them later. When you are on your own."

No let up. No encouragement. No praise. No wonder, sometimes, discouragement could not be avoided. There came periods when she lost sight of what she was there to do, where she was going, losing faith in what she could accomplish, even knowing that she was accomplishing. Do what she might, exert what power of will she could command, energy would drain away, spirit would flag.   Her posture would change.   The vital tension normally held between her broad shoulders would slacken, and they would begin to slump.   This was Savocek's cue.   He knew to watch for it, and never failed to pick it up.   Brusquely he would interrupt her with the directive that, in later years, she would use upon herself:

"Stop.   You need to be reminded of what great drawing is all about."

Heaving a sigh, she would set paper and pencils aside to make room for the reproductions to follow.   Photographs of old master drawings he would reverently place before her, silently at first, as much it seemed for his continuing edification as for her own.   Saying nothing, he let the marvels of great draftsmanship shine into her eyes, the light of genius reaching into that secret place where he knew inspiration grew.   Watching her enthusiasm grow, he pointed out fresh subtleties for her to admire, stimulating her appreciation and desire until her fire to draw, which had momentarily been extinguished, would ignite again.

"The greatest teachers are all dead.   Or are they?" he would ask as the great examples proved irresistible to Kate once more.   The glories of the past became incentives in the present if only she would stop wasting time and get back to work.

No longer able to contain her impatience she would stop his teasing:

"Enough! I've seen enough. Let me alone!"

Obediently Savocek, would collect his reproductions and quietly retire while Kate, absorbed in a new drawing, would not even notice him go. Each time he did this for her, performed this miracle of resurrection, bringing her dying spirit back to life, she would appreciate anew the power of inspiration that Old Masters could provide. Preserved so their voices could be kept alive, they spoke to her across centuries, recalling her back to her own love of creation, exciting her to go forward.

To draw.

Chapter Twenty-Five
THE FUNERAL

Dearest Kip--

On receiving it, I read your letter over many times, each time wanting the meaning to sink deeper in so I could share with you your depth of loss. At last, deeper I reached, but not where I sought or expected, arriving at a cause for sorrow I did not know I had, releasing tears I could not stop from flowing. For who? For Savocek? For you? For me? For what?

It felt more like bleeding than crying. Your letter cut to an untended injury of mine, pried me open, revealing a wound I had inflicted on myself. Perhaps this letter back can help me in the healing that I need. Some has already been done. Some has been done for you. It was this way.

All afternoon, I lay in my small room weeping as much in bewilderment as in pain I could not fathom. Gradually feelings calmed and confusion began to clear. I thought of you. The double loss you have sustained. The blow that severed you from Savocek also cut off that part of you no longer shared with him. I felt sorrow for never coming to like the teacher whom you grew to love. My lack of devotion to him keeps me from adequately grieving with you now.

Emotional distance from him and physical distance from you, have both caused separation when I wish we could be close. I'm sorry for that. And while I'm grateful Joanne and Galen are there to support you, I feel guilty I am not. Your news brings home to me the self-absorption of my exile here. In pursuit of advancement, I have abandoned those I love and have left behind. I know you do not fault my absence. However, I do. Where is your Kate during this time of need?

Tears of remorse. They must have betrayed my desolation and explained my absence from the studio when I came late to the kitchen table that night. How I looked was how I felt. Stricken. Compelling all three to violate the usual privacy we give each other and search my face for explanation. Unable to answer their concern in words, I resorted to mime.

Lifting the long warm loaf of bread from its basket I pulled it to my heart, beloving it, then extended it arms length, sadly broke it in two, and laid it gently back to rest in its wicker casket, the small ceremony flushing fresh sorrow from my eyes. They understood. Death had paid me a visit, taking some of my life away. I could not eat. They did not either, but sat in silence waiting while I waited, not knowing what I waited for. An agony of time crept by. In vain I sought some sense beneath my turmoil to guide me toward what must happen next.

Galen was right long ago when he told me I was a doer like himself, not a reflector like Joanne. For me, the solution is taking action. I scanned the faces facing mine. Jesus is impassive, Marcella resonant with pain, and Riablo is tense with expectation. To the Master's energy I fastened in hope. Either his own impatience or mine would break the paralysis of grief with the movement we could follow.

He did not fail me. Struck with a sudden idea, he started up, reached forward, and tilted the great earthen pot with one hand, sliding the other underneath smudging it with soot. Lowering the pot he rubbed two fingers into the palette of his blackened palm and stepped over to Jesus, that man who is surprised by nothing in this world, perpetually at peace with what comes next.

Kip, you wrote there was no funeral because none but yourself would attend. No. There _was_ a funeral for Savocek. It was the least I could do for him, the most I could do for you, and the start of what I needed to do for myself.

Riablo began the beginning of the ceremony. In this house where language is unspoken, actions become the medium through which meaning is conveyed. My bearing and expression were sufficient. Stiff from a long afternoon of crying, the muscles of my face felt cramped and set into a facade of affliction that I could not remove even though my weeping had subsided.

It was to this design of my features that Riablo responded. Standing before the seated Jesus as he would before an easel, Riablo lifted the musician's head and proceeded to draw his blackened fingertips across the upturned face. What he created was an actor portrait, oriental in execution, a mask painted on a face to catch a certain attitude, in this case of devastation from human loss.

How to give you a picture of that altered face when you do not know the face itself? How to help you appreciate the change a mask can make. In repose, the only guise I've ever seen Jesus assume, the man appears expressionless. The lines of his mouth neither draw up nor down. His eyebrows neither raise nor furrow. There are no wrinkles etched across his forehead. His face is smooth and unconcerned as a child's. His eyes always half opened or half closed, attentive and yet dreamy, a balance of inner and outer states that reflects a temperament not easily upset.

Of the three, he has been the least knowable because his disposition seems so invariant. Light changes daily, weather alters, seasons pass him by, yet he remains the same. Anchored to himself by some connection that is fixed and flexible, he accepts the larger rhythms of existence as if they were his own. Perhaps they are. To the world, his face communicates no affect beyond content. Stoic? Yes. And no. It is no stoic who plays the pipes with such range and depth of feeling. Through music, he channels his inner aspects out.

Who better to paint than one whose face appears so vacant? Why the Master selected him. Darkening the sockets to enlarge the eyes, bereaving their expression by drawing down the mouth, Riablo reconfigured the entire face into an incarnation of human grief. Through those hollow eyes and gaping lips I saw and heard the loss of Savocek for you, of you for him, of your loss begetting mine. Emptied of tears, but still full of feeling, I wanted to do more. But what? Instinct came to my rescue. Gesturing to Riablo, I pointed to my own face. He understood.

On his way around the table he stopped to freshen his palette hand with soot and then stood above me gazing down less as he would at a person than at some pliable material he was about to fashion to his will. Looking up, my eyes were blasted by his concentration. Like staring into the sun, except I did not avert my gaze, determined to accept whatever alteration his hands designed. Although his fingers burned lines and sculpted hollows into my face to which I was blind, my skin, my surface memory, shall not forget the mask that was inlaid. And while the ocean has since removed the external traces, my features have not felt the same.

When he was done, his drawing hand fell limply to his side as he appraised its work. Whatever he beheld seemed to satisfy because he withdrew to his seat. Shifting around in mine, I turned toward Marcella who was leaning forward eager to discover what the Master had made of me. Her mouth dropped. A cry of disbelief escaped her lips.   She clapped her hands then reached for mine squeezing with such force of consolation I had to squeeze with equal strength or else been crushed with comfort.   She was smiling as she sobbed.   What manner of mask was I wearing?   What mix from me was causing such a mixed response from her, a grip of solace and a clap of triumph?   As wearer of the mask, I was concealed from seeing what I wore.   No matter.   Emboldened by the face upon my face, I chose the role to which I felt entitled: Chief mourner.

Leading us outside, I placed us in procession. Myself first, Marcella next in line hands upon my shoulders, then Riablo likewise attached to her, we three the bearers of Savocek's loss, Jesus following with music to lead us on. A slow canon of solemn notes he played, the melody finishing where it began to start again, over and over, rising and falling into itself, a dirge for us to carry my old teacher to his final rest.

A carrying dance we did, and a heavy weight it was. Not the weight of the man, but of his lot in life. What a weary weight! Supporting it caused me to feel how laden with suffering was the life I bore. And I had two others to share the load, while he upheld it all alone.   From side to side we swayed, our backs bent, staggering forward from one faltering step to the next. A slow progress we made, laborious and exhausting, out to the bluff and over, down the path by now familiar, keeping to the unquickening music, fighting the pull which steepness made upon our legs. Obeying and resisting gravity, we were determined to descend at our own reverent pace, deliberate with care, finally reaching the rubble of rocks on the flattened shore. The footing more treacherous, stumble added to stagger, as we struggled to keep our brother aloft, until stones gave way to sand, sand to beach, and beach at last to sea.

By water's edge we stopped. Almost low tide. The turn still to be taken. Barely any waves. Scarcely a ripple, breeze, or sound. Only the lingering remains of subsiding swells, wafer thin sheets of water overlaid on one another, lapping up and giving up and pulling back, the mild respiration of a gentle sea.

In unison, we halted while the ocean gradually withdrew from where we stood, planting our feet like pillars into the liquid sand. As I dropped to my knees, so did the others, all of us as one, laying whom we carried down. Freed from the physical oppression of his weight a sense of lightness levitated me, while I could see the other two welcoming a similar relief. I could see them clearly because this night the moon, although not full, shone with a searching power that exposed every detail of ourselves and our surroundings. Not a bright light, but an extremely invasive one, cool and noticing, devoid of daytime color, the sea a wash of silver, every other earthly thing a shade of brilliant gray.

So here we were where I intended. But what did I intend? Something I wanted. Something beyond delivering his spirit to the ocean that has come to matter so to me. Then I noticed the music had ceased, my three companions having wandered away. Stooping over, I extracted a shard of broken shell from where it lay embedded and, because it was a shape he much admired, drew a large oval on the sand for Savocek to occupy. However slightly, I wanted to draw attention to the human spirit that had been lost. On such a night, I knew the moon would see my faint delineation with her unblinking eye.

Loud breathing coming up behind me, I glanced around to find Marcella lugging a load of rocks, large like the ones she uses to enclose her gardens. Carefully, she laid them on the line that I had drawn, beginning the foundation of a wall, urgently beckoning for me to help her with this task. I followed quickly. We didn't have much time before the tide reclaimed the land it had forsaken.

Heavy work it was. Trip after trip we made, up the beach to gather rocks, back down to lay the oval wall, back up again, no pausing, moving faster when the sound of waves told us the turn was taken and the ocean closing in. My arms were spent, my shoulders ached, the muscles in my thighs quivered from the strain. My body begged to stop, but my mind would not listen. In this part of the ceremony, I had become indentured to Marcella. I was hers to order, and she ordered by untiring example.

Taller the wall grew until an enclosure was contrived, a stone building of some kind circumscribing a special place in which a spirit might peacefully dwell before passing on. This will sound strange, even profane, yet it felt like she and I were erecting a sanctuary of some kind to enshrine this unbelieving man. The walls of our church were sufficient because the roof was already in place. Overhead was an enormous vault of blackened sky, candlelit by stars.

With my last load of stones, I evened out the church's walls. My part felt done.

Then Jesus, who must have been biding his time, stepped forward from behind me and with a tremendous downward thrust harpooned into the sand a long wooden pole, a broken spar or mast, stripped of rigging, the survivor of some shipwrecked

sailing boat. Affixed to the top, was a stiffened piece of tar-stained cloth, tattered but in tact, a rudimentary flag of victory and defeat.

Standing together, he and I and Marcella watched the water advancing, no more than ten or fifteen minutes left before it would begin undoing what we had done when, frantically gesturing us back, from out of nowhere leapt Riablo a pointed stick clutched in his right hand. Turning his back to us and crouching down he began sidling crab-like, engraving in the sand at first a single stem then curling tendrils clinging to the ground. A vine was winding around what we had made, a creeping plant to ornament the crude architecture we had built with a growth of leaves and flowers to adorn the cloistered walls. Although used to watching Riablo work, I had never seen him draw so swiftly, racing the immanent destruction of what he was creating.

The beginning of the end came with less warning than we expected. Instead of sheets of water gently overtaking one another up the beach, a single wave attacked our small cathedral. Rolling in with breaking force, it breached the lower wall, flooded the interior, drenched the four of us and, as the wave receded, thoroughly obliterated the fragile decoration that had been drawn. Then all was lost as even larger waves continued the assault.

Retreating before this onslaught the others headed for the bluff, back to the house to rest. Scrambling up a boulder with seaweed sides, however, I chose to stay and see the ceremony through. The mood of the ocean had changed. What she had peacefully let go, she was repossessing with a temper. The sky grew dark, smudges of clouds distancing the moon and dimming its light.

A rising wind urged the tide to shore. Still, my eyes never strayed from the temple of Savocek's remembrance. Completely covered now, the flag kept lowering as the ocean rose until I was marooned and the flag waved no more. Still I marked the place, ignoring the water crashing about me until it calmed as the tide began to change its mind. Having its fill of land it now decided to abandon the shallow for the deep, undertowing down the beach any debris that would be pulled along, wiping the sand smooth, removing the vestiges of our labor to who knows where?

Swept away, Kip, but not destroyed. Scattered, the dismembered remains thrown up on another beach or tumbled deeper out to sea. Departed, but not gone because what has been created cannot be destroyed. Only altered. Gone, yet still with us. Like Savocek. Still in you. Still in me. Still in his reluctant students. Still even in the Countess, his beloved enemy, he remains. In how he affected us. In the history we shared. In what we remember. In what we do not.

And when we are scattered in our turn, that part of him that is part of us shall be dispersed once more. We are like links in a chain connecting us to our inheritance, to us and through us and to others so long as someone, anyone, is left to carry on. This is not a matter of choice. I carry his influence, much of it hidden in places I shall never discover. Nor appreciate. He gave so harshly it has been hard to value the gifts for duress of the giving. I do so now. May he rest in peace. And may I make peace with what he taught me: that a dedicated artist never rests.

How he kept my eye on the horizon. No matter what possibilities I conceived, he was always finding others to fulfill. New ideas to follow. New challenges to master. New problems to solve. 'There is no end, is there?' I once asked, wishing I could limit the terms of my commitment. He surprised me. 'Yes,' he answered. 'There is an end. When the brush becomes too heavy. The hand too feeble. The will too tired. When excitement is lost. When stamina declines from want of use. When giving up feels easier than keeping on. When the last picture has been finished because there is no interest in creating any more. That is the end.' I remember wishing I hadn't asked. How he was, unsympathetic and unyielding and instructive. Even now.

I wasn't going to add this, but I shall, though it puts a selfish ending on a letter meant to comfort you.   News of the death of Savocek has made me heart and mindful of those dreadful losses that even as I write are gradually approaching.   Losses, uninvited and unwelcome, that I know shall one day visit me.   Of Galen, of Joanne, of yourself.   My three supports upon whom I've relied for constancy at home, more so since being here.   While anger drove me to exchange that place for this, it was love from all of you that let me go.   Assurance of your indestructible presence and devotion gave me the strength of independence to leave.

Then came your letter and my world of security came tumbling down.   Death happens. Love is no protection.   Disease carries Savocek away.   You are bereft.   Your world diminished.   My world shakes and is diminished too.   Although unbeloved, he was part of me and mine.   Savocek dies, and you and Galen and Joanne and, yes, even the Countess become mortal.   And I am troubled by this question: what <u>really</u> matters?

Two years.   Time we could have spent together I have appropriated for my selfish use.   How I have been indulged is how I've come to indulge myself.   Being put first, I have put myself foremost.   Kip, I have received out of proportion to what I have given.   I have not credited the sacrifice of others on my behalf, but have taken those gifts for granted, as my due.   Worse, I have repaid in anger those who gave most beneficially.   The thankless gifts of getting me to do what I did not want, of telling me what I did not want to hear.

I <u>showed</u> them, Joanne and the Countess.   For betraying how I wanted them to be, I punished in return.   Scorning their efforts at reconciliation I justified my spite by feeling wronged.   Then Savocek dies, and with him righteousness of how I have behaved.   Here's a question, Kip. If I knew Joanne or the Countess were going to die tomorrow, would I want to cherish toward them anger that I feel today? Would it satisfy to know I had remained revengeful and resentful to the last? Is that the knowledge I want them to carry to their deaths? Is that how I want to live? Oh Kip, I never wanted permanent estrangement, only to show them hurt for hurting me. But what magnitude of hurt would they and I experience if how things are between us is how things ended now?

What, after all, if they did <u>not</u> betray me? What if I betrayed myself? True, they failed to live up to my standards, but it was I who set the standards that they failed. Who am I, Kip? Who do I think I am? Some perfect person? Some ideal friend and daughter that they should be ideal friend and mother in return? Who am I to dictate how they should live, faulting them when they violate my expectations? See how your friend's death has made a shambles of my selfish world. A shambles of confusion and regret.

Suppose none of us are perfect nor were meant to be? Only a mix of good and bad, of strength and frailty, of wisdom and stupidity no matter how we try. Kip, I am frightened by the error of my unforgiving ways. I have put so much I care about at risk. All those irreplaceable relationships that once gone, are gone forever. Kip: keep yourself safe 'til my return. Tell Galen. Tell the Countess. Tell Joanne. Tell them all. Promise me you will. I have had death enough. Life is too short to spend it staying angry.

I love you,

Kate.

Chapter Twenty-Six
THE COUNTESS FINDS A WAY

The Countess was troubled. And when the Countess was troubled, LaValle experienced the effects. With him, she would intimate distress which from anyone else she would conceal. In this case, LaValle could feel her agitation. The electricity of her impatience with a frustrating problem amply conveyed her charged state of mind.

"To business as usual, Elena, or do you wish to clear the air first? Myself, I would prefer to discuss our transactions free from the influence of your irritation. At what?"

"Not only do you put up with me, LaValle, but you penetrate my disguise."

"Pretenses have no place between two such old acquaintances as you and I, Elena.   Knowing this, you lower your guard with me. Which I appreciate. A gesture of ---"

"Of nothing more than habit, LaValle, of nothing more than that. Please, let us not resurrect the tired old topic that no discouragement from me seems able to discourage in you."

"As you wish. Now tell me, what is so pressing it interferes between a woman of business and business at hand?"

"The girl."

"The Germaine girl?"

"Who else? What other would I mean? I won't have it, LaValle. Next year she's going to study at the University. I tell you, I won't have it. She has a scholarship to study Studio Art. No. This won't do!"

"Why not?"

"Because I want something more for her than education."

"Is this decision not usually between the child and the parents?"

"When was I ever content with the 'usual', LaValle? No. Ordinary paths only lead to ordinary destinations. If you and I had followed ordinary paths, where would we be today? The exceptional opportunity is what I want for her. Some experience that could empower her artistically beyond what any mere university could teach."

LaValle took time to consider what the Countess was saying.

"Yes. Too bad the old etalier system is no longer in place. Or Ruben's painting factory. Through diplomatic channels you might have arranged to place her there. If the Old Masters were still alive. If they were apprenticing aspiring artists. If---"

" 'Ifs' offer no practical solutions, LaValle, only conditions that cannot be met. Come now. Of all people you, with your myriad connections, should be able to provide the opening I seek."

"There are always art schools and academies in other countries."

"Be it here or there, a school is still a school. She has been schooled enough. After three years with that petty tyrant Savocek, her tolerance for further instruction is exhausted. Even she is not enthusiastic about attending the University. Following her parents and her uncle through there is its greatest recommendation, I believe. Well: is this what you are telling me? There is no extraordinary alternative available?"

"What magic do you wish me to perform, Elena?" and he paused long enough to capture her full attention. Then, as though he were becoming impatient with her impatience, he shrugged and appeared to make a throw away suggestion. "Send her to study with the last surviving modern master. Send her to study with Riablo. Is this the kind of fantasy you would have me suggest?"

"LaValle, what a preposterous idea!"

"I only offered it in jest," he said seriously.

"So you did. Well, enough of this idle banter. To business. I thought all extant drawings by Hokusai were already catalogued and unavailable. What is this story of an Australian sea captain's clandestine collection?" But she only half attended his explanation. As the two negotiated their arrangements, the mind of the Countess raced ahead.

Gambrell was the key. From what little she had been able to infer, Kate's current relationship with her mother was disaffected and so not likely to support more separation than was straining it already. One vote against. As for the father, although he had considerable merit as an artist, he was a minor figure in the family and would follow his wife's lead. Two votes against. This left Gambrell. If he could be persuaded, then he might persuade the father and together they might sway the mother into allowing what she would otherwise oppose. It was chancy, but the Countess had taken chances all her life.

After a hard bargaining transatlantic phone call to a number only she knew, the dinner arrangements were comparatively easy to make.

For Phillip it was deja vu of the worst kind. There he was again, seated at her right hand. There she was again, at her most stunningly beautiful and charmingly persuasive. It was no good. He tried to keep on his guard. However, certainty that he was object of her intrigue could not withstand the flattering pleasure he took in his own seduction. As course followed course, he became more deeply bound by the spell of her fascinating company. Entranced, he felt powerless to break it.

At last the crystal finger bowls were silently removed. Guests pushed back their chairs to adjourn for coffee and aperitif. Once again, he felt the pressure of her hand restraining him from rising with the others. Once again, he remained seated, this time with a chill of anticipation and a smile of submission. She smiled back.

"Years ago, Museum Director, I was indelicate enough to exploit the hospitality I offered you for personal gain. To my request, you graciously yielded none-the-less."

"I remember." (How could I forget?)

"It would ease indebtedness I feel if you would consider what I have to offer now as belated payment for what I owe."

"Of course I would be delighted to listen to anything the Countess has to propose." (She can't be sure I'd accept or else she wouldn't be so indirect about it.)

"This opportunity, it concerns your niece."

"Kate?" (My God, what is she after now?)

"Yes. It bears on something dear to you, since she is dear to you. Her future."

"We are all, her parents and I, very hopeful for what her gifts and continued education may allow her to accomplish." (Does Kate know she has become ensnared?)

"I am sure you want what is best for her. An interesting question: what is

best ? Consider it for a moment. If you could place her anywhere you choose these next two years, where would it be? Anywhere you choose."

"As you are no doubt aware, she is planning to attend the University. On scholarship." (Already knowing this from Kate, she must have something else in mind.)

"In your judgment, Museum Director, would any teaching there be of the caliber which she has received these past three years?"

"No." (At least she credits her enemy's talent.)

"Yet you would not advise her continuing with Mr. Savovek?"

"No." (Poor Kate has endured enough from Jan.)

"Can you conceive of her receiving instruction of comparable distinction at any other institution with which you are familiar, here or abroad?"

"No. I can think of none." (What is she leading up to?)

"If this is true, and you as much as anyone could authenticate this truth, would you concede that further direct instruction might not be in the girl's best interests _if_ a superior alternative of a non-ordinary kind might be found?"

"I would consider whatever the Countess would have me consider." (Better to call her hand than continue playing at hints.)

"Then consider this!" And sliding long fingers into some recess hidden in the dark folds of her luxuriant gown she withdrew, as a triumphant gambler might a winning card, an airmail envelope that she ceremoniously laid before him, face up on the table. "You may open it now."

Doing as he was commanded, Phillip gaped in disbelief at the brief message and the signature that he knew authoritatively enough to verify in a court of law. He read it twice over:

'The artist Kate Germaine. She is

permitted to join my household. Space

in my studio. Materials provided.

My conditions--

She remain a full two years.

She not leave to visit.

She not accept visitors.

She comes to work.

To this I agree.

RIABLO'

Phillip shook his head.

"It's impossible."

"Of course it is. The man's a determined recluse. His final years are dedicated to what remains to be produced. Why would he permit such an intrusion from the outside world? He never has before."

"Why would he?" Phillip knew he was being led along.

"Because what is impossible is imagining a problem that imagination cannot solve. LaValle originally fantasized this opportunity for your niece. I have made it a reality."

"How?"

"By way of an exchange. In my collection I had -- it doesn't matter what -- that which Riablo was willing to give up his precious privacy to gain."

"Then this agreement is to be taken seriously?"

"So seriously, word of her flight arrival would confirm acceptance."

"And the expense?"

"Riablo does not want for money. Having little use for it, he has far beyond his needs. Simple luxury has always been enough."

"Why me, Countess? Why do you approach me with this information and not the parents? I am only a vitally interested party. They decide."

"Come, Museum Director, let us not parry over what both of us know too well to deny. I have not been the mother's favor these many years. Through no fault of hers. The error was mine. I overstepped my bounds. She drove me back and out. I have not trespassed there again."

"Until now."

"Yes. Until now."

"And you suppose I shall act your agent in this?" He was caught and he knew it.

"This is my expectation. In tricking me three years ago, you tipped your hand. There is not much you would not do to advance your niece, including manipulating me. Only afterwards did I appreciate how you juxtaposed myself and Savocek to gain her access into his instruction. It was prettily done. Understand, I harbor no ill will at being outwitted. It only raised you in my estimation. You have a capacity for guile not much inferior to my own. I was well trapped. Now it is my turn. Willingly or not, you will act my agent in this because if you do not your niece will lose -- what will she lose Museum Director?"

Phillip reflected. For no particular reason he could think of except it struck his curiosity, he asked:

"Did you ever play chess, Countess?" Then he knew why he asked.

She laughed sincerely, not as a ploy.

"Yes. Once upon a time. Many years ago I had the rudiments explained to me and was told, after much practice, I should never get beyond them. Why?"

"Because I feel your pawn in this."

"Not a pawn! Do yourself justice, Museum Director. A knight at least, perhaps a rook. In any case, the one essential piece without which I could not proceed. Esteem your own value. I assure you, I do."

"There is an opponent, I suppose. Riablo? Is he the king that you have mated in this game?"

"No. Only another of my pieces. All my opponents play for me, except the One."

"Would you entrust me with his name?"

"Why not? The game, as you call it, is between my ambition to get my way and Life's reluctance to let me have it all the time. Always across the board the same adversary is always out to confound me. Luck or Fate, call it what you will. More often than not it has won, yet overall I have not done badly. You are fortunate to witness one of my smaller victories."

"Then to answer your earlier question, if I do not act your agent in this Kate shall lose whatever influence working with Riablo can inspire."

"Whatever that may be," agreed the Countess.

"Yes. Unless he chooses to instruct her."

"He will not. Self-taught, he despises the sham of teaching art. As to the letter, he will honor these conditions to which he has signed his name. Not because of any code of honor, hardly that. But because of pride. He is too proud of his precious name to break his word to me."

Now it was Phillip's turn.

"Yet you are not being entirely open with me. Offering Kate a priceless opportunity you have not mentioned price. You have a price?"

"A small commission. Call it a finder's fee. Talk to the father to persuade the mother. Do what you must. When you are all agreed, then send the father to me."

"And Kate?"

"I do not think she shall need much persuasion. What is required, I have enough to give. Now, shall we join the others. In the pleasure of your company I fear I have neglected them."

"By all means." By what means, Phillip wondered? How to carry out the next move it was his to make?

His first step was to hand deliver the letter of agreement to Galen within the privacy of the artist's studio. At first excited on Kate's behalf, then saddened by the prospect of her absence from his life, finally troubled how the loss would further injure Joanne, Galen appealed to his old friend for help. But first he was curious.

"Of course this is an incredible opening for Kate. How do you think the Countess contrived it?"

"She alluded to something in her collection that Riablo would give up privacy to gain. Since he's more passionate about creating than collecting, I don't think it is an art object he covets. No, something else. An extortion of some kind would be my guess. He must have blundered into her web. This is the price he pays for getting out."

"It's the price Jo will pay that bothers me. Insult to injury, knowing the Countess is behind Kate's leaving. I promise you, Phillip, Jo won't take this lightly. Not after all she's been through already.

You don't know how it's been here. Studying with Savocek tore their relationship. Sometimes I wonder if we weren't wrong to recommend it. It cost Jo so much to get Kate to go and Kate so much to keep going. When she got home she'd take it out on her mother. Acting uncaring. All the old warmth was gone. Inexplicable, when I think how they used to be so close."

"Yes," Phillip confessed. "We have a lot to answer for, you and I. First Savocek, then encourages Kate's visits to the Countess. Now this."

"What's the best way, Phillip, do you think?"

"Head on. We owe her that. Nothing harder than hurting one person you love to help another."

But Galen disagreed.

"No, what Jo has done is harder. Acting out of love, only to be treated as unloving. The most thankless parenting I can imagine. I've talked to Kate, but she won't listen. Blames Jo. It's all Jo's fault. Talk to Jo about it, not to her. And yet, as affectionate with me as ever."

"And with me. On our trips to the Museum, nothing's changed. There's the cruelty of it. Only her mother has been shut out."

" 'Shut out' describes it. But not closed off. Whatever Kate says. However she acts, the change she's going through is not so deep as it appears. My recent portraits of her don't lie. She's chided me for painting her as the old Kate. Swears that's not who she is any more. Phillip, I don't make mistakes about people who sit for me. You know I don't. When I study Kate at leisure and in depth, it's the old Kate whom I see. Distant on the surface, true, but devoted as ever underneath."

"Have you told this to Joanne?"

"I haven't had to. The portraits speak for themselves. I catch her looking at them sometimes, so I know she sees what I am saying."

"That's one comfort, then."

"Yes. Too bad there's not another to soften the blow this letter brings. Phillip, you've always been so good at smoothing out roughness between people. Is there no way to soften this?"

"None. Not at the moment. In time, perhaps, if she consents Joanne may experience some relief from Kate's absence. Although the gain would still be offset by not having Kate around to mother. Joanne has been expecting her to live at home through college, so leaving would be premature. No, Galen. Head on. Are you ready?" he asked. "Good. Neither am I."

The scene was one that Joanne would long remember, a watershed event dividing one phase of her life from another. As soon as she entered the studio and saw both men lower their eyes she knew this was no ordinary social invitation. For an instant it felt like she had walked in on two repentant sons, guilty over some misdeed they were reluctant to confess. This was not the first time she had included Phillip and Galen, along with Kate, into the circle of children it was her responsibility to parent.   Hers were the multitude of invisible tasks and endless small decisions too small for others to consider, but upon which creation of home, household and family utterly depended every day. All hers. It was when Galen and Phillip were most dependent on her unseen labors, taking them for granted, that husband and friend seemed most childlike and she felt most maternal.

"Well," she demanded. "Who's going to tell me? Whatever it is."

Galen handed her the envelope.

"Jo, this comes through the Countess to us."

Had it not already been in her grasp, Joanne would not have accepted what she now felt was a missile aimed directly at her heart. That old enemy was mounting yet another incursion into her home, placing her once more upon the battlements to repel whatever attack this letter contained.

"Suppose I don't choose to open it?" If she ignored the contents would the message go away?

Phillip was first to break the silence.

"It concerns Kate."

"So," Joanne turned full face upon Phillip, away from Galen, confronting the man who was almost her husband, whom she loved almost as dearly. "What does the Countess pay you to be her stalking horse?" This insult in response to loyalty she felt he had betrayed. "What incentive does she offer for enlisting in her service?"

"Kate's future."

Phillip had known he would be tested, but not how severe the test would be. Blamed for standing in for the Countess when he was actually standing up for Kate hurt him as deeply as anything Joanne in her rising fury would accuse him of. While Galen, speechless from horror at seeing another division rend his family, watched helplessly as friend and wife fought over who would determine Kate's destiny and what that destiny would be.

Having risked thus far, Phillip was resolved to commit himself completely.

"Open the letter, Joanne. Read it. If we must fight, at least let's do it both knowing what we fight about."

"I hate that woman! God how I hate her! My answer's 'No' to whatever she proposes. For the misery she's caused me I'd say 'No' even if she offered Kate the opportunity of a lifetime."

"I believe she has. Read the letter, Joanne."

"Damn you, Phillip! Of all people why you?" And she tore the letter from the envelope comprehending its contents in a swift glance.

"Because I care,' Phillip answered.

"Damn her too! Did she tell you she was making an offer I can't refuse? Well she's wrong. I can. I will." She paused, struck by a new thought. "Why should I? Why should I be the one, Phillip? Why should I have to decide? You know how I feel. You decide. Choose between us. Send Kate from me or let her stay. That's your choice. This time there's no room for compromise. No place to hide. No secret ballot. I shall count your vote and know exactly where you stand."

Galen murmured something in pain that the other two ignored.

Phillip chose the honest way out.

"You're lying, Joanne."

"I'm what?"

"You're lying."

"How?"

"By pretending my choice or even Galen's weighs in this. You make all the parenting decisions, you always have. Advise is all we've ever been allowed to do. The final responsibility is yours. Why pretend otherwise, except you are so angry?"

Joanne took up the challenge.

"Because I'm tired, Phillip. And you too, Galen. Because I'm tired of parenting alone. Doing it all, and what is my reward?" Self-pity now spoke openly and unashamed. "What do either of you men know about parenting? Careers first, and what's left over devote to family. If it's convenient. How dare you presume to look out for the child whom you have left me to raise? How dare you scheme against me as though I was enemy to Kate's interests and not the one who has fought my whole life for her to get ahead? Where were you and Galen when I lay awake at night worrying through those dilemmas about Kate for which there were no simple solutions? Praying my decisions turned out more right that wrong. You were away, asleep, at work where both of you have always been. Yes Phillip, it is _my_ decision. No thanks to you or Galen." And here she looked at her husband slumped over in despair, unprotesting of the lashes he had just received.

Phillip stood unbowed.

"Are you ready for me to give you this decision back?"

"Almost."

Joanne walked over to Galen and rubbed a comforting hand on his collapsed shoulders.

"I'm sorry Jo. I just don't have what you do emotionally. Never have. Not able to get involved with Kate as you have done. The upset is too disturbing. I can love her. Talk with her. Paint her portraits. But I can't get into it with her. Too deep. Too scary. I just can't."

"I know. It's the work, isn't it, that steadies you so? That keeps you from rising with the ups and falling with the downs. No matter how I rock, you never capsize. Thank you for that."

"Thank you." Galen felt grateful to be welcomed back. "It's the faith I was brought up in. My parent's religion: work. The one sure thing to count on. To hold onto when all else fails."

"It's a good faith. Not one I would ever want you to give up. Nor you," and here she turned to Phillip to reconcile with him. "Thank you for standing up to me the way you did. Kate was well represented. I know it wasn't easy."

"No."

Stepping back Joanne surveyed them both for a long moment, husband and friend, two different men who together comprised the one complete man in her life.

"My condition for accepting this offer from the Countess is that I tell Kate."

Both men readily agreed.

The door closed quietly behind her and then Phillip discharged his final obligation.

"Galen, the Countess requests you call on her to take care of whatever details remain. I don't know what she wants."

"I do. I'll bring it to her directly." And he did. Actually, he was only surprised it had taken her this long to euchre the object from him.

"Yes, this will suffice," was all she said.

Meanwhile, Joanne had gone in search of her daughter, found the cloister of her bedroom closed, opened the door without knocking and entered in the old forthright manner she had not been allowed, or allowed herself, to do these several years.

"There you are," spoken as casually as if there were no history of opposition between them, startling Kate with the easy familiarity. "Read this, would you?"

Kate unfolded the piece of paper then looked questioningly, suspiciously up at Joanne who appeared to treat the invitation as one of no great matter.

"I don't understand." Kate truly didn't. Why would Riablo want her?

"The Countess arranged it. Since you are going to see her later this morning, no doubt she will explain the offer further."

"Does Galen know about this? Does Kip?"

"Yes."

"Do they want me to go?"

"They think it would be an extraordinary experience."

"And you?"

"I think it's your decision."

"That's all?"

"That's all." Leaving the room Joanne called cheerfully back over her shoulder: "Whatever you decide, when you decide, please let me know." With that, the mother's store of self-possession was thoroughly exhausted. Retreating to her little study she closed the door. Then, in welcome solitude, she began the first of what would be many long meditations about the end of motherhood and what would happen to her now.

In a very different mood was her daughter. Surprise, disbelief, but overriding these was anger. Controlling her world had become increasingly important since school and Savocek left so little lifetime to call her own. And now, with a single letter, the Countess redefined life's possibilities beyond what Kate could comprehend, so certainly could not control. It was happening again! Not exactly the same way, but like Joanne pushing her into service with Savocek. Now the Countess was pushing her to Riablo. Trust in the older woman now gave way to feelings of betrayal. Immediately upon arriving at the Villa, she bluntly charged the Countess with this offense.

"You have no right to meddle in my life, to create this chance!" And she flung the letter at the Countess like an accusation.

"I don't create chance, Miss Germaine. I only take advantage of it."

"Of me, you mean. Perhaps I don't wish to be taken advantage of?"

"Perhaps you don't. In which case you can refuse. The offer shall not be renewed, and you can enter the University come Fall."

"I can still become an artist."

"You can. A lesser one for the risk you hesitate to take. Rebel now, regret later. Or---"

"Or what?"

"Grow up. Rebellion is for children sacrificing self-interest for the sake of momentary power. You are seventeen. There are no second chances in life, Miss Germaine. Other chances, to be sure, but not second ones. The race belongs neither to the swift nor to the strong, but to the opportunist. In a single lifetime how many great chances do you suppose a person is given? One, if they're lucky. Two at most. When shall fortune ever present you with such an opportunity again? Throw it away and you shall always be less than what you might become.'

"You don't know that."

"But you do."

"Oh, leave me alone! You're just like my mother, trying to get me to do what I don't want!"

"Am I? That there was any similarity between us never occurred to me. How interesting. I shall have to give this some thought. Now, come along. I have something to show you. A new acquisition."

To see the family treasure hanging on a strange wall was enough provocation for Kate to want to immediately tear it down and take it home where it rightfully belonged.

"What is this drawing doing here?"

"It ransoms your going to Riablo's."

"Then I won't go. Give it back. It is my father's!"

"Not any longer."

"If I don't go, you'll have to give it back!"

"Yes. But you will go all the same. You will go knowing that for every opportunity taken, there is payment to be made. The greater the opportunity, the greater the price for accepting it. Are you ruthless enough to pay the price,

Miss Germaine?"

"Am I like you, do you mean?"

But the Countess would not be diverted.

"I await your response to the letter."

Stricken by more confusion of feeling than she had ever known Kate felt hopelessly conflicted. Needing to get away she closed her eyes to think, to feel, to clarify what she must do. At last came the question: what did she want <u>most</u> of all? Then, like a grail, the answer beckoned: to be all the artist she could be. Sighing deeply she opened her eyes only to discover the Countess looking in.

"Well?"

"You may tell Riablo I shall be coming. When may I go?"

"As soon as you like."

"That is when I wish. Soon. Even though I shall hate myself for going."

"For a while."

"And I shall hate you for the manner in which my going was arranged!"

"Yes, that too. For a while."

"Well, since I have served my purpose," glancing at the drawing, "and am of no further use to you, I shall be leaving."

"So you shall."

Working her way back into a fury, Kate did not notice the catch in the older woman's voice.

"Years ago my mother warned me against you. She said you had no heart. She spoke the truth!"

"Did she say that? The more you talk about your mother, the more eager I am to get to know her."

Kate laughed bitterly.

"That is as likely to happen as my forgiving you. <u>Never</u> !"

"It is time to say good-bye, Miss Germaine. You may see me at the airport. One parting word of advice. 'Never' is a promise no human being is empowered to make."

Unwittingly, the Countess had spoken truth about herself.

Chapter Twenty-Seven
ʟɪᴋᴇ ᴘᴀʀᴇɴᴛ, ʟɪᴋᴇ ᴄʜɪʟᴅ

Dear Kate--

not to worry you but I am worried about your uncle. Beyond the loss of his friend, I sense that he is suffering from something more. Has he caught Savocek's disease? Gaily dismissing my concern he tells me I worry too much. Perhaps. But worry is an early warning system I have come to trust over the years, an instinct for danger that has rarely played me falsely. No doubt naturally come by. Show me a mother who has not relied on worry to protect her young. Now worry tells me Phillip is not himself. Well, you can judge when you see him. Add your observation to my own and we'll confer. May you prove me wrong.

Your return is an event we all look forward to, I am with some trepidation since our parting was distant and the silence of your absence has been unbroken. All Phillip will promise, and LaValle faithfully affirms, is that you are growing well and I shall be surprised. Your uncle fills with gladness at his old companion coming home. Already he gains strength in anticipation of your arrival. As for your father, two years without a portrait of his daughter has left him quite at sea, so sight of you shall be like sight of land. He can rediscover how you have changed and how you have not, and update the map of his Kate. No doubt a sitting shall be one of your first orders of business. As for the Countess, although changed toward me she is otherwise the same. Imperious. Brutally frank. As devious as ever. She is ready to receive you at court when you are ready to present yourself.

My friendship with the woman remains a rocky road to understanding. There are still many jarring confrontations of an unexpected kind. Toughened me up, has the Countess. She seems constitutionally incapable of speaking without conviction. All her opinions are strongly held. Yet to her credit and true to her word, she does not insist I change my point of view to match her own when we disagree. Some requirements for intimacy have been met. We share our similarities and express our disagreements, but accept our differences.

While I talk very little about you directly, and gather you spoke sparingly of me, the Countess inferred from this reticence the strain our relationship has been under. I did not confirm this, however, until recently when she made a comparison to which I took offense. In passing I had contrasted your assertiveness to my compliance to my mother as a child, how I quietly deferred and you would not. Even when I resented your defiance I envied your courage. How unlike we are!

This is when the Countess called my hand. 'How alike, you mean.' Not what I meant at all. But she would not be put off. 'Mrs. Germaine, having come to know mother and daughter, I assure you some of the similarities are quite pronounced. You are both extremely headstrong. It's just that she acknowledges willfulness and you do not. Take responsibility for the example you have set.'

Responsibility? That hated word! Had I not carried responsibility enough? Here I was being obligated to take more. 'Damn you!' I swore defensively. She had touched a place where I was raw. Then, moved by my curse, she said an awful thing. 'Mrs. Germaine, I am already damned. I was damned when I was born."

Hurt of my own gave way to hurt for her. I looked for further explanation. 'I am my father's daughter. Like a parent, like a child, Mrs. Germaine. The connection can't be broken. As I sickened of my father, so I have sickened of myself. I have been made unfit for caring.'

Such self-contempt! So full of loathing for the similarity she bears. 'Countess,' I pleaded, 'there is no need to be so cruel. Neither Kate nor I see you in the dreadful terms you see yourself. We both consider you a friend.' But she would not relent. 'To get to know me better, Mrs. Germaine, is to come to know me worse. Sooner or later you too shall sicken of the inhuman way I am.'

So I tried another tack. If she could come to see her father in more generous terms she might become more generous with herself. Perhaps he was a better man than she gave him the blame for being. Perhaps he had hard cause to be as hard as he became. Maybe his faults were not of his own making. Maybe he was shaped by a painful history he could not overcome.

But she would have none of these suggestions. 'No, Mrs. Germaine, don't play villains are victims with me. Not all devils are fallen angels. Some are born to evil. My father, he was one. I tell you there was no good in the man. No kindness. No generosity. No love. No caring except for himself. No purpose except to gratify his lust for sensual pleasure and material gain. The only rule I know of he obeyed was the rule of impatience: anything worth waiting for is worth having now. The one time he strayed from that command he lost his chance for me. He believed life was too short to do without. One of the takers of the earth, my father, and I became another. Why? Because I will not be one of the taken.'

Was she declaring she was evil too, I asked? 'I am his daughter,' she replied. 'You be the judge. At least I have not committed the sin of family, damning a child of my own to be like me.' Is that why you have not remarried, I asked, wondering if she despaired of marriage too? Here is what she answered. 'Marriage is just an excuse for infidelity. Promising to be faithful, a man cheats on one woman with another who is flattered into believing his love is true. How gullible to credit such nonsense! Men are generally liars, Mrs. Germaine, and women are generally fools.'

Was she trying to provoke me? She had succeeded. 'There is such a thing as true love,' I retorted. 'In fiction yes,' she agreed, 'but not in reality. At least not in the one that I have known. Make your way as I have had to do, and convenience counts for much more than commitment.'

"At least commitment has gotten me happily married and with family. Can you say the same for convenience?' Anger gave sharpness to my reply that drew water from her eyes. She looked away. Instantly I regretted how harshly I had spoken. When she looked back her eyes were dry but red from where my words had wounded her. 'At close quarters, Mrs. Germaine, you are not to be underestimated. I shall not do so again. Meanwhile, I stand reproved.'

As you can tell, our friendship is not a gentle one. Becoming heated, injury is sometimes given. As for apology, that would only cheapen honesty of what was said, both of us too proud to ask forgiveness. We have the freedom to be thoughtless with each other.

A freedom I once abused with your uncle. I tell you this because, particularly now, you and I and Galen have a special responsibility for the love Phillip has for us. It was shortly after Savocek's arrival at the Museum school when we began to notice a change in your uncle. Their early morning coffees over art began to take precedence over traditional breakfasts with us. More change than this. Your father sensed it first, as you'd expect. Everyone being a potential portrait to him, their shifting poses do not escape his notice, although he usually keeps his insights to himself. On this occasion, however, he casually confronted Phillip at dinner one evening with the observation he had taken. 'This new happiness becomes you, Phillip.' 'Yes,' your uncle laughed, 'I wondered when you'd find me out.' Then he smiled with a radiance of contentment far beyond the perpetual cheerfulness for which he is known.

'Why Phillip,' I said before I could catch myself, 'and all this time I thought you were truly happy. What have you been keeping from me all these years?' Oh to have snatched that question back! Galen, with all his quickness, did not catch the look that swiftly sped and fled across your uncle's face. A cloud of sadness so fleeting sunshine had no time to appreciably diminish before it passed and brightness shone again. Kate, I swear until this moment I had no idea he still loved me in the old romantic way when both were courting me so many years ago. The flame I thought had died had burned in secret ever since. As dear to me as family he became, while I remained dearer to him than that.

Later, as he was leaving, I walked him to the door. 'Phillip,' I asked, 'would you accept an apology from a very devoted but very stupid old friend?' Then he smiled the smile with which he has disarmed the world. 'Joanne, you are not responsible for being ignorant of what you were not told. There is nothing to forgive. Besides, you know I am good at pretending when it matters, and as a good friend you graciously accepted my pretense. And did us both a kindness. Remember, you, all of you, have given me such joy.' 'And pain as well,' I added. He laughed again. 'Well, I don't suppose you can have one without the other, do you?'

But I found it no laughing matter, as I told Galen to whom Phillip's lingering attachment came as no surprise. 'Face it, Jo, you'll always be the woman in his life, I the friend, and Kate the child. The three of us together were the family that he wanted. Surely we can love him enough to give him that.'

Your father is usually a man of pictures, not words. However, he has a way of saying what needs to be said. At least what I needed to hear, guilty over Phillip loving me too much, realizing this was the love he wanted. All of us idealized, Phillip loving us to that extreme. This is probably why I chose your father and not Phillip, knowing I couldn't measure up to your uncle's ideal of me, yet could not keep from trying if we married. While with Galen I could be ordinary and accepted for myself. It was the right choice. I have been content.

Phillip. None of the three of us knows him as deeply as we are known. Usually, I haven't minded his greater privacy. Now that he appears unwell, however, I do. I worry. Your father refuses to be drawn out on the subject, bound by some pact, I believe, he and your uncle have made. So lend me your eyes. Hasten home. May we reunite better than we parted.

I love you,

Joanne

Chapter Twenty-Eight
GETTING IN THE DOOR

It was a bright mid-afternoon in the Spring following Kate's departure for Riablo's when a tall stately figure strode up the walk to the Germaine home and, refusing the courtesy of a bell, gave a glove-covered knock hard upon the door. Apparently unused to waiting the woman shifted impatiently from foot to foot until the door unexpectedly pulled open just as her fist was descending, about to strike again, now poised not six inches from the startled face of the very person she was coming to see.

"What? Oh, it's you. What do you want? If it's business with my husband ---"

"It is not," interrupted the Countess awkwardly lowering her hand. "I have come to see you."

"Me?"

"Yes. To personally invite you to the Villa for tea. To see the daffodils blooming in my courtyard, as I promised last Fall at the airport. Do you recall?"

"I do. Do you remember what I answered? That I refused. Besides, we have nothing in common."

"Too much in common don't you mean?"

"Countess, I don't wish to be rude. Your invitation may mean well. However, the past between us is too painful for me to overcome. And despite what you say, our worlds are very different."

"Are they? I think not, Mrs. Germaine. Consider your daughter. Was not her departure a loss for us both? You miss your child. I miss my friend. Why, shared loneliness itself is enough to bring two strangers together."

"If I am lonely, I prefer to suffer it alone."

The Countess signified she understood.

"Yes, we share that too. You are good at this, very good, Mrs. Germaine. Yet I have been at it far longer and could give you lessons."

Joanne's curiosity was piqued. She felt drawn into further doorstep conversation in spite of herself.

"What lessons are those?"

"At what some would call a vice. Others a virtue. I prefer to think of it as an indulgence."

"Common to us both?"

"I believe so. And why not? It is common enough in life, this matter of pride. Pride, Mrs. Germaine. Self-righteous, self-justifying, self-isolating, self-punishing pride. Here: I'll make you an offer. I'll relinquish my throne of pain if you'll relinquish yours."

"This is hardly an equitable exchange, Countess, since I have suffered at your hands while you have only been inconvenienced at mine."

"What is it you are holding against me, Mrs. Germaine?"

"Your influence. First over my husband then over my daughter. Because by extension both were over me."

"If I am guilty of any offense against you in the past it has been indifference. Beyond that I have never tried to influence you. Until now. My dealings with your husband have been only that, dealings. While with your daughter, friendship came about through no intention to hurt you. We were attracted by mutual dislike of one another and in the process came to appreciate what had initially put us off. If either of these relationships have caused you pain, that was not my design. I was only pursuing my self-interest as I usually do. Unmindful of effects on others as I usually am. For that I apologize. Only for that."

In this frank declaration Joanne glimpsed a hint of humility that moved her ever so slightly, and something in the younger woman began to relent.

"I never thought I'd hear the Countess D'Allessandro Ricci apologize."

"You didn't," the Countess smiled. "That is, if the fact were reported to me for confirmation by someone else I should deny it."

"Why? Is apologizing so damaging to one's reputation?"

"Just say it is an admission at which I am not practiced. My father never gave into it himself. Apologizing requires depending on someone else for forgiveness and he preferred to keep the upper hand where it belonged. With him."

"I've always imagined you loved control more than anything or anyone else."

"I have, Mrs. Germaine. And I do. Only recently, from your daughter, have I come to appreciate what this preoccupation has cost me. Now she is away I have no one in whom to confide as I learned to do with her. As I am doing with you now."

The unanticipated length and growing intimacy of their conversation caused Joanne to want to continue it in a less public place.

"Won't you come inside? You said you take tea, I believe?"

" Asked back into the house from which I have been banished? This is a day for surprises."

"Yes. Yes it is. I never thought I'd invite my nemesis to tea."

"Have your feelings really been so hard set against me?" Still they lingered on the stoop. "You must have given me a great deal of your thought and energy, Mrs. Germaine. More than I ever devoted to you."

"When one is unhappy as I have been these past few years it helps to have an enemy to blame. I have learned a lot about anger through being angry at you."

"I'm glad I was of service. What have you learned?"

"That anger offers an escape from pain. When I was in deepest despair about my relationship with Kate I could rage against you, the woman who did this to me."

"Did what, Mrs. Germaine?"

"Took my daughter. It worked better when I didn't see you. In person, you are less monstrous than I imagined."

"Well, I'm glad for that."

Stepping through the door held open for her by Joanne, the Countess paused, uncertain of where to proceed, waiting to be led. Her hostess obliged by going first, through a living room casually kept, down a long hallway on the walls of which the Countess noticed an empty spot where memory told her the great drawing, now hers, had hung for so many years. Walking by the place she pillaged the Countess felt a momentary attack of emotional discomfort which she suppressed and followed on. Joanne, however, seemed not to notice the loss of treasure, neither pausing nor turning as she passed the desecrated place, stopping only when they entered the kitchen. Here she gestured toward the small table set against a paned window, the waning sun casting a grid of shadows on the well- worn wooden surface. They sat down.

"Why don't we visit here. This is Kate's old drawing table, at least it was when she was younger. Where she spent her early years after school you know. Or perhaps you didn't know. I really don't know what you know." Picking up the conversation in a new location felt awkward.

"More about her than yourself, Mrs.Germaine. She talked very little about home and family."

Joanne was surprised.

" Really? I supposed she shared all her complaints about my mothering. While from listening I assumed you turned against me."

The Countess shook her head.

"No wonder your dislike of me has grown. Actually, she seldom spoke of you in loving or unloving terms. Mostly you were implied by omission. As a presence she depended on so fully your importance had become invisible. You were completely taken for granted. How else could she afford to treat me the way she did? So self-assured we conflicted right away. We truly 'hit it off'. She didn't like how I spoke to her and I didn't like how she returned the favor. Right away we clashed. Perhaps she told you?"

"Only that the first meeting was not a pleasant one. Then she announced her first visit to the Villa. How things progressed between you after that I was never told."

"And did not inquire?"

"As you said, I have my pride."

"Quite so. Your daughter can be prideful too. Right now she punishes me for the exchange I made at her expense, the drawing for her access to Riablo. At first she refused to answer my letters. Now she has written once. I have kept writing, in concession to her sulky mood. She may write more, then again she may not."

"And is your visit to me a concession to mine?"

"Certainly, Mrs. Germaine. Would you have even opened a letter bearing my return address?"

"No, I would not."

"So I come in person to persuade you to come to me. Returning to the house from which I was cast out. Do you remember?"

"I remember. It wasn't the drawing I was defending, it was my home. Even though he wouldn't have parted with the drawing had I said nothing, Galen was extremely angry at my treatment of you afterwards. While he avoids confrontation, he tolerates no interference with his work. Later we had a terrible fight. His defending you made matters worse. So we compromised. I would stay out of his business with you, and you would stay out of our home. Beyond that we agreed the less said about you the better."

"Yes, I begin to see what a thorn I have been in your side. Of course I knew arranging for Riablo would cause you loss of Kate. Hard for me to have her go, it must have been more difficult for you."

"It was. You stripped me of my purpose and brought my mothering to an early end. This last year I haven't known what to do with myself. I still don't know."

"Is there life after children, Mrs. Germaine? Never having my own to hold on to I can't say. However, I can tell you this. There is life without children. My own, for example. Although I have known what it is to struggle with letting go."

"Not with a child?"

"No. At least not literally. A grown man who has managed to remain a child."

"A lover?"

"<u>The</u> lover, Mrs. Germaine. The one to whom all others never could compare, no matter how many I tried. It was a disappointment, I confess, to discover that with all my resources I could not recreate the accidental chemistry of ecstatic love. Strange. Men are so easily lead by their arousal, yet I could not manage this. But, you know how lovers are."

"No. No I don't. I've never had a lover except my husband, and then only after we were married."

"Really?" The Countess was not feigning her surprise. "Well now, there's a difference between us. No doubt you find my experience as foreign as I do the experience you lack. In any case, to keep from being consumed in the relationship I had to break if off, but could not bear to tear myself away. I suppose I had become obsessed."

"How frightening. Were you scared?"

"Fortunately yes. For the first and only time in my life I began to be truly afraid because I was truly out of control. That night as he lay sleeping in bed, the knife in my hand seemed the only solution. But I came to my senses in the nick of time. Judgment intervened. Destroy his life and I would destroy my own. When he awoke next morning I had fled, and a crime of passion had been averted. From his letters afterwards I discovered he had been no less desperate than I."

Joanne was aghast.

"Do you mean you almost killed him?"

"Yes. I confronted the murderess in myself who is in all of us and almost set her rampage loose. Don't worry. Since then I have kept her under lock and key. Only twice have I let her out upon restraint. Once to threaten, once to commit a crime of reason."

"A crime of reason? I don't know what you mean."

"To employ violence as a measured response when someone will not abide persuasion of any other kind."

Joanne shivered at this last remark.

"Countess, there is much more about you to dislike than I supposed."

"Only because I am telling you more about me than I have told anyone else."

Now there was silence between the two women, both gazing out of the window as evening began to fall. It was at this juncture Galen strolled in for a snack. Seeing the Countess he stopped dead in his tracks, at an absolute loss of what to say. The Countess, however, was perfectly at ease.

"Why Mr. Germaine. What a pleasure. So good to see you."

Pleasure? Galen stammered a greeting back.

"And you. Good to see you, Countess," casting a worried glance in the direction of his wife. Of all the people he hoped never again to meet under his roof it was these two together. "Did you come," he began again, addressing the older woman, "to see me?"

"No. Although of course I'm gratified that you looked in. No. I came to see your wife who has been graciously entertaining me. We have been gossiping the afternoon away, as I believe women are prone to do. Please don't let us interrupt you." And the Countess turned back to face Joanne whose face was a study in controlled amusement.

Feeling relieved all was apparently well Galen left without the nourishment he had come for. He was grateful to be gone, yet had the distinct impression he had been dismissed. Back in his studio he briefly pondered over what had occurred, then picking up his brush promptly forgot as he went back to work.

"So you left him," began Joanne picking up the loose thread of conversation where it had been broken.

"Yes. I never saw him again. Although we corresponded for many years, even occasionally do now. There are some matters of business that still lay between us. As for the two years of our terrible attachment, we felt stuck at the time. Now I know better. We were in struggle and struggle is progress."

"Yes, like Kate and I feeling at a standstill but actually in forward motion. I think she still feels stuck with me. At least she hasn't written back. Maybe it's as well to let the distance grow between us. How did you fill your life after separation set you free?"

" It took time, but finally another purpose came to replace my passion. At last I took up collecting. A safer obsession, although like the first, the craving is insatiable because there is no enough. LaValle, with whom I had some slight acquaintance in years past, offered to act as my advisor and agent. The Villa itself was architected from plans he found for me in a private library of old designs to which only he had access. Now, thirty years later, my collection attracts enthusiasts from around the world. All my visitors have come away impressed. Except for one."

Joanne laughed.

"I can guess who."

"Yes, your daughter. After touring the Villa that first day do you know what she had the impudence to say?"

"What?"

" 'Is this all you have?' I answered with a question of my own. 'Is this not enough?' She shrugged: 'I was hoping for more.' How insulting! But then I reconsidered what she had said. She had not come to be impressed by my possessions, but to get acquainted. So I invited her back again, promising not to show her a single picture if she would return. Now I see why she agreed. Momentarily cut off from intimacy with you, she was willing to try companionship with me."

"What did you talk about those Saturdays together?"

"Mostly our opinions. How they differed. Actually I know very little about her growing up. This table, for example. Is it significant?"

"Yes. This whole room in fact."

And Joanne, drawn out by the older woman's curiosity, began to tell the Countess about Kate's early years. The story of Kate's infancy and the magic crayons. Her drawing on the floor and then the butcher paper. Fighting with Kate's school for her right to dual handedness, then arguing with Galen to respect his daughter's talent. Equipping the very table at which they sat and maintaining the gallery of drawings in Kate's room. How the violation of the Benefactor's portrait admitted Kate into her father's studio. And, most difficult of all, the final battle for her instruction with Savocek.

This was a story that Joanne had never told anyone because what was there to be told?   Only a tale of ordinary mothering, and who would be interested in that? Yet telling it now felt affirming. If she had to do it over again, she would do mostly the same, despite the hard way it had ended. But now she felt embarrassed. She had not meant to talk about herself in such boring detail.

"I didn't mean to rattle on," she apologized.

The long thoughtful look from the Countess was not reassuring. Then the woman clapped her hands and burst into applause.

"Bravo, Mrs. Germaine! Bravo! Mothering is certainly not for the faint of heart!"

Now Joanne <u>was</u> embarrassed. Her cheeks colored from the tribute she was receiving, slightly bowing, none-the-less.

"Thank you. I've never had my mothering applauded. I'm not sure many mothers have. If it's not too late, I'd like to accept your invitation to the Villa."

"I should be delighted. And when you come I shall show you some recent acquisitions, the Master's own selections from your daughter's work to date."

"How did you come by these?" Despite what she already knew about the Countess this offer came as a surprise.

"By arrangement, how else?"

"Does Kate know?"

"Certainly not."

"Won't she be angry with you when she finds out?"

"Of course she will. But she'll get over it. After all, Mrs. Germaine, it's not as though I've never done this kind of thing to her before, now is it?"

Chapter Twenty-Nine
LAST LETTER HOME

*D*earest Kip--

I do not understand time. How can the days pass so slowly while the weeks and months speed by so fast? Already it is time to leave.

My last letter. Are you sorry? I am. I shall miss the absence that has brought us closer to together. I shall miss the opportunity to reflect and share what I discover with you. For whom have these letters really been written? Galen would know the answer. Letters really to myself.

Do you know what he once told me? He thought it a great joke. People were paying him to do their portraits when in actuality each portrait was of the artist in the likeness of his clients. I didn't understand what he meant then, but I do now. Whatever we express about others is really something said about ourselves.

Getting away has illuminated so much that daily living with family had obscured me, while this separation has blessed me with a measure of perspective that has eased my heart and mind. I come home at peace and with resolve, both possessions I was lacking when I left.

Writing this in flight, suspended between here and there, I wonder to whom I am returning. From letters sent to me I know transformation has occurred on both sides of the ocean. What the Countess once took me to task about when I complained how no adults could truly understand a child. Being grown ups, they had forgotten what growing up was like. This provoked one of the first corrections I received. "Miss Germaine, growing up is something we do all our lives. We are born unprepared and we die unfinished. In between we develop as choice and circumstance allow. Preoccupied with your own changes, you reckon older people are standing still. I assure you they are not."

Older now, I can agree with what she said. A little frightening, however, wondering about you and Joanne and Galen, and the Countess. Have my constants changed? If her letters have been honest, and she has always been that, Joanne has journeyed on. Your life has been tragically altered. The Countess. Hard to think of her changing. Eroding perhaps. She may not be too old to change, but she is too old to change very much. Like Riablo, she has become distilled into an essence of herself from living many years according to her wants. Galen? No. His changes are confined to the progress of his work. The worker is invariant. He keeps faith with the old quotation mounted on his studio door. Did you know he had me commit it to memory before I left?   He wanted me to take it in me.

Yesterday I wrote and posted it on Riablo's easel for a goodbye:

> "Certain it is that all other ambition
>
> whatsoever seemed poor in his eyes
>
> compared with work which he had in hand;
>
> seeing that the matter at issue was either
>
> nothing or a thing so great it could well be
>
> content with its own merit, without seeking
>
> other recompense."

Whoever Francis Bacon is. I never asked. But that's Galen: content with work in hand. And Riablo.

What surprises shall reunion bring? Here's one. I shall not be drawing again for a while. No. I have not given up my artwork, I just need a different challenge. These last six moths at Riablo's have made me restless to move on. I want another medium to try so I am going to begin to paint.

Where? Not in my mother's kitchen nor by my father's side. Not any more. I need a space apart from home to work, but one that still has the feel of family. In the vastness of her Villa, the Countess surely has one room to serve my needs. To my request she can only refuse, except if I know her she can't. The opportunity is too full of profitable possibilities to turn me down. Besides, if she can exploit our friendship for personal gain then why can't I?

The last dance. Unless I tell you now I shall forget it in the joy of arriving home. Begin the morning of my last full day. There was no hint from anyone about my leaving, not even a crack in household routine. One solitary sign when I came down to breakfast, my ticket laying on the kitchen table. Marcella paid it no attention. Jesus came in, glanced once at it and once at me to show he understood, then he was off about his business, while I returned to my loft to pack. It would require an early start next morning to get me to my evening flight.

Dragging suitcases out from underneath the bed where they had lain unopened these two years, I wondered what to wear on my trip home. What would most fittingly introduce me back into your lives? As I was about to unclasp each bag, I hesitated, struck by ignorance of contents they concealed. So accustomed to slipping on the same uniform here each morning, I had forgotten wearing anything else.

My curiosity was mixed with some anxiety. What would I discover? I wanted to know. Did I want to know? It's a little scary opening a time capsule of artifacts when the history to be revealed is your own. For the first instant, sight of what I found seemed utterly improbable. These belonged to me? I to them? Surely they were costumes for another girl and not myself. Then memory began to claim each piece, where I had purchased it, where it had been worn before. Yes, I remembered now.

Trying them on, however, was most perplexing. Either I had outgrown my past or my past had shrunk too small to fit my present. This was like the tricks of changing size played on poor Alice in Wonderland. Not only did each dress look peculiar, but each felt uncomfortable, squeezing my shoulders and my chest, my waist and hips to suffocation, while not one of them reached below my knees. Zippers refused to zip. Buttons refused to reach the holes for which they were intended. Really, how aggravating!

Laughter behind me.   Indignantly I turned around to find Marcella leaning against the open doorway, heaving with delight at the joke someone had played on me. Wiping the tears from her eyes and straightening her smile as best she could, she innocently shook her head denying my implied accusation of blame. Then with an upraised hand she signaled me to wait while she disappeared and returned shortly with a purple garment folded over her arm. Holding it out for me to take, I saw it was not a single piece but two, a dress of royal purple with shoulder straps, a gathered bodice, fitted waist, flaring into a long free falling pleated skirt. And a broad shouldered jacket to match, both pieces carefully embroidered with decorative stitching along the seams.

'For me? I gestured.' As her eyes glistened my vision blurred and when it cleared I was alone with the gift she had made for me. What I am wearing home.

Oh Kip, have you ever felt divided? Torn apart? Feeling there are two selves in which you can live happily, neither of which can be inhabited at the same time? To be in one necessitates being absent from the other. Iliana is who I am, Kip, who I am here. When I leave I must leave her behind. I shall miss her, Kip.

Now I resume the life of Kate. But what kind of a girl is Kate? As unfamiliar as the clothes I used to wear. While I am anxious to see you, I am equally anxious to see myself. Eager and worried. I am coming home with a glad, sad heart, leaving these three spirits to dance without me, to share silence without me, to explore the night without me, to remain together without me. Shall I be missed? Not in a clinging way. When I came I was welcomed like I 'd been here before. In leaving, I am let go as though I shall be coming back. While the Countess or LaValle may have arranged my entry, now I am welcome whenever I return for my own sake.

I do dread one adjustment, having to speak again, getting used to my own voice and the chattering of other voices too. Hearing the clamor of society after two years seclusion! I must exchange the silence I have come to love for the noise of speech. No more quiet contemplation for writing letters, now I am back to saying what is on my mind.

My last day here was difficult, a series of frustrations. Wishing to visit each location to which I had become attached, I was content to stay in none very long. From my garret window the view recalled me to the studio, from the studio to the kitchen, from the kitchen to the courtyard, from the courtyard to Marcella's gardens, from her gardens to the bluff, from the bluff down to the shore, the rocky shore as jumbled as my thoughts where I found sympathetic company in the restless sea. In constant motion, she cannot decide whether to flood or ebb and so keeps choosing one and then the other. For her, moving on is moving back and forth, and perhaps that's how it will be for me. Unable to choose otherwise because I have become divided. Divided, Kip. Arriving here I had one home, but now in leaving I have two.

A wandering day I had of it, meandering back at last to Riablo's studio where he interrupted his work as soon as I entered and gestured me over. A clown's face he was wearing, with a rueful smile. Turning to his cluttered table of supplies he reminded me of Galen and the wild assortment of materials that becomes an artist's store. A profusion of tubes and jars and cans of pigment in liquid, paste and powder form. Of capped and stoppered bottles and lidded jars containing oils and varnishes, thinners and other solvents. Surrounded by containers of implements for mixing and applying paint, all the tools by which he plied his trade scattered in apparent confusion, but carefully ordered for him to find what he needed at a moment's notice.

Reaching for my hands to shake them good-bye, I supposed, he turned them palm up and carefully began placing in each a selection of brushes from those he used, trusted brushes that had served him well. Such was the confidence from him I felt, they would also prove of worthy use for me, if I strove to be worthy of them.

Gripping them tightly, I felt his energy infuse my hands and glancing up noticed the quotation I had left, pinned to the wall. Riablo gestured to it with an upraised fist affirming power of what was written there. Then he pointed across the room to my easel that supported, instead of a drawing board, a freshly prepared canvas awaiting my next visit. So this was not good-bye, but until I came again.

Back in my room I carefully laid out Marcella's dress for next morning's wear and wrapped and packed the precious brushes to keep them safe. Then I went down to supper.

Our last meal together was reminiscent of our first. What was fresh with newness for me then was fresh with fond familiarity now. My appreciation for the ordinary has been deepened by the ritual power they give it here. I have learned how commonplace events become important in proportion to the care and reverence that they are paid.

Eating over, I was last at the table as usual, curious what music would invite me out that night, waiting to hear how Jesus would call. It was not what I expected.

There was the sound of music, sure enough, but of a distinctly un-pipelike kind. More human it was, yet muted as if a hand were being alternately cupped and released over a mouth creating a vibrato for the voice, urging me to bring my voice and join the song.

On the ground they were seated, now the four of us forming a square. Jesus, whose voice I had first heard, began wordlessly blending one vowel sound into another, the song rising and falling, creating a simple melody that we picked up and began to follow not in unison but like a round, each of us lagging behind another so that unexpected harmonies emerged. Once established, the repetitions began to vary not in tempo but in feeling tone, as though we were playing the entire emotional scale from great joy to great sorrow and back again. It felt like celebrating the depth and range of union between us, how close we had grown, how attuned to one another we had become. Feeling the loss of leaving, my voice was the first to break and the sound of weeping became our song of loss, grieving what we would miss, at last softly subsiding, preparing us for what came next.

First the parting, then the party. Jesus struck up the pipes and one spell was cast over another. To our feet we jumped, Riablo's arm around me from one side, Marcella's from the other, I in between holding each of them, and off we charged at gallop speed reeling this way and that, one-step, two-step, leap, and land, bend way back and forward lean, round and round so long as we could dance until drenched in perspiration, laughing, giddy with exhaustion, our bodies begged to stop, in need of cooling down. Stumbling out, tumbling down the bluff, tripping over the rocky shore, hanging onto each other to keep from falling, at last, we threw ourselves into the calming sea. Gently, patiently, she recovered us, her riotous children, rocking and refreshing us back to our senses, convincing us that now we all had need for sleep.

Next morning I never would have woken up had not Marcella shaken me and shaken me again. Hoisting myself to sitting, I reached for a ribbon to tie back my hair and stared at the bright yellow color to bring me round. Slowly coming to, I slipped on the dress and jacket my mother here had made. The fit was perfect. I started to reach for my suitcases but they had already been taken. Then I noticed part of me was still undressed. My feet were bare. No shoes! I had to civilize my feet for travel. Whereupon I noticed on the floor a pair of sandals -- braided straps affixed to leather soles so cunningly I could not tell how the joining was accomplished. Another perfect fit, as though he traced the outline of my feet from my footprints in the sand.

While Jesus loaded my bags onto the car I lingered before climbing in, greedy for each last remaining minute in this beloved place. The motor starting told me it was time to go. Marcella rushed into my arms and I gave her a tight embrace, letting her go as she pulled away and ran inside. I wanted to run after. One final look at the great house and at a figure waving from an upstairs window. Waving back. I slid into my seat closing the door, and we drove off.

The silence that we shared was much closer than when he brought me here. The good quiet company we were the whole day through, ending our trip at last at the airport where I checked my bags and verified the gate and time only to turn and discover Jesus was gone. Oh, I had counted on him being there to say goodbye! Suddenly I felt very empty, very tired, and very alone. Walking slowly up the crowded concourse among the bustle of strangers I felt disconnected until, within the unfamiliar babble of voices, I recognized a sound I knew. No, it must be my imagination. I trudged on. No, I was not imagining! I stopped and looked around me. Not there. Then up ahead. Warmth swept through my body like a flush of joy. Crouched down against the wall and bending forward, straw hat concealing what he played, was a lean figure of a man from whom a sprightly melody softly escaped, a tune I recognized from the night before.

Brushing past I touched him lightly on the shoulder, rose to my toes, and skipped the remaining distance to my gate. Whether the music actually kept me company so far I cannot swear, only that I heard it clearly in my head. Farewell Jesus! Farewell Marcella! Farewell Riablo! Farewell Escampobar! Kip, I am coming home! Bringing the music with me. Shall we dance?

When you receive delivery of this letter look well at the carrier. She will be looking well at you.

Kate

Chapter Thirty
THE FINAL CONQUEST

Although Galen, Phillip, even the Countess, had offered to accompany Joanne to the airport, she had declined them each. Resolved to bear her anxieties without their support, she would go and meet Kate alone where they had parted company two years before. Brave, but mostly selfish, was this determination to claim right of first reunion with her daughter. Who more than she had earned it?

Arriving at the terminal, however, she began regretting the decision she had made, wishing for companions to divert her from the growing insecurities she felt.

Suppose conditions were no less antagonistic now than when Kate left? Would life regress back to where it was between them? Would her own frail hold on independence be lost by an outbreak of those old hostilities that bound them in the past? My God, how she did not want to mother any more! Yet if Kate acted the child, what else could she do but act the parent?

The lobby was crowded, which was a help. At least she was not without the company of strangers. After checking at the airline counter for information, she joined the stream of people flowing down one walkway that branched into a second leading to the lounge where it appeared everyone was awaiting the delivery of some loved one from the sky.

Not wanting to sit for fear of becoming unsteady getting up, Joanne stood off to one side facing the door from which the flight would empty. When a disembodied voice announced the touching down of 'Overseas Flight 406' and the momentary deplaning of those aboard she felt the quickening not of excitement but of dread. Deeply breathing to calm the disturbance and gather courage, Joanne began searching the long line of passengers filing out for the familiar figure of her daughter until the last stragglers had emerged and only the crew remained unaccounted for. A panic gripped her. Had she met the wrong plane? Pulling the crumpled telegram from her pocket she checked the flight and time against the arrival she was meeting. All was correct. Yet no Kate.

The area was clearing now, the last few raucous groups of reunited friends and family departing, celebrating the recovery of some missing person in their lives. Lowering herself down on an empty chair, among a row of empty chairs, she decided to rest a few moments before making inquiry about the failed connection.

"May I join you?" asked a husky voice. Staring at the floor Joanne limply consented. Why not? An unknown for company felt better than no company at all.

"Mother?"

Even then it did not occur to Joanne she was being personally addressed. Certainly not by that designation, never having been called 'mother' even by her own daughter.

"Mother, it is I. Kate." The words were gently spoken as would a parent awakening a sleeping child.

In disbelief, Joanne glanced round to behold the speaker at her side.

"Kate?"

"Am I so changed you don't recognize me?"

Joanne studied her daughter.

"Yes. Yes, I believe you are. How else could I forget how you sounded?"

"Remembered, you mean. I speak differently now. My voice has lowered as I have grown. How <u>are</u> you?"

What a question! What was she supposed to say? Nothing came to mind so nothing was what she said. Searching Kate's face for any of the old animosity Joanne found none. Here was no stubborn child withdrawn behind a wall of silence to lock her out. Her was no adversary to fight over control. Here was --- what?

Kate seemed to understand this need of Joanne's to physically rediscover this long lost offspring. Tentatively the mother reached over and with the back of her fingers softly touched Kate's long hair, lightly stroked her cheek, then, frightened, stopped and pulled away embarrassed by such bold intimacy with one so unfamiliar. Still Kate did not move, reading in her mother's wary hesitation, trembling mouth and furtive gaze Joanne's timid caring. She did not want to startle her mother away.

"Yes?" asked Kate as Joanne began to form a request with her mouth but could not couple it with sound.

Thus encouraged Joanne tried again.

"Would you," she faltered and began over, "would you --- stand?"

"Of course."

How tall she stood! To Joanne looking up, Kate seemed a giant figure of a woman, closer to Galen's stature than her own, with the same broad muscularity and solid stance. Yet clearly not a man. The girl had grown into the fullness of her features. What had detracted from the child's appearance now flattered the young woman.

"My goodness!" was all Joanne could manage to say.

Kate smiled at this response.

"You look different too. Lighter or younger or freer. I can't tell exactly."

"All of that. Where do we begin?"

"We already have."

"Where do we go from here? I no longer know your way."

"You don't have to. That's not your job anymore. It's mine."

Unburdened of the one responsibility she feared, Joanne breathed a huge sigh of relief. Independent at last!

"Mother," Kate paused, awaiting Joanne's full attention. There was so much she wanted to say to this woman but could find no better words than these carefully chosen few. "Thank you. Thank you for everything."

To the simple words of gratitude Joanne made a simple reply.

"Your welcome, Kate. Often I wasn't sure that I was doing right. But I tried the best I could."

"I know. Thank you for never giving up. Now, can I have a hug?"

Standing up to embrace her daughter Joanne fully appreciated for the first time their disparity in size, marveling at the improbability of birthing someone so much larger than herself. Each enfolded the other and when they released it felt for both as though the bond between them had been reforged, bringing them closer and making them more separate than before.

"I'm glad you came by yourself. I hoped you would. You were the first one I wanted to see."

"And the next?"

"Galen." I want to walk into his studio unannounced. Does he have a sitting today?"

"No. At the moment he's working from much less data than he likes. Two or three chance photographs is all he has to work from. But it's a commission of great importance. Not for the money or prestige it carries, but for the obligation he feels to do it well. It causes him to miss your presence, particularly your advice. A posthumous portrait of Mr. Savocek for the Museum. He wants to get it right for Phillip. A gift from the Countess who apparently feels in Phillip's debt."

"To paint a man he never saw. How difficult."

"Yes. I've never seen him make so many sketches, unable to decide which study captures your old teacher best. He will welcome your help and you home at the same time. As for your uncle, he is doing better but not well."

"I'll call him right away. We have a whole museum to rediscover. I intend to devote myself to his recuperation. Whatever time it takes."

"And the Countess. I was commissioned to deliver you this message: 'Tell Miss Germaine I expect a visit at her earliest convenience.'"

Kate laughed.

"This afternoon. Will you call her? Will you come with me?"

"If you like. Then what? Have you thought about what you shall do next?"

"Yes. I am decided. If I can depend on your support a while longer. I want to begin learning to paint. Mr. LaValle agrees that it is time. He has offered to represent me and I have placed myself in his hands. So I'm afraid you shall have him in and out of the house twice as often as before. Will you mind?"

"No. Things have changed between us. I thought it was the Countess, but perhaps you are why. Although I don't know him any better now, he feels like an old friend. Here, I'll let you in on something. Your father swore me to secrecy, but since you're going to rely upon LaValle I'll break my promise. A number of years ago Galen offered to execute LaValle's portrait. No fee was involved. It was an open, generous gesture of appreciation for the representation your father had received. But LaValle declined. I thought Galen might be hurt, but instead he was amused. The rejection had apparently confirmed some suspicions he had. I was curious. He only told me that LaValle did not want to be 'revealed' in that way. What way, I asked? But Galen wouldn't say any more."

Kate understood.

"He is the same with me. Preserving his mystery is part of our contract. Whoever he is, he is not entirely the man he seems. Yet I trust him entirely."

"He obviously thinks you have great merit."

" He trusts my dedication to develop what I have been given. I have come to trust this too. Time with Riablo has taught me I have what it takes."

Joanne stepped back and surveyed this woman who was her daughter.

"Yes," she declared, "yes I believe you do. Shall we go home?"

And arm in arm they meandered toward the entrance chatting like two best friends immersed in catching up, while the Countess fretted impatiently for the phone to ring, relieved at last when it did. From Joanne's voice she could tell the meeting had gone well.

"Love," she pronounced to LaValle later that day, "love did not desert them as it did my mother and I. It is almost enough to make me a believer again."

"A believer, Elena?"

"Yes, in the power of love to bring together people who have been broken apart."

"So this is important to you, that the mother and daughter should be reunited."

"I have wished for it as much as anything I ever wanted."

"You must care for them a great deal."

"I do."

"Would I be misinterpreting this caring to call it love?"

"What are you getting at, LaValle?"

"Only that if you have grown in sympathy to their love, through your love of them, perhaps you would reconsider my love of you."

"You are a persistent man, LaValle."

"Perhaps 'constant' is a better word."

"Constant?"

"In love," he answered.

"What love is it to love someone who does not return your love? This is not love. This is folly."

LaValle stiffened in anger.

"Does it feel like folly to be loved so truly, Elena?" he asked. "Or is rejecting my love only a protection against allowing yourself to love again?"

The question was perfectly timed. His words slipped through some momentarily unguarded chink in the proud woman's armor striking her a felling blow. Her rigid posture collapsed. Something moistened her eyes. Her body slumped forward then caught itself as instinct for control fought for composure and won. She straightened up, a rush of warmth coloring her whole body, although LaValle could only see her face, a flaming red. Carefully he lit a cigarette and contemplated the impact of his question with genuine amazement.

"Why Countess," he finally observed, "if I didn't know you better I should accuse you of --- of blushing. If I didn't know you never let your softer feelings show."

Although her accustomed reserve was now restored, the departing redness had left a slight perspiration glistening on her skin, evidence of the breach of emotional decorum that had occurred.

"Do not triumph over me at such a moment as this, LaValle. It is unworthy of you. In answer to your question, no it is not folly. Or if it is, the folly has been mine. Forgive my display of weakness." And from her sleeve she withdrew a silken scarf, blotting her eyes and face until her complexion returned to its normal pallor.

LaValle reached over and clasped her hands in his, he the petitioner, she the petitioned, restoring the Countess to her ruling role in their relationship, signifying he wanted her to occupy no other position.

"Elena, Elena, isolation is such a lonely place to live. I know it well. Consider: with no sacrifice of independence or self-respect we could make our lives less lonely, you and I."

The Countess signified she knew where his meaning tended, a weary nod conveying her surrender. Why not?

LaValle nodded back thus sealing the contract. At last.
"The girl, Elena. I think she changed you. When you let her in you let yourself out. Missing her, you became open to the mother and then to me. Is this true?"

Freeing a hand the Countess waved mention of Kate away.

"We can speak of her another time. LaValle, I am not capable of offering devotion in equal measure. I am a taker not a giver. And I must be in control."

LaValle indicated acceptance of her terms.

"Giving comes in many forms, Elena. Receiving is one."

"Taking as an act of giving? Really LaValle, this hardly seems a fair return for having loved me so long."

"Return? How little you understand the return I have already received. These many years you have given me someone to love. But you, Elena, in all this barren time who have you had to love? And which of us has been the poorer? True, you have never admitted my love mattered until now, which is encouraging.   However, if your fondness goes no further, this is enough."

"Enough?"

"Yes. How can I help you understand? Love does not have to be equal between us. The benefits of loving far outweigh the benefits of being loved. Remember, I have loved art all my life and it has never loved me back. Love does not have to be requited to be rewarded. It is its own reward. Although the return you give me now adds immeasurably to the pleasure of my love."

"I fell in love once, you know."

"Yes. But it did not grow anywhere. Otherwise you would still be together. You and I, however, have continued our association over many years. Now, I need to know. Am I right? Was it the girl opened you up to me?"

"You could say so. Two generations between us and we became friends. Perhaps because of this. It took some reaching to accomplish. She is a remarkable girl, LaValle. So full of herself at such an early age. As true to her nature as I am true to mine. What we liked and disliked about each other from the first: our shared intransigence. Our willingness to pay the price for being individual and damn the eyes of the world. Even more impressive, there is talent of a high order. Originality no instruction can teach. And enough discipline and commitment to last several lifetimes. You should get to know her work, LaValle, you really should."

"I have."

"You should represent her."

"I do."

The Countess eyed LaValle with fresh interest.

"I wrote her once how there was much about your dealings that I did not know. Apparently I have underestimated my ignorance. You continue to surprise me, LaValle."

"Do you like surprises, Elena?"

"Not usually. However, they become you. I have always found your capacity for intrigue attractive."

"Then perhaps this shall pleasure you as well." And reaching across his vest into a concealed inner pocket on the other side LaValle withdrew a slender oblong block of ebony which appeared to the Countess to be of middle eastern manufacture. How ancient it was she could not tell since there was no ornamentation upon it of any kind, only the sheen of wear from being passed from hand to hand over many, many years.

"What is this?"

"A token of my esteem."

"What manner of token?"

"One that requires a certain subtlety of understanding if its true value is to be disclosed."

"A box, then. What does it contain?"

"Find out."

"How is it opened?"

"With a secret, of course. Discover it if you can."

"Is this a gift or a challenge?"

"Both."

The Countess turned the block in every way, her long fingers searching the surface to detect any irregularity or seam. She could find none.

"It feels like a solid weight of precious wood," she concluded, doubting it was any more than it appeared.

"That impression was the maker's intent. His instructions came on such high authority he could hardly do otherwise. Speculation is the best we can do, however some knowledge of the customs do survive. Today we think of craft as meaning skill.   Back then it had another connotation: secrecy. Even magic, since craft masters of the day kept their technology to themselves. This was their only power in an age when one's value to one's ruler determined the length of one's life. Only fragments of the story survive, and not all in a single place.   It took me years to gather them together. A dealer in antiquities and a scholar here, an archivist and a collector there, unlikely sources in over a dozen countries, none realizing the full implications of information I coaxed from them. Even then, with all the pieces in my hand, I was not absolutely sure I had not gathered the making of a myth and no more. Until last year when a lover of curios in the Vieux Carre laughingly referred to a recent acquisition intentionally purchased as a hoax upon himself. He called it the Box of Eliaph. I laughed too to make him think we were both laughing at one of those legends of lost wealth that treasure hunters waste their lives fruitlessly pursuing. Inside, however, excitement at what instinct told me nearly shattered my poise. At such times I am extremely grateful for the sedative affects of nicotine. I asked to see it. He obliged. Then we drank to the foolishness of foolish men. He drank more than I. Before you is the outcome of the transaction to which he foolishly agreed."

The Countess smiled.

"But surely the story is not finished. A master of crafts makes a magical box. What then?"

"The ruler was preparing his tomb, ladening it with those precious possessions that were to accompany him into the existence to follow. Since he himself had plundered many tombs in his time, he expected no less to happen to his own and was resolved to play at least one trick upon those he knew would eventually disturb his final rest. The box was to contain what even then, a period of decorative opulence, was beyond all other triumphs of the jeweler's art: a piece upon which a kingdom could be founded. Sealed into a plain casket of its own, of wood too hard to rot, of a construction which defied opening, of an appearance too ordinary to waste tampering with, the ornament would remain safe from whatever desecration took place. When Eliaph, for such is the name of the craftsman history gives us, delivered himself of the box and its secret he also delivered himself to the death he expected as payment for his final commission. Laying the precious object in the box the ruler closed it as he had been shown, only to discover that the old artisan had played the final trick. Instructions that opened the box the first time did not work upon the second trial. Needless to say the ruler was extremely pleased. As he anticipated, no sooner had he been laid in state than the burial chamber was broken open by his successor seeking above other treasure the prize that was nowhere to be found since the box was casually flung aside. Tales of the necklace lived on, however, symbol of the unbelievable richness of that reign, while word of the box was occasionally linked to its hiding place, but only years after the successor's death. By then it was too late. The box was now proceeding down its chain of collectors to the present."

"An arresting story, LaValle. Is it true?"

LaValle shrugged.

"I don't know. It might be. Fiction and history both have ways of telling truth. As for the specifics, I made them up. A lie especially created for you, Elena, a connoisseur of fine lies."

"I'm flattered. Thank you. But this box. A lie, or is it truly a box?"

"Permit me."

He reached over and carefully lifted the object from her grasp. For the moment LaValle's hands stopped shaking and the Countess noticed strength swell his fingers with unexpected muscular power as he pressed opposing corners toward each other with extreme exertion to elicit a soft click. Then, from rotating the box forward and back and forward again, came the muffled sound of small tumblers sliding free. All the while she watched his hands in fascination, his eyes never left her face.

"Put out your left hand, Elena," he ordered.

She did as she was commanded. Gently he lowered the box onto her outstretched palm.

"Now clasp your other hand upon the top."

Again she did his bidding.

"Squeeze the box and as you do so slide your top hand forward and your bottom back."

The Countess applied what pressure she could, according to instructions. Startled, she felt the block separate between her hands and shot a questioning glance up at LaValle.

"Why look at me and not the contents?" he asked.

With apprehension she slowly lowered her gaze and then in shock let go the open box that fell into her lap.

"What is this, LaValle?" Her shaking fingers gingerly lifted the pearled chain until the pendant, an enormous stone of ruby brilliance surrounded by sparkling stones of emerald green, swung back and forth between them like a pendulum counting time, marking the suspenseful silence before LaValle chose to reply.

"Consider it a royal gift to a royal lady from a faithful suitor pledging his eternal love."

"Romantically spoke, LaValle, but I am a practical woman and no neophyte in this business in which you trade. Where did you get such a replica made?"

"I did not."

"Come LaValle, you trained my eye. You educated me too well to be fooled by copies. Besides, I know where the original is kept. I know who holds the lock and key. Don't offer me any artificial tokens of real affection. Don't toy with me!"

LaValle recoiled from the accusation then attacked.

"Countess, I do not traffic in imitations, forgeries or paste! So: you know where the original is placed. Do you indeed?" Gone was the usual even temper. Now he altered beyond her recognition. First the eyes became cold and remorseless, then the mouth, a savage slash across his lower face. The mask by which she had long known him completely fell away. Revealed was an expression of absolutely ruthless intent that reminded her not of LaValle, but of another man. Her father. Involuntarily she shuddered.

"Countess," the stranger enunciated very clearly so that each word was given full opportunity to impress. "Do not insult me. Do not demean me. Not ever again. Now: look well at what is before you and do not cheapen its value with a superficial appraisal."

The Countess yielded. Summoning all the judgment and experience in her possession she examined the intricacies of the setting and assessed the quality of the stones. When she was done it was the old LaValle whom she addressed. The stranger had vanished.

Her curiosity craved answers.

"What is this? How did you get it? Who are you?"

"What it seems is what it is. I arranged to receive it and paid for the arrangement. I am the man you see before you."

"This is not possible. Even you, with all your access and influence, could not induce the release of such a treasure. It is beyond price and can only have been abducted. Am I not deserving of a fuller explanation?"

"Elena, I consider you deserving of the necklace. Is this not enough? Do you accept it?"

"To agree, wouldn't I then become --- your accessory?   Even your accomplice?"

"You would. We would be bound in this way."

The Countess threw up her hands in delight and laughed.

"LaValle, I have had many proposals over the years, but never one like this. I believe marriage is the usual offer."

"But we are not usual people, are we Elena? So the usual will not do. Now, your decision?"

The Countess lifted the heavy ornament and deliberately fastened the clasp behind her neck.

"I accept," she smiled, radiant with pleasure.

"One request," LaValle added.

"Yes?"

"A trinket of this kind wears better in private than public."

"I understand. Yet why was the loss not reported?"

"Because there was no loss. Better to suffer some crimes in silence than face the public outcry over their shameful discovery. Still, they have their eyes out looking everywhere. They have even begged the favor of my assistance. Of course, I agreed. So, in deference to the life of one who loves you, be discrete. I believe when they catch the thief the penalty is death."

"I shall be circumspect. And yet, I am still curious."

"About the necklace? Would you like me to fabricate another lie?"

"No, about yourself. You cause me to wonder, LaValle, if you were so badly injured years ago as all the world has been led to suppose?"

"Perhaps not <u>quite</u> so badly."

"I should like to find out."

"Now?"

"No, later. I have a previous engagement. Miss Germaine and her mother are arriving within the hour. She returned early this morning. Her mother called to see if I would receive them today. The first time for all three of us to be together. It was the daughter's wish. Precisely what she has in mind I cannot guess. One letter in two years! Fortunately, I have not been without my informants. She has been a faithful correspondent in spite of herself. Her drawings have confided much. No longer a mere child artist, to that I can attest. A young woman. But what manner of young woman? You see, LaValle, how my mind is too distracted to concentrate on intimacy at the moment."

"I understand. Myself, I am in her debt since she was agent of your release to me. Before knowing this, I contracted to represent her and would have done so well. Now, however, I shall consider it a trust. Until later, Elena," and LaValle shuffled out. Although it seemed to the Countess that he was less bent than usual, and there was more spring to his step.

"How the world changes about me," observed the Countess out loud to herself as she entered her bedroom in search of something suitable to wear. Usually, she dressed to be the center of attention at whatever occasion she graced. For this small gathering, however, this was not her ambition. Rather, she wanted to downplay her natural theatrics so they would not detract from whatever Kate was planning.

"Since this is Miss Germaine's idea,' she reflected, 'then I want to see what that idea is. Let her lead the way. I shall be follower for once.'

And so resolved, she selected a full length gown of velvet black, unostentatious in design yet fashionably cut, which accounted for the simple garment's extravagant cost. With regret she noticed how the dress enhanced the necklace she had not yet taken off.

"Such a shame to conceal what was meant to be displayed!" she observed to her reflection in the oval mirror, admiring the ageless beauty of the jewels compared with the aging beauty of herself. Shaking her head she removed the necklace and reluctantly returned it to its box.

"Ah well," she sighed as she left the room, "I suppose this is just one of the sacrifices one must make for love."

Thus resigned, she descended several flights of marble stairs to the courtyard below, taking her place at the small white table there. Although fall had arrived outside, she had ordered the interior freshly planted with daffodils. The expense was less important than the desired effect, to create a sense of season to match her mood. The long winter was over and she was ready for spring. Surrounded by flowerbeds of blazing yellow and warmed by rays of sunlight beaming through the skylight overhead, she felt the promise of new life beginning. She felt in bloom herself.

Three stories up, leaning over an inner balcony adjoining the Countess' private chambers, LaValle secretly admired the lady at the table, poised as though she sat upon a throne.   While he continued staring she stood up in response to some signal he could not hear and glided to the center of the courtyard. Commandingly tall, she stretched her long arms out to those she was about to receive. The gown she wore fell like a dark robe richly about her and to the man who truly loved her she looked like a queen, and he felt disloyal witnessing what he had not been granted permission to see.

Then she did the unanticipated. Cocking her head to one side she caught his confusion in the periphery of her vision holding it long enough to let him know he was discovered and that she approved his presence. Then she quickly returned to whatever ceremony was about to begin. His attendance now officially sanctioned, LaValle relaxed.

Next, onto the small stone stage entered mother and daughter, their difference in bearing and physique belying the birth connection between them. Much larger now, the daughter's forward motion was propelled by a confidence the mother lacked. Of slighter build, she had more hesitation in her step, as cautious as the daughter was bold. Yet each accepted the hand held out in welcome, now all three standing still exchanging words LaValle was too far removed to hear.

As the conversation continued LaValle noticed how their constellation began to change, not accidentally but by the girl's design. She had let go of her hand of welcome and stepping back several paces was apparently directing the older two to pose for her, although there was no camera in evidence. Indulging her in this charade, the mother and the Countess moved side by side, but this was not near enough. The artist apparently wanted something more. Waving her hands inward toward each other, she directed them to stand closer still until they clove together, an arm around the other's waist, each free harm reaching out just so, to suit the gesture that the girl required. There! The living sculpture was completed.   And LaValle saw why and what she wanted.   In the presence of these two women to make them one because they were one for her, albeit very different.   And as she bowed before the sacred image they resembled so did he, paying homage to that ancient symbol of giving and receiving, the little two headed goddess worshipped once upon a time for the powerful mix of femininity that she possessed.

Then the girl, rising from her stoop and looking up saw LaValle gazing down from high above.   She smiled.   Now the other two followed her glance as well. At last it was over.   No longer feeling any need to masquerade, LaValle straightened up.

"Welcome Miss Germaine," was all his heart could say. "Welcome home!"

Chapter Thirty-One
INTO THE FUTURE

Dismounting from the early morning bus at a deserted stop marked by a solitary street lamp, the young woman waved goodbye to the driver with whom she had been chatting and, departing the circle of light, began climbing the long-terraced stairway to the massive building spread out across the summit of the hill. As she crested the final rise there, dimly visible in the shadow of the entrance, was a figure she would recognize anywhere who instantly recognized her.

To Phillip, Kate was a miracle to behold. He was awed. From the infant, child, and young girl he had known here was a woman born in seeming confirmation of the dream that he had given her at birth.

"Catherine!" he gasped.

"What?" She was startled at being addressed by a name he had never called her before.

"Kate," he quickly corrected. But it was Catherine whom he saw.

Next moment they were in each other's arms.

When they finally separated it was the old Kip, Kate held. Changed not much but some, slightly more subdued and frail than she recalled. Otherwise the same. Except in his eyes. There was less vitality, Joanne's worry. Kate looked closer, deeper, seeking the source of loss, expert now at seeing into dark.

Phillip did not waver under this examination because while she was searching into him, he was evaluating her. While she diagnosed some differences of a declining kind, he noticed how she was redefined by her experience. So much gained was what Phillip saw, while Kate sensed the beginnings of infirmity. 'Unwell' was how Joanne described it. 'But not serious,' Kate now reassured herself. After a few months of devoted attention, she would have him right enough.

Elation from their reunion overcame momentary concern as with the blithe confidence of youth, Kate banished foolish doubt. And, because he did not want to sadden the joy that filled them both, Phillip did the same.

She clasped his hand. He clasped hers. Just like old times the man and little girl were back together. Old times remembered old times returned as once again they entered that house of inexhaustible marvels, the museum that they loved, hunting for treasure.

The great doors opened and the great doors closed behind them as another adventure began. The same doors for them both.

A different door for them each.

THE END

$\mathscr{S}$YNOPSIS

Set in the world of fine art and collecting, the novel **RIABLO, Three Variations On The Theme Of Love** (475 pages), is several love stories woven into one, each of the three relationships depending on episodes in the other two to reach fulfillment.

The plot follows the estrangement, separation, and reconciliation of artist Kate Germaine and her mother Joanne; the growing attachment between museum director Phillip Gambrell and the troubled art teacher he hires, Janovar Savocek; and the long and finally successful courtship of collector Countess Elena D'Allessandro Ricci by her confidential agent, the art dealer Eduard LaValle.

The chapters alternate between letters exchanged over the two years Kate is apprenticed with the artist Riablo and narratives describing the background and events in the lives of the characters. The first letter begins after Kate departs for Riablo's, while the first narrative describes her early childhood. The last letter is written by Kate on her way home from Riablo's, while the last narrative describes her reunion with Joanne and LaValle's final conquest of the Countess.